CODE

BREAKER

CODE
BREAKER

Katherine
Myers

SALVO PRESS
Bend, Oregon

This is a work of fiction.
All characters and events portrayed in this novel are
fictitious and not intended to represent real people
or places.

CODEBREAKER

Salvo Press
P.O. Box 9095
Bend, OR 97708
www.salvopress.com

Cover Designed by Scott Schmidt

Library of Congress Catalog Card Number: 00-100781

ISBN: 0-9664520-9-7

Printed in U.S.A.
First Edition

Acknowledgments

Special thanks to: Jay Minor, DEA agent (ret.); Ron Kern, president of Shadow Trackers Investigations; Paul Grabe, Boise Police Officer; Randy Arthur, Boise Police K-9 handler; and Kelly Myers, computer specialist.

PROLOGUE

"Look. That bird has a broken wing," the father said to his little girl as they walked along the shoreline. The previous night there had been a violent storm, but this morning it had cleared and the sun was shining in a pale, cloudless sky.

"Maybe it got caught in the storm," the little girl said, filled with concern. She hurried over to the gray gull which flopped on its side. It stirred in alarm but had little strength left to do more than flap its good wing. Its beak was open, its black eyes glassy with imminent death.

"Poor thing," the child said, stooping down and carefully touching the startled bird. All her concentration was focused on the gull. She slowly stroked the hurt wing, gently folding it in. Then she ran her hand along the bird's head and back. A moment later it flapped its wings, breaking free and soaring heavenward.

The little girl stood and her father rested his hand on her glossy dark head. "Very good," he commended, then grew thoughtful. "I wish the world were full of children like you."

"I know," she responded gravely.

It was then that he made the decision which would, in time, proclaim him as either a hero or a villain. He reflected that at this particular moment in history the media was full of excitement because NASA was preparing to launch the first manned mission to the moon. All the world knew Earth was on the brink of change though no one, except for himself, knew of the greater change in history's course which had been decided this day on a solitary beach.

Chapter 1

Meg Parrish made the substantial error of being asleep at two-forty-five in the morning. By three o'clock the nightmare she was experiencing took on such substantial dimensions that it woke her. It had been fifteen minutes or more in the heart of purgatory, and she had no one to blame but herself. A large mark on the calendar and a prescription for sleeping pills would have remedied the situation, but now it was too late.

She awoke coughing, choking on the acrid smells: smoke, pine cleaner, crushed geraniums. "It's over," Meg told herself in a weeping voice, sitting up in bed and hugging her knees in a semi-fetal position. The darkness in the room seemed to press down on her, a leaden blanket which made each movement difficult. "It's over, it's over...." She sobbed the mantra that usually calmed her, willing the smells to go away. Instead there was another surge of the odors and she gagged. It's over, it's over, it's over....

Her heart hammered wildly, making her feel as if she had been running a race. Blood pounded at her temples and her breath was so shallowly rapid that she had a feeling of suffocation. The sobbing turned into hyperventilation and Meg couldn't catch her breath. Bizarre gasping sounds came out of her mouth in a steady rhythm and a part of herself seemed to stand aside, recognizing with detachment what was happening. She cupped her hands over her mouth and told herself to calm down and breathe slowly, mentally repeating the assurance that the dream was over. It didn't matter that it was only a dream, that the images of yellow flames in a second story window, and of a form sprawled in death on a flowered carpet, were ghosts. At this moment she was reliving the horror, experiencing the original shock and disbelief. The echo of screams haunted her.

Meg's hand flew out, hitting the touch lamp. She nearly knocked it over but the contact of her fingers turned it on and quivering light flooded the room as its glass shade rocked. The horror was still fresh in her mind, but the images began to fade and in time her breathing slowed. The jerky gasps eventually calmed to normal, although it took a long time to feel even halfway normal because of the tightening in her chest. It felt as if she had swum two laps underwater while holding her breath. Her muscles were straightjacket tight, her body clammy with sweat. After a moment she slid from the bed, pulling on a terrycloth bathrobe.

In the medicine cabinet were some painkillers. She took three of them, knowing the headache which would follow was inevitable. The face in the mirror seemed ancient, like the ink drawing of a young woman which, from a different perspective, could appear to be an old hag. That's how I am, Meg thought, turning away from the sight. The dreams made her feel as though she had lived through a hundred lifetimes.

Throwing off her robe and nightshirt, she turned on the water in the shower and stepped in. Gradually the cool spray became warm, then hot, and she stood beneath the spigot letting the water sluice over her head and down her aching muscles. The steaming water and murmuring white noise of the shower were calming, washing away the nightmare. "I should have known," Meg sighed wearily. "Why wouldn't this demonic mind I have use my twenty-sixth birthday to flagellate me?" She felt an odd kind of shame at being so unprepared for the obvious.

After she had been in the shower long enough to become waterlogged and more relaxed, she got out and dried off. Her apartment seemed even more quiet than usual, with an air of sad isolation. She sat on the couch, wrapped in her robe and with a towel around her damp hair.

Starting at the age of six, Meg Parrish had been dealt out tragedy at such precise intervals that it seemed as if the Fates had gloatingly smiled and said, "Let's synchronize our watches." She wasn't beyond recognizing the irony of her situation; tragedy often left people with a black sense of humor. In spite of this she still couldn't help but think that this morning's rude wake-up call was only a brooding forecast of what was to come.

While most women would probably look forward to their twenty-sixth birthday and make special plans, Meg dreaded its arrival more than a fortieth birthday party rife with black balloons and Styrofoam grave markers. Briefly she wondered if she would still be alive come her fortieth birthday, or if life would have decided to take its final payment by then. The thought of dying was only a little more scary than the thought of living through the arrival of more systematically delivered tragedies over the course of the next two or three decades.

She made herself look away from the past, trying to ignore it. However, like most human thoughts forced into suppression, hers struggled even harder to return to the surface—an air-filled beach ball shoved under water but buoyantly working its way ever upward.

Part of Meg's personal shame came from the fact that she was an intelligent woman, as proved by her nascent career in cryptology. She handled logistics all the time and thought of herself as a highly rational person. Yet despite this she was still unable to rid herself of the superstitious fear that had haunted her since childhood. For the thousandth time during the last five years, Meg reminded herself of the logical interpretation of her situation, of the statistical averages involved, and of the law of probable coincidence. All of them asserted, undeniably, that no evil entity was waiting like a trapdoor spider for her to stumble into its camouflaged hiding place. Yet that was exactly how she felt, as if no matter how carefully she watched her step there was no way of avoiding the eventual pitfall.

*   *   *

The afternoon of that same day Meg was busy working at her desk. She finished the document she was typing and then began proofreading. On the surface the work she did seemed routine, a forty-hour-a-week job doing skilled office work for the Signet Corporation. In reality there was nothing routine about her job because she was a field operative for the Central Security Service working undercover at Signet. She paused, briefly wondering if her CSS supervisor, Richard Hammond, would have sent her on this assignment had he known about her obsessive fear. Would he have even recruited her in the first place if he had known?

The exhaustive background check CSS had done before hiring her, via its parent organization the National Security Agency, had no doubt given extensive details of the tragedies in her past. They had certainly gone over every psychological evaluation of her experience with post traumatic stress syndrome and analyzed her ability to cope. Perhaps that had even been a plus, from their point of view. What they didn't know, what their personal profile of her was unable to outline, was Meg's compulsive fear of five-year intervals. She had managed to keep that to herself.

Her thoughts were interrupted by the appearance of Beverly Holbrook. "Margaret? Could you make copies of this outline for Mr. Dent's meeting?" Beverly was the executive secretary to Signet's chairman, Willis Dent. She was a thin, neatly dressed woman whose hairstyle probably hadn't changed in two decades. "Can you run off four copies and take them directly to Mr. Dent? He's in the conference room."

"Sure thing," Meg answered, taking the papers and efficiently heading to the copy machine. While the Xerox hummed and collated, she took time to scan the documents: a brief outline of Signet's current security measures, a copy of security system updates, and suggestions for in-housing a research staff to do background checks. Security at Signet was extensive.

She knocked on the conference room door before opening it, then slipped inside. "Beverly asked me to give you these," she said, smiling slightly. Without waiting for Willis Dent to reach for the packet of papers, she handed them to each man in the room. The extended time gave her an opportunity to study who was there.

Dent and three others sat around the table. The first was Alan Scorzato, head of security—a man, who, in Meg's opinion, was memorable for his complete lack of attractive qualities. His sharp features, balding red hair, and goatee were accents to an even less attractive know-everything attitude. He had tried on more than one occasion to win her interest. She handed him the papers, then moved around the table.

Another man, whom she hadn't seen before, studied her. He, like Scorzato, was probably in his early thirties. He had a square jaw and Sean Connery eyebrows set over pleasant enough eyes, though the rest of his features were ordinary.

A third man caught her attention as she withdrew the papers. She had seen him before but not here at Signet. She knew this instinctively, and quickly analyzed why he was familiar. Meg had what her mother used to call "one of those memories." It took her only a moment to sort through a mental file of faces which were similar to his: mid-forties, blond, blue-eyed, attractive because of an open, friendly expression. Then she remembered. She had seen him in the hallway at the CSS field office here in Portland. Perhaps twice. This was the first time Meg realized there was another field operative working at Signet, and it surprised her. Coming to Signet was her first field experience, and Hammond had made it seem routine. Was there more going on in the cogs of this corporation than she realized? Another thought came to her. What if her placement at Signet were only a routine exercise and this operative was here to observe how well she was doing? She hoped this wasn't the case because in two month's time Meg had been unable to locate what she had been sent to find.

Moving on she came to Dent, who sat at the end of the table. Although many of the women on staff perceived themselves attracted to him, in reality it was his executive aura and wealth that made Willis Dent desirable. He was five-foot-ten with a slender build and sandy hair not much different in hue from his skin. Washed out blue eyes and thin lips completed the picture. His personae came across as aloofly cool, which Meg thought was unwarranted by his appearance. Meticulous, competitive, demanding, he had a withering stare for any employee who made a mistake.

At the moment, Dent did not express disapproval. In fact, he and the other men were all staring at her, not even a little bit annoyed that she was taking more time than normal to hand out the papers. Although she was dressed in a conservative blue suit, it did little to downplay her looks. If anything it was too much of a contrast to her appearance, for she was the kind of girl who would have looked best in something flowing and gauzy.

If Meg was cursed, then she was also blessed. She was a knock-out with excellent features and skin, toffee brown eyes, thick golden hair she kept cropped short, and a great body. Added to Meg's physical assets was a gifted mind. It was almost as if life were putting on airs, making a display of its generosity to belie the cruel hands it kept dealing her.

Dent turned his attention to the papers and the others did, too. Meg slipped out of the room, wondering again about the blond man from CSS. Within her field group the "need-to-know" policy was well established, and her boss probably hadn't planned on her recognizing this other agent. She walked away from the conference room puzzled but unaware that the triad of men meeting with Dent, and Dent himself, were to be factors in a chain of events which would alter her life.

The entire staff on the corporate floor of Signet left work that Friday afternoon at five, as was customary because of Willis Dent's specifications. Overtime was frowned on because Dent didn't want his employees to have unsupervised access to the offices. Meg left with the others, responding politely to several suggestions that she have a good weekend. There would be no after work get-together with the secretarial staff to celebrate her birthday because the personnel file on Margaret Wilson, Meg's alias, was full of falsehoods. Everything, including her birth date, was phony.

That evening she dined alone in her apartment, eating a birthday dinner of leftover chicken salad and sesame bread. Meg watched the news while she ate, thinking how nice it would be to have a cat. If she had a cat it could sit on her lap while she stroked it, or curl up on the foot of her bed at night. Unfortunately, cats had a tendency to run into the street and get hit by cars. So instead of owning a pet, Meg filled her apartment with houseplants and lovely pieces of art glass, objects easily replaced if destroyed. A dead fern might be reason for concern, but it didn't cause grief.

After dinner she went to her computer, accessing the Internet and locating the bookmark which would take her to CY-FI, the chat room she frequented the most. Her alias, CodeBreaker, was immediately recognized by the two people already there and they interrupted their pun-filled debate about aliens in the White House to greet her. Cyber Guy was a graduate student at MIT while XenX was a professor's assistant at Berkeley. At least that was what they purported to be. With the Internet you could never be sure. They both might just be really smart fourteen-year-olds who knew how to type.

Cyber Guy: Hi, there, C-B. Where you been?
XenX: She's been prepping her little code brain for my newest cryptogram, haven't you, Code Girl?
CodeBreaker: Actually, I haven't thought about you all day.
XenX: Too cruel, girl of my dreams!
Cyber Guy: Not cruel enough.
CodeBreaker: So what's your cryptogram?
Cyber Guy: Time her. See how fast she can do it.
XenX: It's a simple one. Basic transference from numbers and symbols to letters: 25$ 393 750 @59%4#10@#& 1@#&& 750 @#63?

Meg quickly studied the seven groups of symbols, then scanned the entire line a couple of times. She glanced at the repetition of 750 and worked directionally from there. It took her thirty-nine seconds before she smiled to herself and retyped the cryptogram in English.

CodeBreaker: I don't know, XenX. "Why did the rhinoceros cross the road?"
XenX: Dang, girl, you are fast! He crossed the road because there was a chicken on his back.
CodeBreaker: We all have our burdens.
XenX: Will you marry me, Code Girl?
CodeBreaker: Sorry, I have this problem with rhinos...
Cyber Guy: Okay, it's time for your confession. How did you do that?
XenX: What program are you running on a second computer?
CodeBreaker: Nothing to confess. I'm innocent! But, here's a hint for next time:
CodeBreaker: Don't pick a sentence which repeats the word THE or use any words with double consonants.
XenX: Okay.
CodeBreaker: Leaving the question mark unchanged was a good one, though.

Cyber Guy: I think you should go on Wheel of Fortune.

Codebreaker: No thanks. I'm scared of what might happen...

Cyber Guy: Hitting bankrupt?

Codebreaker: Worse. Buying a vowel.

These people and several others, whom she'd never met in real life, had become Meg's main source of social activity during the last couple of years. She liked the playful banter and discussions, and she also liked the fact that there was nothing much to lose if one of them quit writing, because she didn't have a deep relationship with any of them. Meg never accepted their invitations to have a phone conversation or to send them a scanned picture of herself.

She thought of the Internet as a kind of marvelous equalizer. In a media-dominated society where physical appearance now seemed to be everything, the standard of human judgment had taken a unique turn away from Barbie dolls and body builders. The Internet didn't care if a person were plagued with acne or excess weight, or stuck in a wheel chair. It also didn't care if you were great to look at, as in Meg's case. As long as you didn't go to the next step, to actually meeting the people you were talking to, then all anyone cared about was what you had inside your head.

Working with cryptograms at CSS had allowed for little human interaction on Meg's part, and in time even chatting on the Internet wasn't enough. This was one of the reasons she had actually come to enjoy her two months at Signet, despite the mundane work. She was able to talk to others in a more human setting and regain some of the skills for face-to-face conversation which she had slowly been losing. The staff at Signet knew nothing about her abilities, or history, and had accepted her as a secretary. Except for Alan Scorzato's supercilious advances, and Willis Dent's aloof demeanor, most of the people had been refreshingly pleasant.

Originally, when Hammond had asked her to accept the field work, she had been reluctant. Not that there was a problem with going undercover, but it would have taken her away from the work she had become devoted to.

"You're doing this because you want me off the DES project," she had accused. Richard Hammond had scowled, making him look even more like an English bull dog than he already did. "I can do it," she'd defensively continued before he could answer. "You know if anyone can find that backdoor, it's me."

"If is the key word, Meg. We've all been going on the assumption that the cryptographers intentionally left a mathematical vulnerability in the encryption code. What if they didn't? What if you've been circling the pyramid trying to find an entrance to the sphinx, so to speak, and there isn't one? What if the builders didn't want to get back inside the pyramid and didn't want anyone else to get inside, either? Think about it. The DES algorithm is so unusual that it's even resistant to differential cryptanalysis." This latter was a newly discovered mathematical attack format which cryptologists were now using to break crypto-systems. "The creators of DES already knew it would withstand the probe. They probably even planned it that way to protect national security. I don't think they did anything by chance, and if they didn't leave a backdoor, you're not going to happen on one by chance."

Meg had slouched down in her chair, looking defeated, and Hammond's tone softened. "We could debate this all day, you know, and I didn't ask you here for that. I want your help in the field, kiddo, even though you haven't been trained as a field agent and it's not what you were originally hired for. I've gotten special approval because no one else has your ability."

She had eyed the folder on his desk. "Is that the profile?"

He handed her the folder labeled Signet. "You'd be working as an office secretary. That would be your cover, anyway. I know this is like asking a physicist to sit through high school chemistry classes, but we need your eyes inside this company. It's important."

Thumbing through the file, Meg's interest had begun to grow. Her work with DES and the suspected events at Signet were uniquely related. It was suddenly clear why Hammond was asking her to accept this assignment.

That had been two months ago, though, and disappointingly Meg had been unable to substantiate Hammond's suspicions about the firm. Perhaps that was why another field agent had been sent to Signet, she thought, turning off the computer and feeling discouraged. This was twice she had failed. First with the backdoor into DES and now with Signet.

The previous night's interrupted sleep had left her feeling tired for most of the day, but it was still nearly midnight when Meg finally climbed into bed. She drifted off quickly but sleep lasted for only a short while before she awoke with a start. No nightmare this time, but still she was awake. Was she afraid to relax enough to fall deeply asleep? It was natural to be fearful of bad dreams, especially after last night. Meg lay on her back, staring up into the dark. She seemed to see figures there, retinal images from a long-ago past. There had been happiness back then, too, and some of those images danced like drifting shadows in her mind. She took in a deep breath then let out a long, slow exhale.

When Meg was only six years old, the first tragedy had happened, leaving its mark on her family. Ed Parrish, her father, had died. He had worked for the local power company as a lineman. The crew was working on 6-K high-voltage lines and he had been up at the top of a wooden power pole installing a new section to the line. The wire he was working with accidentally flipped up into the high-voltage lines. There was a brilliant flash of light and the wire became instantly cherry red with heat, the 6,900 volts burning through his rubber glove and electrocuting him.

If the jolt had knocked him to the ground, perhaps the impact would have started his heart beating again. In a few rare instances that sometimes happened to electric shock victims, but Ed's safety harness held firm and he didn't fall. Instead he had died on the power pole, dangling far above the ground.

Meg's memories associated with that time were of family members and friends gathering in their home, murmuring quietly with helpless expressions. She could still hear their voices intermingled with the ticking kitchen clock, and all the smells of food that had been brought into their home. There were strange casseroles unlike anything her mother cooked, and a multitude of Jello salads with bright colors seemingly too festive for so much sadness.

Meg's mother and sister had grieved and wept at this terrible loss. Meg had cried, too, even though she couldn't really comprehend that her daddy was truly gone. It wasn't until the days and months began to pass, until Ed Parrish never came waltzing through the front door in his heavy boots smelling of wind and damp flannel, that she realized he wasn't going to come home again. "How're my girls?" he used to ask, his big, open face grinning even when he was tired. "Hello, pretty Robyn," he signed with his large hands to Meg's older sister, who was Deaf. His fingers had been thick and awkward. No matter how much he practiced he would never have signed fluidly. His hands would always have been heavy with the sign language because his fine motor skills were more adept at using a screw driver or ratchet. It hadn't mattered, though. He was trying hard, and Robyn knew he loved her.

Then one day their daddy just stopped coming home. Even though Meg had previously seen him lying in a casket, dressed in a suit he had never worn before, she still expected her father to come through the door when it grew dusky outside. At six years old she had possessed a remarkably logical mind, but that hadn't stopped her from years of learned habit. It took a long time for her to quit glancing at the front door while her mother was cooking dinner.

The death of Meg's father had been a terrible tragedy but at six she had still been resilient. At twenty-six she was not.

Five years passed and the little family worked hard to get by, to be strong together and happy. Meg grew even closer to Robyn, who had lost her hearing to meningitis as an infant. Their mother, Estelle, had spent most of Robyn's life learning how to sign so she could communicate with her daughter. In spite of this she was still a little stilted and tended towards a more English sign system, while Robyn attended the nearby Institute for the Deaf and became fluently ASL. Although Estelle had to work hard at signing, Meg's learning had flown. The syntax and grammar of the language created by the Deaf had taken on a clear and perfect meaning for her. When signing, the subject was established in the beginning of the conversation and then expounded upon. The pictures and expressions were so complete for her that English words became unnecessary. It had seemed like a magical secret code to Meg, with doors that were always opening to new signs. She and Robyn had often conversed with so much excitement and speed that Estelle sometimes felt she was living with two lovely, alien beings.

When Meg was still ten, before five years had elapsed since her father's death, she and Robyn became friends with two girls who moved in next door. Stacey and Claire Green were nine-year-old twins who lived with their mother, Donna, and their step dad, Warren. The two girls had become fast friends with Meg, and it had been a wonderful school year having them always at her side, especially after school when Robyn was still on her way home from the institute. Before Stacey and Claire's arrival Meg had spent many listless afternoons waiting for Robyn. Now she played with the twins until her older sister came home.

Even though Robyn was twelve she was patient with Meg and her little friends. Sometimes she would make treasure hunts for them, leaving pictures or written codes for them to follow. Their houses were close together and the girls had strung a cord between their bedroom windows which were upstairs. Sometimes, while playing at Claire and Stacey's house, they would find a note being sent across the string by Robyn. She would draw pictures that were playful: an eye, a can, capital C and U. Meg had loved those days. Then she had turned eleven.

Late one night in March she was slowly awakened by a strange smell. It was like an elusive snake weaving its way into her dreams, slithering quickly beyond the grasp of recognition. The smell wouldn't go away, and in time it was joined by the sound of hissing rain and the glow of early sunrise. When Meg opened her eyes she saw little bits of light drifting through the window. At first it seemed like fireflies, until one of the pieces of glowing ash settled on her face.

Meg threw back the covers and went to the window. There was no sunrise, only odd yellow light shining through Claire and Stacey's bedroom window. Flames were licking upward, causing the crackling sound she had mistaken for rain. Smoke poured from the roof and there were eerie shapes behind the window, shadowy forms of frantic movements and a hand sliding down the pane of glass before disappearing. She heard the sound of choking screams which were suddenly cut off by the distant wail of sirens. Meg had stood frozen at the window, pieces of glowing ash dancing towards her. When the original shock faded she bolted out her bedroom door and down the stairs. A fire truck pulled up outside, its swirling lights flashing and bouncing red beams off the darkness and smoke.

That moment of time was forever fossilized in her mind, like an unexplained phenomena encased in amber: the arc of water sprayed at the house from the fire truck, firemen in alien garb running past, the feel of cold cement under her bare feet, smoke making every breath she took sting, glass exploding out of the front window of the Green's house, the heat from the fire as it seemed to sear through her nightgown, her mother and Robyn holding her and crying, and her own tears like slow trickles of ice in the March breeze.

Meg believed the older she became the less resilient she was to pain. Tragedy at six had been very hard. At eleven it was devastating. She had grieved over the loss of her friends and their stepfather, even as the entire community had grieved. Donna, the girls' mother, had strangely escaped the fire, having spent the night with a friend. In time there was an investigation and Donna Green was arrested in the arson deaths of her children and husband. She had taken out large insurance policies on Warren and the girls. The police looked into her past and found that ten years ago, in a town across the state, she had lost another child in a fire. A son died and she had collected on a large premium. It had been suspicious at the time, but the police hadn't found enough evidence to convict her. Now it was different. A man working for an early morning newspaper delivery service had identified her car leaving the neighborhood shortly before the fire erupted. Donna was found guilty of murder and sentenced to life in prison.

Meg was haunted by the death of her friends and plagued by a thousand uncertainties. She had spent much time over at the girls' house and had observed their mother's behavior. Donna had seemed nice enough to Stacey and Claire. Sometimes she'd been grouchy, but no more than any other mother Meg observed. She was an ordinary-looking woman, not pretty like Meg's own mother, but pleasant enough. On the outside Donna had done all those things which seemed like what a caring mother would do. She had fixed her family's dinner, picked up cookies and other treats when she bought groceries, gone to school programs for the girls, and provided gifts at Christmas. Had Stacey and Claire been unhappy, hiding secret abuses of a cold-hearted mother? If that side of them existed then she hadn't seen it, and this thought haunted her even more.

When Meg was eighteen she had gone to the library and looked up the news articles Estelle had tried to shield her from at the time. She read all the sickening details, but none of the articles could explain how a woman was able to pretend to be a nice mother while inside she was really a monster. Donna had taken out life insurance policies on her family with premeditated calm, knowing exactly what she planned to do. All her outward actions had been a charade.

Meg could still remember how the Green's house looked afterwards, the charred black bedroom window staring back at her like an empty eye socket. At school it was not much easier. Every time she entered the building she passed a bulletin board with large school photos of the twins matted on light blue construction paper. Die cut letters stated: In Memory of Stacey and Claire Green. After that fateful day in March, Meg sat alone at school; she ate lunch by herself and ignored anyone who tried to become her friend.

Even though the Green house was eventually rebuilt to look normal, the place continued to haunt the Parrish family and the following year they moved to a new house across town. Unfortunately for them, it seemed that death had no trouble finding their new address.

When Meg was sixteen, she and her mother were excitedly planning a party for Robyn who was graduating with honors from the Academy for the Deaf. After Estelle got off work that Friday in May, she and Meg spent the evening shopping for party supplies. They returned home with a bag full of pink, teal and lemon-colored crepe paper streamers, decorative ribbons, and balloons. That day, too, was to become forever frozen in Meg's mind, the moment of giggling pleasure turning into one of horror.

She had walked through the house and into the family room, where disbelief made her waver on the threshold. Her mind was unwilling to accept what her eyes took in. Books and papers had been knocked from the desk and the coffee table was askew. A pot of geraniums was smashed on the floor, dirt scattered across the flowered rug where Robyn lay. The smell of crushed geraniums assaulted her senses, mingled with other odors which came from death.

Robyn was sprawled in an awkward position, clothes shredded, head to the side, her unblinking eyes staring as if fascinated by an overturned chair. Strands of strawberry-blond hair lay across her face, her mouth open, her hands lifeless. Those hands had almost never been still. They had flitted with excitement, flowed with compassion, signed a hundred stories, and drawn pictures with ease. More than any other thing, the stillness of Robyn's hands bespoke her death. Meg tried to scream but no sound came out except for a high, thin wail. It was like stepping inside a nightmare where screaming was necessary, where it was demanded for survival, but nothing happened. She just stood there, her mouth open like Robyn's. Then her mother had come and screamed for her, a scream of such misery that it had opened Meg's throat, too.

The police never found Robyn's rapist and killer. To this day Meg wondered who it had been. Was Robyn's murderer some hideous man with grizzled hair and tatoos, or was he just an average-looking person walking around with a monster inside, the way Donna Green had been? Whenever a serial killer was arrested and his neighbors were interviewed on t.v., they usually said the same thing: an ideal neighbor, quiet and polite, kept to himself, never bothered anybody. Except when he was out killing, of course.

Was Robyn's assailant someone they knew? Was it someone who smiled and came to the door, pressing the buzzer which made an inside light flash to alert Robyn there was a caller? The police said there were no signs of forced entry. Maybe it had just been a harmless-looking murderer asking to borrow a cup of sugar. Meg and Estelle were never to learn the identity of the man who killed Robyn. Fate was not going to offer them that balm.

A grief more overwhelming than anything she had experience overcame Meg and she was barely able to hang on. She and Estelle clung to each other in their misery, sitting in silence. In time Estelle went back to work, and Meg back to school, but life was never the same for them. Meg's hands felt strangely idle, as if an odd malady had caused them to become leaden and useless. The sign language which she had loved so much ceased to exist for a time.

Since they were unable to tolerate going back inside their home, or into the room where Robyn had died, friends and family helped them move into an apartment. They stayed there for a long time with unpacked boxes. They existed but never healed. Sometimes they talked about the terrible events that had plagued their lives, though mostly they just sat quietly together like two survivors of a holocaust. It was during those hours of solitude that Meg recognized tragedy had managed to strike in five year increments. At sixteen this was still a theory. At twenty-one it became reality.

In the beginning she had hoped, and even believed, that the avenging angel of death would pass them by because there was already so much sacrificial blood decorating the doorways of their past. In fact, at first it seemed as if she'd almost won. The month of February arrived, and her twenty-first birthday came and went without incident. Nothing happened until late November.

Even now she could clearly remember her mother sitting on the couch, holding her hand. Meg had gone away to attend the community college in Ellensberg, a couple of hours away. Almost every weekend she came home to be with Estelle, unable to leave her for long.

"It's been too much, you know," her mother said that day. "I loved Robyn with all my heart and was very proud of her, even though in the beginning I mourned her deafness. I blamed myself because I didn't recognize how sick she was. At first it just seemed she had the flu, but then the fever didn't go away. Even the doctor wrongly diagnosed the meningitis on her first visit to his office, so how could we have known? That was little comfort, though, when we realized she had lost her hearing. After that it seemed so important to communicate with her, to make up for my failure as a mother. Your dad and I learned to sign and she seemed happy enough. Even so, there were many days, when you were both napping, that I would go find a dark corner somewhere and just sob the whole time."

Meg was stunned by this revelation. She had never heard this side of the story or seen evidence of it. Of course she had lived her whole life with Robyn's deafness and couldn't have envisioned her any other way.

"She wasn't sad, Mama," Meg had protested. "Robyn was happy. She told me once how her friends were always surprised because you signed so well and could chat with them. Most of their parents couldn't sign anything except about eating or going to bed. You signed well enough for Robyn to tell you what she was thinking and how she felt. She knew you and Daddy loved her."

"She was such an angel," Estelle said, her eyes filling with tears. Neither of them had shown tears in a long time. "It's been too hard, losing your father and then losing Robyn. Dr. Marden keeps saying it's a shock I'll never completely get over, especially since parents aren't supposed to outlive their children." Meg thought that her mother's therapist had little help to offer by making such obvious statements, but it had been a long time since Estelle had said anything about those days and so Meg only nodded.

"I don't want to live through losing you, too," her mother confided. "I couldn't stand going through it again." Meg had been puzzled by the sound of apology in Estelle's voice and her guarded expression, despite her own reassurances that they both had years ahead of them.

What Meg hadn't know was that Estelle had chosen to ignore her medical doctor's caution to switch from the glucatrol tablets to insulin because her diabetes was becoming much worse. A few days later Estelle's blood sugar level soared, and while driving home from the store she had slipped into an unconscious state. Her car rolled several times and she was killed. Like the others, this last tragedy was burned into Meg's mind: the phone call at college, the frantic drive home, the coroner's straight-forward explanation, standing in the small room and looking at the television monitor to identify her mother's body in another room, Estelle's face looking so oddly serene in death, the smell of pine-scented cleaner on the damp floor, and the sensation of falling into darkness.

A week later, having made it through the funeral, Meg was sorting through items in her mother's bedroom when she found a nearly empty box of chocolates. Suddenly she understood her mother's apology. Estelle Parrish hadn't wanted to go on living because that meant facing the delivery of more traumas, and she couldn't handle the parcels life had already handed her.

Anger, frustration, and helplessness had filled Meg. She couldn't be angry at her mother because how could she blame someone she loved so much? She could be angry with life, though, and how it had dealt out such continuing suffering. That had been nearly five years ago and Meg still felt angry. Not the burning, furious rage of those early days, but a cold knot of hard anger deep inside her.

Meg lay still with her eyes closed, tears leaving damp lines down her temples. Mentally reviewing the past had done nothing but let heartache resurface for a time. There was no resolution, no answer, no brink of misery which she could step away from.

Before finally drifting off to sleep she thought once more of her mother. Meg had loved Estelle with all her heart. She also understood her mother's desire to escape the daily pain of remembering, but Meg could never follow in her footsteps. Life may have pummeled her unmercifully and perhaps there was another traumatic event just waiting around the corner, but she wasn't going to give up the same way her mother had. Very possibly another tragedy would come after this recently completed five year respite, or show up when she least expected it during the following year. After all, that was the pattern, and both Meg's hobby and occupation were analyzing patterns. If it did come, that couldn't be helped. She couldn't really prepare for it anyway, or call the shots, but she could go down fighting.

Chapter 2

Sunday evening Phil Allred was dining with his girlfriend, Marita, at an Italian restaurant on the north side of town. He was particularly pleased with himself and the recent turn of events, as he deserved to be. His work as an operative for CSS didn't allow him to tell any of the circumstances to Marita, though, so instead he kept the news to himself and smiled like the cat who had managed to finally snag a goldfish after numerous attempts in the fish bowl. Phil had been working undercover at Signet for several weeks. While there he had finally procured the file his boss had sent him looking for. It hadn't been easy because of the company's intense security measures, but he was much more clever than his broad Danish features made him seem.

After dinner he and Marita left the restaurant and headed across the street to the parking lot. The sun had set an hour ago and cone lights from the building left smears of bluish luminescence near the edge of the road. They started across the street and heard the angry sound of an engine gathering speed, tires spinning, and loose gravel spewing. A dark blue car, with no headlights on, sped towards them.

Pushing Marita ahead of him, Phil tried to get out of the car's path but it mowed him down, the tires rolling over him. He lay on the pavement in numb agony as the car sped away. Marita began to scream and there was the added sound of voices and people running, some of them coming closer, others calling for help. Phil had always hated irony, and the irony of this situation was that he'd been taken down by a basic hit-and-run, just like in a hackneyed cop movie. Spasms of pain knotted his abdomen. Phil thought about Marita and how much he was starting to like her, how much there still was left to learn about her. He thought about his family, and especially his two nephews, Corbin and Justin, who would miss him terribly. Then shock's cold mantle settled over Phil Allred, and he thought about nothing at all.

* * *

Monday morning Meg rose early and left her apartment with a canvas bag, planning to exercise and shower at the gym before heading to Signet. A couple of minutes after she shut and locked her door the fax machine in her apartment came to life, spitting out a message: Please come eat breakfast with me.—Aunt Agnes

Had Meg seen the fax she would have been concerned. This kind of message from pretend Aunt Agnes could have had only two suggestions. If the fax had invited her to dinner then she would have known to attend work that day, but to also make arrangements to take some time off, hence leaving an open door. However the word "breakfast" was the key signature in this communication. It meant she was to immediately cease her involvement in the current case and report back to the field office. Meg would have done that had she seen the fax. By so doing she also would have missed the opportunity she had been waiting for.

Throughout the morning her work at Signet was routine, but she didn't mind because it helped her forget about her own private birthday party which had been hellish. During the afternoon she turned over a few typed documents to Beverly Holbrook who was looking unusually pale.

"Are you all right?" Meg asked.

"I don't think so," Beverly replied with enough composure to belie this statement. "I must have caught some kind of flu bug."

Meg encouraged her to go home and rest but Beverly was meticulously conscientious about her work and didn't want to leave. Obviously years of working for Willis Dent had caused her to feel that she couldn't take advantage of the sick leave she must be amassing. At four o'clock Meg checked back with her and found she looked worse than ever.

"You've got to go home, Beverly. You've gone from pale to flushed."

"Mr. Dent's expecting an important call from New York. I need to take that message when it comes."

"You can forward your calls to my desk. I'll take care of it and you go home."

"I will, as soon as I finish this prospectus Mr. Dent outlined. He needs it for tomorrow morning's meeting." Most routine letters and documents were passed off to Meg and some of the other secretaries, but a few important pieces Beverly took care of herself.

"Let me finish it. It looks straightforward enough, and all my work's done."

"I don't know..." Beverly said, her voice trailing off. Her hands slid from the keyboard and she sighed. "I'd feel better about it if Mr. Dent were here so I could explain why I'm leaving."

"I'll explain when he comes back. Is he due before the end of the day?"

"Yes. In fact I've been expecting him any time." Beverly looked up with red-rimmed eyes and a flushed face. "This is very nice of you, Margaret. There's not much left to do, just follow the outline in the first draft. Proofread it twice and then print out three copies and put them in these envelopes."

Meg assumed her most confident air, reassuring Beverly there would be no problem in finishing the proposal. After a few more instructions, Dent's executive secretary gathered her things and left Signet forty-five minutes early. Meg sat in Beverly's chair and began typing, continuing to do so for a while until she felt sure Beverly had left the building. One or two people passed by, but no one questioned what she was doing at the desk. The corporate floor was laid out in a maze of cubicles allowing privacy for the workers. It also left them unaware of when Willis Dent might walk by and stop in suddenly just to check on what they were doing. She wished there was a clearer view of the elevator from here because there would be only a few seconds warning when he came back to the office.

Meg minimized the document she was typing, then used the mouse to open Network Neighborhood. The computers at Signet used Novell Network, which allowed anyone on staff access to the company's database and the other files. Soon after Meg arrived at Signet, she realized there was little information of interest there, and definitely not what she was looking for. The next week she had arranged for her computer to have problems. The computer technician who arrived to take care of her networking problems had typed in the password needed to enter the company's server. Although the four digit password had shown up as a series of asterisks on the monitor, she had ignored that and instead been able to read it from the keyboard as the tech typed it in. Not everyone could do this, but Meg's eyes were quick at following the movements of his hands. She had gleaned the password which was 1987, probably the year Signet was incorporated. Once these numbers were attained, she accessed the server. At every spare moment she scanned for the code system Hammond had sent her to find, but during the last two months her search had proved fruitless.

Now, browsing through Beverly's computer, she was pleased to see that Dent and his secretary had a secondary program linking their two systems. She surmised that the code she was looking for just might be in a file on Dent's computer. Until now Meg hadn't had a chance to get near this computer because Beverly arrived promptly at eight in the morning and left at five, seldom leaving the work area during the day. Nearly every day she ate lunch at her desk, and sometimes Meg wondered if she even took a break now and then to go to the ladies' room. Not that her absence would have allowed Meg access to the computer with Dent's office right next door. Besides, had she been able to get at Beverly's computer before now, it still would have been a much more difficult task because of the initial password required to enter their system. This problem was bypassed, at the moment, because Beverly had allowed her to take over the task at hand, and the prospectus she was typing was being saved to a data folder on Dent's computer.

Meg pulled up the programs list on his computer, a thrill of anticipation running through her. Looking at the data, she wasn't surprised to find that he was meticulous about how he arranged the files inside each folder. His tendency for exacting order was going to make her task easier because each folder was laid out and labeled according to the programs which were used to create them. There were folders for Excel, WordPerfect, Daytimer, Internet Downloads, Graphics, and myriad others. Her eyes scanned through them and she opened any which caught her attention. Seeing nothing of importance in these, she started at the top and opened the files she hadn't checked out before.

When she opened Excel she found quite a few folders inside, as she had in the others, but the name of one file caught her attention: Kronek's Coding. She clicked on it and a request for a password came up. This was strange because none of the others had asked for a password. A new rush of excitement filled her, and for a quick moment she reflected on Dent's foolishness in putting a password on this file. It was a red flag signaling there was something he was trying to hide. She heard footsteps and glanced up, her heart racing. A colleague walked by and smiled, and she thought about how easily that could have been Willis Dent returning to his office. What would he have thought if he'd seen Beverly's computer screen displaying his files? Maybe she wasn't cut out to be a field operative. It took strong nerves, and Meg's nerves seemed frayed these days.

Passwords were not as easily broken as movies made them seem, but neither were they impossible to figure out. Few human minds were so complex that they came up with bizarre choices. The fact that Willis Dent was an exacting and pragmatic person gave her a chance. She had studied his profile and memorized the important information about him before entering Signet, so she started with the basic facts. Quickly she typed in his birth date, with no luck. Next she tried his Social Security number, driver's license number, even his Mercedes' license plate number, all with no results. She typed in variations of his name, his middle name, the street he lived on, the name of the boat he owned, his height and weight. The fact that he was divorced and had no children or pets eliminated a large variety of choices. She tried all the common electives such as the current year, then the current month, and even the word *password*. There were many variations of this, such as *secret, secrets, top secret* and *private*. None of these worked. Another common one was the word smile, though she didn't bother to type this one in since she couldn't imagine Dent choosing something so frivolous. The password line sat unmoving, staring back at her with blank secrecy.

Meg glanced down the hallway again, her ears straining for the sound of footsteps. In the distance she could hear a few murmuring voices, a phone ringing, the sound of someone answering it, and keyboards clicking. She felt her anxiety level rise, her heartbeat having chosen a quick and steady rhythm; every sense seeming to be heightened. Turning her attention back to the screen she told herself that stepping inside Willis Dent's tidy mind and finding his password was not impossible. She still had more time left to try and find it.

Next, in the process of elimination, was the reminder factor. Many people liked a secret reminder and left themselves physical clues, designing the password from an object which was in view of their computer. This was especially handy if the person was amassing a series of passwords. The door to Dent's office was kept locked, and even if it had been open she probably wouldn't have gathered the courage to slip inside. Watching a suspense movie where the heroine was searching the villain's desk, knowing he could pop in at any moment, tended to make her feel nervous. She wasn't ready to try such a stunt in real life. At this moment she was about as far out on the edge as her courage dared let her go. Besides, it wasn't necessary.

Meg was able to pull up a mental image of his office, having been inside it on three or four occasions. Her near-photographic memory was a plus, and she toured his office in her mind. She started with his desk. It was an unusual piece composed of a large slab of inch-thick glass set on two faux marble pillars. Atop it was his computer system, a white phone, a large notepad inside a leather folder, a square crystal container which held Cross pens and mechanical pencils, and a pyramid-shaped paperweight. Meg typed in the words *paperweight* and *pyramid*. No luck. Behind his desk, and covering the left wall of the office, was a bank of windows looking out on one of Portland's lush parks. She couldn't think of anything from that scene which might have given an idea for a password. To the right of his desk was a large medieval tapestry depicting a hunting feast with hounds. It covered the entire wall and fell in folds on the floor. She tried *tapestry*, *hounds*, and *medieval*. Again no luck.

The phone on Beverly's desk jangled and Meg jumped, her adrenalin taking another step up. Even though the ring was soft, at this moment it sounded like a shrill scream. She jerked the receiver from its cradle, answered the queries from the client in New York, and jotted down the message. The phone call had taken less than two minutes, but by the time she hung up it seemed as if a huge chasm of time had passed.

Meg felt her palms turning damp. Her underarms were already soaked. Apparently, she told herself, the flopping feeling inside her stomach was what people referred to as butterflies. She didn't care for the sensation and paused a couple of seconds to take in a deep breath. A few more tries at breaking into this folder and then she would have no choice except to get out of here and back to typing the prospectus. The thought of being so close filled her with anxious frustration, and the time ticking away brought to bear a feeling of incredible pressure. She made her mind focus on the final wall in Dent's office which was directly opposite from where he sat. Perhaps this would be her best bet yet as it was in his line of sight.

On that wall were two expensive pieces of contemporary art. It had seemed strange to her that someone who was so exacting and conservative could throw away ten thousand dollars or more on a pair of such ugly works of art. They were smears of gray, blue and brown acrylic paint, mixed with primers, rock salt, and sand for texture. Her mind focused on the painting to the left. The artist's signature was illegible, but there was a small brass plate on the bottom of the frame which named the artwork. Meg forced her mind to pull in closer to the memory and the name surfaced.

She typed in the word *eclipse* and the folder magically opened. Bingo! She had broken the password. A moment of exhilaration filled her until she caught herself and glanced down the short hallway again, relieved she was still alone. Turning back to the screen she saw that inside the folder was another single folder, this one labeled *Codes*. Her excitement began to rise. This must be what she was searching for!

Meg clicked on the folder and another password request came up. You've got to be kidding! she thought, clenching her jaw in irritation. Talk about paranoid! Another deep breath and she again sent her mind back into the mental image of his office, recalling the second picture on the wall and the brass plate on the bottom of its frame. Dent's fetish for neatness would force him to follow up with the twin picture's title as a second password, especially since they both had the same amount of letters in each name. Doing something more random would probably be intolerable for the guy, she realized, and this thought made her feel more confident as she typed in the word *shadows*. The folder opened.

At this point Meg's exhilaration and anxiety were so entwined that she felt more finely tuned than the tautest string on a violin. Inside the folder were numerous files. The listing numbered them at a hundred and forty-three, and each was labeled with a date. She clicked on the first file and a window appeared which said, "Click on the program you want to use to open this file." Meg then realized that Beverly's programs didn't include Excel, the spreadsheet program needed to look at the files. This meant there was no other choice than to save the data and take it with her.

The files were similar in size which would require about two-and-a-half megabytes per file, adding up to more than three hundred and fifty megs for the total folder. One this size would require more than just a few floppies, she thought with an ironic slant. Looking at the setup of Beverly's computer, she realizing it had a writeable CD ROM. Searching through the desk drawers she found a stack of blank writeable CDs and picked one up. Meg inserted it in the drive, then used the mouse to grab the icon of the folder and drag it to the CD Rom icon. At this point her fingers were nearly trembling with excitement.

She meant to copy the files to the CD, but in her haste accidentally clicked on "move" instead of "copy". In one second the folder was moved out of Dent's computer and into the drive. Meg gasped and realized her mistake. What had she done? At this point there was no time left to stop the process and restore the folder to his computer. The minutes were ticking methodically towards the five o'clock checkout time, much like the timer on a bomb. She had no other choice than to let the information move out of his computer and onto the CD. He probably isn't going to like this, she said to herself, then bit down on a smile that nervously jumped to her lips. She felt overwhelmed by a desire to giggle, recognizing this as a new onset of nerves.

More than fifteen minutes had already elapsed during her search and it would take at least that long to store this large a folder onto the CD. In her haste to get it copied she had thrown up a red flag. Actually, she'd done more than that. She'd stolen the information. It wouldn't matter that Dent had it backed up somewhere, and probably more than one copy, too. The fact remained that she had been intrusive and was leaving a trail. So much for discretion. Okay, so big deal, she mentally said. I got into the system, didn't I? I'm getting what CSS needs, right? Dent could burst a blood vessel, for all she cared. At this point she just wanted to get herself and the CD out of Signet without being apprehended.

While the data was being saved Meg maximized the proposal and began typing furiously, glancing down the hallway several times. It's okay. Even if he comes back and turns on his computer he won't know what you're doing, she reassured herself. Not unless he tried to access his files, or noticed the hard drive light flashing. There were more butterflies in her stomach. She finished typing the prospectus, proofread and saved it, then printed three copies.

Fifteen minutes elapsed and her heart rate slowed a bit. She checked again to see if the computer was finished copying, and found it had saved more than ninety percent of the files. Meg slid the three documents into the manila envelopes and set them in a neat stack, her fingers fidgeting with nervousness. She recopied the phone message in a neater script, the first one having been scrawled and shaky. One more glance at the screen and she saw it was done copying. Relief flooded her and she removed the CD, putting it in a jewel case and sliding it into the pocket of her suit. It was ten minutes to five. The sound of footsteps startled her, and she looked up; Dent was coming down the short hallway. Quickly she pressed the master switch on the computer, shutting it down to immediately exit his program files. Two seconds later he was standing at the desk, looking down at her with a puzzled expression.

"Beverly's sick," Meg hastened, looking up at him with an innocent air. She knew for the time being he would be unsuspecting, especially if she didn't babble because of the adrenalin overload she was experiencing. Most people didn't think she was capable of doing more than typing a few letters because she was pretty, blond, and looked younger than her twenty-six years. Dent was no different.

"She felt really ill but didn't want to leave, so I offered to finish typing the prospectus. She said you would need it for tomorrow's meeting. Also, here's the information on that call from New York."

Dent took the items from her, glancing over the message and then pulling out one of the documents. "Okay, this looks good." He didn't inquire about Beverly's well being. It wasn't in his nature to be concerned.

"Do you need anything else before I leave?"

He glanced at his watch. It was nearly five. "No, this is fine. Have a good evening." His tone was dismissive as he headed into his office. Meg stood and pushed the chair in, her muscles feeling achy from the tense pose she had held during the last forty minutes. Going to her own cubical, she shut down and turned off the computer, put away a few items, and got her purse. Then she headed to the elevator where others were gathering. She smiled and acted nonchalant, never letting on that the CD in her pocket felt like it was burning a hole in her side.

*   *   *

Willis Dent sat at his desk, reviewing the prospectus while his employees left for the day. He liked the way the busy typewriters and phones became still at five o'clock, the voices of his employees drifting away, eventually swallowed up in the elevators. Only a few minutes passed before the cleaning staff arrived. One of them immediately came to his office as per the arrangement he had set up several years ago. She was a woman in her mid forties who did a thorough job cleaning his office.

He vacated his desk so she could clean the glass top which she did quickly and conscientiously, careful to replace each item where she thought it belonged. She dusted, vacuumed, and emptied the trash while Dent sat in a corner chair occupying himself with the recently typed prospectus. This cleaning arrangement suited him well because the thought of custodians invading his office without supervision was intolerable. He didn't perceive himself as obsessive, but rather as having achieved a higher level of perfectionism than most ordinary, less capable, people. The truth was that Dent's compulsion for orderliness stemmed from an early environment which had been out of control.

His mother was an unusual alcoholic. Drinking made her a much nicer person and so, for this reason, Willis had both pardoned and despised her weakness. The times which had been the worst were those when Vivian Dent Hartman had decided to be sober. The longer she was dry the meaner she became. He could still remember an early episode in his life, before he had taught himself to wear the armor of detachment, when her self-inflicted rehabilitation was at a peak. He had been seven years old, and standing in the hallway in his underwear. She was looming over him, her fingernails digging viciously into his arm.

"I should never have had you," she hissed with narrowing eyes. "I should've gotten rid of you before you were born." At the time her cruel words had dug into him far worse than her fingernails. Today, remembering, they were powerless to hurt him.

Over time, when he and Vivian had endured all they could of her dry spells, she would thankfully start drinking again. Like a dying fuchsia finally being watered, the return of liquor had brought her back to a sweeter and more pleasant personality. She never drank to the point of seeming drunk, but instead came to life—a bright, flamboyant flower that needed to be frequently watered. It was a pattern that was to repeat itself throughout his childhood.

When he was eleven she married well and they began living an affluent lifestyle. Willis was devoted to his stepfather, Marvin Hartman, who eventually paid for his topnotch education, and a few years later gave him the capitol needed to buy the small, floundering software engineering firm that had become Signet. Despite the improved circumstances in his life, Vivian's influence continued to leave its indelible impression. There had been no way to predict his mother's mood swings. One day he might be filled with dread, terrified she would pounce on him because of a mistake he had made. When she only shrugged, or ignored him completely, he would be flooded with relief and amazed by this gracious reprieve. At those times he felt genuine gratitude and love for Vivian. The next time, though, when he had done nothing of consequence, his mother might fly into a rage and rain hatred down on his head. No matter how he tried there was never any way to predict what slight incident might incite her wrath. There had been no control in his childhood, and no order. This was why Willis Dent made sure there was plenty of it in his adult life.

The cleaning woman left and he shut the door. He returned to his desk and carefully adjusted each item the few centimeters required to put them in their proper places. In time the crystal pencil holder, leather notebook, pyramid, and phone were all in their places. It always annoyed him that she was never able to get them exactly right, and that he had to adjust them himself each time. He didn't say anything to her, though, because he was also very good at accepting the limitations of others when it came to this kind of situation. They just didn't see how things were supposed to be. Willis always knew exactly how they should be, though, and it gave him a sense of well-being to have things in order. Today, more than most, he longed for that feeling. It had been a rough weekend with a mess that needed to be taken care of. Willis abhorred messes.

Like many people who felt distanced from love and affection, Willis tried to fill the void with possessions. He liked the prizes he had gathered as self-rewards, and one of the recently acquired things he had gotten was on his computer. Turning on the master switch, he gave the entry password to get into his system, and accessed the program folder. At the moment his anxiety level was still high because of the mess-up in Signet's security this weekend which Alan Scorzato was still cleaning up. He disliked dealing with abnormalities in his company; problems like this current one left him feeling vulnerable.

Reviewing his recently acquired code files would be a pleasurable experience, as it had been each time before, and one which could ease his anxiety. He had studied the codes several times since receiving them. Although they weren't decipherable in the least by the human eye, just knowing what he had was immensely enjoyable. It was, in fact, the culmination of a two-year search by his investigative staff. It was also the proof that the situation he'd happened on two years ago had really occurred.

He entered Excel and immediately clicked on the folder labeled Kronek's Coding. The request for a password came up and he typed in *eclipse*. The folder opened and Willis Dent stared at the empty computer screen in puzzlement.

Where was the Codes folder? A dreadful apprehension grew inside him; he closed the first folder, and then re-entered it. There was still nothing there. This was no computer glitch. Someone had deleted or stolen his files!

In furious desperation he closed out the computer, turned off the power, then restarted it. He ran through all the steps, just to make sure, because he couldn't believe it was gone. He had almost convinced himself it was a visual error on his part when he again opened the Kronek folder. It was still empty. Willis Dent felt stunned by this violation. Who had gotten inside his computer? Who the hell had been able to circumvent the two passwords which only he knew! A chill tightened his scalp. What was happening? What the hell was happening? First the theft this weekend, and now the loss of these extremely valuable coding files. It didn't matter that he had two back-up copies of these codes. What mattered was that he was no longer the single owner of the most important find of his life!

He stood, strode around the desk, and jerked the door open. The corporate floor was empty. It was nearly six and the cleaning staff, along with their security supervisor, had left. The place was completely quiet. He closed the door to his office, examining the lock. It seemed to be untouched, and since he alone knew the five-digit electronic code to spring the latch it was nearly impossible for someone else to break into it. He had made sure of that. Besides, there was a nearby camera which would have alerted the security staff to anyone suspicious trying to get into his office.

In frustration he turned away from the door, looking over at Beverly's desk. His chest tightened. Her computer tied into his. It was set up to enabled her to save documents directly to his system's WordPerfect folder. When he had come back from his meeting this afternoon that new secretary, Margaret something, had been typing on Beverly's computer. Could she have broken into his system and stolen the files? Impossible. She was just a secretary, good at typing, good to look at, nothing else. After all, he alone knew the two passwords! She couldn't have gotten into his system and used them. He'd never told them to anyone, said them out loud, or written them down. How could she have known what they were? Then he recalled the source of his passwords, the small engraved nameplates on the framed acrylics. Maybe he hadn't been as careful as he'd thought. Pushing back feelings of turmoil and disaster which threatened to overwhelm him, Dent sat down in Beverly's chair. He pressed the master switch and her computer came to life, displaying a message: Windows was not properly shut down. One or more of your disk drives may have errors on it. Press any key to run ScanDisk on these drives....

The simple white text on the dark gray background couldn't have stood out more vibrantly if it had been flashing chartreuse and purple. To him it was the signature of haste. The woman must have shut off the computer at the master switch to quickly sever her tie into his system when he showed up. She had seemed a little startled when he entered the hallway and headed towards her. At the time he had assumed it was because he was the boss and she was a mere typist sitting at his secretary's desk; obviously she was the thief. A new kind of rage welled up inside him at this deceptive woman who had used her pretty face and innocent gaze to lie, cheat and steal from him. He fervently wished he could have her throat inside his hands at this moment. He envisioned those big brown eyes widening in alarm as he squeezed tighter and tighter, her mouth gaping in fear, and her hands helplessly clawing at his fingers. He would find her and get back the stolen files. Any other answer was unacceptable. Besides, it had taken him two years to find the codes in the first place, and although the search had been expensive and tedious it had paid off. His security staff would apply the same techniques and he would find her. It was only a matter of time.

Dent grabbed the phone, dialed Alan Scorzato's number, then changed his mind and hung up the receiver. No doubt Alan was still taking care of this weekend's breech. He flipped open the company directory to the security section, finding Ross Ecklund's pager number. Ross was one of Signet's newer security employees but had an impressive history. Dent had hired him because he was very good at what he did, and right now he needed expert help. He dialed the numbers with angry exactness, a cold knot of rage making him feel as if he'd been punched.

Chapter 3

Evan sat staring out the window, seeing nothing. Flecks of rain decorated the pane of glass; he let the droplets blur in front of his eyes until there were twice as many as before. The ten-year-old was small for his age and had angelic features beneath a cap of whey-colored hair. He was a child of unique talents with a sweet temperament; however, at the moment he felt very low and melancholy. The sadness crept over him like a slowly rising tide of hopelessness.

"Come on, Evan," Chris said, his voice echoing concern and exasperation. Chris was also ten, though half a head taller than his brother. He was African-American, with short black hair and skin the color of a melting Hershey bar. Chris slipped off his gold-rimmed glasses and rubbed one of his eyes with the heel of his hand. "Let it go, okay?"

Evan didn't answer and Chris put his glasses back on. "Oh, man!" he said at last, heading downstairs where several of the others sat. "It's Evan."

"I'll take care of it," Marvin said, rising from the couch. The young man went to the foot of the stairs.

"No, let me go," Bethany offered, hopping up.

He looked back at the fourteen-year-old girl and shook his head. "It's okay."

"You're not the kind he needs," she worriedly commented.

"She's right," Jerry added, not bothering to look up from his physics book. He wasn't being critical. There was no criticism from any of them.

"What can you or Bethany do for Evan that he can't do for himself?" Marvin softly asked. "I can at least get him through it without physical damage."

The others looked at him; Bethany's eyes became awash with tears. She wasn't hurt by Marvin's statement. It was her compassion for Evan which made her feel like weeping. She sat down and Marvin went upstairs.

Evan had moved to the bed. He was lying with his arms rigidly by his sides, tears trickling down his temples. "Hey, buddy," Marvin said, sitting beside him.

The boy didn't move, although his eyes flicked over to the young man with auburn hair and a sunburned nose.

"You having a rough time?" Marvin asked.

Evan slowly nodded. "It's so bad," he murmured, his voice sounding full of tears. "Why do they have to hurt so much? There's too many of them."

Marvin put a comforting hand on the boy's forehead. "Let them go, Evan. It's not for today."

"Some are hurting real bad," he whispered. "And some are bent all wrong. Even some of us."

"That's true."

"Aren't you worried?"

"No, buddy, I'm not. I'm just doing what I can, which for now is going to school and studying, and learning everything there is. Today I can only be twenty, just like you can only be ten-and-a-half."

"You help them, though," Evan sighed, his voice jagged with emotion.

"I help more than I did at ten, and less than I will at thirty. A lot of them have to help themselves, just like you do."

"I know," Evan said, still emotional but feeling more logical now.

They talked for a while until the boy closed his eyes, physically less tense. Marvin talked on and on about the stream of life. He had a wonderful voice which could sooth and comfort. Evan became drowsy even though the heartache and concerns were still there. They never really went away, it was just that his older brother's voice was so calming, like the ocean tide sweeping out the hurt. His pulse slowed, as did his breathing, until he eventually drifted off to sleep.

Marvin slowly stood, feeling drained. He went to the door where Bethany was watching him, this time with tears of gratitude in her eyes. "You were right," she whispered, hugging him.

* * *

It took Meg forty-five minutes to drive from Signet to her apartment. The first thing she did when she got home was to fire up her computer, change into comfortable clothes, and grab a bottle of juice. The anxiety of breaking into Dent's system had made her mouth feel like cotton. She sat down at the computer and put the CD into the drive, then entered Excel. Once there she opened the Codes folder to view the files. She paused for a moment, thinking how peculiar this seemed. In the excitement of getting into the folder she hadn't even thought about how odd it was to have the codes in so many files. She had assumed the information would be in a single file, or maybe in two or three volumes. Dent's project must be much larger than she had originally guessed. Studying them she saw each file was titled with a date, the first one 18 JUN 75. They all had different dates, the years ranging from 1975 until only two years ago. She clicked on the first file and it asked for a password.

With a sigh Meg tested every file and found that each was encoded. It was frustrating and annoying, but not overwhelming. The experience of breaking through Willis Dent's folder passwords had been exhilarating, and she was currently filled with confidence. This was only a detour, not the end of the road. Besides, now that she was safely ensconced in her apartment, with the doors locked, the only butterflies she felt were from excitement. She sat back, looking up at the framed watercolors above her computer desk and letting her mind drift off as she analyzed the situation. The trick about passwords was in recognizing the needs of the user. Nobody who set up a password to encode a file would choose something that would be a hassle to use. If it were a single folder they might choose something unusual or hard to guess, as in the case of Dent's paintings *eclipse* and *shadows*, but this wouldn't be the case for each of the hundred and forty-three files. No one could memorize that many different passwords. There might be a single password which fit them all but Meg doubted it. She didn't have any real reason to feel this way, just her instinct when working with codes and passwords. Instinct, she had found, went a long ways in her business.

She tended towards the belief that Dent had an individual password for each file, and actually hoped this was true because passwords for many would be easier than one common key shared by them all. It was like looking for one hundred and forty-three needles clustered in a haystack as opposed to one needle by itself. The fact that there were so many, and that they each had an encryption, actually worked to her benefit. With that many files it would be impossible to remember the passwords without a written list, which would defeat the purpose of the encoding. The only way to automatically know the password would be to use the title of the individual files. In this case they were dates. Twelve months, thirty-one days, and the spanning years gave her sixty-three numbers to work with. That was too many numbers for an easy encryption. Meg didn't believe Dent would have wanted to memorize a complex code of symbols just to secure the files. Whatever symbols he used had to be right in front of her on the keyboard, and easily transposed with the dates.

The phone rang and Meg pulled herself from the computer, picking up the receiver. "Don't you check your messages or fax machine anymore?" Hammond asked gruffly on the other end of the line.

"Hi, Richard," she answered, scooting over to the fax machine. She picked up the paper it had spewed out this morning not long after she left. In her excitement to look at the computer files Meg had forgotten to check for messages. The fax displayed a single sentence request from Aunt Agnes that she come to breakfast. "Uh-oh...was I supposed to have breakfast with you? If you wanted me to come you should have said whether we were having omelets or croissants." Her heady triumph about finding the encoded files obviously made her feel frivolous.

"That's not funny," Hammond said. "We've been trying to get a hold of you since this morning, you know. Where were you?"

"At Signet until an hour and a half ago. I left early this morning and missed the fax, or I would have called in. What's wrong?"

"We'll talk about it tomorrow morning when you come into my office. Don't go back to Signet. You're being pulled from there."

She fell silent and neither of them spoke. What was going on? "Just like that?" she finally asked, wondering if in some bizarre way he had found out about the code she had just stolen. That seemed pretty impossible.

"Don't call in sick, either. You'll do that from our office so it'll be screened. Be here at eight o'clock."

"Okay."

"And next time, check your messages and your fax machine. You had me a bit worried." His voice was still gruff but had softened a bit.

He hung up before she could say anything else, not even giving her a chance to tell him about the code system she had found on Dent's computer. It was just as well, she thought, turning off the cordless phone and setting it down. Tomorrow she could take the CD in with her, hopefully with the passwords broken. She went into the kitchen and dug some leftover stroganoff out of the fridge, warming it in the microwave. Then she sat eating it in front of the computer screen. An hour ticked by as she played with the dates, searching for passwords. In time Meg decided to simplify the numbers to ten single digits, zero through nine. Instead of fourteen she would use a one and a four, and so on. This gave her new ideas but all of them seemed more complex than necessary, and none of them broke through the passwords.

"Look at the keyboard," she told herself. "How could those dates be typed in without memorizing a code or having a written list? I have ten numbers. I need ten characters or letters."

On the standard qwerty keyboard the bottom row had seven letters, the middle row had nine, and the top row ten. These last were beneath the numbers and offset to the right. The letter Q was below the number one, W was below the two, and so on to the P which was offset beneath the zero. If this were the key Dent used then it would be simple enough to look at the date as a set of single digit numbers and type them on the letters directly underneath. Meg held her breath and typed in the date of the first file, which at this point she had memorized from all the repeated attempts at finding it's password. It was 18 JUN 75, simplified to 18 06 75, and which typed in as QI PY UT. The file opened.

"Yes!" she cried with elation, hugging herself. "Way to go, CodeBreaker! You are hot, girl! You are so hot! XenX would be proud of you. "She was laughing, feeling giddy with the euphoria of the moment; however, her triumph faded to intrigue and awe at the images lining up on the spreadsheet. Meg stared at a code system unlike any she had seen before. Almost perfect in its structure, it was also amazingly simple and based on patterns of four letters. Q, S, C and Z cascaded across the spreadsheet like complicated beadwork on a Hopi necklace, a variety of patterns repeated and merging in multiples of the letters. She moved the cursor to speed past the images and for a few seconds it seemed as if she actually saw something in the lines of code, as if they formed a kind of complex and beautiful visual rhythm. Then it was gone and Meg found herself staring at a code which she instinctively knew she would not be able to break.

The initial pleasure of the moment began to fade, and with a jolt she realized the file she had stolen had nothing to do with DES or its sister replacement. It was not the code she had been sent to Signet to find. This realization was like having a glass of cold water thrown in her face. What had she done?

"I'll tell you what you've done," she said with growing apprehension. "You've broken into Willis Dent's computer system and stolen a code that isn't the one you were looking for. You didn't find it, verify it, and then turn the information over to your boss so he could use a search warrant. You didn't even just take a discrete copy of it. You moved it. You wiped it right off his system, and it isn't even what Hammond wanted you to look for in the first place."

Meg was quiet for a few seconds, then closed the file. "Shit."

She looked at another file, 12 DEC 76, then typed in the password QW QW UY and said, "Open sesame." It obliged. The spreadsheet was filled with a similar code based on the same letters, but it was also quite different. It had its own kind of rhythmic beauty with longer repetitive patterns. At the moment, however, she was hardly able to appreciate it. She closed the file, closed the folder, and exited the computer. What was she going to tell Hammond? It didn't seem likely that he could know what she'd done, but if he did there was no doubt he would bring it up first thing tomorrow. He was very straightforward that way. However, if he was pulling her out of Signet because she hadn't found the DES related program codes, and she wasn't going back there again, then maybe he didn't need to know about the mistake she'd made.

"Don't be stupid," she sighed, stretching out on the couch and massaging her tense scalp. "You've got to tell him. Even if he gets really upset with you, it's better if you tell him."

First, though, she would wait for him to bring it up, and have the CD in her purse as proof of her desire to confess. There would be no harm in waiting to see what he had to tell her, and why Aunt Agnes had felt the urgent need to invite her to breakfast.

*   *   *

At ten o'clock Tuesday morning, Ross Ecklund, one of Signet's security investigators, was just finishing up with Beverly Holbrook. Dent had seen her first thing before going to his meeting, and she still looked stricken. Her skin had taken on a grayish hue, and her eyes were red. Some of that was probably from yesterday's illness, he guessed, but most of it was from knowing how close she had come to being fired. "Is that everything you can tell me?" he queried.

"I can't think of anything else." Her gaze seemed distracted by the inner turmoil she was experiencing. "It's just so strange. I wouldn't have guessed Margaret capable of something like this. She seemed so nice and helpful..." her voice trailed off. "I mean, all the other secretaries liked her."

"I'll talk to them," he said, feeling sorry for the woman who had been outmaneuvered by the skilled Miss Wilson, or whatever her true name was. "You really couldn't have foreseen this," he reassured her.

"I was so careless."

It was clear that she was not going to forgive herself for this breech any more than her employer was. Ross sat down on one of the chairs, waiting for his boss. Willis Dent and Alan Scorzato should be showing up soon. For the fiftieth time Ross flipped open Margaret Wilson's file and looked at her employee picture. It didn't do her justice, that was for sure. He remembered seeing her last Friday, during the security meeting, when she had brought in a stack of papers and handed them out. She was a woman easy to notice, and Ross had enjoyed looking at her. It was amazing that this lovely face, and those wide brown eyes, housed such a cleverly devious mind. She was smarter than Dent, Scorzato, or even himself, Ross mused. He pretty much had proof of this though it wasn't something a man liked to admit. He couldn't have accomplished what she had done, nor could any of them. Just because she was clever, though, didn't assure her escape. Ross was also smart, but more importantly he knew how to couple his brains with dogged investigative work. She'd been here two months and must have left behind some small clues about herself that he could follow. He didn't believe she was going to be impossible to find. Just really, really hard.

Dent and Scorzato arrived and they all went into the office which looked out over one of Portland's city parks. Ross and Alan sat down in chairs opposite their employer. "Okay," Dent said. "What have you found out?"

Alan reached for the file, taking it from Ross. "It's all fake. Every bit of it."

Ross glanced at Alan who had come into the office for only an hour this morning before leaving to do who-knew-what. Last night Ross had come in as soon as Dent called him, then stayed at the office until eleven. He had also been working on the file since six this morning, going over it with a fine-toothed comb. Alan had barely scanned it.

"You're telling me everything in that file is phony?" Dent queried, his voice taking on an even harder edge. "What does that say about the company we've been using for background checks? You assured me that ProFilers was the best, Alan, and that they were thorough."

Alan glanced down at the file, readying an answer, when Ross stepped in. "Actually, they're very good at giving us what we ask for. They did a complete search of her background, or at least the alias Margaret Wilson. We can assume that's not her real name. They verified everything on the application, and our personnel office also followed up by calling all of her references which were impeccable, by the way." He retrieved the file from Alan and pulled out some letters, each with impressive company letterheads. "They sent great reference letters, too. Of course each of the numbers I called on this list have since been disconnected, as were the numbers on her original application. Her home phone listing has also been disconnected. I've been told there were times someone on staff called her at this number and got hold of an answering machine with her voice on it, but it's my guess nobody ever talked to her directly at this number."

He got ready to drop the bomb. "Not only that, but she called in this morning."

"What?"

"Why didn't you tell me?" Alan asked.

"It happened at eight-thirty while you were both gone. It gave us no help, though, since the number wasn't traceable."

"What did she say?" Dent queried.

"Her mother, in Denver, has had a stroke and she's flying out this morning to be with her. She doesn't know when she'll be able to make it back into the office."

"Convenient," Alan said with sarcasm.

"No, this is good," Dent observed with controlled excitement. "It means she doesn't know we've found her out. She's assuming we haven't learned her file is a fake yet, or figured out that she broke into my computer."

"Don't get your hopes up," Ross cautioned. "I'm not clear on why she called in, but she has to know it's only a matter of time until you discover what she's done. Maybe this is her way of trying to postpone suspicion when she doesn't show up, just in case we haven't yet found the files are missing. She's too smart to believe that won't eventually happen."

Dent leaned back in his chair, the closest he would ever come to slouching, and Ross continued. "Her address doesn't check out either. I went there at seven this morning and talked to the manager of the apartment building. Number G30, at this listed address, has been vacant for a month which doesn't surprise me. The tenants who lived there before were Korean, so we know it's not as if she were there and recently move out. It's another set-up."

He flipped through the papers in the file and pulled out a photocopy of her driver's license and Social Security card. "These are fake. DMV has no existing number for this driver's license, and it must be the same with the Social Security card though that's taking a while longer to verify. I haven't contacted WSU yet, either, but my guess is that they have no record of this particular Margaret Wilson ever having attended their university. Her resume, references, and college transcript are clever forgeries."

Ross straightened the papers in the folder. "It had to be difficult and expensive to come up with this cover. What I mean is that not just anybody has the resources to pull this kind of thing off so well, coming up with a useable Social Security number and phony college transcript. For this reason I'd guess that whoever set her up here as a plant has some funds to work with. You can eliminate any of your small competitors who might be dying to get their hands on your files. They may have a motive but don't have the financial backing to play at corporate espionage on this level. We need to look at your biggest competitors, and also to consider the government."

"The government?" Dent repeated. "Why would the government send somebody to spy on me?"

Ross Ecklund saw paranoid alarm spring into his boss' eyes. He didn't have time to respond because Alan snorted in derision at this suggestion. "We don't have anything that the government wants. I think you're blowing this out of proportion. How can you even be sure she was the one who stole the files? I mean, look at her," he said, reaching over to the folder in Ross' lap and flicking the picture with his finger. "She's just a secretary with a great body and probably not enough brains to even access a security system. You really think she broke in here and got through two passwords? I don't think she could have done that without help. Maybe someone else in our company gave them to her."

"Don't be dense," Willis said with cold annoyance. "No one could give them to her. I was the only one who knew them!"

It was clear Alan hadn't thought of this but had instead assumed a few others must have shared access to the files. Ross glanced at Alan and noticed a flush of embarrassment rising above his reddish goatee. He guessed that the greatest success Alan Scorzato had ever attained at Signet was the interview which had landed him his current job.

Ross closed the folder and looked at Dent. "Now that the passwords have been broken, and are useless, do you mind if I ask what they were? It might help explain how she did it."

Dent seemed hesitant at first, then shrugged. He pointed to the two paintings on the wall behind them. They turned to look at the artwork in fancy ebony frames. Ross thought the swirls of gritty acrylic color were ugly, but he also recognized he wasn't an art buff. "I don't get it," Alan said with a puzzled expression.

"Their titles, *eclipse* and *shadows*," Ross explained, pointing to the small nameplates. "Clever girl."

"The office was locked, right?" Alan reminded. "She wasn't even in here to look at those pictures."

"Had she been inside your office before?" Ross asked.

"Yes, but only two or three times. She seemed interested in the room and the furniture, even commented on the tapestry," he admitted, obviously embarrassed at being duped.

Ross sensed his employer's discomfort and nodded. "There's nothing about that which would have seemed suspicious, though."

"What about the security videotape?" Dent asked, changing the subject.

"There's nothing there," Alan answered. "It's not that good a film, anyway, because it's a profile shot of her in the lower half of the video. The camera is mainly focused on your office door, you know, and doesn't even catch what's visible on the computer screen. It looks like she was just doing routine office work."

"Actually, I picked up on a few things," Ross interjected, feeling annoyed with Alan's efforts to show he was in charge. Alan may have been his supervisor, but he really didn't know jack about how to investigate. This morning he had watched the tape only once, while last night Ross had replayed parts of it more than a dozen times, even studying a majority of the footage frame by frame.

"What did you find?" Dent asked.

"Nothing concrete enough to use as evidence, but still some suspicious behavior. She typed for the first few minutes, then started using the mouse. For nearly fifteen minutes she worked back and forth, using the mouse and then typing a few letters on the keyboard. I'm guessing that's when she was trying to break through the passwords." He remembered the intent look on her face, the worried glances down the hall, and finally an exultant expression. He didn't mention this.

"After a while she seemed to be looking for something in one of the drawers off camera. I'm guessing it was a writeable CD which she then inserted into the drive. Not long afterwards she began typing again, stopping only to use the mouse a few more times. Near the end there seems to be a partial shot of her sliding something into her pocket, but it's hard to see. A minute later you showed up."

"Which is when she hit the master switch," Dent stated. "Then it's conclusive. She did break my passwords."

"That's mostly speculation on Ross' part," Alan said with irritation, trying to show who was in charge.

Ross didn't respond or say what he was thinking, that it wasn't speculation because his gut instincts told him there was no doubt she'd broken into Dent's system. He had seen her worried glances, how she bit her lower lip while intently focusing on the computer screen, and how her hands had nervously fidgeted with the envelopes and papers while waiting for the files to be saved. Margaret was probably skilled at breaking codes, but she wasn't an unflinching corporate spy. She had been a bundle of nerves.

"Like I said, it's not evidence," he explained. "It was only suspicious behavior."

"Then there's no way of knowing if she did it or not," Dent sighed.

"I think there is," Ross answered. "While you were gone this morning I checked out the record log on the server. During the last seven weeks it was accessed fifty-four times from the computer system in her work space."

The two men stared at him, realization dawning. "The secretaries only have clearance to enter the database," Dent stated. "The server is restricted to upper level managers who have access to the password."

Ross slowly nodded. "Somehow she got that password, too, because she entered the server tons of times between January 12th and last Friday. Sometimes she was digging in there two or three times a day. My guess is that she was systematically searching for the files you had hidden on your computer." He really wanted to know what the secret files held, but knew better than to ask. Whatever information was in them it was obviously valuable and this loss could possibly cost Signet huge benefits in the long run. He had seen smaller companies destroyed by internal thefts and understood his employer's frustration.

"I want you to find her," Dent said, his mouth drawing into a tight line.

"We'll do it," Alan stated.

"Don't make promises you can't keep," his boss commented with cold reserve. "Ross, what are our chances of getting this girl, and getting back those files?"

Ross let out a slow breath and shrugged. "It's not going to be easy but I'll give it everything I've got. I took prints off her workstation last night, and will turn in a police report of corporate espionage this afternoon. My guess, though, is that the prints won't turn up anything because she's got no record. She wouldn't have been hired by her current boss if she would have been that easily traced. There is one plus, the simple fact that she worked here for two months. She seemed well liked, according to Beverly, and I don't believe a person can work at a company, socialize with other people, and leave no clue about their true selves. If she's unwittingly left behind some piece of information about herself then I'll find her. Just bear in mind that I'm not a miracle worker, and if we do track her down she may have already passed on the files to her true boss. Anyway, I want to start by interviewing the other secretaries." He stood, anxious to start this secondary process.

"Tell them they're to give you full co-operation under my orders," Dent said. "If you find her there'll be a major bonus in it for you. I want that woman taken care of."

A strange feeling came over Ross at Dent's choice of words, and at Alan's closed expression. He studied them both, eventually deciding he had seen too many mafia dramas. Signet's president no doubt meant that he wanted her arrested, and Ross couldn't blame him.

"I expect to have ongoing reports of your progress," Dent stated.

Ross nodded, started to leave, then turned back. "One other thing. There's something that I can't figure out. Why did Miss Wilson, or whoever she really is, remove the file from your computer? She had to know you would keep a backup. Stealing it off your system was stupid because it threw up a red flag. She could've taken a copy and you'd probably never have suspected her."

Dent looked thoughtful, even concerned by this new puzzlement. "I don't know."

"Well, I guess I'll ask her when I find her," Ross said. With that he left the room.

Chapter 4

The young woman sat on the porch swing, tired from rising so early and working hard all morning. The sky was blue and filled with thick white clouds, which was a delightful sight after so much rain. The breeze was cool on her face and she fastened the top button of her quilted jacket. Then she closed her eyes, letting her hands rest on the swell of her abdomen. The movement of the baby was like the slow roll of an ocean wave.

Soon she drifted off to that place which was neither sleep nor wakefulness, and found herself twelve years old again, standing on a dusty road lit by a lopsided white moon. Behind her was the main highway; further behind that was both grief and loss. Ahead of her, just down the road, was something evil. There was also something wonderfully good which beckoned to her. Tucking her short red curls beneath a baseball cap, she continued forward until the tent came into view. It was surrounded by parked cars which sat like silent stones, worshiping the ratty canvas tent with faded paint declaring: Brother Voltry's Hands of Faith. A few yellow and blue flags atop the tent snapped in the night wind, and beyond that were the sounds of an organ, a voice rising in sermon, and many voices crying hallelujahs.

She drew near. Sallow light spilled out of the mouth of the tent, and the voices grew louder. Inside it was stuffy and warm, sweaty people crammed together on metal folding chairs. There were people with infirmities lining up before a man wearing a long black suit coat and a string tie with silver tips. His loud voice reverberated off the taut canvas walls, swelling with importance. He was healing grateful people who begged him to take their money. They were poor folk. Most didn't have enough money left for the doctor, but they could hand over their last paycheck, or most of their social security nest egg, to be healed. She recognized right away that he was the source of the evil, a kind of blasphemer who made a profit from people's misery. He refused to recognize that life was full of marvelous things, and that mankind had been given a beautiful world for which God never charged a cent.

In a moment her attention was drawn to a boy behind the back row of chairs who was walking in her direction. He was probably a couple of years older than she was, with dark eyes and an easy smile. There was nothing shy about him, and he seemed to have an open, genuine expression of pleasure. A few seconds more and he was standing beside her.

"It's about time," he said over the noise, his smile easy and infectious.

"Why do you help him?" she asked, her voice tinged with accusation and not a little disappointment.

He glanced towards the dominant figure of the tent, then indicated the throng of people who sat with their hope, and their last few dollars, in their hands. "I'm not helping him. I'm helping them."

She nodded, understanding and feeling relieved. "You ready to get out of this place?"

"Let's go," he grinned. They headed towards the opening and he said, "I'm Jack, by the way."

"Nice to meet you, Jack-by-the-way," she joked, stepping into the cool night air which was delicious after being in the poisonous draft.

Inside the tent Voltry commanded an old man to rise from his wheelchair. "I invoke the pow'r of the Lawd and declare unto you, arise!" he cried with frenzy. Nothing happened.

*   *   *

A couple of hours before Ross and Dent's meeting at Signet, Richard Hammond sat in his office which was overloaded with organized clutter. The CSS field director's desk was a mess. He never really had a problem with misplaced papers, though, because of an instinct about where he had last put things. At the age of fifty-eight he was very involved in his work and the work of his underlings. He loved what he did and knew enough to recognize how fortunate that was. Richard also had a wife who loved him, which proved life had genuinely smiled on him. He chose to ignore the fact that he was overweight, not much to look at, never comfortable in the suits he had to wear, and required an arm-brace cane because of a jerky gate when he walked. He had survived childhood polio which was now exacerbated by arthritis. The pain was miserable and slowed him down, but even in spite of this Richard's attitude was 'you can't have everything.'

At the moment he was meeting with Daniel Trenery, who had come down from NSA. Although Richard was never intimidated by anyone, he felt somewhat off-balance because of the recent turn of events. Both of them were waiting for Meg Parrish who should arrive soon.

"I don't think it's necessary to pull Miss Parrish from this assignment," Trenery said. "We're still not sure that what happened to Phil was more than just an accident."

"I'm not willing to take that chance. Meg is the most creative cryptographer I've got, which actually is irrelevant when it comes to the safety of one of my people. Besides, we can't have her in two places at once, and if you want the boy approached then who else are we going to use on such short notice?"

"That's true," Trenery ceded. "I guess if she's been unable to find that code system after two months then we need to give it up."

"Maybe Willis Dent doesn't have it anyway," Richard suggested. "Maybe he only had the file list and was never able to get his hands on the actual codes." Trenery nodded but neither of them really believed this.

"Everything's taken care of, as far as Phil's cover story?" the senior agent asked.

"Yes," Richard replied. "The story of the hit-and-run is in today's paper, and it used his cover name, Phil Black. Then tomorrow there will be a fake obit."

"Good, then," Trenery said, though both of them felt the situation was anything but good. They hoped there would be no need for a real obituary a few days from now.

Richard studied his superior. He had a slender, homely face centered with a sharply arched nose. His dark hair was clipped short, his charcoal gray suit was neatly tailored to his trim form, and his trousers had pressed creases down both pant legs. His shirts were always white with button-down collars, his solid-color ties perfectly knotted. Some of his exactness in dress and attitude came from a military past, and Richard often felt sloppy in comparison to this NSA supervisor. Daniel Trenery's outer appearance mirrored his exactness of mind. He often had the ability to work over details like a methodical field commander setting up military zones.

"I read through a profile on Miss Parrish though I haven't seen a picture of her," Trenery said. "She's not very old, is she?"

"Just turned twenty-six." Hammond swivelled in his chair and began digging through the mess of files on the top of the cabinet behind him.

"What did you mean when you said she's your most creative cryptographer?"

Hammond pulled out one of the files and opened it, turning back around. He removed a photograph from the inside cover of the folder, handing Meg's picture to Trenery. "She has a good analytical mind, but so do all my staff. I'd say it's her gifted thought process which sets her apart."

"What do you mean?"

"When she first came to work for me, there were several highly skilled mathematicians also on staff. At the time they were avidly working on blocks of coding to try and solve a difficult cyphertext. Right away Meg bypassed their block analysis and looked at the whole as it was composed of the blocks, explaining the patterns she saw and they later found. They'd been dogmatically focused on the segments, then she came along and pointed out how the whole had patterns. 'Like a quilt,' she said. She was right. It was surprising to say the least."

"How did your mathematicians take it?"

Hammond chuckled. "Not well. Can you imagine what it was like? Say you're a skilled pianist who has a degree in music. You've spent years reading musical notes, studying music and music theory, plus hundreds of hours practicing the piano. You've gone to every competition, recital, and concert that was required of you. You've paid your dues and have the papers to prove it. Then she comes along. No credentials. She can't even read notes very well. What she can do, though, is play by ear. She can play extremely well. Rachmaninoff is a snap for her. Not only that, but she can compose with incredible ease. You've been working your heart out, and she shows up at the last minute to take the blue ribbon. For a while it was pretty chilly around here. A couple of them started calling her 'teacher's pet' but she just smiled and shrugged."

"Cute pet," Trenery said, indicating the picture.

Hammond nodded. "Her looks didn't help the situation, either. Anyway, it's not like she can always see the patterns in codes. It just depends on the cyphertext and how the algorithms or the coding fall. Even when she can't immediately come up with a pattern it's amazing what she can still do by using her basic analytical skills."

"How did she end up working for you?"

"Lloyd Weston, at the National Cryptologic School, called me. He was teaching there and I was still in Maryland at HQ. He heard about the plans for me to head up this satellite program, and called to tell me about Meg. She was his student, whom he'd met the year before. One of the classes he teaches is a course in advanced encryption which she had signed up for along with a bunch of other students. The first day he always gives them a code to break and bans any computer help. If they don't figure it out on their own, in an hour, then they're dropped from the class. For this particular test he used an encryption which could be resolved two different ways, and he required they show the process on paper. It was hard and knocked out three-fourths of the students who had enrolled. She was one of them.

"The next day he met with any students who wanted to appeal. There were always a few who thought their answers were right or that their previous work and transcripts were impressive enough to give them entry. Lloyd's never been easily dazzled and he almost never makes exceptions, just tells them to try again next semester. Meg was his last appointment that day and he pulled out her test, surprised to see it was blank. She hadn't even written anything down. According to Lloyd she was tentative about meeting with him and apologized for taking his time. She explained she wasn't appealing the test. Said it was clear she'd flunked it, but just out of curiosity she wanted to have him check her solution. Apparently she'd been thinking about the encryption during the night. It was eating at her because she'd been unable to find an answer during the test. For her own curiosity she asked him to look at her solution and see if she had finally figured it right. He watched her write out a decryption and recognized it was the correct answer."

"Wasn't he concerned she'd just gotten her hands on one of the test answers and was trying to pull the wool over his eyes?" Trenery asked.

"No, because her decryption was different from the original two solutions. She had come up with a third correct formula that Lloyd hadn't even seen."

Trenery let out a low whistle. "I'm guessing she got into his class."

Hammond smiled. "He took her under his wing, so to speak, and the next year called me about her. Seems she was planning on dropping out of school."

"Why?"

"She was top of her class in some of the courses, while she was flunking others. Go back to my analogy of music. Meg had this unique ability to perform and compose by ear, so to speak, but had a lot of trouble reading the basic musical notes. Yet a majority of the classes were based on that practical knowledge which was extremely frustrating for her. Anyway, after we talked and he told me some more things about her, I decided our team needed her, really needed her. So I begged upstairs, asked them to let Meg join us. I even ended up talking to the director himself, and he suggested that we set her up in our satellite program under an educational internship; his criteria was that she must finish the school year because she had been recruited to NCS and was on scholarship there. She did, then flew out here. She's been with me ever since."

Trenery was thoughtful, handing back the photo which Hammond paper-clipped back inside the folder before closing it. "What about her personal background? I read through her history on the way here, as I told you. Doesn't any of that make you concerned?"

"Why should it? She went through all the 'jazz' the same as the rest of us."

Jazz was Hammond's term for the extensive background check, polygraph tests, and in-depth psychoanalysis which all NSA and hence CSS personnel were expected to submit to. He didn't add what he'd sometimes wondered: when CSS recruiters found her, how much had their division been willing to overlook because she was such a great find? "You should already know, from having read her history, that she was given a clean profile in spite of those early traumas."

"Almost too good to be true. I wonder if either of us could have come through those experience and been unaffected."

"She's not unaffected," Hammond said, his voice taking on a slightly defensive edge. "Who could be? Instead I'd say that she's coping and doing pretty well. Along the way she's also managed to become a more valuable employee than most."

"I can't argue that."

There was a light knock and the door opened, interrupting their conversation. Meg smiled tentatively and came in. She was dressed in jeans and a thick teal sweatshirt against the damp air. It had been raining most of the morning, not unusual weather for March in Oregon. She also had on thick-soled boots and a leather carry-all hung from a shoulder strap, which Hammond hardly ever saw her without. She looked tired this morning, her face a little pale.

Hammond motioned to a chair and she sat down, then he introduced her to Daniel Trenery who shook her hand.

"In about a half hour, when we've finished here," Hammond said, getting right to the point, "I want you to call Signet and tell them your mother has had a stroke and that you're flying to Denver to be with her. Tell them you don't know how long you'll need to stay there."

Meg let out a slow breath, wondering again if he somehow knew about the files she had stolen. "Why are you pulling me out of Signet?"

"A couple of reasons, the main one being that one of our field agents, who was also undercover at Signet, was seriously injured in a hit-and-run. We're still not sure if he's going to make it."

Meg looked at them with surprise. This was not the reason she expected to be given for being pulled from Signet. "Was he about six feet with blond wavy hair, blue eyes and a square jaw? Kind of friendly looking?" she asked.

The men glanced at each other. "His name is Phil Allred, an operative from HQ who came in only a couple of months ago. Do you know who he is?" Hammond asked.

Meg shook her head. "I saw him in the hallway here, and then in a conference room at Signet." Hammond looked at Trenery with an I-told-you-so expression.

"It kind of unsettled me to see him there," she confessed. "You didn't tell me you were sending in another operative."

"Phil was working in a different area of Signet, not one related to yours," Hammond explained. "We didn't think your paths would cross."

"Are you assuming someone working for Signet was the one who ran him down?" Meg asked. What would Willis Dent do to her if he figured out what she had done, and if he was able to find her? She pushed away this initial concern. The experts in their organization, who had set up her cover file, really knew what they were doing. He wouldn't find her.

"We're not sure. Maybe it was just a drunk driver who took off after he struck Phil," Trenery answered.

"It looks like there's also a chance someone searched his home," Hammond added. "It wasn't ransacked, or anything like that, but things look like someone might have been there. So at this point I'm not willing to take any more chances with my people."

Meg realized that the only way Signet's security corps could have found Phil Allred's home was to have followed him, since there would have been nothing in his personnel file to give him away. If someone at Signet had followed her, too, she would have had a visit from them before now. Even so, the thought of this sort of danger coming from someone at Signet left her feeling a little nervous. At this point it seemed the best thing to do would be to reach inside her purse, grab the CD, and hand it over to her boss. Explaining wouldn't be fun, but maybe it was necessary.

"Besides," Trenery said, interrupting her thoughts, "We need you somewhere else. We've got another field case which should only take a few days. It's nothing like your stint at Signet. According to your file you're quite skilled at sign language."

Meg was startled by this off-beat query. Why was he asking about that? Hammond read her expression and leaned forward in his chair.

"We need a field operative who can sign. We also need someone who is young, attractive, observant, and who can pass as Deaf."

She stared at him, saying the first thing that came into her mind. "That's a big taboo in Deaf culture. It's the number-one rule with them in regards to hearing people. You're never, ever supposed to pretend to be one of them." Both of the men stared at her as if this were totally irrelevant, and she took a defensive posture. "Besides, I haven't signed in ten years."

A memory flooded back to her of sitting in a white birch tree, hands flying, Robyn laughing. She couldn't tell them the whole truth, that although she loved and missed sign language there was a bitter-sweet side to it because of Robyn. It filled Meg with sadness to sign without her sister. She couldn't tell them that, though, could she?

"I'm sure it's like riding a bicycle. Once you've learned how, you never forget," Trenery observed.

"Hardly," Meg scoffed. "The phrase you hear most from people who have experience with signing is, if you don't use it you lose it."

"You're not most people, Meg," Hammond said, silently concerned because of her reaction. He recognized they had hit a nerve. "I don't think you've ever lost an ability to do anything."

"Ten years, Richard! I haven't done it for an entire decade."

"Actually, according to your file, you participated in silent lunches when you were attending school in Ellensburg, and you also had some Deaf acquaintances in Maryland that you visited with every so often."

"What else does my file have in there?" she asked incredulously.

"Just about everything," Hammond smiled.

Well, not everything. It doesn't know about my nightmares, does it? Meg thought. She had worked through the syndromes of post traumatic stress with a therapist long ago, and later come through the required psychoanalysis with good results. According to the psychologist her survival mechanisms and tendency for self-healing were almost too good to be true. Of course she'd never explained to him about the nightmares. Not because the bad dreams were something she wanted to hide, but because they were so intensely personal. She didn't want to share them with others any more than she wanted to pose in the nude.

"This field operation will only be for a few days, and you don't need to start until Saturday," Hammond explained. "That will give you this entire week to review some sign language videos and the file we're giving you."

They were both staring at her and she let out a slow breath, having momentarily forgotten about the CD in her purse. "What is it you want me to do?" she asked with resignation.

*   *   *

Ross Ecklund, at Signet, was currently interviewing a fifth secretary, and his optimism at finding the elusive Miss Wilson was beginning to lose its edge. The consensus from the other workers had been the same: she was pleasant, nice to talk to though a little bit reserved, and a hard worker. He sat across the desk from Karen Wickerson, a secretary in purchasing who seemed full of office news. She was a thin woman with long hair in need of a trim. It was obvious she was excited to be interviewed, and he could only imagine how the speculation around the coffee pot must be flying.

Most of what Karen had to tell him was useless gossip, but he listened to it all. He never knew when a stream of mundane information might actually hold a vital nugget.

"She was a helpful sort, you know," Karen stated.

Ross thought it interesting that she had switched to the past tense in referring to Margaret. In Karen's mind the other secretary would no longer be working here. "Helpful?" he repeated.

"Well, yes...like last week. It was Shirley's birthday, you know. She's worked in our department longer than anyone, and she was turning sixty. It was a double celebration for her birthday and for her being here at Signet fifteen years. We'd all pooled our money to buy her a gift, but the secretary who had taken the money home with her called me the day before Shirley's birthday. She was kind of in a panic because her little boy was sick and she hadn't had a chance to get the gift yet. She wasn't going to be able to make it into work the next day for Shirley's birthday, either. It was a problem, you know, because she had the money with her, and one of us would have had to drive out to her place and get it after work, then go shopping."

"So Margaret helped you out?" he asked, hoping to hurry the story along.

"Yes, that's right. She said she could stop on the way home from work and pick something up. She'd bring it in the next day, and then when Wanda came back to work she could reimburse her. We all thought this was very nice because it was sixty dollars, and, well, you know how it is on a secretary's salary. Anyway, Margaret picked up this beautiful glass container for Shirley. It was a real hit with her, and she keeps it on her desk with a plant in it."

Ross nodded, looking down at the list and finding Shirley Orzano's name. "Thanks for your help," he said, standing. Ross realized he might have been handed a needed clue for tracking down Miss Wilson.

He left Karen Wickerson's cubicle and a moment later arrived at Shirley Orzano's. The woman was sitting at a desk which was well organized in spite of the stack of work. It also held framed photos of her family and a few plants. One of the plants was inside a small pitcher made of opalescent blue glass. Ross introduced himself.

"I know why you're here," she said, looking up from the open folder in front of her. "It's the only thing the others have been talking about since this morning."

He smiled at her forthright manner. "May I sit down?"

"I don't know any more than the rest of them," she shrugged. "But if you want to interview me, too, I don't care."

Shirley Orzano looked all of her sixty years. She was casually dressed, neither heavy nor slim, and wore her hair in a short permed style that required no work. Her face was round with a pointed chin, and he doubted she had ever worn makeup in her life. Shirley was one of those what-you-see-is-what-you-get kind of people.

Ross sat down, deciding he would do better with Shirley if he skipped the small talk. "Anything you can tell me about Margaret Wilson?"

She smiled at his equally straightforward manner. It made her chin more pointed, giving her an elfin-grandmother look. "Sure. I can tell you several things, but nothing of much use."

"Did you like her?"

This wasn't what she was expecting. Her smiled faded and she turned thoughtful. "I liked her a lot. She was a real sweet girl. I don't know what kind of trouble she's in, but whatever you're thinking she's done it must be a mistake. The poor gal has already had enough problems in her life."

"What do you mean?" Ross asked. None of the others had said anything like this.

"She's not very old to be left alone without family. Most of the others, maybe all of them, don't know she's an orphan."

Now things were really taking a different direction. He nodded as if he knew what she was talking about. "I guess Margaret didn't feel comfortable telling the other secretaries about that. How did you find out?"

"It was a month ago. I was feeling down because it was the anniversary of my husband's passing. Thought I was keeping it to myself pretty well because nobody noticed I was blue. Except Margaret noticed. I was eating lunch right here at my desk when she showed up with her sack lunch. She asked if she could sit with me and we started talking. It was real good. I didn't cry or get maudlin, or anything like that. Just talked about Herve and the kind of husband he'd been. You ever lost anybody close to you, Mr. Ecklund?"

Ross studied the delicate glass pitcher on her desk. "Yes I have."

"Then you know the worst part is that nobody wants to let you say a thing about the person who died. Maybe they're afraid that saying something, or mentioning their name, will make it hurt more. Truth is, ignoring them like they never even existed is way worse."

Shirley's observation was keen and it brought up long buried feelings inside Ross. "That's true," he replied.

"It was then she mentioned that her dad died when she was little, and then her mom passed away a few years ago. She said it left her feeling 'cut off.' I remember those words because it described how I felt. Anyway, right after she told me this she seemed kind of nervous and asked me not to talk about it with the others."

I'll just bet, he thought. The real Margaret must have slipped up, because according to her file her parents were divorced and her mother lived in Denver. Hence the call this morning to say her mother was in the hospital suffering from a stroke.

"She explained how she's a real private person," Shirley continued. "She didn't want everyone feeling all sorry for her."

"I can understand that," Ross commented. He then pointed to the decorative glass pitcher. "Is that the gift she picked out for your birthday?"

"It is," Shirley answered, puzzled that he would know about it and be interested in it.

"Very pretty. Were you happy to get it?"

"Yes I was. It's so delicate and fancy, though, nothing like what I'd get for myself. Margaret said I needed something that wasn't practical. Something I could look at everyday and enjoy because it was pretty. Look, Mr. Ecklund, I don't know what you think that girl did, but you must be wrong. A few of the other women here are jealous of her because she's so pretty. But she doesn't see herself like that. She's not uppity at all. What she is, I'd say, is a good, sweet girl. If you just get a chance to sit down and talk to her you'll see that."

"I'm hoping to get that chance," Ross truthfully answered. "I'd like to get that chance before the police find her."

Shirley's eyes widened in alarm. "The police?"

"I'm not supposed to discuss this with anyone, Shirley, but you seem to know more about Margaret than the others, and to care about her. What I'm going to tell you is confidential, but it seems to me you are more capable of keeping a confidence than most of the other secretaries who only want to gossip."

"True," she managed.

"Margaret stole some files off of Mr. Dent's computer. We have her on video tape. In fact, as soon as I'm finished here, I'm going down to the police station and file a complaint against her for corporate espionage. I'll also be turning in her fingerprints."

Shirley's lips parted in alarm and her eyes filled with uncertainty. "I can't believe it."

"If I can find Margaret first, and convince her to return the files, it will go a lot better for her than when the police get involved." He didn't add that there was little chance of them actually apprehending her with nothing to go on but a file full of forged papers. He also doubted they would do more than take down his report.

Shirley's gaze wandered, distraught. She was torn between her affection for Margaret and her loyalty to Signet. "It's so hard to believe," she said, although her tone stated that she did, indeed, believe him now. "I don't know what to say."

"Why don't you start by telling me abut this glass pitcher?"

"The pitcher?" Shirley asked, a little bewildered.

"Margaret was the one who bought it, didn't she?"

"Yes. She picked it out, anyway. It's Fenton Art Glass. Margaret told me that when she's feeling blue she goes and buys a new piece. I guess she's got quite a collection of it in all different colors."

Ross felt a growing excitement. This small bit of information might be the clue he had been looking for. "May I?" he asked, picking up the pitcher which had cut-edge faceting. He checked the bottom but didn't see a tag. Shirley opened the bottom drawer of her desk, lifting out a square box of dark green cardboard with a gold crescent moon embossed on the top. She pulled off the lid and dug through the tissue.

"This is the tag that was on the pitcher, and this is the box it came in."

The tag was a folded piece of printed card stock detailing the history of the glassware. He picked up the gift box and turned it over. On the bottom was an oval gold sticker which said Half Moon Gift Shop. The address was printed in smaller letters beneath the name of the store. He read it twice to memorize it, then handed the box back to her.

"Thanks for your help, Shirley. I'm guessing I can trust you to keep this conversation confidential." If Dent knew Ross had let information slip, he would be hopping mad. Ross also realized that you sometimes had to trade a little knowledge to get a lead.

"I don't care for gossip," Shirley stated, and he realized her concern for Margaret would probably keep her lips sealed.

He nodded and smiled at the most likeable woman he had yet interviewed. "Is there anything else you can tell me?"

"Nothing to tell, only to ask. If you find her, give her a chance to explain, will you?"

Ross was thoughtful. "Okay," he said. "But only because she's got somebody like you vouching for her."

Shirley smiled again, the elfin chin reappearing.

Chapter 5

Wednesday morning Ross drove across town to look for the Half Moon Gift Shop supposedly located along the Willamette River near Ankeny Park. Since it was about a forty minute drive from Signet, he thought there was a good possibility Miss Wilson might actually live in the area. He couldn't envision her driving very far after work to pick up a gift for Shirley Orzano. The shop was probably convenient to her home. If this were the case then he might have a chance at finding her, unless she had already packed up and left after getting what she wanted from Dent's computer. Soon enough he would find out if this lead were valid or not.

The previous day Ross had finished interviewing the secretaries, not surprised to have gleaned nothing else which might lead him to his quarry. He had then spent the final hours of the day at the police station, going over the incident with a detective who seemed pleased enough to leave the investigation in the hands of Signet's security force. Ross had realized from the beginning that they had no real evidence against Margaret Wilson, although the detective did agree to run her fingerprints through ISIS.

Ross didn't see any of this as a setback, though, because he was enjoying his job for the first time since accepting employment at Signet. He found this hunt a challenging diversion, a salve to an earlier disappointment of running into another dead end in his decade-long quest. He had interviewed at Signet, and accepted the offered position, because of a lead he was following for personal reasons. Curiosity and hope had brought him from California to Portland. He had ended up staying here because there were no more leads to follow and no reason to go back.

He located the small store in a row of trendy shops and parked his car. The cloud cover overhead had parted, showing patches of blue sky. Not far away the river glided by like an iridescent green snake among the surrounding trees, sequins of sunlight scattered on its back. The day was still cool and the blue sky would probably not last, but at the moment it brought with it a rare promise of spring.

Ross entered the store and immediately smelled the mingled scents of potpourri, candles, and decorative soaps. Nearly every space in the shop was filled with tables and displays of saleable items, each section taking on a theme of color and coordinated goods. There were fancy objects of every kind and a myriad of merchandise. Baskets abounded with flowers and scented gifts. He hated stores like this.

He scanned the interior and saw shelves of art glass lining one wall. Ross worked his way over there and recognized the same kind of glassware that had sat on Shirley's desk. There were glass baskets, bells, tiny tea sets, figurines, pitchers, and vases of every shape. Much of the glass was opalescent pink, blue, and green, though there were also pieces in deep shades of purple or milky white with flecks of color.

"May I help you?" a woman in her late forties asked, coming up beside him. She was slender with likeable features and ash blond hair styled in a pageboy. Clad in a rose print skirt and matching sweater, she wore a name tag which said Belinda.

"Fenton Art Glass," Ross verified, greeting her with a smile. He was one of those people whose features came to life when he smiled. It softened the lines of his jaw and made his eyes look warm. "This is what I wanted to find. You have a lot of nice pieces."

"Yes we do," she said, returning the smile. "We have one of the largest collections in the city. Collectors come here from all over the Willamette Valley to buy from us. Do you know much about it?"

"No," he answered. "I'd never even heard about it until the other day."

"It's shipped to us from West Virginia. The Fenton Company has been making this kind of glass for eighty years. These pieces, here, are also hand-painted and signed by the artist," she said, indicating some of the solid color glassware. "From what I understand the glass is made with special silica found only in West Virginia, which is why their pieces have this excellent color. They're all hand-crafted, too."

Ross smiled again, this time more hesitant. "I met someone who has a collection, and she was trying to describe what it's like. The colors are great. I can see why she likes it so much."

"The opalescent pieces are the most popular because you don't see a lot of glass like this, except for some rare pieces shipped from Italy."

At this point Ross had learned more about the glass than he cared to know. Now was the tricky part. "My friend was saying something about that. She's a customer of yours, I guess."

"Really?" Belinda politely inquired. "What's her name?"

"Well," Ross said, pulling up his most sheepish expression, "I don't know." He lowered his voice and leaned slightly nearer in a confidential manner. "I met her at a business seminar. We were at the same table and started talking. Actually, when the speakers got really boring, we wrote notes to each other."

He stopped and looked embarrassed. "As bad as high school study hall, huh?" he said. Belinda chuckled and he knew he had her interest.

Ross wasn't a liar by nature; however, in a situation where showing his investigator's license wouldn't help, he became a convincing storyteller. "During the luncheon she told me she was going to reward herself for sitting through all these dry speeches by going shopping. I asked what she was going to buy and ended up learning about her glass collection and your store. Anyway, it's kind of a long story and I'm probably boring you."

"Not at all," the saleswoman encouraged.

Ross grinned again, maintaining his male-who-screwed-up expression. "She agreed to go out to dinner with me last Friday, and wrote her name and number on my notepad so I could call for directions..." he let his voice trail off.

"What happened?"

"I've torn my office and house apart looking for that notebook. I haven't been able to find it anywhere."

"You stood her up?" Belinda asked with an amused smile.

He nodded slowly, appropriately ashamed. "I couldn't call her because she only told me her name once, when we first met, and I forgot what it was. I didn't ask her again before we left because it was embarrassing not to remember her name. Besides, it was written down in my notebook, so I thought it'd be no big deal. I've been trying really hard to remember it, but I'm lousy with names. Faces I never forget, but names I blow all the time."

"I'm the same way," she said, and Ross thought it interesting that most people claimed this problem.

"I have a picture of her, though."

The sales woman lifted her eyebrows in surprise, her voice turning playful. "You don't know her name, but you have a picture of her?"

"Each of us had to bring a photo for a workshop game they were doing. Before we left I stole hers off the table," he admitted.

Ross realized this was where his story was getting pretty thin. At this point it didn't really matter, though, because the saleswoman had already bought it. He felt a twinge of guilt lying to her. Ross wouldn't have lied for personal gain, but since Miss Wilson had lied and stolen from Signet it seemed that all had become fair in the heat of the chase. He reached into his jacket pocket and drew out the company photo which had been in Margaret's personnel file at Signet. He showed it to the saleswoman.

"Well yes, of course! She's one of our customers who comes in quite often." Belinda paused for a moment to recall her name. "Meg Parrish, I believe."

Ross managed to smile with an expression of relief instead of triumph. "That's it," he said with genuine excitement. "Meg. I knew I'd remember her name when I heard it again." He turned his attention back to the glassware, picking up a large and beautiful fluted vase in iridescent shades of lavender. "If I were to purchase her a piece of glass, as an apology, would you be able to help me get it to her?" He knew better than to ask directly for the newly identified Miss Parrish's address or phone number.

"We do have a delivery service available for an extra fee. You could have it delivered to her, perhaps with a note inside."

"That would be great," he said with genuine pleasure. "How soon can we send it?"

"We only deliver once a week, on Saturday afternoons."

Inwardly he was irked at coming this close to finding her then having a delay, though Ross was smart enough to let only a little disappointment show. Besides, he now knew his quarry's real name. Between now and Saturday he might be able to find her on his own. "Will you help me pick out a piece she would like?"

"The one you're holding is very nice," Belinda said.

Very nice, and very expensive, he knew. Ross didn't flinch, though. Dent would think the vase a worthwhile expense if it led to the capture of their corporate thief.

He picked out a small card, pretended to write in it, then sealed the blank card in its envelope and handed it to the saleswoman. "If you see her before Saturday you won't say anything, will you? I'd like this to be a surprise."

"Of course," Belinda agreed. "I'm sure she'll be delighted to get this delivery."

You have no idea, Ross thought. He paid for the vase and also purchased a bouquet of spring flowers tied with raffia. He handed the flowers back to her. "For your help," he said before leaving the store.

The saleswoman smiled at him with pleasure, delighted to have been involved in what she believed to be a romantic episode. Of course she had no idea that her helpful deed would put Meg Parrish in the most deadly situation of her life.

*   *   *

"Hi Benny. I need you to go for a walk with me tomorrow morning," the voice on the other end of the phone-line said.

"Don't call me that," the young man replied, his voice static with anger.

There was a pause. "Sorry, Ben."

"Another walk, huh? That's twice in one week." His voice had flipped from dangerous to cheerful with surprising alacrity. "What're you trying to do, make me rich?"

Another pause. "We need your help."

"Okay, but before we go I want to explain something to you." The cheery sound was gone again. "Have you ever heard of the Chinese fairytale about the five brothers who all had special powers?"

"No, Ben, I haven't," the caller said, being careful not to sound patronizing.

"Well, let me give you the abbreviated version. This one brother is a fisherman who has the ability to drink up the whole sea and hold all the water in his mouth. That's how he's able to get special fish nobody else can find. This one little kid from the village begs the guy to swallow the ocean so he can get some rare fish for himself, and the guy agrees. He drinks the whole sea and holds it in his mouth while the kid goes picking up starfish and crabs, and all these great fish he's never seen before. Are you with me so far?"

"Yes."

"There's a problem, though. The Chinese brother can only hold the sea in his mouth for so long before he has to spit it out again. Pretty soon he signals the kid to come back because the time's up. The kid is so excited that he doesn't pay attention to the man who is waving his arms, trying to warn him it's time to leave. Does this sound familiar?"

There was an uncomfortable pause. "What are you getting at, Ben?"

"The Chinese brother is holding the whole sea in his mouth, desperately letting the kid know he has to get out of there, but the kid doesn't listen. In the meantime the poor guy's head is pounding from the pain of holding onto the ocean for so long. He gets to where he's ready to explode and finally has to let it all go. Do you know what ends up happening to the stupid little kid in the story?"

No answer.

"Are you there?" Ben softly asked.

"Yeah, I'm here. I'm guessing the kid drowned."

"That's right. Afterwards, the guy ends up being tried for the crime, even though it wasn't really his fault. Lucky for him his four brothers come to the rescue with their special abilities. The problem is, I don't have any siblings who

want to come save me, do I?"

"No."

"Do you get my point?" Ben asked, his voice taking on a subtle but threatening edge.

"I get it."

"Good."

                              *   *   *

After two days of endless rain, Portland's deluge temporarily stopped. The sidewalks and streets were almost dry except for shallow puddles left as evidence of the downpour. The sky was still the color of gray wool, though, and it wasn't smart to go anywhere without an umbrella. Saturday morning Meg donned a pair of jeans, warm shoes, a white turtleneck, and a thick pink sweatshirt. Pink wasn't her favorite color, but this shade looked good on her. It also made her appear younger, especially when she fluffed her hair in a messy, more carefree style. Apparently Hammond thought she looked young enough to pass for twenty, and though she didn't believe it for a second she was doing her best to fit his profiled cover. Obedience, Meg realized, was not necessarily an indicator of genuine acceptance. She alternated between extreme levels of doubt and irritation about this assignment. Couldn't he just let her go back to work at the CSS office, maybe writing another code or something? This undercover stuff wasn't anything she felt capable of doing well, especially after the last fiasco.

With a sigh of annoyance, at both Hammond and herself, she thought about the files purloined from Dent's computer. Meg had ended up leaving her boss' office without telling him what she had done. This was partly because she'd been distracted by the details of the new assignment, and partly because of nerves. Perhaps if Trenery hadn't been there she would have felt more comfortable admitting her error to Hammond. As it was they had discussed the new field assignment—argued about it, in fact—and then she'd been dismissed. Nearly a week had passed and Meg realized she wouldn't be going to her boss anytime soon to confess. Signet was history. If it weren't for the codes on the CD which continued to intrigue her, she would just forget about the whole thing. Although most of this week had been spent prepping for her new undercover assignment by voraciously reviewing sign language videos, she had still managed to check out most of the files on the CD. They were all different and yet the same—flowing streams of enigmatic codes which were like impractical but lovely works of art.

The phone rang and she picked up the receiver. "Hi Richard."

"How did you know it's me?"

"Who else would call? I think you're the only one who ever calls me, anyway. Are you checking to see if I'm going?"

"Kind of," he chuckled. "Do you feel more comfortable with this assignment since you've had a chance to study the videos?"

"No," she replied, picking up the folder on the night stand and looking at the photo of the young man. It had obviously been taken during surveillance and wasn't a very good picture. "Gee, Richard, he's just a kid! I'm seven years older than he is. Ten years ago I could have babysat him. You really expect that he'll be interested in me, strike up a friendship, and invite me home to meet the folks? It's not gonna happen."

"Think positive."

"I hate this. I'm not good at being a field operative," she complained, closing the folder and sticking it inside a drawer in the night stand.

"You told me several times you didn't mind being at Signet. You were even enjoying it, you said. I think the difference is, kiddo, that you were still working with computers and looking for codes. Now we're asking you to get personal. That makes you uncomfortable."

She didn't answer for a minute, then sat down on the bed, retying her shoe. "Don't analyze me. You're lousy at it."

"Sorry."

"I'm going now," she curtly stated.

"Meg?" His voice turned hesitant. "Just find the kid and where he lives, get in and see who's there, then get out. Keep it down to one day, if you can. No more than two." Hammond wanted to tell of his concerns, that there was more riding on her efforts than what she'd been told, and that a lot of pressure was being sent to him from upstairs. The info he had been given was classified, though, and he wasn't authorized to tell her more than she absolutely needed to know.

She sensed his concern. "You sound kind of worried. This isn't a dangerous assignment, or anything, is it Richard?"

"No, of course not. If it were, then we'd be using a trained FBI agent, wouldn't we?" He didn't tell her that this second plan had been put into effect because the FBI's best surveillance team hadn't been able to keep track of a nineteen-year-old Deaf kid. In spite of Daniel Trenery's assurances, this fact alone made him wary. "Take off, now. Just don't forget to check in."

Meg hung up the phone, stuffed a small umbrella in her backpack, then headed out the door.

* * *

Ross sat in his car. It was parked next to a few employee vehicles behind the row of stores near Ankeny Park. His car was far enough away from the back door of the Half Moon Gift Shop that no one would notice him, though he could still watch the place. He had been here since ten o'clock this morning, keeping an eye on the car belonging to the store. Surveillance was the part of investigation which he found extremely tedious even though it was necessary.

Wednesday the saleswoman had promised him the package would be delivered to Meg Parrish today. When that would actually happen was anyone's guess. He had originally hoped it would be in the morning, though this hope disappeared as the lunch hour came and went. Ross spent the time in his car with a bagel sandwich and soft drink.

It had been a frustrating couple of days for him. After his accomplishment of finding out the true name of Signet's thief, everything had gone downhill. He had started his search for Meg Parrish by doing the first and easiest thing he'd learned as an investigator; he looked in the phone book. It was surprising how many people ignored this basic step when they went searching for someone. Unfortunately there had been no Meg, Megan or Margaret Parrish in the Portland directory. There were, however, three listings for an M. Parrish. Two turned out to be men, and the other one was Mary Parrish, a young mother who ran a daycare. There were fifty-nine listings under the last name of Parrish in the Portland directory, and this roster he turned over to Signet's background research firm, ProFilers, for follow-up calls.

With nothing but a name to go on, Ross had been unable to use credit headers because they required both a social security number and the signed permission of the person whose credit was being checked. DMV hadn't been much better, either. Without a driver's license number, date of birth, or social security number to go on, it took far longer than normal to process the paperwork. He filed three separate forms asking for information on the names Meg, Megan and Margaret Parrish, but was told it would take seven to ten working days to get a response. If he'd still been living in California, Ross could have gotten the info much easier because of the inside contacts he'd made there over the years. Having lived in Portland only six months, and doing straight security work for Signet instead of private investigations, he had no such contacts established in Oregon.

Some of his time had been spent looking for Meg Parrish using ProFilers vast database. It allowed him to search for her by name, requiring neither address or date of birth. Ross had used every variation, spelling, and combination of the young woman's first and last name he could think of. Her name was surprisingly uncommon, and because of this he was able to come up with only six possible variables. Two of these were immediately eliminated by the Social Security

Death Master List. One of the women had died four years ago, the other two-and-a-half. The last time he had seen Meg Parrish she had definitely been alive and breathing.

The third name was eliminated because the woman had moved to Albany, New York ten months ago. The fourth was in the county jail on drug charges, which left only two more names. He had taken their addresses and searched them out. The most likely choice, a Margaret Parrish on River Street, lived only thirty minutes away from the Half Moon Gift Shop. He went there first, driving up in front of a large brick house with tall trees. Feeling hopeful and excited that this was her place, he had pulled into the circular driveway and seen the sign: Pleasant Valley Private Care Center. His optimism had faded. A quick check told him that this Margaret Parrish was over eighty and had been at the nursing home for two years. The woman was nearly blind, cross as a badger, and irritated with him from the onset. She had bitingly assured Ross, "I have no grandchildren, you idiot!"

The final name, Megan Ann Parrish, showed an address in Tigard which was on the outskirts of Portland. She was twelve.

Late Thursday afternoon the fingerprint check came back. When she had first been hired as Margaret Wilson, she had signed several application forms including a waiver giving Signet the right to conduct a background check and process her fingerprints. He had used that form to submit her prints with ISIS, the state-run program which covered Oregon, Washington, Nevada, Idaho, Utah and Arizona. Margaret, or Meg, had no prior criminal convictions in these states, which didn't really surprise Ross. It did mean, however, that police involvement in Signet's search for her would be minimal.

His final efforts to find her took him dumpster diving. Wednesday and Thursday night he had driven behind the Half Moon Gift Shop, checking their garbage dumpster for possible leads. No self-respecting investigator would ever be above picking through trash, he had reminded himself after accidentally sticking his fingers into the oozing remains of a milkshake. Friday night, when he checked the garbage bin, he was rewarded with two trash bags stuffed with paper. It was amazing what pieces of information the American public threw away, he reflected.

He had spent the evening in his apartment sorting through the papers, discovering a real boon. The shop had discarded the previous month's credit card receipts. He checked each one carefully, excitedly finding a three-week-old receipt for a fifty-seven dollar purchase by Meg Parrish. To his annoyance and dismay, the paper showed only her city and zip code. Great! he'd thought with irritation. An hour and forty minutes spent sorting through garbage, and all he knew for sure was which zip code area of Portland she lived in. With further irritation Ross realized he could probably get her address from the number on the card, except that it was 11:30 on a Friday night, and the next day the delivery from the gift shop was going to be made.

All the tricks of the trade he had learned in tracking down people had turned out to be useless. He reflected that whoever the real Miss Parrish worked for had managed to keep her life very private.

Half Moon's back door opened and an elderly man came out. He had a cardboard box in his arms which he put inside the hatchback of the shop's car. The saleswoman, Belinda, also stepped outside, handing him a list and nodding as he asked questions. A minute later she went back into the store, and the man fumbled in his pocket for keys. He had the look of a friendly grandpa in a zip-up cardigan and English driving cap. Ross started his engine and followed the delivery car out of the employee parking area, careful to keep his distance. At last the chase was underway.

*   *   *

Meg stepped off the MAX light rail transit system and into a crowd of people. The heart of Portland's Old Town was filled with activity. Street vendors, artists, entertainers, and tourists mingled together. It was the first day of the Portland Saturday Market which began in March and ran every weekend until Christmas Eve. Oregon proudly boasted the largest open-air market in continuous operation in the United States, and on this opening day it had drawn a huge crowd. The market stalls and vendors were situated along the Willamette River and the Tom McCall Waterfront Park in the heart of Portland; hundreds of people strolled past canopied booths which sold exotic wares and festive foods.

There were couples with children, couples alone, friends walking together, and sisters with shopping bags. Meg wandered with them, solitary in a society which liked couples. She stopped near a booth which sold velvet jester hats, looking at her map. There were more than four hundred vendors, which meant it would take her a little while to find the booth she was looking for. She moved past stands which sold batik fabrics, glass beads, fleece outerwear, and leather goods. It was going to be a long walk.

*   *   *

Ross sauntered by the parked delivery car and glanced at the condominium. The delivery grandpa, as he had come to think of the elderly gentleman, was inside the manager's office with the first package. Ross lifted the unlocked hatchback, and looked inside the large cardboard box to check the names on each gift-wrapped item. The package with Meg Parrish's name on it was still there, and Ross memorized its size in relation to the others. He closed the hatchback and headed back to his car. A few minutes later the grandpa in the English driving cap reappeared, getting behind the wheel.

From this point on it was even slower going. The traffic from the nearby Saturday Market was thick, and Half Moon's delivery man was not a speedy driver. After a while Ross wondered if every package but the one designated for the elusive Miss Parrish was going to be delivered. His car phone buzzed and he picked it up.

"How's it going?" Alan Scorzato asked. "You're still working on the case, aren't you?"

Ross hadn't told Alan what he'd learned about Margaret Wilson's real identity. He didn't like to share the loose details of an investigation until he had solid proof. Although the saleswoman had identified the picture, he himself hadn't actually made visual contact. Until he finished following this deliveryman to her home, and knew where she lived, he wasn't going to jump the gun and tell Alan he'd found her. A lot of things could have already happened that would make this just another dead end. If her sole reason for being in Portland was to steal those files off Dent's computer, then she might be long gone. Besides, if she was still here Ross wanted to do some further investigation before turning her over to Dent. For one thing, he wanted to learn which company had hired her.

"I'm working on it, Alan. It's just slow-going." Ross looked at the line of traffic, meaning this literally.

"No weekends off until we find her. That's from Willis himself."

Ross smiled, thinking this must really stick in his supervisor's craw. "I'm doing my best. Every lead I've had during the last two days has gone nowhere." That was true enough. They talked a few minutes more while Alan asked to meet with him that afternoon. Ross didn't want to but had no choice. He made a mental note of the time before extricating himself from the phone call.

It took more than an hour to finish the delivery route, and Meg Parrish's package did end up being the last one delivered. The elderly man, still unaware he was being followed, pulled up in front of a large three-story apartment complex which was painted Cape Cod gray with white trim. Although the buildings weren't new they were well-kept, with a grassy area and a pool central to the complex. Ross parked his car in the visitor's section and casually followed the older man who seem to have no trouble finding the ground floor apartment.

Ross pretended to be looking at the swimming pool; in reality he was learning which door belonged to Ms. Parrish. When there was no answer the elderly gentleman left a note, headed back to his car, and drove away. Ross stepped into the partial hallway and went to the door. He knocked, even though he knew there would be no answer. After scanning the shop's printed notice about an attempted delivery, he snatched the paper off the door and stuck it in his pocket. He wasn't disappointed Meg Parrish was out. If she still lived here, and hadn't moved on, it gave him an opportunity to search her place.

The front door had a deadbolt, so he knew there would be no easy access here. He casually walked back around the corner, counting the patio areas to figure out which one was hers. He also scanned for anyone who might be watching. The other exit from her apartment was a sliding glass door which looked out onto a small redwood patio surrounded by a low fence. A few terra-cotta planters edged the deck, and a wind chime hung from the eaves. Ross glanced at the other apartments, saw no one watching him, and went to the patio door. He examined it, realizing it was one of the older sliding doors which were easier to get through. Meg Parrish may have had a deadbolt installed on her front door, but she should have been more concerned about the patio door and put a stop bar in the bottom track.

He grabbed hold of the glass door, lifting it up a few inches and out of its track. It came free from the lock and he slid the door to the side before letting it fall back into the slotted aluminum track. Doing this had actually broken the lock, but it was too late now to change that. Pushing the draperies aside he disappeared into the apartment. Ross stood listening for noises. Thirty seconds of quiet and he felt certain no one was home. He slid the door closed behind him, letting the curtains fall into place. He examined the apartment's interior, pleased to know that the young woman hadn't moved out of the area after all. This meant she might still have the stolen files somewhere in her apartment. He felt excited at the prospect of winning this half of the game.

Ross also knew that what he had just done was illegal, regardless of his motives. It was breaking and entry, for which he could definitely be arrested, though this didn't worry him much. He actually found it exhilarating to venture close to the edge, and also held to the premise that all was fair during corporate war. Meg Parrish had been the one to start this battle by stealing from Signet in the first place. He doubted that his adversary would be anxious to call the police if she came home and found him here. His presence in her apartment, if she came back, might actually be enough to spur a confession from her. Ross was hoping that before this happened he might be lucky enough to find the stolen CD on his own. If so, he and Signet would be one giant step ahead in this game of corporate espionage.

He scanned the interior of the apartment, making mental notes of all he saw. The first thing he noticed was the computer. She had an impressive setup with every piece of electronic equipment anyone could want, including a scanner, a DVD and writeable CD Rom, two modems, a liquid crystal monitor, a cordless mouse, a LaserJet color printer, and a fax machine. Not bad for someone who was supposed to be getting by on a secretary's salary. Ross didn't bother to turn the system on. He wasn't a hacker and it would be a waste of time to try and get into her computer. Instead he continued to investigate the place.

The furniture was simple and comfortable, the white walls decorated with a few tasteful watercolors. There were houseplants and colorful pieces of Fenton glassware, which he now recognized, both on end tables and shelves. She had a small television, a stereo system, and a large collection of music CDs. He thumbed through the discs, seeing her tastes ranged from Bjork to Kitaro, with a lot of different artists in between. There were even a couple of classical orchestrations.

The kitchen was sterile with only a few counter-top appliances. The cupboards held a minimum of plates, bowls, and drinking glasses. There were boxes of cereal and crackers, and the small freezer was stocked with single-serving microwave dinners. There was a carton of milk and some fruit in the fridge, not much else. A cereal bowl and spoon sat in the sink, otherwise there were no dirty dishes. The rest of the apartment was also neat. Her bedroom was more uniquely decorated than the rest of the house, with plants and art glass atop an attractive wardrobe and dressing table. The bed was the most unique piece of furniture in the place. It had a delicate wrought-iron headboard, and tall posts which formed the skeleton of a square canopy. This was entwined with rose vines and gauzy fabric. The bed's comforter was a floral print over white eyelet, topped with lots of pillows. It was feminine and impractical, a contrast to the rest of the place.

Ross began searching the apartment, hoping to find the stolen CD. It was important to be methodical and yet move quickly. He started his search in the livingroom, carefully exploring every space and drawer, then moved through the rest of the apartment, ending up in the bedroom again. He checked the closet, which was filled with casual clothes. A few suits hung on the left side, like the one he had seen her wearing at Signet. It seemed as if the real Meg preferred jeans and sweaters rather than a corporate look.

In the top of the closet there was a folded quilt, extra blankets, and an album. He lifted down this last item, which was dusty on top, and opened it. The first page had a wedding portrait of an attractive couple. Carefully scripted beneath the picture was the date June 11th, 1967. Following this photo, and other snapshots of the couple, were baby pictures of a little girl named Robyn. Several pages later there was another baby picture. This one had Meg's name and birth date printed beneath it. Ross did the math and noted that Meg Parrish was twenty-six, older than she looked, and had celebrated her last birthday on that same Friday when he had first seen her at Signet. An odd coincidence, he reflected. Further inside the album there were family pictures of the father, mother, and two little girls. A few more pages and there were school pictures, but no more family photos of the four of them together. There were snapshots of the girls on their birthdays, and one or two of them with their mother, but no more pictures of the father. Ross remembered his conversation with Shirley Orzano, and assumed Meg had spoken the truth to the other secretary about her father's death.

Despite his role as an investigator, Ross felt uncomfortable. This was prying on a more personal level than what he was used to. Even so he continued to turn the pages, seeing glimpses of Meg Parrish's life. There were photos of the two girls playing at a river's edge, jumping on a trampoline, opening Christmas gifts, riding on a horse together, and dressed in Halloween costumes. He skipped some pages. They were older now; the photos showed Meg in ballet costumes and her older sister playing sports. There was a definite resemblance between the two sisters who both had long hair. He flipped more pages and saw an eight-by-ten portrait of the mother and two daughters when the girls were in their teens. It was a winter pose, and they all wore sweaters. He checked the date written on the bottom and calculated the numbers. Meg would have been almost sixteen. One more page and there was her senior picture. She looked different. For one thing, her long hair had been cropped short. Ross flipped the page and found the next one blank. The rest of the album was empty. Thoughtfully he closed the book, put it on the shelf, and shut the closet door.

He checked the dresser drawers and found more personal items, though no hidden CD. She was orderly and folded most of her clothes, the kind of girl every mother would love to have. Ross kept searching. In a drawer by the phone he found a folder which he flipped open. Inside was a five-by-seven photo of a young man walking down a street. He hadn't posed for the picture; it looked like a surveillance photograph. Carefully he read the information about the young man named Parker Briggs, and the instructions on the following page. He re-read the papers.

After a minute Ross sat down on a chair near the bed. He assembled the facts. It was surprising what you could learn about someone from touring their home. Meg Parrish had probably never been married. She lived alone and didn't cook.

She had no pets and didn't decorate her place with photographs, neither were there any framed pictures of herself or anyone else on the walls. Something had happened to Meg, or to her family, between the time she was sixteen and eighteen. He didn't know what, but she owned an album full of pictures which quit abruptly in her teens, the only follow-up photo being the obligatory senior picture.

Other than this mystery her personal life seemed simple. She was orderly though not a neat freak, as attested to by her somewhat messy computer desk and the damp towels tossed on the bathroom floor. She didn't watch much t.v., didn't rent movies, and didn't read. He assumed her main sources of entertainment were listening to music and working on the computer, this latter being outfitted like the starship Enterprise. He also assumed much of the hardware came from her employer, who obviously supplied her with anything she needed.

She was a cautious person, too. There was a deadbolt and chain lock on the front door, an extra-wide peep hole, and a good-sized fire extinguisher in the kitchen. He looked at the file folder again, and at the surveillance picture and info sheets. It was also highly probably that Meg Parrish worked for the government. He recognized the info sheets of confidential material as a government profile. Ross closed the folder and put it back in the drawer. His investigation had just taken a very different slant.

*   *   *

Jugglers threw colorful balls in the air while excited craftsmen displayed their wares at the market. A variety of smells wafted from the food court, where everything from American pronto pups to African sambusas were offered to hungry patrons. Further ahead there were more displays from every kind of artist. Meg passed booths selling paintings, clothing, metal sculptures, feathered masks, jewelry, toys, and musical instruments. Eventually she stopped, seeing the artist's booth she had been searching for. It was situated near a cluster of trees next to a stall which sold flavored vinegars in decorative bottles. Meg stood back and watched the artist paint a watercolor sketch of a little girl who wore a cotton hat with a large sunflower on it. He was very good at what he did, and people stopped to watch, making comments he couldn't hear.

Meg recognized Parker Briggs from his photo. He had a large nose and thick eyebrows set in a lean face. Lanky and angular, he had no doubt recently evolved from the awkward phase of his earlier teenage years. His brown hair was conservatively cut; he wore a dark green cotton sweater and jeans. She studied him and he glanced up as if sensing her stare. It was then that Meg saw what the photo had failed to show. His deep-set eyes were a piercingly clear gray. They were the pure color of newly cut granite or Virginia marble, yet in spite of the stone color they were anything but cold. In the photo they had been flat. Not necessarily lifeless, but ordinary, causing no notice. Here, in a more dimension form, they were full of so much awareness and curiosity. I must be crazy, she thought. He's going to know right away that I'm a fake. They continued to look at each other for a second, then he returned his focus to the watercolor sketch of the little girl.

Meg watched him work, surprised at how artistic he was. His portraits weren't anything like those garish chalk or ink caricatures which were found at county fairs. His were delicate watercolor portraits, lovely to look at. She had always thought portraits must be difficult to paint because the artist might have the features right, but seldom captured the personality or true look of the person who posed; however, the picture of the little girl showed he had created an excellent replica of her. He had painted her round cheeks, blue eyes, and rosebud lips. The single tear on her cheek was in contrast to the bright flower on her hat, and made a touching portrait. The two-year-old must have been crying in the beginning, though now she seemed content to sit and look at the artist. He smiled at her as if there were an ongoing conversation via their eyes. A moment later the portrait was finished and he lifted the little girl off the chair. Her thrilled grandmother thanked the artist and counted out the bills she owed.

A man stepped forward, signaling Parker. He was middle-aged with a round nose, black hair, and a large, crooked mouth. The artist stood and smiled as they greeted each other. Their hands flew with speed, signing an instant dialogue. There was never any innuendo with sign language—no niceties, small talk, or protocol. Conversation usually started off at a staccato speed and eventually wound its way into storytelling, the participants thirsty for interaction.

Most of the patrons who stood in line drifted off, deciding to come back later. Sign language usually tended to both fascinate and alienate hearing people, who generally preferred to watch it from a distance, hoping they weren't being intrusive. The Deaf were so used to people gawking that they could ignore the stares, focusing on the conversation. Meg watched the signing and felt herself plunged back into that magical time when ASL had been a way of life for her, when she had understood everything Robyn had signed. It had been ten years, though, and she was rusty, only grasping pieces of the conversation rather than the whole. This didn't matter, though. She was fascinated by the Deaf boy's hands. Despite their bony structure they had a natural fluidity born from years of signing. To the untrained observer they must seem like the movements of moths which swirled and darted, calmed and startled anew, pausing only for a brief moment before again taking flight.

"Your business is disappearing. Sorry," the older man apologized. "You need to paint. See you later."

Parker Briggs made the "no-big-deal" sign. "Dinner, my house? Next week, Friday?"

"Yes. Fine. You call, TDD?"

"Sure."

That was the end of the conversation and the man walked past Meg. "How're you?" she signed. These two movements were probably the most common introductory greeting in ASL.

He lifted his eyebrows in surprise and interest. Meg had immediately been elevated from the status of a non-signer to a signer. "Fine. You Deaf?" he queried.

That was always the first question unless there was clear evidence a person was either Deaf or hearing. Meg hated to lie and squirmed internally, even as she nodded her hand in assent. The artist drew near, studying her with a bemused expression. Did he know she was lying? The older man was throwing questions her way, and although she missed a few of the signs she grasped enough of the content to answer him. Where was she from? Maryland. Second lie, though a partial one. If she told him Portland had been her home for the past three years it would be suspicious. The Deaf community was tightly knit, and it was unlikely she would have lived here long and not known some of the people within that circle. Meg winged her way through more lies, losing count of how many, until the artist stepped in and smiled at her. For a second she thought he knew she was sinking and was kind enough to help her, but then decided this was ridiculous. If he knew she were hearing, pretending to be Deaf, he would be chastising her instead of chatting.

He introduced himself by quickly fingerspelling his name, and for the first time she noticed that the name Parker was spelled fluidly, like finger poetry. Meg was grateful she already knew his name, because she had been missing all the spelling the older gentleman was throwing her way. The signs she could grasp, but fingerspelling was almost always the most difficult for hearing people to read.

After more conversation she asked to have her portrait painted. The older gentleman, whose name she'd been unable to catch, left after using the "see-you-later" sign. Meg sat down on the chair and the artist put a new piece of stretched watercolor paper on the easel. His eyes studied her with open curiosity. She had seen that look on the faces of children exposed for the first time to the sights of a planetarium or the acts of magicians. She had never seen it in regards to herself. He seemed curious about her, even intrigued, and for a brief moment Meg was sure it had nothing to do with her appearance.

Parker Briggs didn't sign to her while he worked, so she began to relax. He started with a light pencil sketch, the briefest outline which would enable him to paint her in proportion. Next he mixed colors from watercolor tubes, deftly blending the hues that would match her skin and hair tones. He also blended red, white and a touch of vermillion to get the right shade for her shirt. People passing by began to stop and watch, and in time a small crowd had gathered. She sat very still, overhearing their comments but trying hard to ignore them, acting as if she were Deaf, too. Meg liked watching the fluid strokes of his brush, and the way his eyes moved back and forth between her face and the paper.

Letting out a slow breath, she began to relax and allowed her mind to wander. Being immersed anew in the sign language stirred feelings in Meg which had been long-buried. She thought about Robyn, the signing they had done together, and how they had also taught Claire and Stacey Green to sign. An unbidden memory surfaced of the four of them sitting under a tree in the back yard, signing stories until they eventually became involved in other diversions. Meg hadn't thought much about the girls in a long time, though now she recalled them with clarity. The twins had been uniquely different from each other. They both had brown hair and straight-cut bangs, but that was where their resemblance ended. Stacey's face was round, with a smattering of freckles, and she wore glasses. Claire's face was heart-shaped and her eyes were green. "Like my name," she had often said with a sense of pride. Stacey was playful. Claire had a tendency to dream.

The four girls had all been drawing pictures together, but by noon the paper and colored pencils were set aside. It was a sunny Saturday in spring and they decided to have a backyard picnic. In a strange way Meg felt herself drawn back to that place and time, as if she were again sitting on the old quilt. She remembered the dappled shade cast by the overhead tree, the slight breeze, and the feel of the soft, time-worn quilt beneath her hands. Meg could suddenly taste the red Kool-aid, and feel the anticipation of eating the chocolate cupcake with the little white icing swirl on top.

Robyn put down her half-eaten sandwich and picked up the paper, finishing the sketch of a butterfly. Meg looked at her sister, whose long hair was pulled up in a ponytail. She saw Robyn's features from both her childhood self and the adult she had become. Her sister had a perfectly arched mouth, like those in Renaissance paintings of angels, and large, beautiful eyes. Those eyes were looking down at the paper, her long eyelashes casting shadows on her cheeks. The shadows seemed like an embodiment of the butterflies they were drawing. The lashes fluttered and her sister glanced up; Robyn looked at her and smiled. The adult Meg felt a welling of deep love. With it came intense grief, the hurt so real that it felt as if her heart were being squeezed in a cruel and merciless fist.

The afternoon light began to fade, gray clouds gathering overhead. The cloud shadows darkened the day, falling like an ominous presence across the marketplace. In a few more minutes there was the sound of scattered raindrops hitting the overhead canvas. People pulled out their umbrellas, others headed to more sheltered areas. Parker ignored the rain, finishing the painting. It had taken him about thirty minutes. He turned it around for Meg to see, and she sucked in a startled breath. It was Robyn.

Chapter 6

Daniel Trenery opened the glass-paneled door and stepped into the CSS division office just as he had many times during the past week. Today he paused, his trained senses coming alert. He had a strange feeling something was wrong even though everything looked normal. The only sound in the place was that of a copier machine spitting out papers. He glanced around the office. The secretary at the main desk sat unmoving, staring at her computer screen with a slightly puzzled expression. Her hands were idle. There was a swirling screen-saver design on the monitor, and she seemed fascinated by it, frozen in her study of the moving patterns. He felt his scalp grow tense in alarm, but did nothing to distract the receptionist from her odd trance. Instead he moved forward with stealth. After serving in Nam he had later been recruited by the Department of Defense, eventually ending up in the NSA. When Daniel Trenery's instincts told him to be cautious, he heeded them.

Moving quietly forward, he stepped through the open doorway where three other workers sat at their desks, each one still as a mannequin. His eyes were drawn to the only movement in the room, the copier which was spewing out papers. A tall man in a charcoal gray suit stood at the Xerox, his back to Trenery. He was the only person in the room who was moving, and at the moment he seemed in a hurry. The NSA agent looked through another open doorway and saw Richard Hammond sitting at his desk. The field director was staring straight at him, and relief flooded Trenery. What was wrong with him, anyway? This most recent case must be getting on his nerves, he thought, before another chill of apprehension swept over him. Richard wasn't looking at him. Richard was looking through him. Hammond's eyes didn't move, except for an occasional reflexive blink. His round face was waxy, his bulldog features etched with frozen concern. Both his hands rested on either side of an open, empty file folder.

Trenery heard footsteps and turned, seeing a man step out of one of the offices.

He was fairly young, blond, and dressed casually in jeans and a white t-shirt. His fine hair was neatly parted on the side and slicked down, his pale skin highly flushed. His close-set eyes, edged by pale lashes, were the same unexceptional slate blue as most newborns. Daniel Trenery wondered if the guy had been born with eyes which had failed to change to either brown or blue as he grew. The NSA agent felt an impulse to laugh, then recognized it as out-of-control fear. Every instinct in his gut was screaming at him that this red-faced kid, with a trickle of sweat running down his temple, was dangerous. Trenery slid his right hand inside his suit coat, reaching for the gun he was licensed to carry. The young man smiled at him. It was a frightening grin completely devoid of mirth.

A blank space of time, unmeasurable and eerie, slipped by before the NSA agent again became aware of the sights and sounds around him. He found him-self sitting in a chair in front of Richard Hammond's cluttered desk. In the back-ground he heard the sound of typing and people murmuring to each other. A phone rang and someone picked it up. Hammond was staring down at the closed file folder on his desk which was full of important papers. His face was colorless except for a bright spot of red on each cheek. Trenery felt wrung-out and sweaty, a headache starting behind his eyes. He glanced at his watch, trying to remem-ber what time he had come into the building. Hammond slowly looked up from the folder, and the two men stared at each other.

*   *   *

"If you still haven't found out anything about Margaret Wilson, or where she is, then what exactly have you been doing?" Alan Scorzato asked Ross, his voice accusing. "You've been logging a lot of hours on Signet's time."

Ross stared at his supervisor, feeling a growing dislike for the know-it-all lit-tle weasel. He especially didn't like being dressed down in front of Alan's two security watchdogs, who were staring at him as if this were an inquisition. He took visual note of the flunkies, not particularly liking what he saw.

The older of the two, Martin Wimer, was an ex-cop and ex-private eye who currently did grunt work for Alan. He hadn't been good at either of his previous occupations but was apparently useful to Alan. He had small, mean-looking eyes and greasy hair. Martin was about forty pounds overweight, the bulk of which hung over the front of his belt.

The other man, Leo Fromm, was as muscularly toned at his cohort was flac-cid. He was a weightlifter with bulging muscles and a bull-like neck. No doubt he was the kind of guy that girls would fall for because he fit the mold of male attractiveness, especially the kind shown in glossy bodybuilder magazines. Leo was tan, wore a small gold earring in his left ear, and had pretty good facial features beneath a neatly trimmed haircut blended into a ponytail. He was also dumb as a post.

Leo had been hired by Alan strictly for his muscle mass. He had no investigative ability and very little experience in security work. Martin had experience, but few successes to recommend him. Despite the fact that Ross didn't think highly of either man, he recognized Alan must have had his reasons for hiring them.

"You're right," Ross said at last, addressing Alan's accusation. "Guess I've really blown this whole investigation." He had no intention of giving Alan any further information until he knew what the heck was going on. If Meg Parrish worked for the government, and he was sure she did, then why had she been undercover at Signet? "Maybe you should pull me off this case and turn my responsibilities over to Martin."

The three men looked at him. "That's not necessary," Alan replied in a calmer voice. "I don't want to switch over in the middle of this. What I do want is to know why you haven't been able to come up with anything, especially after practically promising Mr. Dent that your interviews of the staff would turn something up? He's expecting results, and wants them now."

"I guess I was wrong," Ross shrugged. "Maybe you should conduct another set of interviews."

"We already are," Leo said.

Ross nodded. "Good. Maybe you'll catch something I missed." He knew this was unlikely, especially if Leo were in charge of the interviews. "Have you come up with anything?"

"Not yet," Alan replied with a closed expression. "Maybe we should go over everything again. I'm supposed to give Mr. Dent an outline of the investigation and what we've done so far. This needs to include your itinerary, too."

Ross nodded and opened the personnel file on Margaret Wilson. Alan and Leo got out their notes, though Martin chose this time to go to the restroom. Ross wished he could find a way to escape the meeting, too. Instead he went over every fact in Signet's possession, patiently waiting while Alan made notes. The rest of the information—who Margaret Wilson really was, where she lived, and who she worked for—he decided to keep to himself for the time being. He would investigate this case for one more day on his own. If he didn't figure out what was really going on, or find the stolen files, then he'd have no choice but to turn over his findings to Alan.

*   *   *

Richard Hammond's secretary leaned through the doorway of his office.

"Meg's on the phone," she said.

He nodded and reached for the receiver, but Daniel Trenery stopped him. "Hang on a minute. Before you talk to her, I want to be clear on something. You do not have my permission to pull her from this assignment unless she's already gotten the info we're looking for."

Hammond glared at him with consternation. "I'm not leaving her in a potentially dangerous situation."

"We don't know if she's in danger."

"How can you ignore what happened here this morning?" Hammond incredulously asked.

"We don't really know what happened, do we? I don't have a clue what went on and neither do you."

"That's exactly what's so alarming."

"Yes, it's alarming, but it's also why we need every edge we've got," Trenery replied. "We can hope she's found out something. If not, you're to leave her where she is."

"You can't be serious."

"Tell her differently, and I'll have you removed from this position," Trenery vowed. There was no nastiness in his voice; it was a direct statement without emotion, and Hammond knew he meant it. The NSA agent reached over to the phone and hit the speaker button, ending any further debate.

When no one said anything, Meg cleared her throat. "Is anybody there?"

"What have you found out?" Hammond queried.

"You know, Richard, you need to work on your small talk skills," Meg sighed. "It makes common conversation so much easier if you start off with 'how are you?' or 'hi, what's up?'"

In spite of receiving the half-serious reprimand, Hammond felt deep affection for Meg. She was like the gifted student with a prickly personality whom the teacher loves anyway. He was highly fond of her, though she had long ago rejected any of his attempts at genuine friendship. In the beginning he and his wife, Jeri, had invited her to their home for dinner on several occasions. Meg had always been prepared with good excuses, and in time they quit trying. He could see she was afraid of becoming friends with an aging man who was clearly plagued with health problems, and whom she would most likely outlive. Hammond had come to terms with the fact that her fear of loss kept him at an emotional distance; that didn't stop him from caring for her, though.

"Small talk's not my style," he patiently explained.

"I know," she said. "Okay, well, you'll be happy to know I met Parker Briggs today, just like you wanted. It went pretty well in spite of my weak signing skills."

"What's your opinion of him?"

"Hmm.... Well, he's very talented, for one thing. His watercolor portraits are exceptional." She didn't say anything about the picture he had painted which looked so much like Robyn, unwilling to share something for which she had no logical explanation. "He seems like a really nice kid, and it's hard for me to understand why you're even investigating him." Meg was curious about this assignment, but was also willing to accept the rules of classification. They may have needed her to work as an operative, but they didn't need her actual input about classified information.

There was another silence, then Hammond said, "We want to know about the people he's staying with. Any progress there?"

"He's invited me to his house tomorrow after the market closes at four-thirty."

The two men looked at each other. Trenery was clearly satisfied despite his effort to look impassive. Hammond, on the other hand, scowled.

"Okay. Get in, check the place out, then head on out of there as soon as you can. We'll use Brian and Pete as our surveillance team, and they'll keep an eye on you. If something happens and you get separated, get to a phone and call in. I'll have a car pick you up and bring you in for debriefing."

"Just like in the spy movies?" she chuckled, then her voice grew serious. "You know, Richard, I'm not the greatest judge of people. We both know that. I also know it's a fluke that you're using me in this field operation instead of an experienced probe. If I didn't have the signing skills, I wouldn't even be on this assignment. Maybe I'm not a whiz at interacting with other people but I have to tell you, this boy seems like a genuinely nice person. It's hard to imagine he's involved in anything illegal, though there's probably no way to know about his family. Anything's possible, I guess." She thought about Donna Green's harmless smile which hid a malignant soul. "Anyway, you wanted to know what I thought of him, and that's my open assessment. To be honest, I'm also a little nervous about going to his house. It's one thing to fool him, you know, and be able to carry off the role of being Deaf. I'm just not so sure about a whole group of strangers I'm expected to sign to, not to mention understanding what they're signing to me."

"You'll do fine," Hammond said with an assurance he didn't feel. "You fit right in at Signet, didn't you? And obviously you're better at signing than you think, if he's asking you home for dinner."

"I suppose so."

"Then don't worry about it."

Meg thought her boss' voice sounded a bit worried in spite of his counsel. It couldn't be too big a deal, she decided, or he would have pulled her out. They discussed a few more things and then the phone conversation ended.

Hammond pushed his chair away from the desk. He forced his stiff muscles to move, catching up his arm-brace crutch and fitting it into place. Trenery also stood, his expression apologetic.

"I didn't like making that threat, Richard."

Hammond moved around the desk with an awkward, jerky gait. "Anything happens to that girl, you won't have a chance to fire me. I'll be out of here so stinking fast your head'll spin."

*   *   *

Meg sat down at the table, opening the cardboard sheath to reveal the portrait. Again she was struck by the definite thought that it was Robyn, and not herself. The hair may have been short and honey-colored rather than strawberry-blond, but the face was Robyn's. On second thought, maybe it was a combined portrait of both Robyn and herself.

She went into her bedroom, bringing down the photo album that she hadn't looked at in nearly a year. It wasn't that she didn't still have feelings of love for her family. Actually, when she sat down at the table and flipped it open, she was overwhelmed with deep love for each of the three other people in the photos. Yet right on the heels of that love, like an angry wolf snapping at a hapless ewe, came grief.

Flipping to the last half of the album, Meg found the group photo of herself and Robyn taken together with their mother. It had been the Christmas before Robyn's death. She steeled herself against the pain and studied it closely, realizing how much she and her sister really did look alike. They both had large brown eyes, though Robyn's were a bit rounder. Meg looked at the watercolor. It definitely seemed to be Robyn's eyes, though this must be a mistake. Parker had probably painted the eyes a little bit more round than he'd meant to, accidentally making them seem like her sister's. The smile also seemed to be Robin's. Did she smile like her sister, Meg wondered, and was she simply unaware of it?

She looked back and forth between the two pictures, sometimes gazing at the faces in the photograph, sometimes at the watercolor portrait. The painting became like one of those holographic pictures that change shape when they're moved. Sometimes she saw herself; sometimes she saw Robyn. At last Meg sighed, putting the portrait back inside the cardboard sleeve and coming to the logical explanation she desired. Parker must have inadvertently painted her looking younger than she really was, since that's how she was dressed and how he perceived her. After staring at the family photo it became clear how much she and her sister had looked alike, more than Meg had ever realized.

The renewal of sign language had obviously brought her sister more clearly to mind than before, and she had also been daydreaming while she posed, thinking of Robyn. This fact was then coupled with the events of the day. When Parker had turned the portrait around for her to look at, she had mistakenly seen her sister. Meg was used to the cruel tricks her mind played. It was just another subtle punishment for having lived when the others she loved had died. She took the painting and album back into the bedroom, sliding them both onto the shelf and shutting the closet door.

*   *   *

The massive amount of people attending the second day of Portland's weekend market actually made Ross' work easier, letting him blend in unnoticed. He walked past stalls selling ceramic wares, air-brushed t-shirts, stained glass, hand-painted watering cans, and tons of other things which held absolutely no interest for him. The people at the market drew his attention more than the artistic items for sale. Ross found other human beings more fascinating than inanimate objects ever could be, and the nice weather had brought out a vast variety of shoppers. He strolled along, pretending to be one of the browsers himself, but most of the time he was watching Meg Parrish and the young Deaf man, Parker Briggs.

Ross had waited outside her apartment since early this morning, though she hadn't left until this afternoon. It had been a boring wait, though now he found his time well-spent. His intrigue about the elusive Miss Parrish had doubled. He watched her signing with the young man, their conversation animated and fascinating to watch. His respect for her many talents increased. Not only was she smart enough to break into Signet's server and Willis Dent's computer system, she was also apparently a skilled signer. He was sure the FBI, or whomever it was she worked for, were highly pleased to have someone with such a broad skill base working for them.

The surveillance proved to be interesting, for in spite of staring at her picture numerous times during the last week, he had only seen her briefly at Signet. This afternoon's work gave him a fresh perspective. That day in the office she had worn a navy skirt and blazer with a white shirt, and her short hair had been neatly combed in place. He preferred the more casual Meg Parrish over the corporate Margaret Wilson. Today she was dressed in a sea-foam green sweater which had multicolored flecks of teal, fuchsia, and emerald. She also wore fitted jeans which gave Ross an ongoing view of her adorable butt. The breeze ruffled her hair and moved her dangling turquoise earrings. She smiled at the young guy, and Ross pitied him. He had to be a lost cause when a girl like that smiled at him.

Ross had been watching them since arriving at the market in her wake early this afternoon. Starting at two o'clock, they had stayed for an hour at the booth where Parker Briggs was painting. The boy was surprisingly talented. It was amazing how he could paint such detailed portraits in such a relatively short span of time. The hour wait had been the most difficult part of the surveillance because Ross had been forced to circulate to the many different booths in the area without going very far. At three o'clock she and the kid had left the booth and gone to the food court where they ate fajitas. At three-thirty they'd gone strolling, and it was then that Ross had discovered he wasn't the only one following the couple.

Two men were trailing Meg and Parker, and they were highly skilled at surveillance. In fact, it was to Ross' credit that he had even picked up on them at all. One of them was a slender man, probably in his late forties. He had a narrow face, wore wire-rimmed glasses, dressed casually, and had a camera bag slung over his shoulder—every bit the convincing tourist. The other one, a big Samoan, wore a Portland Trail Blazer's cap and a Far Side t-shirt. Larger than his companion, he was more easily noticed.

The two men had strayed into his line of sight several times, until Ross knew they were tailing Meg and the Deaf boy. He assumed they were the follow-up surveillance team, keeping an eye on her for safety because she was undercover.

At a little after four o'clock Meg stopped at a stall selling hand-blown glassware, and the boy moved to her side. They appeared to be discussing the glass, but Ross couldn't be sure since he knew nothing about sign language. Neither of them seemed to be aware of the men trailing them, or of himself. Most of their attention was spent on the signing, and he could see how it wouldn't allow for more than a few glances outside the circle of conversation.

They moved on, passing a group of street musicians. Then, at about four-fifteen, there was another incident, this more eye-opening for Ross than all the rest. Meg and Parker rounded a corner and came to a stall full of bright red geraniums in glazed pottery. The flowers and painted pots were stacked everywhere, even spilling out into the walkway. The thick clusters of petals swayed slightly in the breeze, the bright crimson flowers seeming to nod their heads.

Meg's steps faltered and a young mother pushing a stroller almost ran into the back of her legs. The woman managed to veer the pram around Meg, who gave her no notice; she stood frozen in a sea of shoppers who flowed around her. Ross slowed and moved to the edge of a jewelry stall, glancing at the two agents. They did the same thing Ross had done, further proving they were following her.

Ross returned his attention to Meg. He couldn't see her face, but her stance was rigid. Her hands, which had been signing only a moment ago, were fisted at her sides. What was going on? Something in her demeanor showed alarm, even fear, though this was hard to understand. It was a bright, breezy day with sunlight breaking through the cloud cover. The air was cool, but the sunshine was a rare delight and everyone seemed happy. Music drifted on the breeze and mingled with the voices of the shoppers, while a variety of wares, including bright geraniums, greeted the browsers. What was she seeing in this festive scene which made her afraid? Momentarily forgetting the other agents, Ross moved forward.

Meg turned around, stumbling in his direction. He felt shocked by her expression. The face which had been smiling and flushed only a moment ago was now white with misery. In a brief span of time he caught an expression of such horror that it stunned him. Others in the area noticed, too, staring and making way for her to pass through the crowd. The Deaf boy hurried after her, catching her arm and guiding her to a bench.

Ross moved back, avoiding the attention of the other men following her. He needn't have worried. They paid him no heed, turning their gazes on the young woman seated on the bench. People began returning to their pursuits as Parker Briggs sat down beside her. He looked concerned, but not alarmed, even though Meg's expression, itself, was alarming. Ross watched him catch her chin with his fingers, turning her face towards him. The young man slid his hand to the side of her head, his thumb resting on the back edge of her jaw. His fingers slid beneath her hair and up the side of her head.

Meg's haunted expression began to fade and she sat still, her features unmoving. The Deaf boy was gazing into the distance, not even looking at her, though his expression was intent. Her own eyes fluttered closed for a moment, a calm mask falling into place and color slowly returning to her face. Eventually she opened her eyes. The fear was gone, her expression now a mingling of puzzled wonder and relief. A grateful, embarrassed smile crept to her lips.

Ross felt as if he were inside a spinning vortex, the only person standing still while the rest of the carnival scene was caught in a fun-house centrifuge. He had seen this kind of thing before, had in fact experienced it himself during times of suffering. The scene with Meg Parrish and Parker Briggs brought up an indelible mental image from his own past. A decade seemed to melt away and once again he was a twenty-two year old college student sitting on the bunk-bed in his old room. "I'm sorry, Ross," the childish voice sadly stated. "I have to go now. It's not safe for either of us if I stay here." A delicate hand reached out, her thumb resting on his jaw, her fingers pressing against the part of his head where the cerebrum sorted out emotions. "Don't worry. We're both going to be okay," she whispered, her voice thick with tears and love.

He blinked hard and the memory faded. The spinning stopped and he let go of the edge of the jewelry counter which he'd been gripping. The artist in the booth was looking at him with a worried expression, obviously concerned that Ross might be a lunatic. He moved away, finding a shaded spot beneath a tree. The childish voice in his head kept echoing the promise that they would both be okay, but he wasn't okay, was he? Ross thought. He hadn't been okay in ten years. Starting at this moment, though, he now had renewed hope. He marveled at the bizarre coincidence which had brought him to this point and allowed him to see Parker Briggs and what he had done. The young man might possibly lead Ross to the one person he had spent ten years searching for.

During the last decade he had chased shadows and myths, and followed information which led no where—just like the clues which had brought him to Portland. Finally, when he had given up all hope and turned his attention to chasing down stolen computer files, he now found himself stumbling onto the lead he had been searching for. Suddenly Ross no longer cared about his job at Signet or Willis Dent's missing CD. His investigation had dramatically altered during one brief moment in an open-air market.

He gathered his senses and looked back at the bench where Meg and Parker Briggs had been sitting. They were gone. A second glance through the crowd told him the two agents had also disappeared into the throng of shoppers. He bolted forward, moving quickly through the crowd, scanning the clusters of people for a girl in a speckled green sweater and an average-looking teenage Deaf kid wearing a denim shirt.

*   *   *

"You lied to Mr. Jensen," Chris accused. "You said we were going to the lost and found to look for your soccer ball. You don't even own a soccer ball."

"I had to lie," Evan said, undaunted. "How else could we have gotten the hall pass?"

The ten-year-olds passed a bulletin board filled with paper flowers made by Mrs. Wogle's first grade class. The centers of the blossoms were circles cut from school photos. Die-cut letters above the flowers boasted "Spring Has Sprung!" Immediately past the bulletin board were two offices, their closed doors centered with square panes of glass. The boys looked in the first room which had a large conference table. Around it sat the principal, the school nurse, the school psychologist, the school counselor, the teacher heading the resource program, the

*first-grade classroom teacher, and a distraught mother holding a copy of the IEP.
Evan ignored this group of people, looking inside the counselor's room next door.*

A little boy sat at the child-size table. "You gotta be kidding," Chris said.

*"It's the first time he's been alone," Evan answered in a low whisper. "I been
waiting for this a couple of months."*

*"Marvin and Jerry both said you shouldn't do it any more, remember? They
said wait a long time, maybe years, before doin' more stuff. They know what
they're talking about, too."*

*"I don't want to wait," Evan said, opening the door and pulling Chris in after
him.*

*Inside the room the first grader sat at a small table with a box of crayons. A
coloring book lay in a heap on the floor while the crayons on the table were
being denuded. The little boy was carefully using his fingernails to peal off the
crayon papers before snapping them in half. He was also talking to himself.
"Hoop, hoop, hoop..." he softly said.*

"No way," Chris whispered, staring at the little kid.

"I can't do this one myself," Evan patiently stated. "He needs both our kinds."

"You don't expect to get done during recess, do you?"

*"Can't do a whole lot with him anyway, can we? Just make it a little better,
that's all." Evan smiled his impish grin, looking at his darker-skinned brother.
"Come on."*

*"I don't want to miss recess, or computer lab," Chris complained, sitting down
beside the little boy.*

*Evan sat on the other side of the skinny child with curly brown hair. "Hi,
there," he softly said. "I'm Evan, and this is Chris. We're in the fourth grade.
What grade are you in?"*

*The little boy didn't look at them. He dug his fingers under the crayon paper
and pulled off another piece. "Hoop, hoop, hoop!" he said, his voice rising in
alarm.*

*Twenty minutes later Craig Jensen walked down the halls of Mary McPherson
Elementary, looking for his two displaced students. He should have been irritated because it was cutting into one of his specials. The class had gone to the computer lab, and he had planned on using the vacant half-hour to get a cup of coffee from the teacher's lounge before spending the rest of the time in his classroom
correcting math tests. He was in a very good mood, though, which abated his
annoyance at the missing kids. He had met with the principal before school, and
she had gone over his formal evaluation. It had been very good.*

At the beginning of the school year he had come home distraught, telling his wife that this year he truly had the class from hell. Five were slated for resource room help twice a day, one was emotionally disturbed and wouldn't open her book when he asked, let alone pay attention, and one was hearing impaired, which required him to wear an FM system for broadcasting his voice to her hearing aids. Three of the kids were slow learners struggling with basic writing and reading skills, one was a gifted ball of rage living in his fourth foster home in two years, and six of them were loaded with ADHD, each a bundle of hyperactivity with an inability to pay attention unless they were on medication—heaven help him if even one kid's parents forgot to dose them before school. The nurse kept an extra supply of medication on hand, just in case this happened.

In the beginning he had been concerned about surviving the year, though now he was doing much better than that. He was actually teaching, and by this last quarter of the year things were very good. Normally it was the hardest time of the school year, but the whole class was doing well. Sheila now opened her book when he asked, while Justin had stopped slugging other kids. The slow ones were learning, the hyperactive ones were paying attention, and the principal, Mrs. Miller, had given him excellent scores on his evaluation. He would have been thrilled if it just weren't so damned eerie. He glanced inside the counselor's room and saw his two missing kids sitting on either side of a little boy. After rapping on the glass they looked back at him, leaving the table and slipping out the door.

"This is getting old, guys."

"Sorry Mr. Jensen," Chris mumbled, embarrassed at being caught again. "He's kind of a friend of ours."

"Sorry Mr. Jensen," Evan sincerely echoed, looking up at him with an innocent smile. "We got sidetracked."

"I don't understand why this keeps happening. If it were some of the other kids I could understand it, but not you two," the teacher stated, hoping his stern demeanor would influence them. "The rest of the class has already gone to computers, so I guess you'll miss out. Go back to the classroom and put your heads down on your desks, then this afternoon you'll spend recess with the safe school aide since I have duty. Maybe that'll help you remember to make it back to class on time."

Neither boy complained or argued, as was so often the case these days when a student was reprimanded. Instead they quietly headed back down the hall, the teacher watching them go before he took off for the lounge to grab a cup of coffee.

The young mother stepped out of the conference room, stuffing the damp tissue into her jacket pocket. She hated herself for losing it in front of these snotty professionals who thought they knew what her son needed. Ignoring their pity-ing glances, she opened the door to the counselor's office, then stopped in her tracks. Her son was sitting at the table, coloring a picture in the coloring book. He was staying in the lines, too.

"Cody?" she said, his name slipping from her lips despite years of training herself not to expect a response.

The boy looked up, actually making eye contact. He smiled, and her hands flew to her mouth.

Chapter 7

Willis Dent sat in a leather wingback chair in his comfortable study. It was his favorite room in the expensive condominium where he lived. The interior decorator had designed it to be a room rich in maroons, indigos, and antique golds. It was where he liked to come when contemplating business deals and company plans. At the moment, though, he wasn't able to focus on work because he felt overwhelmed by anxiety and anger. For the hundredth time during the past week he thought about how Margaret Wilson had sat at his secretary's desk, looking up at him with an innocent expression while she was secretly stealing from his company. The thought enraged him.

Since the incorporation of Signet, Dent had made sure his company was safely ensconced within his control. He had felt protected by his advanced security measures, but now all that had changed. A week-and-a-half ago there had been the suspicions about the Kronek file lists being photocopied and snuck out of Signet, though Alan had never found any proof of it in Phil Black's apartment. Maybe Martin Wimer had been mistaken about what he'd seen, and all of their troubles, including eliminating the suspected thief, had been for nothing. Even more alarming, was there a chance that the two incidents of corporate thievery were tied in together? He knew it was very likely. Either Phil Black and Margaret Wilson were working together, or there were two separate groups of people illegally spying inside his company. Either one of these posed a nightmare, and it again came back to the same question he had wondered over and over again: who were these two corporate spies working for? This thought had plagued him constantly for the entire week.

At least the first thief had been taken care of, but what about Margaret Wilson? She had managed to disappear, and despite Ross and Alan's reassurances he felt extremely concerned that they might not be able to find her. Not only that, but compared to the photocopied file list, what she had taken was far more important. Her actions had also been more intrusive than simply photocopying a few papers taken from a file folder. She had actually broken into his private computer system; the very thought made him feel violated. He again recalled her innocent expression as she had sat at Beverly's desk. Her true actions only reaffirmed his belief that women were never what they appeared to be. They might look innocent, be attractive, or even be flamboyantly enticing like his mother, but underneath they were all the same—cloying users only concerned with themselves.

This was a bitter conclusion Willis Dent was to arrive at repeatedly during his life. He had not been without romantic interests during his adult years, and had actually been involved with several women. He preferred the kind who chased him, flattered him, and eventually catered to his wishes. He also preferred women who were less intelligent than himself, those that might be considered a step down because of their common natures. It was important for him to feel superior to them, though he never put this reasoning into words. Eventually, though, these romances all fizzled because the women ended up revealing their true selves. They became clingy, demanding, and usually nagged at him to trust them. It seemed an obviously impossible task to trust someone who had to ask you to do so.

He closed his eyes and leaned his head back against the chair. His thoughts repeatedly hovered on the attractive Miss Wilson and what she had done to him. Her misdeed was more than just that of stealing from him. She had changed everything, making his past concerns into a reality. He had spent years locking doors and setting up safeguards, none of which had ever proven vulnerable. Then she had come to Signet and surpassed his company's security measures. Not only that, but she had taken something of great value which he desperately needed back. Dent no longer kept the codes on his computer; he didn't dare. Instead he kept copies of them on two CDs, one locked in the wall safe of this room and the other one in his bank's safety deposit box. He hadn't looked at them since the theft, as if they had somehow been tainted. Depressed, he wondered what they were really worth after all. It was like the fisherman who caught a mermaid and didn't know what he should do with her. She wasn't a fish he could eat, or a woman he could marry, but still she was something wondrous. The tricky part was figuring out how to take the one-of-a-kind discovery and capitalize on it.

It was possible the codes might never benefit him directly, but indirectly they could be of great value. Besides, if what he had seen two years ago on a deserted country road had really happened, then it was also possible that the codes were the key to freeing him from his greatest fear. If they could do that for him, then how many others would pay to have the benefit of them as well? Since acquiring the code files he had spent a great deal of time thinking about how to use them. There were still a lot of unanswered questions, though one conclusion had been evident. To continue to have the required leverage, it was imperative that he be the sole owner of them. That was why the thought of Margaret Wilson, or her employer, possessing the codes filled him with self-righteous rage. He was the one who had spent two years searching them out, including purchasing the source from which they'd come. By all rights they were his!

This thought, coupled with his anger, circled inside his head like a growing cyclone. The only way he had been able to even partially assuage his rage was by visualizing Margaret Wilson tied to a chair while he dreamed up ways of interrogating her. He would like to start by slapping her until she dropped that innocent expression. Then he would find out who she worked for and what she had done with his codes. He mentally devised different means of how to persuade her to confess, some of them erotic.

After a while he reached for the phone. Alan and Ross had better come up with something soon. It was clearly justifiable to expect them to stand by their assurances that they could find her. Willis Dent wanted the codes back. He also wanted to make Margaret Wilson pay for what she had done to him.

*   *   *

The Tri-Met bus finally left the busy inner-city traffic behind, which made the ride less jerky. Meg was signing with Parker, learning about his schooling and art studies. Her eyes were tired from constantly staring at his hands and facial expressions in the process of deciphering the communication. As a hearing person, she was used to listening to conversation while glancing away, but if she looked away during signing, for even a couple of seconds, the meaning of the dialogue would be lost. It required a different kind of focused attention than what she was used to doing, and was hard work to continually follow his gestures with her eyes. Several hours of non-stop signing for an out-of-practice person was definitely fatiguing. Added to this was the strain of the baffling experience in the market.

She thought about the potted geraniums and the flashback they had initiated. One minute she had been walking along, signing with Parker and examining the wares in the booths; the next, she had rounded a corner and come upon the display of flowers. The bright red color and bitter odor had simultaneously assaulted her senses. Meg wondered if there were ever a more horrid scent than that of geraniums. Roses and lilacs smelled wonderful, but geraniums were a deceptive plant pretending to be a pretty flower at first glance, until you bent to smell them.

She thought they had a nastier odor than the bitterest gall.

Today a new memory had surfaced upon seeing the flowers; the bright red blossoms had reminded her of blood. She had been flooded by the vision of Robyn lying in death's grip, and had remembered the sight of red blossoms scattered across the rug. Until today she had forgotten that ten years ago, when she had first seen the red on the carpet, she had thought it was blood. She had been mistaken, though, since the coroner's statement had later explained that her sister's death was caused by strangulation. The scattered geranium petals had merely seemed like red drops of blood to a sixteen-year-old girl in shock. Today, while reliving the initial moment of finding her sister's body, she had recalled this forgotten first perception.

Meg wished the memory had stayed buried. She also wished she'd never caught sight of those sickening flowers, or smelled their stench. Embarrassedly remembering how she had staggered away from the flowers, she realized it was a miracle she had even been able to make her way to the bench. Parker had helped her sit down, and he had also somehow been able to ease the moment. What had he done to bring an ensuing peace which had erased her near-hysteria? She could find no logical explanation for what had occurred.

Although the flashbacks rarely happened, Meg was familiar enough with them to recognize their blueprint. Their pattern was always the same. They emerged out of nowhere, in the blink of an eye, and then took time to ebb away, just like the nightmares. Today, though, the trauma had been swept away almost as quickly as it had come. She had gone from two extremes: frantic fear to serenity. How was this possible?

*   *   *

Parker was watching Meg, but he was also wondering if the three men were still following him. He felt certain that one of them had been lost in the crowd not far from the place where the red flowers were. The other two had been harder to elude, but he had taken every precaution. He hoped that they'd been left behind, and felt pretty sure they had been. Even so, it was a risk to bring Meg home considering who she worked for. Parker hadn't been able to help himself, though. Gram had once accused him of bringing home stray folks the way other people brought home lost animals. He guessed she was probably right about that.

Meg looked up and found him staring at her, his hands still. "Sorry," she signed. "Mind diverted."

"No-big-deal," he signed back. "You think about today?"

She hesitated, then nodded her hand. "Yes."

"You afraid, red flowers. What-for?"

Hearing people might avoid an embarrassing issue, but questions and answers were succinctly given and received in the Deaf world. Meg didn't want to discuss the flashback, although she knew her odd behavior needed to be explained. Besides, she had some questions of her own.

"Ten years ago, terrible event," she set up the factors of the story. "My house...Mother, me, come home. See my sister dead. Near her, red flowers...." She showed the action of a toppled plant strewn on the floor.

"Why sister die?" he signed, his face concerned.

Meg let out a slow breath, again lifting her hands. "Man (don't know who) rape, kill."

He made the "wow" sign which had a dozen different meanings ranging from awesomely dreadful to great. His current expression gave it the appropriate designation of something unbelievably bad. He used the "sorry" sign, this time signed with great empathy.

"Today, flowers...see red, smell sick/gross." She lifted her hands above her head, making a ballooning circle which indicated a mental image. "Remember sister...dead." She put her fists over her heart, grinding them around each other in the motion which indicated grief. Her heart felt heavy retelling the story, yet in some ways it was far easier to sign than it had ever been to tell out loud.

He accepted her story as complete, asking no more details. It was her turn now, and she knit her brows to indicate a pending question. "This afternoon, what do you? Don't know how, but you help me. First, felt fear. Next, calm. You touched my head." Meg copied his earlier gesture, struggling to remember if there was a sign for the word she was now looking for. Finally she fingerspelling her question: h-y-p-n-o-t-i-z-e?"

Parker stared at her, apparently not understanding the word. He rerouted, trying to answer her question. "Explain...difficult. My family, what? Healers." Meg wondered if she had understood the last sign right, but he was continuing to gesture, his gaze momentarily diverted. She had seen this a few times with other Deaf people. They sometimes tended to break eye contact which allowed for the signed completion of their thoughts without interruption.

"Soon, you meet my family." He ticked them off on a finger list. "Grandma. Three sisters: Leah, Amber, Shannon...Shannon's husband, Jack, also brother Keith." At this point she was getting lost in the fingerspelling, not sure if Jack was the brother, or brother-in-law. What he said next made her forget the rest. "Happen, you come my house...not pretend Deaf. My family, hearing, none Deaf. Easier if you talk."

He knew she wasn't Deaf! Meg felt a wash of guilty embarrassment. How long had he known, and why was he being so calm about it? This infraction should have caused a barrage of chastisement the moment he figured it out. The very best she could have expected was chilling indifference from this point on, but his expression and demeanor were unruffled.

"You know."

"Yes."

Meg didn't understand why he wasn't demanding an explanation for what she had done. He couldn't be happy about her trying to trick him. "You mad?" she hesitantly queried.

Parker shrugged.

"How long you know?"

"Since we met."

Meg felt chagrined. "Why say nothing?"

He smiled, his gray eyes piercing. "Interesting game," he signed; or "Interested in game." She wasn't sure which he meant.

She felt a resurgence of embarrassment, then a quick rush of annoyance at Hammond for making her accept this assignment. Parker said nothing else and she let it rest. If he wasn't going to go further, then neither was she.

They got off at the next bus stop, in an older residential area of town, and walked past several run-down houses until they came to one in worse repair than the rest. It was an old home with peeling yellow paint and an enclosed front porch bearing battered screens. The eaves sagged and the shingles were curled with age. A rusted chimney vent on top left red-brown streaks down the width of the roof. A speckled cat sat on the porch step and Meg bent down, scratching its head. Almost immediately it stood and rubbed against her leg.

"What your cat's name?" she asked.

"Not our cat," he signed, opening the screen door. The cat followed them inside as if he belonged there, and Parker held the door for it.

Once inside the porch, he opened the front door, allowing Meg and the cat to enter. She was immediately greeted by an odd aroma of steam, baking bread, laundry soap, and damp mildew. It should have been nauseating but was strangely beckoning after the first startling whiff. They stepped into a kitchen that was cluttered from one end to the other. She had never seen so many dirty dishes in one sink before, and the single large window was streaked with steam rivulets. There was a microwave on the counter, oddly in contrast to the oldest kitchen stove she'd ever seen in actual use. An aluminum pot boiled on the burner, no doubt the source of the steam. The floor was a hideous green linoleum which was warped with age, and the cabinets were painted a color which must have once been salmon. The cat, which according to Parker didn't belong to his family, immediately went to a bowl of milk sitting near a yellow refrigerator. A dozen magnets held crayon artwork on the front of the fridge. Charming and simplistic pictures were drawn in red, yellow, green, and purple.

"Who drew the pictures?" Meg asked, wondering if there were a child in the house.

"My sister, Leah."

"How old?"

"Eight," he signed, leading her along.

To the side of the kitchen a doorway opened into a laundry area where an old washer churned away, a pile of clothes at its base. They passed through double doors and entered a large living area filled with furniture. There was an over-stuffed couch, two desks, several oddly shaped chairs, and a large bookshelf. In the center of the room a quilting frame was set up with a small quilt, and two women sat working at it, their backs to Parker and Meg. One was old, with knots of gray hair bobby-pinned in swirls on top of her head. The other was young, with red hair that fell in curling waves down her back. They were bent over their work, fingers carefully weaving needle and thread through cloth and batting.

Meg studied the room which was more organized than the kitchen but which still seemed contentedly settled into a state of disarray. The floor was of aged hardwood topped by a very old Persian carpet. Two skinny brass floor lamps, with discolored silk shades, sat on either side of the couch while the windows were draped in faded red brocade edged with gold fringe. The draperies looked as if they had been hanging at the windows for at least five decades. Nearly everything in the room seemed old, and there was a dusty smell that supported this conclusion. The strangest thing in the room, however, was a hand-painted mural on one of the walls. It stood out in sharp contrast to the rest of the place because it was decorated with wild artwork that was eerily fantastic. It depicted a huge map like something from the inside leaf of a fantasy book, with make-believe names and strange, elfin villages. Funny, whimsical creatures unlike any she had ever seen before were drawn on the map. Good grief, Meg thought. It's like Ma and Pa Kettle meet Dr. Seuss in here. What would Hammond and Trenery think if she put that in her report?

A beam of afternoon sunlight slanted through a streaked window, carrying with it a dance troupe of swirling dust motes. The light cast varying shadows on the wall mural, making it seem almost animated.

"Hi, Parker," the older woman said, not bothering to turn around. "Did you bring a guest home?"

Meg's attention focused on the woman. She felt sure the old lady hadn't turned around to see them. How had she known they were there, and why was she talking to Parker with her back to him so he couldn't read her lips?

"Just one minute more," the woman continued, her voice taking on a tone of laughter. "Just a few more stitches...."

"You've been saying 'a few more stitches' for half an hour," the younger woman chuckled, putting down her needle and pushing away from the quilt. She turned around and faced them, her laughter fading. Meg studied the girl who seemed attractive, perhaps more for the way her features melded together in such unison rather than for their actual individual shapes. Her eyes were bright blue and surrounded by spiky lashes; she had golden skin with a smattering of freckles in keeping with her red hair, and a small half-moon scar in the hollow of her throat just beneath her Adam's apple. Most noticeable of all, though, was that she was very pregnant. The young woman looked straight into Meg's eyes. It was a disconcerting gaze—not threatening or judgmental, but probing none-the-less.

Meg thought her age was hard to tell. At first glance she looked quite young, but the more Meg stared at her the more she sensed a persona of maturity. Ancient eyes in a young face, Meg thought, then had an echoing reply inside her head: Oh, see, the thought chuckled. You've got a poetic streak.

It was an odd moment, and for a brief second it almost seemed to be the other girl's teasing thought and not her own. "I'm Shannon," the young woman said, stepping near.

"Meg."

"Welcome to our home," she said. "Gram, put down that needle and meet Parker's friend."

Gram did as she was counseled, tucking the needle into the fabric and stretching as she stood. "So you're Meg," she said with a pleased smile that was charmingly infectious. "Parker was telling me about you yesterday, and I'm glad he brought you home."

Parker's grandma was strange, though at this point it was pretty much expected she would be, Meg thought. The elderly woman had one of those faces you immediately liked because, in spite of the tired eyes and time-worn facial features, it had a kind of charming charisma. Her skin was wrinkled in pleasant furrows, as if the lines had formed from expressions of excitement and pleasure rather than worry. Her gray hair must have been quite long, as it was pinned up in funny circles atop her head and kept in place with a dozen bobby pins. She wore a faded sweatshirt, bleach-stained jeans, and Keds.

Meg chatted with Parker's grandmother and sister, observing details about them and their home. They were peculiar, she thought, but then so were half the people she'd ever met. Gram was friendly and excited to meet her. Shannon was pleasant but seemed more reserved. For a fleeting moment Meg thought she was even a little worried, though this might only be a natural offshoot of her pregnancy. They showed her the baby quilt they were working on, talking about the impending birth. "A little girl!" Gram beamed.

During all of the conversation Meg made sure she signed because she didn't want to eliminate Parker from the dialogue. It automatically made the signing more cumbersome because of the English use of articles and helping verbs, not to mention placement of subject. At least Parker could switch to the more English sign base and follow the discussion, she thought. His sister and grandmother, however, made no such concession. They never raised their hands to sign and didn't even bother to make sure he could clearly see their faces. Sometimes they included him in the discussion, but to Meg it seemed useless if he couldn't read their lips or, preferably, have the benefit of signing. Both the women stepped into the kitchen and Meg sat down on the couch, following Parker's invitation.

"They don't know sign?"

"No."

"That bother you?"

He smiled, shrugged, and gave the "don't-care" sign.

Meg said nothing else, thinking it was none of her business, anyway. She wanted to ask about the wall mural, but before she had the chance a little girl came hopping down the stairs, singing in tune to the jumping.

"Jesus said...love ev'ry-one...love them...oh, yes...do. When your heart...is full of love...others...love you...too!" The last word brought her to the landing and she looked at Meg and Parker, immediately coming over to them.

She began using sign language with Parker and introductions were made. This was Leah, his littlest sister. There was no resemblance between Parker and either of his sisters, Meg noted. All three were different in both facial features and coloring. Leah had large brown eyes, a button nose, and very dark hair cut in a short pixie. If it weren't for her ears being pierced she could have passed for a boy. She wore a paint-streaked shirt and pants, and her hands were stained with flecks of dried paint.

There was more chatting until the little girl paused, crooking her head as if she were listening to something. "Shannon wants to talk to you in the kitchen," she informed Parker.

Meg glanced toward the kitchen, having heard nothing. He excused himself and left her alone with the little girl. At first she felt somewhat disconcerted, knowing nothing about children, but Leah smiled and sat down by her on the couch. It seemed as if the child planned on being the one in charge of the conversation. "You're very pretty."

"Thank you."

"Jack says we're not supposed to look at people's outsides. Our job is to see them on the inside only, you know, but I can't help it. When I'm painting I like to paint stuff that's pretty, and animals that are pretty. If you have to choose, don't you want to paint a horse instead of a cow?"

"I'm not very good at painting," Meg confided. "But I've always thought horses were prettier than cows."

Leah seemed pleased. "I think so, too."

"There are lots of animals that aren't pretty but I think they're interesting to study," Meg qualified.

"Like with people. Jack says we should be careful when it comes to people, 'cause if we take time to look at the outside we'll get distracted, or maybe scared if someone is really ugly, you know, like the Hunchback. I love that book."

"Jack sounds pretty smart." There was a lull and Meg asked about the crayon drawings on the fridge. "Parker said you drew them."

The child snorted in disgust. "They stink. The teacher makes us color pictures at school, and then I have to clean out my cubby and bring them home in my backpack. Gram puts them up on the fridge to punish me."

"Oh, I'm sure your grandma puts them there because she's proud of you," Meg reassured, thinking she was getting a handle on conversing with children.

Leah leveled an analytical stare at Meg that made the feeling vanish. She hopped off the couch and went to the wall with the mural. "There's a space right here for you," she said, pointing to an island with a tiny castle. "I'll paint you very small, with butterfly wings, and make you a fairy. Would you like that?"

"That would be fun, but you'll have to ask permission. Is Parker the one who painted it?"

"No, course not! He does watercolors. I used acrylics on this."

"Are you saying you painted that mural?" Meg asked, trying to hide the tolerant skepticism creeping into her voice.

"Of course I did." Leah bent down to the art supplies spread out on newspapers and caught up a pencil. Before Meg could say anything the little fingers began to sketch in the outline of a fairy. Her movements were exact and precise as the art flowed from her with an adult skill that was eerie. Meg came over to watch, her amazement growing.

"How can you do that?"

Leah dropped the pencil and turned to grin at her. "I love drawing. Parker and me are the same way, good at art, you know. Of course we're not the same kind, or I could be with him and help you, even if Shannon doesn't want to."

"I can't even draw a straight line," Meg said, staring at the mural with awe and ignoring the child's odd conversation.

"That's not a problem," Leah reassured. "I never use straight lines."

Meg smiled, still disbelieving the child had drawn it all. "Did Parker help you?"

"He outlined the map and put up the scaffolding. He's very good to help me, and he told Jack that I should paint the wall, even if Keith said we're only renting and it's someone else's house so we shouldn't. But what else can I do, with nowhere else to paint?" she stated with a tone of voice which spoke of the obvious.

"What about school?" Meg asked, recalling the drawings on the fridge. "Your teacher would love to see you do something like this."

"Un-uh! She'd end up showing it to the other teachers, and they'd put me in the gifted program. Then I'd have to do more second-grade projects to learn stuff I don't need to know. 'Sides, Jack says it's best if they don't figure it out, even if Gram wants me to. She says I'm hidin' my light under a basket, but you get to see it, right? And some of the other people Parker brings home?"

Leah's attention became diverted and she grimaced, going to the kitchen entrance and peering around the doorway. A minute later she came back, solemnly studying Meg. "Shannon and Parker are arguing about you," she whispered.

This surprised Meg who had heard nothing and didn't think the child could have been at the door long enough to follow a conversation. Even so, her job in coming here was to get information. "About me?"

"Shannon says he shouldn't have brought you here. If we have to run away again it's going to be hard for her 'cause of the baby." Leah walked over to the couch and Meg followed. They sat down and the child studied Meg for a while, then glanced at the mural. "I hate to leave it unfinished," she wistfully sighed.

"Why would Shannon talk about running away?" Meg quietly asked.

"If you tell on us, then the bad men will come again," Leah replied.

"Who would I tell?"

Leah stared at her. "The men you work for, of course!"

Meg felt a chill start at the nape of her neck. Did they know who she really was, and why she was here? She wanted to probe further but Leah's attention was now riveted in the direction of the kitchen. The child gazed at the wall as if she had x-ray vision. "Shannon is sure worried, but Parker says he had to bring you here 'cause it will take two of their kind to help you."

Meg began to wonder if all conversations with eight-year-olds were so strange and hard to follow. Was it Leah, or was it children in general, and how accurate were her statements, anyway? Obviously she was brighter than most kids her age, but half of what she said didn't make sense. "What do you mean, they want to help me?"

Exasperated, the child glanced at her with a split attention, then returned her stare to the kitchen. "I hate the way grown-ups pretend everything and can't say how things really are, 'specially when they talk to kids. It would be better if you'd just say how things are, you know, and stop hiding everything."

Meg had the eerie feeling that she was being dressed down by a college professor stuck in a child's body. Leah glanced at her and smiled. "Okay, I'll explain it. Parker wants to help you. He wants to do it 'cause you are hurt, but it takes two of their kind. You don't need my kind, or Jack's kind. You need Parker and..." her words faded. Parker and Shannon came back into the livingroom; neither one of them looked very pleased. They were both staring at Leah.

Shannon glanced at Meg, then scowled at her little sister. "I'm sorry she's such a pest. Leah, I think you have some homework to do."

"Oops," Leah whispered, sliding off the couch. Shannon's scowl increased as she slowly lowered herself onto the couch next to Meg. Her face was flushed, and a few tendrils of her hair were damp with perspiration.

"Are you all right?" Meg asked, concerned.

The little girl came back to the edge of the couch, worriedly looking at her older sister. She put her hand on Shannon's abdomen, then rested her head there as if she were an Indian guide listening to ground vibrations. Leah closed her eyes.

"She wants to come out and be with us," Leah whispered.

"No way," Shannon sighed, leaning her head back against the couch. "Tell her she needs to stay there another two weeks at least, until she passes six pounds."

"Are you okay?" Meg asked, concerned. "Do you want me to get your grandma?"

Shannon bit her lip and closed her eyes. "It's just a contraction. Dang, it hurts!"

Meg was concerned with how Leah was sprawled on her sister. She rested her head and splayed hands on Shannon's pregnant abdomen. "Leah, maybe you shouldn't lean on her that way," Meg suggested.

"No, she's fine," Shannon said, opening her eyes and touching the child's head. "Hurry up, will you, honey?"

Meg looked at Parker. "What's happening?"

He pointed to Shannon, explaining she sometimes had contractions but would be okay in a couple of minutes. When Meg asked about a doctor he shook his head, unconcerned.

"Is that better?" Leah finally asked, opening her eyes and pulling back.

"Yes, better now," Shannon sighed.

"Poor little baby Nicole! It's getting crowded in there, isn't it? But your daddy says two more weeks at least, so just be patient," Leah crooned, talking to Shannon's abdomen as if she were best friends with the unborn baby. "Your daddy says wait, and so does your Uncle Keith. You listen to them and then you get to come out."

Shannon tenderly brushed her hand against Leah's cheek. "I love you, Sis."

"Love you, too, Shannon."

Leah smiled and headed for the kitchen, leaving Meg alone with Parker and Shannon. "She's very bright, isn't she?" Meg observed, hoping that normal conversation might actually help things in this strange household seem normal.

"Yes. She's off the chart," Shannon answered, and Meg assumed this was in reference to Leah's I.Q. The young woman looked at Meg with an apologetic expression. "I want to tell you I'm sorry for being self-centered. Parker brought you here for a reason, and I've been selfish."

It had been difficult for Meg to follow Leah's conversation, but Shannon seemed no better. "Does your family always talk in riddles?" she queried Parker.

"This afternoon, remember what happened?" Parker signed. "You remember red flowers? You afraid/sick and I helped you become healed...short healing. You want same, repeated? Your decision."

Shannon touched Meg on the shoulder. "You've had some very bad things happen in your life. Your sister was murdered and you found her body."

"Parker told you?"

"You were so close to her, weren't you?" Shannon asked. Meg noticed how the other woman's voice was gentle and comforting, almost silky in its cadence. "It must have been a terrible thing for you. It must haunt you still."

"Yes," Meg replied, feeling suddenly drained. She wondered about this odd family and about why Hammond had wanted her to come here. Trenery had let her think they might be hackers of some kind, but she saw no evidence of this. Were they hiding something, and if so, what was it? They were definitely eccentric, but she didn't think they were dangerous. Wearing to deal with, perhaps, which would account for her fatigue, but not sinister.

Her thoughts drifted away and she had a hard time hanging on to them. She leaned her head back against the couch and closed her eyes the way she had seen

Shannon do. Her hands lay limply in her lap as if they were now too heavy to move. Meg knew she was being rude but couldn't help it. She was just so tired.

"I've seen lots of sadness, you know," Shannon commented, her voice lulling Meg even deeper into the moment of solitude. "But yours is different. It's left you so alone. Does it bother you, not being close to other people?"

Meg slowly nodded, the weight of isolation suddenly feeling heavier than a lead blanket.

"You've never really gotten over losing your sister and mother, have you?" the other young woman continued. "Or your little friends, and before them your daddy?"

"How do you know about that?" Meg whispered, barely able to move her lips. She wanted to open her eyes but her lids were too heavy. Had Parker told his sister? No, he couldn't have, because she hadn't told him....

I'm dreaming, she thought. I'm just so tired, I've fallen asleep and I'm dreaming.

Shannon must have been in her dream, too, because Meg thought she heard the young woman's voice speaking inside her head. You're so afraid now that another five years has passed. You live with this curse you've created in your mind. The sound was more like a rustling wind than an actual voice.

Meg became aware of other hands touching her, of Parker's hands against the side of her head and on her shoulder. It was like an odd connection joining the three of them in a way she couldn't fathom. In the dream-state Parker was talking to her with a normal voice.

We can take it away, he said. She began to see images that made her smile with joy. They were wonderful, forgotten pictures of the people she had once loved.

* * *

In the kitchen the clock ticked in rhythm to the hum of the old yellow fridge. The stove burner had been turned down to medium and only an occasional burp of steam jiggled the pot lid. Leah sat at the kitchen table with a loaf of bread and the peanut butter can in front of her. The butter knife in her hand was poised above a slice of bread, and she sat very still. Gram had just finished putting in another load of wash when she came back into the kitchen. She paused, catching sight of Leah. The little girl's eyes were round with fear, and she was staring up at the ceiling.

"Good grief, child!" Gram said, jiggling Leah's arm to try and bring her out of the trance. "What is it?"

"Oh Gram!" the girl answered, her voice shaky. "There's someone upstairs! There's someone bad up there, and he's got something evil in his hand."

It took the grandmother a few seconds to catch her breath and deal with her own fear. She always believed everything Leah told her, and because of this her voice now rose in alarm. "We better tell Parker."

"No!" the child cried, tearing her gaze away from the ceiling to look at her grandmother. "Don't bother them. They're busy fixing Meg and they need more time," she said, even though her voice showed increasing fear.

"But if we're all in danger...."

Leah returned her stare to the room upstairs. "He's leaving now," she stated with evident relief. "He's backing out the window and climbing down the lattice."

"What was he doing? Was he a prowler, or was he one of them?" Gram said, a sound of disgust sneaking into her voice.

"Them."

"But he's gone now, you say?" Gram asked, puzzled.

"Yeah. It's still bad, though. He left the sick stuff, and the other ones are going to be coming soon."

"Then we don't have a choice! We have to get you kids out of here!"

Leah bolted from the chair, and any stranger watching would have been mesmerized by the odd play of a child authoritatively interceding with a frightened adult. "They're healing Meg, Gram. Give them a few minutes more."

"Not if the goons are coming," Gram retorted with determination, skirting the table and heading towards the livingroom.

Leah spun back around to face the outside door. She hurried over to it and pushed aside the yellowed curtain, peering out the windowpane. "Too late," she gasped.

Gram stared, too, but saw nothing. Ten seconds passed, then two unmarked cars and a couple of squad cars pulled up in front of the house.

*   *   *

The livingroom had grown dark because afternoon clouds blocked the sunlight that had previously filtered through the window. The room was quiet, and the three people on the couch were still as statues. Meg breathed slowly, aware she was in a dream-like state even though she also seemed more aware than she had been in years. During the span of time within her dream, the length of which she was unable to gauge, she had experienced dozens of buried memories. Recalling the long-forgotten experiences with loved ones had brought a remarkable balm to her soul. It seemed as if her true self had been withered for a very long time— a shriveled, dying stalk of grass in a parched wasteland. Then, a few moments ago, it was as if a flow of water had spread across the dry ground of her life, restoring the childhood she had lost. It was so wonderful she wanted to cry, but the images were moving forward with an increasing speed that left no time for exploring reactions.

Following the flood of memories, Meg was led on to another visual image of the inner workings of her mind. She seemed to sense the remarkable synapses and nerves that shot out impulses with nanosecond speed along her mental network. She moved forward, finding herself within the workings of her brain, seeing it as an incredible light show. The impulses flashed with incomprehensible speed, and she wondered how it were possible to see it. 'Look this way,' a voice said, and she followed the sound. Within the network she saw a dark wedge, almost like a splinter displacing the flow of her brain's activity. She was standing by it now, with Parker and Shannon on either side of her. The huge inverted spiral was a hundred shades of black. They showed her the moving images and she shrunk back with revulsion.

This can't be real, she gasped, and the thought echoed like a cannon blast through her mind. She felt afraid of the black wedge in spite of knowing no such thing existed inside her brain.

'It's just a visual image we're using to help you,' Shannon said. 'Try and look at it, Meg.'

Obediently she moved closer, examining the spinning shard. It was hideous, and in total contrast to the earlier pictures. The darkness of the inverted spire sucked away light as if it were a conical black hole. In spite of this she could still see frightening images which decorated its bizarre mosaic. Charred limbs and sightless, staring eyes moved past her. The splinter began to spin faster, and Meg caught glimpses of destroyed bodies and other ghastly visions. There were flickering pieces of burning ash, corpse faces against satin, fingernails crusted with blood, snakes of smoke, red flower petals weeping drops of blood, a palm print of scorched flesh on a glowing windowpane, a car door crumpling as if it were a wad of aluminum foil, bones protruding from melted flesh, exploding glass, fingermarks on a white throat, strands of hair withering in a dark orange flame, torn clothing atop bruised, waxy limbs, and a blackened glove holding a glowing, red-hot wire.

She was repulsed and yet mesmerized by the nightmarish display. It was every horrid image that had ever haunted her dreams. Meg knew each of the images, recognizing them as the symbols of her grieving.

'Do you want them out of you?' a voice asked.

She couldn't look away, but sensed the other two were no longer standing beside her. Meg pondered the question. 'Can you do that?' she asked, speaking words which seemed immediately sucked away from her and into the dark vortex.

Meg felt herself being pulled away from the spinning images with great speed until she was far from the shard. From this distance it seemed much less threatening; she felt herself grow less tense, almost like switching a radio station from hard rock to soft classical. She smiled at the analogy, marveling at all the offshoots of this strange dream. A few seconds passed and she realized she was with Parker and Shannon in a different place. They seemed to be studying her expectantly, and she sensed they were waiting to see if she wanted to return to the dark image. When she didn't, Parker smiled. 'Some don't want to give it up.'

'We're glad you do, though,' Shannon said, her voice happy.

It seemed as if Meg were simultaneously aware of being in two places within her mind. One was from the distance of standing on a mountainside and looking down at a valley, where the darkness still burrowed. The other was of seeing the sliver much more clearly than when she'd been close to it. She watched it being lifted out, sliding up and away from where it had been lodged. They were pulling out the dark wedge, and as they did so it seemed that the earlier joyous memories seeped into the empty place, much the same way water flowed to its own level when an impediment was withdrawn. It was a remarkable experience.

A small voice intruded into the dream state, a worried sound that drifted into her awareness. 'They're here,' the child gasped, her voice frightened.

A fist hammered against wood—three violent blows that Meg sensed as sound waves washing across her—and a voice shouted, "Federal agents! We have a search warrant for this residence!" There was a moment's pause, then a door banged open and there was the sound of running feet.

Meg felt herself sucked out of the dream state. Her eyes flew open even though she was still deeply aware of the internal images. The bond was cut and the dark splinter returned with a force that was devastating. Like a wooden splinter hammered back into the wound it had been pulled out of, the pain was far more excruciating than if it had never been removed in the first place. It throbbed like a bamboo shoot rammed anew beneath a fingernail having known only a moment's respite. Meg gasped, bending over as if she were experiencing a physical blow.

"I'm so sorry," Shannon whispered. She was weeping.

Chapter 8

A third squad car pulled up behind the other vehicles, and Igor's quick glance took in the scene as they slowed. He looked over his partner's shoulder from where he sat in the back of the car, a thrill of excitement running through him. He chuffed in anticipation. The German shepherd would have preferred to have let out a full-fledged bark to match his mood, but in deference to his partner's human ears he settled for woofing noises followed by a whine.

"You know what's coming, don't you, boy?" Partner asked.

The human tone of expectation primed Igor and made him all the more ready to go. The dog thumped his tail and whined again. He stood, sat, stood, and turned his ears forward to catch any sounds coming from outside the car. Soon he would be able to play. Not practice-play like he and Partner had done last night, but real-play. Practice-play was when Partner got out Igor's toy which had the special smell. Partner would hide it, Igor would find it. Then they would tug and wrestle, which Igor immensely enjoyed. Most of all, though, he loved the times when he could do real-play. This was when they drove someplace, like now, and Igor got to hunt for packages that had the same smell as his toy. He liked it the very best because when it was time for real-play the men were always excited, too. He could smell it in their sweat. Then, if he was able to find the toy-smelling thing, they became even more excited. They would pet Igor, pat his head, and tell him, "good boy!"

Partner stopped the car and climbed out, leaving Igor in the back of the modified squad car. The rear bench had been replaced by a rubber-covered board at seat level with enough room for both Igor and his water bowl. The back door had also been modified. It was outfitted with a remote control door popper which Partner could spring from outside the car in case of an emergency.

At the moment all Igor's attention was focused on Partner and the other men he was talking to. There were two police officers whose scent the dog was familiar with, and one man in a dark coat whose scent he had never whiffed before. He whined again, a sound which was mostly self-comforting in the face of the frustration he felt at being left inside the car. When would Partner let him out?

Igor was somewhat new to the Portland Police Department's drug task force. He had only been with his human partner for six months and was a relatively young dog. The department had paid more than $4,000 for him, and he had come from Slovakia, the former Czechoslovakia, where he had received the specialized Schutzen training for guard dogs, as had the five generations before him. He had been certified for his obedience, stable disposition, and tracking abilities. European dogs were bred for work, as opposed to most of the U.S. dogs which were bred for showmanship. Igor wasn't much to look at, standing shorter than most shepherds and having a mottled brown coat that would never win a blue ribbon; however, his keen instinct and ability to learn put him at the top of the smart-dog list. The department had also paid another $2,500 for his security training in Riverside, California before he had been flown to Portland.

Partner came back to the car and opened the door. "Prijit," he said, which was the Czech word for "come." Igor needed no prompting. He was out of the car in a flash, and soon they were at the front steps of the house. A quiver of anticipation ran through him. He sniffed each man with Partner, recognizing the officer who ate muffins and the one who always used a too-strong soap. The third man, who seemed dark to the dog because he wore a black coat instead of a recognizable uniform, had an unknown scent. He sniffed the man again, disliking the odor. It wasn't the adrenalin smell of excited policemen—a scent he loved because it told him to be excited, too—but instead a nervous odor which Igor usually associated with humans who became Partner's prey. In spite of the smell Igor sensed this male was different. Partner was talking to the man and nodding his head in an obedient way which Igor had learned to associate with the human pecking order. Igor wasn't quite intelligent enough to actually form a question about human line-of-command, but it would have been much easier for him to puzzle out if people would either crouch down to show respect or lay with their jugular vein exposed in complete surrender. He had not yet come to recognize human hands raised in the air as a sign of surrender, and so instead he followed what was happening by using the blueprint of odors which humans excreted.

The men opened the door and passed through the screened front porch area. "Patrat," Partner said, giving his dog the Slavic command to search. Igor sniffed the air, a quick shudder running through him. They entered the kitchen and Igor smelled many things, the most prevalent being human food and wet soap. He didn't like the odors. They hurried through the house and came to a place where people were gathered. He smelled/sensed concern but found no fear. Most of the time when they did real-play Igor smelled fear, the fight-or-flight pheromone which usually made him want to chase. Not here, though. Igor sniffed again and identified the different human scents. He recognized which sex the people were and sorted out each previously unknown human odor: four females, one male. He already knew the policemen's scents and recognized each, along with the new other-male smell of the dark man. More important than all of these scents, though, was his favorite smell which threaded its way through the room: the toy scent. It was time to play!

Igor turned his head to the stairs and was ready to bound up them when he was suddenly overwhelmed by a flood of human emotion. Until this moment Igor had never experienced anything like it, and with a whine he turned back to the group of people. Immediately he located the source. It came from a human female pup who was staring at him. Igor stared back, overpowered by the boundless sense of love which came his way. He whined in confusion, glanced at the stairs, then back at the female pup.

"Patrat," Partner said again, repeating the command to search and find the toy. Igor didn't want to right now. Instead he wanted to stay with the human pup. With her there were no human actions to decipher or commands to follow. The pup's love was clearly understandable to him. It was better than ear-scratching or toy-getting, better than the red meat Partner tossed to him from the outside burning thing which smelled so good. It was better than running and barking, even better than working with the other dogs, Brunno and Bleck.

Igor had lived his entire life in a balancing place. He was a brilliant creature in a class of non-sentient beings, the Einstein of the retarded. Until this very moment Igor had always been more than happy to please Partner, to give him what he wanted, and to play. There had been nothing else in life. Years of breeding had brought out the strongest strains of loyalty in the German shepherd. His instinct and training demanded fidelity to humans, and Partner's affection had been everything to him. Now he had found something more. The human pup loved him, and also understood him.

Officer Rob Carmichael looked down at his dog. The animal was acting strangely, and at first he thought it might be a case of drugs hidden in two places. Now, though, Igor was behaving in a way he'd never seen before. Officer Carmichael gave the Czechoslovakian command again but the dog ignored him. Igor paid no heed at all, almost as if he hadn't heard the order. The dog crouched on his belly, his mouth open in a strange canine grin, his tongue lolling out. He inched his way towards the girl who was smiling at the dog, her eyes shining with delight. A few seconds more and the child had her arms around the dogs neck, holding him as if he were the greatest prize in all the world.

"What's going on here, officer?" FBI agent Dale Warner asked, annoyed. "Control your dog."

Carmichael glanced at the agent who had stormed into the office of Portland's Drug Enforcement Administration this afternoon with a search warrant signed by Judge Hooper. Agent Warner had been pushy, demanding, and full of urgency. DEA officials and local law enforcement agencies were used to this, though. The FBI were well known for their abrasive tactics and were not always well liked. There had been ongoing jokes ever since he'd joined the force about what the F in FBI stood for. The least offensive substitution had been 'friction.'

The officer approached Igor, taking the dog by the collar and pulling him away from the little girl. The German shepherd whined, glanced at him, then looked back at the child. Carmichael studied the dark-haired kid. She was wearing threadbare pants spotted with paint and a thin top that hugged her stick-like figure. It didn't seem as if even an ounce of drugs could be hidden on her, though it was hard to tell what drug dealers would resort to in a panic. It was his guess she was clean, though, and the others, too. He had gone to hundreds of busts and was used to the persona of drug dealers. This mismatched group of people didn't fit the usual profile, though of course it was hard to tell for sure what people were up to.

"I love this dog," the little girl said, looking at Igor and smiling.

Igor whined and panted in comical response. Carmichael was puzzled because the dog had never behaved like this during the entire six months they'd worked together. Igor had played with the officer's own boys and was good with kids, but he'd never acted like this before.

"Let's remove the child," Agent Warner said, coming forward and putting his hand on the girl's shoulder. A menacing growl came from the dog which bared its teeth, snarling at the FBI agent.

Officer Carmichael was baffled, embarrassed, and at this point a little amused at his dog's behavior toward the agent. Maybe Igor had developed a distaste for FBI agents, especially rude ones.

"Zastavit!" he said, commanding the dog to stop growling. He caught Igor by the collar and reprimanded him, leading him away from the child and the agent. Igor looked up at him with uncertainty and a kind of dog-shame for ignoring his master.

"Patrat!" Carmichael ordered again, and this time the dog sniffed the air, looking at the stairs. He seemed torn between the child and the toy-scent but finally surrendered to his four years of training. Igor headed to the stairs but glanced back at the little girl and whined again.

She waved to him. "Go ahead, Igor. Go play!" With a bark he headed up the stairs. Carmichael and another officer followed the dog, while two others searched and secured the front area of the house.

Officers Carl Gutierrez and Jimmy Lloyd were dressed in street clothes but wore recently donned vests with the word POLICE stenciled in bright yellow letters across the back. They approached the suspects, and Gutierrez patted down the Deaf kid, checking his pockets, waistband, and legs for any odd shape that might be a weapon. He finished with the kid's ankles, making sure he wasn't wearing an ankle holster. The boy was hiding no weapons.

Jimmy Lloyd checked one of the women, carefully following the stringent guidelines for patting down a woman when there was no female officer present. The young pregnant redhead stood quietly in front of him, and he carefully checked her waistband, the neckband of her shirt beneath her hair, then her legs below the knees. Gutierrez left the Deaf kid and checked the grandmother, while Lloyd finished with the other female.

Officer Lloyd studied the young blond woman in front of him. He noted she was extremely pale and wondered if her ashen appearance were from using drugs. He checked her eyes to see if they were dilated, then noted they were normal. The officer let her sit back down beside the redhead.

"Looks like they're clean," Gutierrez said, and Agent Warner gave a curt nod.

"Of course we are," the grandmother commented. "We haven't done anything illegal, and he knows it." She glared at the FBI agent.

Warner stared back at her, impassive.

"Officer?" she said, turning to Jimmy Lloyd. "I'd like to see that search warrant. One of you has it, I presume?"

"Agent Warner has it, Ma'am."

Gram turned her attention back to the FBI agent, not bothering to hide her hostility. "Since you used it to enter my home, I'd like to take a look at it."

He hesitated, then pulled it from his pocket, handing it to Officer Lloyd who handed it to her. She unfolded the legal-sized document with numbered lines running along the side. There was a bold heading announcing U.S. District Court across the top of the document, and an assigned identification number. She scanned the contents which outlined the FBI agent's name and position, and listed his reasons for searching the premises. It was signed by Judge T. William Hooper.

"Look at this," she said, handing it to Officer Lloyd with disgust. "It's fake!

This warrant is a forgery, and he's not a real FBI agent. Judge Hooper never signed this document, either. Call his office and ask him if he issued this warrant, will you?"

Officer Lloyd looked at his partner, seeing Carl was also surprised by the request. He glanced back down at the document. "It looks like the real thing to me."

"Then you have nothing to lose by checking on it, do you?" she asked, nodding her head so sharply that the gray pin curls on top gave a little bounce.

Agent Warner stepped forward and took the document from her. He folded it and slid it inside his coat pocket, standing stoically beside the irate grandmother.

"This room is clean. No weapons," one of the uniformed officers asserted as he finished a search of the front room. Since the officers had found no weapons in the livingroom, they set it up as a temporary holding area for the suspects while the rest of the house was searched.

Parker studied Shannon and Meg, his gray eyes showing concern. He felt far more worried about the two young women on the couch than he did about the presence of the policemen. Meg was staring straight ahead, her features waxy. She looked ill, and he blamed himself. Shannon's face, on the other hand, was unnaturally flushed. Her cheeks were as bright as Meg's were pale, though she was no longer crying. What a mess! With a sigh he looked at Leah, lifting his hands to ask what she knew about their situation.

"What happened?" he queried.

She signed to him about the intruder who had come in the window upstairs, and brought a "bad thing" with him. Parker watched the story unfold on Leah's hands. The room was quiet, the old clock on the mantle ticking softly.

Meg sat on the couch, her head reeling. What had happened to her and what was going on now? Her mind was usually quick to sort out things and find a logical explanation. At the moment, though, she was in a fog. She tried to think about what Shannon and Parker had done to her. She assumed they had placed her in some kind of hypnotic trance, though if that were the case then there were a few things she still had a hard time understanding. The experience, in many ways, was beyond explanation. At the moment the physical pain she'd experienced was ebbing, but the internal ramifications continued to leave her feeling stunned.

"Are you okay?" Shannon quietly asked, her eyes full of concern.

"How could I be okay," Meg murmured.

"We only wanted to help you. Do you believe that?"

Meg was silent for a while. "Yes," she finally answered.

Agent Warner came near and their conversation died. She wondered if he were possibly from Hammond's surveillance team, sent in because she had stayed inside the house too long. She doubted it, as he was unfamiliar to her and his expression seemed coldly unyielding. Although now might be the best time to declare her undercover status, instinct told her to say nothing. Her boss had sent her into the house to observe and that was what she needed to do. If the surveillance team were still following her, then Hammond was already aware of what was going on. Because he hadn't sent someone in to retrieve her, it seemed an unspoken signal that she should stay put.

Meg wondered about the search warrant the grandmother had questioned, and if the older woman might be right about it. If so, then she'd better start getting every bit of information she could, and carefully watch the FBI agent. Meg stared at him, mentally recording his face. He was a tall, unattractive man with lean features and a hawkish nose. He would have been formidable except for a receding chin which weakened his other more threatening features. He walked with a clipped gait and sharp, angular movements. Many things about him seemed sharp, including his glance and the quick way he turned his head.

He moved away from her and Meg focused on Leah who was cautiously signing to Parker. The little girl was talking about a "bad man with a bad thing" who had broken into the upstairs part of their house. Meg watched the child with detachment, trying hard to ignore the confusion and pain of ten minutes ago. It was her job to observe, she reminded herself. In the past she had refused to let her personal problems influence her work, and now was no different. She needed to pay attention to every detail of what was happening.

Leah signed about a man who had climbed in through a window upstairs. She gave a quick physical description. He had short brown hair and a scar running through his left eyebrow. "He had 'the bad thing' with him," she signed, explaining how he had left it upstairs before climbing out the window. Leah's signing was interrupted by Agent Warner who came and put his hand on her head.

"Stop that," he ordered.

The little girl looked up at him. "Why did your friend hide that bad stuff upstairs?"

The agent stared at her as if his gaze were a hot poker and she a piece of flimsy paper. Meg studied the man's face, her inner instinct telling her something was very wrong. He didn't like what Leah had said, and his harsh glare masked an unnatural nervousness.

The German shepherd bounded down the stairs, loping towards the little girl. Officer Carmichael followed in the dog's wake. He was holding a plastic bag full of golf ball-sized crystals. "About a half-pound of crack cocaine," he stated.

*   *   *

"What do you think?" Carl Gutierrez asked his partner as they searched the kitchen.

"This place is a mess," Jimmy Lloyd answered. "But I don't find anything that ties in with the drug dealing. It's a broad search warrant, you know, so where's all the other stuff?"

The warrant granted them the right to not only look for drugs but any items instrumental in the packaging and sale of drugs. So far they'd found no milk sugar or other substances for cutting the drugs, no packaging materials, heat sealers, or scales. There weren't even any zip-lock bags or small coin envelopes normally used for packaging. Most obvious of all was the absence of arms. Weapons and drugs almost always went together because dealers often felt a need to protect their illegal stash. If someone tried to steal a dealer's cocaine, he couldn't exactly dial 911.

"What do you think about the old lady's accusation?" Gutierrez asked.

"I think she's off her rocker. Don't you?" Lloyd replied.

"Probably. But I was watching Warner's face when she asked us to call the judge. He was sure of himself until she said that." They were both silent for a minute. "The guy's been a jerk since he first showed up with the warrant," Gutierrez added.

"He's FBI," Lloyd answered, as if that were explanation enough.

"Yeah, well, how hard would it be to forge a warrant?"

"Not hard. But why forge one, if you're FBI?"

Gutierrez was thoughtful, closing the cupboard he'd been searching. "What if you didn't want to jump through hoops and explain to a judge how long you've been an agent, how many drug cases you've been involved with, and all that? Say you might even have trouble actually persuading a judge about the evidence you think's in a place, or what probable cause there is for letting you search? Another thing, when you have a search warrant issued you're supposed to know exactly who's in the house and what they've been doing. I don't get that feeling with Warner. He didn't know anything more than the rest of us when we came through that door."

"You're forgetting the bag of crack Carmichael found upstairs."

"I'm not forgetting it. Did you hear what that little girl said, and catch a look at Warner's mug when she said it?"

Jimmy Lloyd stared at his partner, wondering where Carl was going with this. They had served together for six years and knew each other well. Carl had always shown a skilled cop's uncanny alignment of facts, and Jimmy trusted his pal's sixth sense when it came to crime scenes. "What's bugging you?"

"My gut. Something stinks, and I can smell it just as much as Carmichael's dog smelled that crack."

They could hear the voice of Officer Knox in the other room. He was reading someone their rights. The two officers left the kitchen, moving back into the living-room and noting that all four adults were being arrested for violation of federal drug laws. Officer Carmichael was sliding the drug package inside a large manila envelope. He wrote his name across the flap and sealed it with a piece of clear evidence tape that would leave signs of tampering if anyone tried to open it. His dog sat happily beside the little girl, panting with pleasure.

Meg stood while the large African American officer continued to address her. She was holding a copy of the Miranda Rights and a pen. "You have the right to have an attorney present during any questioning. If you cannot afford an attorney, one will be appointed to represent you by the court." As per his previous directions she initialed the form after each right was explained. "If you decide to answer questions now, you may stop at any time and request an attorney." His voice sounded a little bored, as if he had said this all too many times before to be able to quote it with enthusiasm.

The moment seemed anything but boring to Meg, though. The officer pulled out the hinged handcuffs which were kept folded and ready for use. He slid them around her wrists and she heard the teeth of the cuffs slide into the ratchet. Then he slid one finger between her wrists and the cuff to make sure they weren't too tight. He took out a key and double locked the cuffs. Meg watched as they also handcuffed Parker. What was going on? She still felt stunned at the sight of the officer returning from upstairs with a bag of cocaine, and Leah's little voice previously asking the FBI agent:"Why did your friend hide that bad stuff upstairs?" The child's question had been clear as a bell, and it had rung with innocent truth. Gram's previous accusations also echoed with a self-righteous indignation which was at odds with a crime scene. The members of this family were strange, to say the least, but in spite of the miserable result of the hypnotic trance Shannon and Parker had put her in, Meg believed they had truly meant to help her. Now they were being arrested, and she sensed what was happening to them was wrong.

Leah broke the silence. "Don't put handcuffs on Parker," she protested. Her voice wasn't childish at the moment, instead her tone was authoritative. "He's Deaf and uses sign language. How would you like it if someone stuffed your mouth full of rocks and taped it shut?"

Officer Carmichael knelt down, looking into her face. "Don't worry, sweetheart, he'll be okay. No one's going to hurt him."

Leah leveled him with a direct stare. "No one can hurt him," she replied, her tone of voice now showing the same impatience with the policeman that he sometimes showed his dog.

Officer Gutierrez watched the exchange and then studied the pregnant redhead as her hands were bound with nylon flex-cuffs because her wrist were too small for regular cuffs. Her face was calm and she didn't seem alarmed. It was odd, but all of the people being arrested were surprisingly docile. He had been at arrests where the suspects fought, shouted denials, ranted indignantly, pleaded their innocence, or openly wept. With the exception of those who went into shock, or those too zoned out on drugs to notice, most people reacted with alarm, which was normal. Today, however, barring the grandmother's initial protest, everyone was remarkably calm. Never before had he been at an arrest where the suspects were so obligingly serene and almost unconcerned. It gave him the creeps.

He walked over to Agent Warner. "Why are you arresting all of them? The Deaf kid and grandmother are outlined in the warrant, but not the other two. Who's visiting this place, anyway, and who actually lives here? Do you have that sorted out?" People visiting a house where drugs were found on the premises weren't usually arrested, unless they were doing something like openly sitting around a table cutting cocaine.

Warner stared down at the officer. His hawk-like features were stoic, but a betraying trickle of sweat ran beneath his jaw and disappeared into his shirt collar. "This is a probable-cause arrest. I want them taken in for questioning."

Gutierrez slowly nodded, ignoring his gut which grew tighter with each development. "Do you want us to find a friend or relative to take the little girl?"

"No," Warner quickly replied. "I want her brought in, too. You can call a social worker after we get to the Federal Building."

Jimmy Lloyd overheard him and glanced at his partner, reading Carl's wary expression. Usually after arrests were made, and whenever possible, the authorities tried to have a family member or friend take the children so that the state didn't have to get involved. If no one could be found, then Child Protective Services were usually called to the arrest site. Why was Warner eager to break from the normal arrest format and bring in the little kid? Lloyd looked at his partner but Gutierrez didn't say anything.

The officers led the suspects outside where the usual crowd of neighbors had gathered. Meg caught a glimpse of Leah hugging the German shepherd as Shannon was put into a squad car beside Gram. A panicky feeling overcame Meg. She had a premonition that she wouldn't see them again. A sudden, clear memory came to mind of Parker and Shannon trying to erase the ugly mental images that had haunted her life. Maybe there was nothing more to the hypnotic state than dreaming, and logically she believed this was probably the case. Yet what if there were a slim chance that this brother and sister had some kind of gift for helping get rid of psychological demons? If this were true, she didn't want to lose contact with them.

A question formed in her mind, echoing through the emptiness she felt: 'Do you want help?' They had asked that when she was sitting on the couch with them, hadn't they? Feeling suddenly frantic, she looked first at Shannon's profile through the patrol car window, then at Parker. He was standing just ahead of her, his hands cuffed behind his back. The fingers of his right hand were moving slightly, and with a start she realized he was fingerspelling. She stared at the letters which were slowly spelled out. Seven letters were drawn with careful exactness, then repeated, almost like a methodical use of morse code. She read the word, forming it in her mind, even though it made no sense. Was it the name of a person, or maybe a place? The minute she mentally formed the word, Parker quit fingerspelling. A moment later an officer put his hand on the young man's head, guiding him inside a squad car.

Meg was put in one of the unmarked cars, and as per procedure sat in the rear seat opposite the driver. Since she wasn't being transported in a regular squad car with the protective grill, another agent would be required to sit next to her in the back seat. Meg squirmed to find a comfortable position, which wasn't really possible because of the seat belt across her chest and her hands cuffed behind her back. Agent Warner climbed in next to her and shut the door. The driver started the car's engine.

At this point she felt certain something had happened to the surveillance team which had been tracking her, because Hammond would have had them intervene by now. Maybe it was time to shed her cover and explain why she'd been in the house in the first place. Meg was ready to say something when the driver turned and looked over his shoulder before steering the car into the road. He had short brown hair trimmed in a military cut and a scar running through his left eyebrow. The thin line of white scar tissue disrupted the hairs of his eyebrow, and although it was noticeable it wasn't severe. It gave his semi-attractive features a rugged look, and under normal circumstances she wouldn't have given it much thought. Yet less than twenty minutes ago she had seen Leah's signed description of an intruder the child claimed had planted a "bad thing" upstairs. Meg remembered the little girl's finger tracing a zig-zag line along her eyebrow. It had been an exacting visual description which matched that of the man in the driver's seat.

He turned away and she stared at his profile as he pulled the car onto the road and accelerated. They had gone less than three blocks when Agent Warner looked her. "Tell me about this family of yours," he said. She listened to the timbre of his voice which was hard-edged, dangerous, but also wary. He was cautiously studying her as if she might have a hidden weapon the police frisk had missed.

Quickly her mind sorted through the small bits of information she had gathered so far. This man, who may or may not be working for the FBI, had arrested her and the other three adults in the house. Now he mistakenly asked about her family, assuming she was one of Parker's relatives. The grandmother had accused him of falsifying the search warrant, and the little girl had accurately described the driver who now sat in the front seat. Leah had stated he had hidden something "bad" upstairs. Meg was sure the man hadn't been in the main part of the house during either the search or arrests, so Leah wouldn't have been describing one of the officers already there. Had the little girl gone upstairs while Meg was distracted with Parker and Shannon, and seen the man with the scarred eyebrow coming into the house through a window? Also, what was the "bad thing" she had signed about with such concern, and later asked Warner about? The only probable item the police had found that could fit this description was the bag of cocaine. Either the drugs belonged to Parker's family, or they didn't. If they didn't, then they had been planted to facilitate a false arrest.

She looked at the hawk-like features of Agent Warner. He returned her stare, watching her cautiously. The eyes of the driver kept flicking to the rearview mirror, not to check on traffic but to look at her. They both seemed nervous.

"I've dealt with other members of your family," Agent Warner said, breaking the silence. "We've been able to come to some very fine working arrangements that can benefit us all. Maybe you could talk to your brother. What do you think?"

Meg changed her mind about explaining she was working undercover. She didn't say anything. He leaned near, his eyebrows drawing together in an expression that made him seem predatory. "This is the U.S. Government you're dealing with. You can't fight us."

"I have the right to remain silent," Meg managed. "I want to admonish that right."

*   *   *

Officer Knox drove the patrol car out of the residential area, heading for the Federal Building where the two female suspects in the back seat were being taken for questioning. Thankfully they were quiet, since he didn't feel up to listening to either of them plead their innocence or whine about how unfair the arrest was. He got sick of hearing that, and besides, he was in no mood to deal with it right now.

During the past five months, Officer Knox was seldom in the mood to deal with anything. He didn't like listening to music anymore, or reading. He didn't want to be around his friends or go on dates, and he'd given up racquetball. His new past-time was brooding.

He had been an officer for nine years. For eight-and-a-half of those years he had loved his job. Now he dreaded it. He dreaded working, dreaded sleeping, dreaded just about everything. Most of all he hated remembering the man he had shot and killed. It didn't matter that Decker Spatten had been six miles high from smoking a dried parsley toke liberally laced with angel dust, or that he was a well-known drug dealer who was a human piece of trash. The only thing Knox now seemed able to remember was the guy's African American features similar to his own. He frequently recalled the shock in Spatten's face at being hit by the bullet. He also recalled those features going slack, a blood-stained thread of spittle sliding from the corner of the man's mouth.

Knox was angry at the jerk for refusing to put down his gun, for pointing the weapon and threatening to shoot, and for being the worst kind of racial slur his people could have—a black drug dealer. Yet none of these facts, or his exoneration in the shooting, could stop his mind from replaying the scene over and over again. Sometimes, while watching t.v., he would be amazed at how easily the main characters in a cop show could shoot someone, then come back next week completely unscathed. Real life wasn't like that. A shooting could stay with a cop forever, and the memory of this one had become a vicious monkey on his back.

'You had no choice,' a gentle voice said, the sound of it echoing through his thoughts. The four words brought with them an overwhelming balm of comfort.

Officer Knox slammed on the brakes, pulling his car over to the side of the road. Out of his peripheral vision he saw the other squad car in front of him doing the same thing. He ignored it, still reeling from the voice which had been like the ring of a crystal chime reverberating through his brain. His scalp tightened with alarm and he slowly turned around, looking at the girl sitting directly behind him. He studied her through the grid which separated them. She was a young Caucasian woman about the age of his kid sister.

She smiled at him. 'I can help you.' He heard the words clearly inside his head, stunned by the way they washed over him and burrowed into the place where the worst memory of his life had laid buried for nearly half a year. He knew the comment came from the girl but couldn't comprehend how, since she was still smiling at him and her lips had never moved.

*   *   *

During much of Meg's life a streak of black humor had often surfaced at the oddest times. It did so now, while she was not only busy with a dozen thoughts but was also being fingerprinted. Officer Flores, the woman who worked in fingerprinting at the Bureau of Criminal Investigation inside the Federal Building, guided Meg's hand to the glass plate and pressed it atop the digital fingerprinting system. She rolled Meg's fingers in much the same way prints used to be taken from an inked piece of glass several years ago. The prints were scanned with a laser and classified by a series of points matched to the whorled shapes on Meg's fingertips. They were then sent directly to AFIS, the Automated Fingerprint Identification System, which searched for prior arrests.

Meg watched the process with detachment, most of her thoughts spent in trying to sort out the situation. She reviewed her earlier analysis of Agent Warner but came up with nothing new. The experience with Shannon and Parker shoved its way into her thoughts. She couldn't forget about what had happened. The dream, or hypnotic state, or just plain weird brain-tampering-thing that had happened more than an hour ago now left her filled with longing. She had the illusion of coming close to winning the lottery, to being free of the albatross which had hung around her neck since she was six, only to have those who could help her end up being arrested as drug dealers. Meg felt concern for the people who had managed to emotionally trash her in their weird effort to help, but above all she was struggling with the lack of a logical explanation about what was going on. Many emotions flooded her, but instead of being panicked she felt like giggling. Everything was starting to seem sickeningly funny to Meg. Her sense of black humor made her think about calling Hammond from jail to tell him she'd been arrested. She envisioned herself asking him for a bonus; clearly she deserved one. Not only that, but wait until she tried to explain about the mental stuff that had happened. It was going to be an impossible task. Maybe that was what seemed so humorous. Here she was getting fingerprinted, and she couldn't keep from snickering. Officer Flores glanced at her as though she were nuts.

It didn't get any better when Meg moved on to have her photo taken. She was backed up against a wall lined with a height scale and was handed a card to hold. It had her full name, Margaret Joyce Parrish, plus the agency and an arrest number. The officer took both a forward and profile photograph and Meg smiled for each, which probably made her look ready for the mental ward. What were you supposed to do in a mug shot? she wondered. If you didn't smile, it made you look guilty. If you did, it made you come across as either cocky or nuts.

Next she was placed in a room for questioning, though no one came in to question her for more than an hour. Perhaps this was a tactic that policemen used to unnerve their suspects. After an hour of waiting on edge most people would want to spill their guts. At this point she just wanted to get a hold of Hammond and have him clear up this mess. She wondered what he would think, and if he would have any insights as to what was really going on.

*   *   *

"This stinks!" Officer Gutierrez said, stalking down the hallway of the Federal Building. He glared at Agent Warner who walked beside him, and bit back a few choice swear words. "I would never, ever send an officer into a situation without letting him know fully what he's up against. You haven't played this square from the onset, so it's time to let us know what's really going on."

"You tell me," Warner calmly stated. "Explain why your officers just pulled over to the side of the road and let our suspects go."

Gutierrez opened his mouth to retort, then snapped it shut. His distrust of the FBI agent had turned to open dislike at having the conversation manipulated. "You know something you're not telling us, and right now I've got two officers who are sitting in a daze, and who are going to have to explain their actions before a board."

Carl Gutierrez didn't add what he was thinking, that the oddest thing about Officers Knox and Ridley's behavior was how calmly they were taking it. They should have been highly distressed, especially considering both men's personal situations. One had just come back to work after a leave of absence because of a shooting where a suspect had been killed, and the other was going through a bitter divorce and custody battle. Yet neither officer was showing any signs of stress at this most recent occurrence which could become a blotch on their record. In fact, Knox had looked him square in the face and said, "I'm okay with this, Carl. It'll work out."

Gutierrez and Warner entered the observation room where a video camera was set up to focus through a two-way mirror looking into the interview room next door. Officer Lloyd was standing by the camera, waiting for them. He studied his partner's face which was clouded with anger and concern. He understood Carl's annoyance. Warner ignored both officers. He turned and looked through the gray glass and into the room next door. The room was set up for the Reid method of interrogation, named for the man who had developed the system used by the police. The square room was painted a pale tan, and there were no pictures or notices of any kind on the walls, allowing no distractions for the suspect. Except for the two-way mirror which was used for observation, and a table and two chairs, there was nothing else in the room. The young woman in a pale green sweater sat in one of the chairs. Her honey-colored hair was a little messy but her previously pale face had regained a more natural hue.

"At least we've got one left," Officer Lloyd commented.

"Yeah, but we'll have to drop the charges," Gutierrez stated with irritation. "Apparently there's no evidence left to book her with."

Lloyd raised his eyebrows in dismay. "What happened to the cocaine?"

"We're not sure. The evidence envelope was in the trunk of Carmichael's vehicle, but it's not there now. There's a sticky black residue and some paper ashes in his evidence box which we're having tested. We think it might show up as burned cocaine."

"Someone charred it, and left it in his trunk? How'd they get inside the trunk in the first place, and why didn't they just take it?"

"That's the big question, isn't it?" Gutierrez asked, looking at Warner.

"Twilight Zone," Lloyd quipped, though neither of the other men seemed to think it was humorous. "So what about the girl?"

"She doesn't need to know we don't have the evidence," Warner stated. "We need to interrogate her, see if she'll tell where the other members of her family may have gone to."

"I'll go talk to her," Gutierrez offered.

"Sure," Lloyd added. "You always take the cute ones."

Gutierrez scowled, wishing his partner wouldn't make jokes in front of the FBI agent. He left the observation room, went out into the hall and entered the interrogation chamber. The young woman looked up at him, her features solemn. He started his act.

"You're Margaret Parrish?" he asked in the friendly, open manner he had often used to garner information from suspects. "I'm Officer Gutierrez. Mind if I sit down?"

He slid out the other chair, covertly studying her body language which was neither defensive nor self-protective. She looked him squarely in the face, and he had a fleeting thought that this one might be a harder case to crack than usual.

"Do you have a tape recorder or a video camera running?" she queried, pointing to the mirror across the room.

Gutierrez smiled. "You've been watching too many cop shows. I just want to chat with you, and hopefully keep what we're gonna talk about between these four walls."

"If you don't have a tape recorder running, you need to get one. I'm going to make a statement, and I don't want to do it more than once. Do you have a tape recorder or video camera going, or don't you?"

The officer hid his annoyance at her pushy attitude. At the moment there was nothing else to do but play along. "We do. Go ahead."

Meg turned to face the glass pane which covered the camera. "My name is Margaret Parrish. I'm an operative for the Central Security Service and was working undercover when the arrests in the Briggs household were made. My RAC supervisor, the Resident Agent in Charge of our satellite division here in Portland, is Richard Hammond." She gave the phone number. "This is the completion of my statement. If you have any further questions you can discuss them with my supervisor after I've been debriefed."

Agent Warner swore under his breath, striding to the door of the observation room and jerking it open, leaving a gaping Officer Lloyd in his wake. He hurried down the hall and to the elevator. When he reached the lobby of the Federal Building, his assistant was waiting for him. The man with the scar who had driven the vehicle hurried to keep up with his boss.

"She's a plant! One of Hammond's people."

"Great," the other man hissed.

They moved past the front desk and through the outside doors. "What now?"

"We might have info on her from some of the items we got out of Hammond's office. She had contact with Briggs and some of his family, so let's set up a system on her. It's a long shot but let's do it anyway. In the mean time, what information have we gotten from the house?"

"Stanton and Koranda are there now. They went in as soon as the police sealed it with evidence tape and left. They're looking for some kind of paper trail."

Both men climbed into the front seat of the car which soon merged with the city traffic. "I was stupid," The man posing as Warner said. "Really, really stupid."

His driver was quiet for a while. "It worked with Benny," he said.

"Sure. They're not like Benny, though, are they? That was our mistake. It worked with Benny because he couldn't maintain it for very long, and once we got him in a cell the only thing he could have done was have his jailors sitting around in a stupor. He got real cooperative when we set out the rules and told him he'd never detect a sniper taking him out if he proved to be a danger to us. It's a whole new ball game with the Deaf kid and his sister, though."

"More of a challenge, that's all. We found them once, we can find them again," the driver said, stepping on the accelerator.

Chapter 9

The sun was just starting to set when two men came out of the rundown house where Parker and his family had been living. One of them carried a manila envelope stuffed with papers. They climbed into a dark blue Plymouth and a few minutes later drove away. The three young people, shielded by the hanging branches of a weeping willow, watched them leave. Amber, Jack, and Keith stared at the house where they had stayed until only a few hours ago.

"They always look for a paper trail, but never find anything," Amber stated with irritated amusement. "You'd think after this many years they'd figure out we're not exactly going to leave them a forwarding address."

Keith glanced down at his little sister. She was five-feet-two and looked several years younger than her true age of nineteen. Amber had classical Japanese features and long black hair that swished against her windbreaker when she tossed her head.

"What now?" he asked.

"I go and question our sweet little old neighbor lady, of course," Amber replied. Before either of her brothers could stop her she scurried across the street.

They watched her knock on the door, then Keith turned to Jack. "Shannon will be okay."

Jack glanced at his blond-haired brother who wore a perpetually carefree expression, then slowly shook his head. "I should have been there with her."

"Shannon has lived half her life on the run, Bro. You know she can fend for herself. Besides, Nicole isn't due for another two weeks."

"That's no guarantee," Jack responded. He thought about his young wife, remembering one of their many episodes spent on the road. In the beginning Shannon had called him Jack-by-the-Way, and had held his hand when they crossed the frightening places. She had been twelve, thin as a stick, and wore short red curls tucked beneath a baseball cap. He had loved her from that very first day. Now that she was in the last stages of pregnancy, he felt more concerned for her than ever. She seemed equally vulnerable as she had that first night at the tent show when she'd used bravado to hide her fears.

"Leah's with her," Keith reminded.

Jack sighed. "Leah's still so young, and not very experienced."

"She's also going to be a whole lot more of an impressive medical healer than either of us, Jack. You know that. Besides, she's already got a real love for Nicole and will do whatever it takes to keep both Shannon and the baby safe."

"Yeah, just like in the tabloids: eight-year-old delivers baby," Jack bit off with a tone of sarcasm that wasn't natural for him.

Keith smiled and clasped his brother on the shoulder. "They're all going to be okay! Let's get out of here and find them. Maybe we can even get to them before they reach the California border."

"Okay," Jack sighed.

The two young men turned their attention back to their sister, Amber, who was having a biting conversation with the neighbor next door.

Mrs. Finch's wrinkled face peered through the half-open doorway. "I told the police all about how your family brings home every kind of homeless wino and loser. It's sickening how those low-life types just keep showing up at your house, coming and going all the time. Dregs of society is what I call 'em. Mabel Watson never should of rented to you people in the first place! It serves you right that the police come hauled your deef and dumb brother off, and your loony grandmother and kid sister. If you don't get outta here, I'll call the police on you, too!"

Amber's eyes narrowed dangerously, and she felt her anger rising. It was her belief that most people had reasons for the way they were, and if you could help them with their reasons they could become better. Some people, though, were like Mrs. Finch, just nasty all the way through.

"Listen to me, you mean old crone, if you call the police you'll regret it. You have to sleep sometime, you know!"

"Get off my property!" the woman screamed, her false teeth half slipping out of her mouth.

Amber took a step back, her expression still aggressively cross. "Do you have good smoke detectors, Mrs. Finch?"

The woman's mouth gaped in fear before she slammed the door shut. Amber could hear the deadbolt turning and the chain rattling into it's lock. She hurried back across the street and down half a block to where her brothers waited.

"That wasn't very nice," Keith said, though his blue eyes sparkled with amusement.

"She had it coming! Besides, I don't want her calling the police, even if there's nothing they can do. We don't need any more complications right now."

"You shouldn't make threats," Jack admonished. He didn't share Keith's sense of humor regarding the situation.

The siblings turned and walked away from their house. Amber linked her arms through those of her two brothers. She looked up at Jack who was taller than either of them. He had a beard and wavy brown hair that hung long on the nape. She knew that soon he would be trimming his hair and shaving off the beard, even as she would cut her long tresses into a shorter style. None of this bothered her. It was Jack's deep concerns which made her want to comfort him.

"Well, I think if they were going to raid us then they did it at a good time. What if they'd taken in you two and Gram, and the rest of us had happened to be gone? You guys probably couldn't have gotten away. We know that since the cops took Parker and Shannon then they must all be free by now and on the road. Not only that, but we know where they'll head, and we just have to get there, too. Before you know it we'll be meeting up with them."

Jack nodded, squeezing her hand which had slipped into his. "Always trying to make everything right, aren't you, Sis?"

"That's our little Amber," Keith added. "Best therapist in town."

"Thank you," she smiled, knowing Keith's teasing had a sincere side to it.

The flaming sky had faded to dull orange atop darkening pewter. Twilight turned the evening light gray, and a cool breeze stirred the tree branches. It whispered through the leaves which seemed to sigh in response. They were on the run again.

*   *   *

The officer on the other side of the counter slid the manila envelope to Meg. She took it and dumping out the cash and coins which had been in her pocket, along with her turquoise earrings, watch, and ring. She initialed each item on the list and signed the form. Hammond patiently waited while she stuffed the money in her pocket and slipped on the jewelry. She was grateful to have her watch back. It had been extremely annoying to sit in the empty interrogation room and periodically check her naked wrist out of habit.

They left the Federal Building and she unconsciously slowed her gait so that Richard wouldn't have to hurry. Outside, the sky was darkening. Soon it would be night. Meg thought it felt much later, as if many hours had passed since she and Parker had left the downtown marketplace. She thought about the young man, still intrigued by what she had learned. He and the others had apparently escaped from the patrol cars. The police detectives were still baffled, though at this point Meg wasn't really surprised. She thought there was little about Parker's family that could surprise her any more.

They hadn't gone far when someone called her name. A moment later Officer Gutierrez caught up with them. "I'm glad you hadn't already left. There's something else we found out that I thought you two might want to know. We checked with Judge Hooper's office. He didn't sign that search warrant."

"So it was a forgery," Meg said, having a renewed respect for Parker's grandmother.

"My partner examined it at the house and said it looked legit, so whoever Warner really is, he had some connections."

"You've checked with the FBI?" Hammond queried.

The officer nodded. "The real agent Dale Warner is on assignment in Miami."

Hammond wasn't surprised. "Thanks for your help, officer."

"Wait a minute," Gutierrez said. "We need to know what's going on. We have two officers who are going to have to undergo review for their actions." His voice wasn't demanding. He didn't have much clout when it came to Hammond's division, but hoped to encourage him to share information.

The older man seemed thoughtful. "Considering the evidence you have from the judge's office, and the FBI themselves, I think you have enough to clear those men. It seems to me your boss has other more serious concerns after this incident. There's not much else I can suggest. You have my number in case he needs to call me."

Richard and Meg turned to leave but Gutierrez followed, walking with them. "Something strange is going on. Can't you let me in on what it is?" He looked at Meg. "You were there at the arrest, so let me run some stuff by you. There's a few things starting to click now that I've had more facts and the time to think about them. For one thing, I've never seen any of the police dogs act the way that one did during the search, and though I didn't think about it at the time, that little girl knew the name of the dog. How'd she know it? The officer in charge of the dog only uses Czech commands, and almost never calls the dog by name. The kid knew his name, though. She called him Igor and told him to go play. Another thing, how did the grandmother know the warrant was a forgery when it was good enough to pass my partner's inspection? It had all the official marks of a real search warrant. We've seen them hundreds of times, and it fooled us. Why didn't it fool her? And why were you working undercover with those people? They're not drug dealers. Who are they?"

Meg smiled at him and shrugged. "Life's full of weird stuff, officer. I don't know much more than you do." Besides, she thought. If I told you what happened to me today, you'd never believe it. "Some things don't have a logical explanation, at least not one that we can figure out. Just shrug it off and be glad you're done with it."

The two CSS agents climbed in their car and drove away, leaving the frustrated officer standing on the pavement.

*   *   *

"Thanks for your cooperation, Kurt," Daniel Trenery said into the phone. He was talking with the Resident Agent in Charge of Portland's DEA. "I'll send two of our men out right away to take depositions from your agents."

He listened further, hesitant to give out any more information. "Uh-huh. Sure. Well, as I explained before, the suspects were skilled hypnotists. Your men could hardly have know that, could they? Right. I think so too. Just point out that since the evidence, search warrant, and FBI agent have all disappeared, it's best to wipe the slate clean and release your two officers from any responsibility. There's not even a file to close on this one, is there? Yes, I understand, but we have no more information than you do on who the fake Agent Warner was. One more thing. Our undercover agent was fingerprinted and photographed, and we definitely don't want her info in the system. Can you take care of that for us? Thanks."

In time Trenery managed to extricate himself from the phone call. Almost immediately his intercom buzzed and he was informed that Meg Parrish was ready to give a statement. He joined her and Hammond in a small conference room, sitting down at the table with a tape recorder in its center. He smiled at Meg. "We're relieved you're back. It gave us a real upset when our surveillance team lost you. Can we get you anything before we start? Something to drink, perhaps?"

"No, I'm fine." Both men were looking at her with a lot of interest and concern, which was understandable. She had said little to Richard while in the car, agreeing it was best if she waited for the deposition before discussing the day's events.

"Then let's start," Trenery suggested, leaning forward and turning on the recorder.

Meg began with her name, the date and time, and her assignment criteria. She then told as many details as she could remember of being inside Parker's house, with the exception of the hypnotic state she had been in. She would save that for later. At the moment she focused on Parker, his family, any of the oddities about them she could remember, and the chain of events leading to the arrests. She ended with a detailed account of her ride in the unmarked police car, seeing the driver previously described by the little girl, and Agent Warner's threatening comments. It took more than forty minutes.

"Can we stop here for a bit?" she asked. "I need a drink of water."

Trenery verbally noted the time and turned off the recorder. "I'll see to it." He went to the door and opened it, sticking his head into the office area. "Brian? Can you bring Meg a glass of water?"

A minute later Brian Moses brought in a paper cup filled with water; the large Samoan agent was Hammond's assistant. "Hi, Meg," he said, setting the cup down in front of her. He had a friendly personality that was a cross between a teddy bear and a bulldozer.

"Hi, Brian. How's it going?"

"Good. Hey, I'm glad you got back okay."

"Thanks."

Brian had also been one of the two agents on her surveillance team. He seemed genuinely relieved she was safe. He left the room, shutting the door, and Meg drank the water. When she was finished Trenery again reached for the tape recorder but she stopped him.

"Before we continue, I want to ask if you've read a personal profile on me, Mr. Trenery."

He hesitated only a second. "Yes, I have."

"Then you know I've lost several family members."

"Yes. Your parents and sister. Also childhood friends."

"That's right. In a minute I'm going to tell you some things which will make reference to those events, and it's not going to be particularly easy for me. I'm a private person. Until today I've never let my personal life cross over into my professional one. If I'm going to tell you everything that happened in that house, then I'll have to make reference to some of those personal experiences."

"We understand, Meg," Hammond said.

Trenery turned on the recorder, stating the time, and she took a deep breath before starting. "I'll now make reference to two different situations. The first happened when I was with Parker Briggs in the marketplace. We came to a stall selling geraniums. I became upset. This is because when I was sixteen my sister was murdered, and I discovered her body. There was a pot of broken geraniums in the room where she was killed, and the sight of the ones in the marketplace caused a flashback. This rarely happens to me," she added, wondering if she would lose her position with CSS now that her personal instability was known. She stared at the tape recorder, watching the slow turning of the cassette tape. The last thing she felt like doing was making eye contact with either supervisor.

"At that time," she continued, "Parker Briggs did something that helped me. What I mean is that he made me feel calmer, without actually saying anything, since he's Deaf. At the time I assumed he was able to put me into some kind of hypnotic trance, because almost immediately the flashback faded and I felt better. Did the surveillance team give a statement about what they saw?"

"They did," Hammond said, his voice softer than normal. "Were you able to question Parker about what happened?"

"Later, yes. He gave no real explanation, though I think he signed something about his family being healers. At that same time I explained to him about my sister's death because he questioned me about my reaction to the flowers." She didn't raise her eyes, instead preferring to watch the dizzying circles of the cassette.

"Go on," Trenery encouraged.

"The second incident occurred inside the house, and from this point on I can't be sure what happened. I can relate the incident from my perspective, though it won't be logical or easily explained. Just my perspective, you know."

She was hoping they would tell her she didn't need to say anything else, but instead Hammond suggested she continue. "Don't over-analyze it," he said. "Just tell us what you think happened."

Meg took in a deep breath and then let it out slowly. "I was sitting on the couch talking with Parker and his sister, Shannon. I felt very tired at the time, and was relaxing my head against the back of the couch with my eyes closed. Shannon brought up my sister's death, and then talked about my friends and parents dying, too. I thought this odd, since I hadn't told Parker about the other family members I had lost. After that it became very strange. They asked me if I wanted help. I said yes, and they began to help me recall all kinds of good memories about my family and friends. After that, I then remembered some of the really bad things that happened, too. It seemed to me Parker and Shannon were helping to ease my painful memories and would have succeeded in somehow dissolving them if the police hadn't shown up and interrupted us."

The tape recorder continued to turn, but no one said anything. She looked up at the two men sitting across from her, and finally Hammond spoke. "Do you have any theories about what you experienced?"

"Theories? Yes, I have three. The first is that I was dreaming. It might be possible that somehow I fell asleep and dreamt the event, especially since it had a very dream-like quality."

"Do you believe that's what happened?"

"No. In spite of being dream-like it was too intense, and I also seemed to be actively cognizant of everything."

"Go on."

"My second theory is that Parker and Shannon used hypnosis. In fact, that was what I originally believed, though there are too many parts of the experience to be explained away by mere hypnosis." She raised her eyes, looking at the faces of the two men. "My third theory is that Parker and his family are telepaths."

Meg watched their faces as she said this. She expected them to raise eyebrows, or look embarrassed at such frivolous theorizing. Instead, both of their expressions were guarded. No one said anything until Trenery switched off the machine after verbally noting the time.

"Thank you, Meg. We'll see you get home now. It's been a long day."

She stared at him, uncertain. "You're not laughing at me."

Trenery lifted his eyebrows in surprise. "Why would we laugh at you?"

Meg felt unsettled, as if even common circumstances and reactions were no longer predictable. "Because I just tossed out a theory that's right up there with alien invaders from Mars, but neither one of you looked at me like I'm nuts. You looked cautious, just like my dad did when I was five and accused him of being Santa. I had guessed what he hadn't wanted me to know. I think it's the same with you two, because I've made a guess at something you know about but want to keep secret."

They continued to stare at her, and their silence seemed to confirm her statement. "It all makes sense now, and I can hardly believe it! Those people really are telepathic." She felt her own face register the surprise she had expected to see on theirs.

"You're jumping to conclusions," Trenery stated.

"Am I? While I was sitting in that interrogation room in the Federal Building, I had a lot of time to think. And what I thought about was how they seemed to know what was going on all the time, and to know what the others were thinking, and even what I was thinking. That's why Leah described Warner's driver after he planted drugs upstairs, and how she knew the dog's name though nobody said it out loud. That's also the real reason Parker and Shannon were able to get inside my mind, and why the policemen let them go from the squad cars. I have always thought everything in life had a logical explanation, but now the perimeters of my logic are getting stretched out of whack because there really is such a thing as telepathy!"

"Meg, calm down. You're jumping to conclusions," Trenery cautioned.

"I am calm," she retorted with enough steam to belie the statement. "For reasons I can't even guess, those people have telepathic powers. Is that why you sent me in with no knowledge of who they really were? Yes, it must be," she said, answering her own question. "If I knew all about them, they would have read it in my mind. They must have known I was spying on them, though, because that's what Leah alluded to. But in spite of the danger I might be to them they still wanted to help me."

She had the strange feeling that someone had thrown a jigsaw puzzle in the air, and that the pieces had somehow magically fallen into place to form most of the picture. "I never would have believed telepathy was possible, because it's too weird, except that I experienced it first hand today. Not only that, but something has convinced you, or the people over you, and it's the reason this case was set up in the first place, isn't it? That's what the whole big deal is, right? If they're really telepathic, and I'm not talking about 1-900-dial-a-psychic or other crap like that, but if they're true telepaths, then there's also a real reason for concern. If someone can read minds, how do you establish government security? It doesn't matter how many codes we write. People who can read minds don't worry about codes, because after one of you reads the classified material, they can then read you."

"Miss Parrish, will you stop?" Trenery crossly asked.

She stared at the two men, wishing they would admit the truth. Why were they letting her stand alone in this, refusing to acknowledge her discovery? She was like that poor guy on the old t.v. show Mr. Ed who knew the horse could talk but no one else knew it. Hammond and Trenery knew it, though, but they weren't going to help her deal with a piece of knowledge that was turning her logical world upside down. Her adrenalin was surging and she felt overwhelmed with emotion.

To her horror, Meg felt her throat tighten and her eyes smart. If she got weepy in front of Hammond and Trenery she would go home and slit her own throat. She took in a deep breath, holding it a few seconds until her lungs ached. Slowly she released the air, feeling a little dizzy but more under control as the flood of emotions receded. "Okay, maybe you can't admit it because of classification," Meg said, making her voice sound more calm. "But let me say something else. Those people aren't dangerous to us. I think all they want to do is to be left alone, then someone like Warner comes along. His driver plants cocaine in their house so he can storm in with a fake search warrant, all to try and get his hands on them. What agency would give him sanction to do that? Is he NSA?"

"No, of course not," Hammond answered.

"Well, I know he's government, because when he questioned me, assuming I was one of Parker's family, he said I couldn't fight the government."

"Everything we have discussed here tonight is classified," Trenery stated, his flushed face showing how disconcerted he was. He was a normally stoic person, yet her many theories had clearly ruffled his feathers. "You have no authority to discuss any of this case further. If you do, your job will be in jeopardy. Do you understand that?"

Meg stared at him, then slowly stood. "Maybe I don't want to work for a government which tracks down innocent people and uses fake warrants to arrest them. Maybe it's time I found something else to do with my life."

"You can't quit," Hammond said, openly concerned.

Meg looked at the boss she had grown so fond of, somehow feeling betrayed. "Of course I can quit. You're not the mafia, you know." The two men stared at her and she sighed in frustration. "I'm going home now. If you don't want me to talk about it anymore, then fine, I won't talk."

"Have Brian take you home," Hammond told her.

Meg opened the door and left the room, feeling overloaded with new discoveries and, at the same time, disheartened and disappointed.

Brian drove her to the MAX transit rail parking lot where she had left her car earlier in the day. "Richard was mad as a wet hen that we lost track of you," he confided on the way there.

"It wasn't your fault," Meg answered, thinking that it really wasn't, since a telepath could have easily helped him lose track of her.

"No kidding! You were there one minute, then gone the next. Pete and I were left looking around like a couple of lost idiots, and neither one of us could find you."

"It's no big deal," she reassured him.

"Yeah, well, it was to Richard. If anything would have happened to you, he would have had our heads on a shish kabob."

Meg thought that much more had happened to her than he could ever know. They said goodnight and she unlocked her car. Brian watched her drive out of the parking lot before leaving. She drove the rest of the way home, feeling isolated and surrounded by the darkness. A few minutes later she was in her apartment and, although it felt good to be back home, she was still oddly aware of being very alone. Too much had happened today, and she ached to talk with someone. She was suddenly overwhelmed by a deep longing to be with her mother. They had been such good friends, always sharing everything. Meg missed her mother terribly at the moment, and was brutally aware of her total lack of friendship with any other human being. After her mother's death she had decided the pain wasn't worth it. Not wanting to lose anyone else, she'd become solitary and isolated. Today, though, she had felt kindness and friendship from two people. Parker and Shannon had opened a door that had been closed for too long.

"What am I doing with my life?" Meg asked herself, aloud. She looked around the apartment, at her many houseplants and the collection of art glass. Would it have been such a bad thing to at least chance getting a cat? She went into the bedroom, taking off her clothes and throwing them in a pile on the floor. Meg felt sweaty and her eyes were gritty from fatigue. She spent ten minutes in a hot shower, trying to wash away the forlorn feeling that had come over her. After toweling off, she dried her hair and decided to dress for bed, even though it was too early to go to sleep. She pulled on one of the oversized t-shirts that she preferred sleeping in and went into the kitchen.

Realizing she was hungry, she checked the freezer. The frozen dinners looked unappetizing. She settled for a bowl of cold cereal and some toast. After that she wandered through her apartment, restless and nervous. The message light on her answering machine was blinking, and she saw there were three calls. This was a little surprising, as she seldom got messages. The first was from Brian at a payphone in the marketplace, about a half-hour after he and Pete had lost her. "Meg, if you get home call in right away, will you?"

The second was fifteen minutes later and from Hammond's secretary, requesting a call into the office. Meg assumed this was after Richard learned the surveillance team had lost her. The third was from Belinda who managed the Half Moon Gift Shop, asking that she call the store. This seemed a little odd, but then Meg remembered the saleswoman talking about a new catalogue of Fenton glassware that was coming in. Maybe that's what she was calling about. She erased the three messages, thinking how hollow her life was. It was pretty bad when she had to lose a surveillance team to get a couple of phone calls.

She went to the computer, turning it on and accessing the Internet. Meg decided to first learn about telepathy, searching for that single word. Nearly seven thousand listings came up, and she was amazed by all the information on a topic she had always felt unworthy of her time. Words like paranormal, clairvoyant, and ESP showed up. These were subjects Meg had previously discarded as illogical fancy, merely the trickery of others. She still couldn't discard that indelible belief, and in spite of her experience she was amazed so many people were interested in it. Some of the data had telepathy tied in with a listing of everything from Area 51 to UFOs, which is where she'd always personally thought it belonged.

Meg clicked on an interview with a professor who analytically discussed both ESP fakery and a few real instances he claimed to have personal knowledge of. Another site discussed paranormal dreams and lucid dreaming, some of their definitions eerily close to what she had experienced, and some of them way off-base. Still another web site had advice on creating mental links and exploring others telepathically. She had looked at less than half a percent of the information out there and already it was too much. Discouraged, Meg backed out of the web sites. She wasn't ready to embrace the onslaught of new-age beliefs in spite of what she had experienced. There must be some kind of logical explanation or scientific reason for what had happened to her.

Parker and his family again came to mind. They may have been weird, but they were also highly likeable. Despite the problems caused to her, the time spent with them had been good. She thought about them with ever-growing curiosity, making a sudden decision to find them. There really wasn't any other choice. First of all, she needed to know why they could do what they could do, and what had really happened to her. The other reason for finding them, and the one which seemed far more important, was that she wanted them to finish what they had started.

Meg could still clearly recall the black splinter. Shannon had said it was a mental image they were using to help her. Whatever it was, now that she had seen a visual of all the misery plaguing her life, she wanted it out. She thought about the word Parker had finger-spelled to her while he was in handcuffs, and she believed it was a possible clue to finding him. That, or perhaps he was telling her the name of someone who could help her. She hadn't told Tenery or Hammond about the word, since somewhere during the conversation with them her loyalties had begun to waver.

She typed in the word Parker had carefully spelled for her: b-e-n-i-c-i-a. Half a minute later a couple of thousand references came up, and Meg realized Benicia was a town in California. She accessed their Chamber of Commerce, learning what she could about the small community north of San Francisco. Was this where Parker and his family were headed? He must have planned on using his telepathic ability to escape the squad car, and then go to some kind of safe house in a prearranged town. If Benicia was that town, then perhaps he had been telling her where to meet him so that he and Shannon could finish what they had started. A sudden surge of hope filled her, and she smiled for the first time in hours. Tomorrow she would call Hammond and tell him she wanted to take a few days off. Her smile faded. They hadn't parted on the best of terms. In fact, Meg wasn't quite sure if she had actually quit her job during those last angry moments. She realized their conversation had been sort of gray, and no doubt her words would be taken more as a threat than an actual declaration. Even so, remembering the scene made her feel unsure. Besides, did she want to continue working for an organization who tracked down innocent people just because they might be telepathic? And, more importantly, were they affiliated with another sector of the government that had no qualms about planting cocaine and making false arrests? Maybe now was a good time to take a little vacation, she reflected. She could drive down to Benicia and see what it was like. Very possibly her efforts would prove useless, and she would never see either Parker or Shannon again. She might walk around the rest of her life with a visual of the nightmare images she had experienced, never finding a way to get rid of it or stop it from haunting her. She would probably go on working for CSS, never completely comfortable there again because of what they had and hadn't done. These thoughts weighed her down, and although she tried to shake them off, the idea of continuing on in this kind of survival mode and isolated existence filled her with bleak discouragement.

With a sigh she went to the Internet chat room where she had so often spent time with faceless friends who didn't even know what she looked like or where she lived. She began a conversation with one of the guys she'd typed to off-and-on for more than a year.

CodeBreaker: Hi, XenX. How are you doing?
XenX: Hello, code girl. Where you been? Not seen you in a week.
CodeBreaker: Yup, been busy.
XenX: Well, I've been working on a new code for you. Want to try it?
CodeBreaker: Not tonight. I have a headache.
XenX: It's cryptography, not sex.
CodeBreaker: Very funny.
XenX: Okay, okay. So tell good old XenX what's wrong.
CodeBreaker: Kinda down, that's all. Some problems at work.
XenX: Sorry to hear it. What sort of work do you do, anyway?
CodeBreaker: Government. Classified. Don't ask.
XenX: Sure, J. Edgar. Heard that one before.
CodeBreaker: I only do it to supplement my career at McDonald's, anyway.
XenX: Finally, the truth comes out. I'll have a milkshake...

After chatting for a while Meg signed off, finding little pleasure in the playful banter. She grabbed a lap quilt off one of the chairs and wrapped up in it, then used the remote to click on her small t.v. Feeling down always lent itself to watching the news. Besides, Meg dreaded going to sleep. When she was under stress she was more prone to nightmares. Today had definitely had a lot of stress.

Eventually she nodded off anyway, too tired to follow the news report about drunk drivers. Curled up on the couch, her half-conscious self gave several reminders that the bed would be more comfortable and that she would sleep better without noise from the television. None of this deterred Meg from slipping into a relatively deep sleep which was, at first, dreamless and heavy. Momentarily it eased her fatigue until a dream started to surface. She heard a scraping sound lace through the droning voice of a t.v. sportscaster, then envisioned a man standing in front of her. Meg tried to wake up, to open her eyes and dispel the realistic fear of a stranger standing in front of her. A few seconds later she dreamed she awoke and saw the image disappear, but then the dream became more intense and she felt afraid. Determined to wake, she pushed herself towards awareness, desperate to open her eyes and prove the room was empty.

The television continued its annoying murmur as she slowly opened her eyes. A man with a large knife was hovering over her.

Chapter 10

A gasp escaped Meg and she sat up as the man moved in, pressing the tip of a five-inch blade beneath her chin. "This could hurt," he said.

Meg stared up into the face of Alan Scorzato, blinking hard to try and understand why he was here and why he was holding a knife to her throat. His slanted red eyebrows where knit together, giving him a demonic look. He smiled and seemed all the more satanic. Alan was near to her, pressing the pointed tip of the knife upwards in such a way that she had to tilt her head back against the couch. If he should decide to give it a thrust, the blade would slice through her flesh and up into her inner mouth, tongue, and on up through the roof of her mouth to the inside of her head. The mental image of it doing so was quite terrible.

"I need some cooperation from you," he said. "Would you like me to take this knife away from your throat?"

"Yes," she carefully whispered, afraid of what he might do if she didn't answer. She was also terrified by what kind of cooperation he meant. Her mind was reeling, trying to understand why and how he was here. How had he gotten past the deadbolt on the front door? Then she remembered the scraping sound that had invaded her sleep. Somehow he had managed to get in through the sliding glass door, even though she always kept it locked.

He didn't remove the blade from her throat, apparently enjoying seeing her fearful. Another evil smile formed on his mouth, and he finally moved the knife tip away from her by just a few inches. "That better?" he asked, his voice playfully condescending. "Now, are you going to be a good girl and do what I want?"

"Yes," Meg managed.

"That's good. This knife is very sharp. It's used for gutting and skinning deer. You wouldn't be smart to try anything, would you, Margaret? Or should I say Meg?" He caught her left arm in his free hand, slicing the blade horizontally across the flesh of her upper arm.

She cried out in pain, and he quickly pressed the knife at her throat again. Her heart was hammering with dread and fear, shocked by what he had done without hesitation. A numbing sense of destiny overpowered Meg. Her five years were up.

"I just want you to have a little taste of how sharp the blade is. I bought it new a couple of hours ago, and had them hone it. You can have that cut stitched up, but if the knife happens to slice into your throat, there's not much anyone could do."

Meg's arm was stinging, rivulets of blood running down its length and dripping onto the heirloom quilt once belonging to her grandma. Her heart was hammering so fiercely that the sound of blood surged in her ears with the noise of ocean breakers. He was going to kill her if she didn't do something to stop him. Her mind raced with thoughts of what she might do. Fear made her discard most of them. She had taken the required ten week physical training course prior to coming to work for CSS, and had learned basic karate and defensive tactics. At the moment she couldn't recall if there had been any insights about what to do if someone had a blade positioned ready to pierce your throat and go up into your brain.

Alan smiled again, moving the knife and himself back a few more inches. "You look scared." Meg said nothing, her head still reeling. Her mouth felt dry, as if it were lined with cotton fibers.

His smile faded. "Let's get down to business, and see if you can buy your way out of this predicament. It seems you have something that belongs to Signet. Where's the CD you stole with the Kronek Codes on it? You do have it, don't you Meg?"

"Yes."

"Then I suggest you get it."

Meg shakily stood, the quilt slipping to the floor. She walked over to her stereo player which had several music CDs stacked next to it. She pulled out the third one, a Kenny Loggin's CD, and flipped it open. Scorzato took it from her.

He glanced down at the writeable CD. "I'd like to check it out, if you don't mind. Turn on your computer."

She walked over to the desk, aware of how scantily she was dressed and of how his eyes scanned the length of her bare legs. She turned on the computer, sat down in the chair, and waited for the virus scanner to run its course. Blood was still dripping from her arm and she glanced at the wound, alarmed by the sight of the straight, deep gash.

He stood near her, his gaze flicking between the computer screen and her lightly clad body. "This is some setup you've got," he said at last, motioning to the computer with the point of the blade. "Who paid for it?"

"I did."

"What I mean, Meg," he said, drawing her name out with the pretended patience of an annoyed teacher, "Is who do you work for?"

She glanced up at him, then back at the computer screen. "The government."

"Do I have to remind you again of how sharp this blade is? How about if I cut you again, this time someplace even more tender? Would that help you tell the truth?"

"Zytex," she said, blurting out the name of one of Signet's largest competitors. She was willing to come up with any answer he wanted. Thankfully he seemed to accept this, nodding his head as if he had expected her to say this.

"That's better."

Relieved it was what he wanted to hear, she typed in the password, then when the main screen came up she selected Excel from the program file. Scorzato inserted the CD into the ROM and soon the contents were displayed on the monitor. He smiled down at her, running his free hand along her jaw. "That's my girl."

Meg turned her face away with a sinking feeling and he chuckled. For a brief moment she had held to the hope that all he wanted was the CD, and that once he got it he would leave her alone. He removed the CD from the ROM and inserted it back inside the Kenny Loggins jewel case, setting it down on the desk.

"Now, how about if you and I have a little chat?" She didn't answer, and he smiled. "Did you give a copy of this to your boss?"

"No."

He moved the knife very near to her face and she gasped. "Meg, I want you to know how important it is to me that you be completely honest. If we have an honest talk, and you tell me what I want to know, then I won't cut you again."

"I didn't give it to anyone, because I took it by mistake," she said, her words hasty. She was desperate to convince him she was telling the truth. "I was supposed to look for codes that could interface with the Clipper Chip."

"What's that?"

She glanced at him, surprised he didn't know. "It's the new security system the government wants to replace the DES with, which was originally written by IBM."

"Go on."

"Basically I was told that Signet had some code files, and if I found them I was to let my employer know and he would take care of it from there. Once I broke into Dent's computer system I only had a little time to check it. That's when I found the file that said Kronek's Codes. I meant to copy it, but made a mistake and moved the folder to the CD instead of just copying it. Once I got it home I decided to look at it instead of sending it straight to my boss. Each one of the files had a password, but I was able to break the system and get inside the files. That's when I realized they weren't the codes my boss had sent me to look for. I didn't give them to him because I didn't want to get in trouble for taking them, especially since they weren't what he wanted. Mostly I just work in the office. It was my first undercover assignment."

He was silently watching her. "Lucky girl," he said at last, his voice caressingly soft. "I believe you. Do you have another copy of this?"

"No, because I realized these codes weren't what my boss wanted. I just put the CD away and went on to another assignment."

"Well, I'd say you've been very cooperative, Meg. Come here," he said, walking over to the couch.

A shiver ran through her. She thought of trying to run, but knew there was no way to escape him. She couldn't make it to the bedroom and shut the door before he would come in after her, and both the front door and the sliding glass doors were closed. She was trapped.

"I'm losing my patience," he said, his voice sharp. "Come here!"

Meg stood, trying to keep her legs from shaking. She wanted to start screaming, to let out a blood-curdling cry that would make her neighbors come rushing to see what was happening. This, of course, would give him a reason for slitting her throat. Instead she walked over to him. He was only a few inches taller than herself, and she wished with all her heart that he didn't have the knife. In some ways it seemed far more frightening than even a gun. A gun's destruction was obvious. It put a bullet through you and you died, or maybe the assailant got scared off and someone came and got you to the hospital in time. A knife, though, could take away bits and pieces of you until you were wishing he'd used a gun.

"Don't look so afraid," he said.

"Are you going to kill me?" It was a stupid, ridiculous question. Killers never admitted that to their victims, so why ask a pathological criminal with a knife for reassurances? Even though she knew it was stupid, she hadn't been able to stop herself from asking.

"Of course not. We are going to have some fun, though. What you did was not good, and you need to be taught a lesson so that you won't do it again." He reached out and slid his hand around her neck, pulling her closer. "You know, when you worked for us I thought you were very attractive. Let's start by having you take off that shirt."

Meg began to tremble. "Please don't hurt me," she said, despising herself for the words which came out on their own.

Scorzato smiled. "I like it when my women beg. Now be a good girl and do what I tell you." She shook her head and his smile faded. "Fine, then I'll have to get rough."

He shoved her back on the couch, leaping atop her. The knife was suddenly at her throat, but in spite of it pressing into her flesh she struggled against his efforts. He was pulling at her shirt and pawing her in a way that filled her with disgust. Meg was overwhelmed by a hundred thoughts. She felt fear and rage at her weakness, and shame at her inability to avoid the inevitable rape. She thought of Robyn, realizing with a wrenching of emotion what it had been like for her sister. For the first time she also understood what kind of man raped. It hadn't been some hunchbacked miscreant that had defiled her sister. It had been the kind of man who was full of himself, who had a swollen ego hiding a raging lack of self-esteem.

Alan's hands were hurting her, the knife forcing her head back against the arm of the couch. His breath was hot in her face, his mouth slobbering on her in a disgusting way. A couple of hours ago Meg had thought about her mother and how much she missed her. Now, for the first time in her life, she was glad her mother was dead. Estelle had been right to want to die before something else terrible happened. She could never have withstood losing her second daughter to the weasel-like prey who stalked and raped women. A sob of rage and anger filled Meg as she tried to push him away. The blade sliced her throat, making a surface cut this time, not nearly so deep as the one on her arm. Even so, it stung.

He became irritated with her. Scorzato started swearing at her, taunting her, calling her every foul, demeaning name he knew. She hated and loathed him, thinking it would be far better to die than to have him rape her. Living with the memory of this creep's abuse would be worse than anything she could think of. Her strength was ebbing; it was surprising how wiry and strong someone like him could be. Hopeless discouragement filled her, and she became aware of all the brash noises of the moment: his vile, sexual comments, her own gasping breath and muffled cries for help, the tinny audience laughter from the television late-night talk show, and a scraping metallic sound. A shadow moved across them, and Scorzato was suddenly pulled off of her. There was another man in the room, Meg realized with shock.

Alan yelped as his arm was jerked backwards, the knife knocked out of his hand with a karate blow. It spun across the room and landed under the front edge of the computer desk. He gaped up at Ross Ecklund with a startled, angry expression. "What are you doing here!"

Ross' face was dark with rage. He pulled back his fist, letting it fly with all his strength. It landed a direct hit on Scorzato's nose, who screamed in pain as bones crunched beneath the blow. Ross dropped him and he crumpled, rolling on the ground. His nose spurted out blood, his hands covering his face. He was yelping like an injured dog, a sound that under a different circumstance might almost be humorous. He then started screaming about his nose being broken, swearing between yelps of pain.

Meg stood and the room began to gyrate, her vision going dim. Ross stepped forward, taking hold of her and leading her to a chair. She sat and he silently guided her head between her knees. "Stay like this for a couple of seconds until the blood goes to your head, or you're going to pass out."

He then looked at her arm, seeing the gash. He took out a white handkerchief from his back pocket, opening up the folded square. He flipped it into a triangle and tied it around the wound, making a tight knot as she lifted her head. "Are you alright?" he asked.

She didn't look at him, instead staring at Alan Scorzato who lay on the floor, his hands covering his bloody nose. His yelps had died down to moans. Ross looked at him, then back at Meg Parrish, whose face was white. Her lips were drawn back in rage, hatred giving her features almost a vixen look. She leapt off the chair, flying atop her assailant. Ross stood with gaping mouth, amazed at what he saw her do. Her hands were around Alan's throat and she was squeezing with all her strength and banging his head against the floor. His arms were flailing and he was trying to get her off. The punch in the nose had weakened him, and he wasn't successful in pushing her away.

"I'll kill you, just the way you killed my sister!" she screamed. Meg dug her thumbs into the soft triangle of flesh beneath his chin, the same place he had pressed the point of the blade on her own throat. She shoved her thumbs upwards with all the pressure she could summon. It immediately cut off his air supply, much faster than simply strangling him with her hands. He gagged and fought wildly, finally knocking her off with a hard blow. Meg rolled to her hands and knees, but Scorzato had already scrambled to his feet, lunging for the open patio door. He shoved his way through the curtains, disappearing into the night.

Meg sat back, panting for breath. She was shaking. She looked up at the man who had rescued her and knew she'd seen him before. In the disorientation of the moment she wasn't able to place him, wondering if he were one of Hammond's agents stepping in to rescue her. He came forward, helping her to her feet. She was trembling, but not dizzy like the first time. "Who are you?" she managed.

"For the next two minutes, a friend," he tersely answered. "That's how long it's going to take him to get back to the two guys that work for him, who are waiting across the parking lot. I'm not going to be able to take on the two of them, and there's no way to block that patio door because the latch is broken."

Meg nodded. He had clean, average features, and at the moment her gut instinct told her to trust him. "I'll get some clothes."

"Hurry," he said.

She ran into her bedroom to the pile of clothes she'd dropped in the middle of the floor before taking her shower. Quickly she pulled on the jeans, barely able to zip and snap them because her fingers were shaking. She put on the semi-damp socks and her slip-on shoes that had been left on the floor, then grabbed a thick sweatshirt lying on the foot of her bed, jerking it over her head. A dozen wild thoughts were running through her mind, and her limbs felt leadenly slow, though in reality she was moving quickly. There was no time to think about who this man was or whether or not she should go with him. He was the definite lesser of two evils, and so the only choice at the moment. She was trembling from primal fear, anger, and amazement at having escaped her attacker. Meg grabbed her oversized purse and ran into the front room.

Ross had dialed 911 with the slim hope that a patrol car might be in the area. "Come on, will you?" he snapped. He had seen Martin Wimer and Leo Fromm across the parking lot and had no desire to meet up with either of them once Alan reached them dripping blood.

Meg ran over to the computer desk, picking up the CD and shoving it in her purse. Ross was standing near the closed patio door, looking through the parted curtain. "Let's go," he urged.

"Wait a second. I'm not leaving my computer open." She quickly used the mouse to shut down to the DOS prompt and typed in 'fdisk.' Then she selected the option to delete the Primary DOS Partition, and hit Enter. In her mind she was hoping this would make it harder for someone else to get into her files. By deleting the partition all the data was gone, and the drive would be blank. Her back-up tape was off-site in a safety deposit box, so she had no concerns about losing her files. When the computer was next fired up, there would be nothing there. It wouldn't even boot. As an after-thought, she also reached behind the computer to the power supply, finding the tiny 115-230 volt switch. With her fingernail she switch it from the standard 115 volt side used for U.S. electrical currency, to the 230 volt connection commonly used in Europe. If someone else turned on the computer, only the LED lights would come on. Nothing else would come up and the computer would appear to be nonfunctional.

Ross was at the front door, undoing the deadbolt. "Are you coming, Miss Parrish?" His voice was urgent.

She ran over to him, pausing only a second when she thought she heard the sound of someone at the sliding glass door. Meg watched him cautiously open the front door and peer out. A moment later they slipped outside into the cool night air. They began running, crossing the open lawn and hurrying around a fenced area. He fled down a walkway and she followed him along the side of the apartment complex. Her footsteps and rasping breath sounded much louder to her than they really were. She was aware of every noise and movement, much like a hunted animal. Nothing seemed more frightening than the thought of being chased, and she hoped no one was following. They ran through an alcove beneath another set of apartments, passing a staircase, then went on through to the far parking lot.

A heavy cloud cover had moved in during the last few hours. The air smelled wet, and a few drops of rain began to fall. Meg tried hard to keep up with the man who was sprinting along just ahead of her. He had referred to himself as a friend, and she hoped this were true. Her legs felt rubbery, and each step she took became harder than the last. Her body was angrily protesting the abuse it had experienced, and it was all she could do to force herself to follow her rescuer. At one point she thought she heard running footsteps in their wake. Looking back over her shoulder she saw nothing and decided it must be the echo of their own footfalls across the asphalt. The stark white lights surrounding the parking lot cast bright circles on the ground. The illumination gave their skin a sickly hue, and sent long shadows scurrying before them as they ran. On the perimeter of the light the nighttime seemed very dark because the clouds blocked the moon. Just when Meg thought she couldn't take another step, he pointed out a Buick Skylark.

"Get in," he ordered, his voice a harsh rasp as he opened the driver's side.

He already had the key in the ignition by the time Meg had rounded the car and opened the passenger door. She sank thankfully onto the seat, then closed and locked the door as he began to back the car out of the parking space. Suddenly large hands slammed against her window and she cried out, staring up into a square, brutish face made even more frightening by the shadows. The man grabbed the door handle, jerking it up, but thankfully it was locked. He hit the glass hard again and it shuddered. For a terrifying moment she envisioned it shattering beneath his heavy fists, and him reaching in through the window and grabbing her. Ross shifted into drive while the car was still backing out. The engine lurched into gear as he did so, then he hit the accelerator. The tires squealed and the car leapt forward, leaving the brute-faced man behind. He tried to follow, slamming the trunk with his fist as the car sped by. It spun out of the parking lot and into the road, continuing to increase speed.

Meg stared over her shoulder, watching the man who had hit her window diminish in size as they moved away from him. He was a bodybuilder type and, if he were one of the men with Alan Scorzato, she could understand why her rescuer had been anxious to get away. Fist fighting him would be like trying to punch a sack of rocks. She turned back around in her seat, the movement making her arm and neck hurt. Sitting still now, her rapid breathing beginning to slow, she started to feel the pain of what she had experienced. Her arm, neck, and back hurt, and she was achy in lots of places. No doubt it would get worse before it got better. The car was still moving at top speed, rounding corners very fast. She studied the man doing the driving, realizing where she had seen him before. He wasn't one of Richard's men after all, but worked for Signet. She had a momentary sinking feeling, fearful of what he wanted. Then she thought of the CD Scorzato had temporarily held. There would have been no reason for this man to put on an act to try and gain her confidence and get the codes. She had been more than willing to hand them over. He flexed his right hand atop the steering wheel as if his knuckles hurt. No doubt they did, from punching her attacker. An image of Scorzato and his disgusting pawing of her came to mind. Meg shuddered.

The rain began to fall in earnest, spotting the windshield like liquid drops of glass which magnified the streetlights. Ross turned on the windshield wipers and sluiced them away. He glanced in the rearview mirror, then at Meg. Her face had more color now, her hair windblown from their run. She was also shivering.

"Put your seat belt on, will you?"

Meg reached for the strap and snapped it in place. She began shaking even more, shivering as if she were freezing. She had to clamp her jaw shut to keep her teeth from chattering.

"Are you cold?" he asked, turning on the heat and directing the vents toward her.

"A little," she managed through clenched teeth. "I don't know why I'm shivering so much, though."

He slowed the car so that it could take the turns more sanely. "It's probably a shock reaction. Your body's letting you know it didn't like what you just went through."

"Great," she replied, the air from the vents growing warm, which felt comforting. She turned to look at him. "I saw you in a meeting with Willis Dent last week. You work for Signet."

Ross was momentarily surprised she remembered him, then recalled who he was dealing with. "Maybe you should say I used to work for Signet. I'm guessing that punching my supervisor and breaking his nose probably means I just resigned."

Meg smiled at his ironic comment, her mouth aching at the movement. "Thank you for doing that," she said, her voice quiet. "What's your name?"

"Ross Ecklund."

They drove through the wet city streets and her shivering started to ebb. Thankfully her teeth were no longer chattering. "You can turn down the heat now if you want, Ross. I'm not cold anymore."

He did so, watching the steady rhythm of the wiper blades. "I have a lot of ground to cover with you," he said, his voice brisk.

"What do you mean?"

"I have questions," he stated, glancing in the rearview mirror again. "I don't think they'll catch us now. Hopefully we're out of their path. Let's clear up a few things before I start asking my questions, though. First of all, tell me where you want to go. You'd probably better report this attack to the police. Do you want me to drive you to the precinct downtown?"

"No, I don't want to go to the police," she responded. Two sessions with the police in one day would be just too much, and the thought of sitting through another bout of questions and paperwork was more than she could bear.

"It wouldn't be just your word against his. I'd be a witness."

She thought of the officers who had come to her home when Robyn was killed, turning the family's t.v. room into a crime scene. "I don't want to go through it." Her voice sounded harsher than she meant it to.

"Fair enough," he calmly answered, coming to the main roadway and turning onto it, merging with the traffic. "Then the next concern is your arm. Do you think it's still bleeding?"

"I don't know. You tied the handkerchief pretty tight."

"Better take a look at it."

Meg slid her arm out of the sweatshirt, exposing the bloodied handkerchief just below the hem of her t-shirt sleeve. She grimaced at the sight, carefully peeling the cloth down. Blood crusted the edges of the wound, but there wasn't much new blood flowing from the cut. It still was a scary-looking gash. "What do you think?" she managed, noticing that he had also been studying the wound.

"It's not doing great, but you'll live. Did that happen during the struggle?"

"No. Before. He wanted to show me the knife was sharp, and what would happen if I didn't cooperate."

Ross glanced at her, shocked anew at the depth Scorzato had sunken to. "What a disgusting creep!" His voice was heavy with loathing.

"That's what I think," she said, putting the makeshift bandage back in place and sliding her arm inside the sweatshirt sleeve.

"Does it hurt?"

"Not so much now. What needs to be done for it? I don't have enough first aid skills to know," Meg said.

"I'd say you can go one of two ways. It could use some stitches, but could also get by with some neatly placed butterfly bandages. If you want it stitched up, it needs to be done within then next hour or so, which means we'd need to get you to an emergency room fairly soon."

"What would you do in my place?"

"I'm tough," he said, smiling down at her. "I'd go for the bandage." She decided he should smile more often. It altered the lines of his face and made him seem far more likable.

"I can be tough," she quietly stated.

"I guess you can," Ross replied. "I thought you were going to choke Alan to death before he pushed you off. You scared the hell out of me."

Meg raised her eyebrows, looking at the man who had punched her attacker and then briskly taken charge of their flight. "I find it hard to believe you'd be scared of anything. Do you often leap into other people's houses and rescue them from attackers?"

"Haven't done it before. I felt kind of responsible, though."

"What do you mean?"

Ross sighed. "After you stole the CD from Signet, I was the one who tracked you down. Yesterday I found where you lived. I didn't tell Alan where you were, though, because I have a few questions of my own I'm hoping you'll be nice enough to answer. What I'm guessing, though, is that somehow he figured out where you were because of me. It's got me stumped as to how, unless the tracking firm I was using sent information to my desk and he got his hands on it. Anyway, I came back tonight hoping to talk to you, and that's when I saw two of Alan's security men in the parking lot, sitting in a Signet car. I parked my own car on the far side of the complex and ran back to your apartment. When I heard muffled cries, and saw you struggling with him through a slit in the draperies, I came in through the patio door."

Meg was very glad he had done so. She shuddered at the memory of Alan's touch, and of how close he had come to raping and probably killing her. "I don't understand how he got in. I almost always keep that door locked."

Ross scowled, hating to confess but thinking it best to be honest if he were going to expect her to be honest with him. "That's what I meant about feeling responsible. Yesterday I broke into your place through the patio door, which damaged the lock. I searched for the stolen CD but didn't find it. Alan was no doubt able to get in because of what I'd done."

She felt shocked and hurt. Her valiant rescuer didn't seem so valiant at the moment. "You were inside my place?"

"Remember, Meg, I thought you were a thief who had stolen something worth thousands of dollars to the president of my company. At the time I didn't know you worked for the government, or I never would have broken into your place, you can be sure of that."

"How did you figure out I work for the government?"

"There was a surveillance folder in your night stand, with government information sheets on your next undercover assignment. The only papers I've ever seen like those were from the federal government. Look, you know I could have lied to you about being in your place and pretended to be some kind of knight in armor who came along and rescued you, but it seems I owe it to you to be square about what happened."

There was something almost boyishly pathetic in his concern. "Did you look through all my drawers?"

"Yes. You're very neat. Your mom must have loved having you live at home. Mine always accused me of having the messiest room on the planet."

They were both silent for a while, watching the road. "You can have the CD if you want. It's got no value to me," she said.

"I don't want it, either. I've had a major change of priorities, and if I'm going to be unemployed for bashing my supervisor, I don't really care if Signet gets it back or not." The traffic light ahead of them turned red and he stopped behind several cars. "Look, I know it sounds low, my breaking into your place and searching it, and all that. But I truly believed you were a criminal involved in corporate espionage. I was making plans to have you arrested until I figured out you were a government agent."

He drove into the parking lot of a major drugstore chain, put the car in park, and turned off the ignition. He reached over to her and lifted her chin, looking at the slice on her throat. "That's not too bad a cut. It'll just take a band-aid. Does it hurt?"

"No, I can't really feel it at all. It's my arm that's aching."

"You sure you want the cut on your arm butterflied instead of stitched?"

"Yes."

"Okay. Wait in the car, and lock the doors. I'll try to be fast."

He left the car and headed for the drugstore. Meg locked the doors as he had suggested. She could hear the sound of cars driving by and see the flutter of passing headlights. It wasn't heavy traffic, though, because it was getting late. Trying to analyze the things Ross had told her, she wondered if it might not be smart to just take off and disappear into the night. Yet where would she go? She couldn't go back home, and definitely didn't want to go to the police. Her parting with Richard hadn't been on the best of terms, either, and other than her boss she had no friends or family to hide out with. She could go to a motel but wouldn't feel safe there by herself. Besides, at the moment her muscles were aching and felt leaden. It just didn't seem worth it to try and even get out of the car.

It bothered her that this man, Ross Ecklund, had broken into her place and inadvertently allowed Alan to come after her, but it was also to his credit that he was honest about it. Added to this was the mental image of his sudden appearance in her apartment, his face dark with anger, his fist slamming into Alan's nose. That image went far in persuading her to stay. He returned a few minutes later and she unlocked the door for him. He slid into the seat and handed her a small paper bag.

"There's painkiller in there, too, and some bottled water under your seat." He started the engine. "I'd like to keep driving for a while before we stop and bandage your arm, since they're probably still looking for us. Not that I think they'll be lucky enough to find us; I just don't want to risk it."

He pulled the car out of the parking lot and headed towards the freeway, looking over at her as she took three painkillers and a swallow of water. "I half expected you to be gone when I came out."

"I half expected to leave."

He chuckled and again the smile transformed his face. "Let's head down city center and drive around there for a while. That'll give us the time we need to think about what to do, and find a safe place to stop and butterfly your cut."

Ross was doing well at putting on a fairly calm personae, but inside he was still feeling the influence of the adrenaline which had permeated his system like a locomotive in overdrive for most of the day. Ever since this afternoon, when he'd seen what had happened at the geranium stand, his mind had been in a whirl. For the first time in many months he had been filled with hope. This feeling had soon been followed by deep apprehension at losing track of both Meg and the Deaf boy in the throng of people at the marketplace. Because he had previously gleaned Parker Brigg's name from the file in Meg's night stand, he then spent several hours trying to get the boy's address from the people who had issued vendor's licenses for the market stalls. They had been uncooperative, and so he had eventually come back to the place from which he had started his surveillance that morning: Meg's apartment. She hadn't been there, though, and after waiting a couple of hours he'd decided to go back to his own place, get something to eat and rest for a while. He'd fallen asleep, and by the time he awoke and drove back to the apartment, the other men were already there. When he first arrived and saw Martin Wimer and Leo Fromm sitting in a Signet car, he was filled with apprehension. That was nothing compared to what he later felt upon seeing Alan trying to rape Meg. Ross had grown up with a strong moral code and that kind of thing disgusted him to the core. He still felt highly justified at punching the scum-bag out. Hopefully he would never have to see Alan or his brainless security toadies again. Ross checked the rearview mirror once more, feeling relief at knowing the three men had been left behind.

He would have felt just the opposite if he had known about the narrow black box attached by heavy-duty magnets to the underside of his car. The Motorola electronic tracking device was eight inches long and two inches wide, with a wire antennae protruded from one end. It was sending out a steady transmission of trackable beeps.

*   *   *

Alan Scorzato sat in the backseat of the vehicle, moaning. The two men in the front seat ignored him. Martin Wimer had just finished screwing two long cords into a receiver, while Leo Fromm pulled the antennas attached on the other end of the cords out either window. The magnetic bases quickly attached to the car roof and gave the appearance of two CB antennas. Wimer put the oversized briefcase in his lap and flipped open the lid. He plugged the receiver's power cord into the cigarette lighter and turned on the switch, watching the fluctuating needle in the dial come to life. His partner guided the car away from the apartment complex and drove according to Wimer's instructions, just as they had done this morning when they first tracked Ross Ecklund to the apartment building.

"Let's get bird-dogging," Wimer said, using the vernacular he had become familiar with during his twelve years on the Las Vegas police force. He navigated, following the beeps, while Fromm drove.

The two black antenna wires were tied into the radio receiver. It analyzed which antenna was receiving the stronger signal from the transmitter, and the gauge's needle indicated which direction they needed to go. The range of the tracking device was anywhere from a mile or so in open areas to only a few blocks, depending on how many buildings might be blocking the transmission.

After Alan Scorzato had happened on the faxes from ProFilers, listing all the phone call searches for someone named Meg Parrish, he had immediately gone to their boss with accusations against Ross Ecklund. Willis Dent's suspicious nature quickly surfaced, and he demanded that they start following Ross. During yesterday afternoon's meeting, when Wimer had excused himself to use the restroom, he had instead gone to Ecklund's car which was parked in the company garage. He then activated the transmitter and attached it to the underside of the Buick.

Wimer and Fromm had followed Ross' car for most of the previous night, which had been fruitless, then picked him back up in the morning. They had tracked him to the apartment complex, and Wimer had been pretty sure he had seen the girl in another car, but they lost them both in the heavy city traffic surrounding the weekend market. Tonight he'd returned on his own to the apartments, wanting to see if the girl he'd caught a glimpse of had been Signet's thief. Eventually she'd shown up, and he had called Alan and Leo, then gone to pick them up.

"This pain is killing me," Alan said from the back seat, lowering the blood-stained handkerchief. "You've got to get me to a doctor."

"Not yet," Wimer said. "We can't lose them now." Neither one of the security men were willing to pass up on the chance of finding the girl when they were this close. The bonus Dent was offering was substantial, and each man had already made plans for the money.

"You'll be okay," Fromm said, glancing over his should. "I got my nose broke playing highschool football, and it didn't change my looks any. Besides, there's not much a doctor can do for you anyway, just tape it. Unless the cartilage is really damaged, then you'll need surgery."

Their supervisor groaned and Wimer smiled, glancing at Fromm who hid a subdued smirk. Both men thought it was funny. Alan Scorzato may have been their boss, but neither of them really liked him. He was too much of a egotist for anyone to enjoy being around long.

"Turn here," Wimer said. "Go faster, will you? The signal's starting to fade." They were passing a large office complex that momentarily cut down the reception. "So what do you think Mr. Dent is going to say when he finds out Ecklund has switched teams? And who paid him to jump ship anyway?"

"It's Zytex," Scorzato's muffled voice announced through the handkerchief. "That's who she's working for. I found out that much before he jumped me."

"He's probably worked for them all along," Fromm added. "I never did like him."

"Turn here," Wimer instructed. "No, go left again.... Oh, man, we're losing them! Pay attention to what I'm telling you, will you Leo?"

The next fifteen minutes were a combination of Wimer's navigation, Fromm's curses when he turned wrong and had to backtrack, and Scorzato's complaints from the back seat. They all became tense when the signal was suddenly lost.

"What's going on?" Fromm asked. "You've got nothing on the screen."

"I know that! It must be interference, maybe from that large shopping complex. Go around it."

"What if the batteries are going dead? It's been transmitting a long time."

"They were brand new," Wimer explained with irritation. Then his voice changed, growing excited. "Okay! It looks like they're stopped somewhere. Go straight down this road, and hurry."

Leo Fromm obliged, but Wimer voice suddenly cut in with a few choice cuss words. "They're on the move again."

A few minutes later they found themselves following the directional needle onto the freeway. "Where's he going now?" Alan asked.

"City center. That stinks! Those buildings are going to throw up a lot of interference and cut down our tracking range. Step on it, Leo, and let's see if we can get a visual before he gets downtown. If not, we're gonna have trouble finding him."

"Don't worry, we'll catch him," Fromm said with the kind of optimism that his partner often thought brainless.

Scorzato sat up, looking over their shoulders. He hoped with all his being that Leo was right, because behind the pain he also felt rage and hatred. "When you find Ross and kill him," he growled, "I want to watch."

Chapter 11

The city streets of Portland were glossy with rain, looking like a black ribbon shining under the glow of the car's headlights. Since it was late Sunday night, and the next morning started a new workweek, there was very little traffic. The closed city offices and stores made the town look sleepy. Meg, herself, felt anything but sleepy. She was exhausted, battered, and drained, but still too traumatized to relax. She and Ross had begun asking each other questions. He had wanted to know what branch of the government she worked for, and she had wanted to know how he'd tracked her down and found out her real name. He was just finishing that story, which explained the call on her answering machine from Belinda at the Half Moon Gift Shop.

"That's all there was to it. So when you get a very nice Fenton vase from the gift shop, don't be surprised."

"I'm impressed you were able to find me from such a small lead. Very clever."

"That's me. Clever. You, though, are probably some kind of genius," he said, looking over at her and smiling. "Yeah, don't give me that innocent expression."

"I'm not a genius."

"You broke into Signet's server the first week you were there, and then managed to break through Dent's two passwords and steal his files, which flipped him out, by the way. No average person could have waltzed in and done that. Which is why I'm guessing you've got an I.Q. that makes the rest of us look like pitiful apes."

"I'm more of an idiot savant than a genius," she said, smiling in self-deprecation.

"What do you mean?" Ross asked.

"I have a skill. Kind of a gift, maybe you'd say. That's all."

"And being gifted is different than being a genius?"

"I think so."

"What kind of gift do you have, if you don't mind an average ape asking?"

Meg studied the drifting shadows that crossed his face as they drove past well-lit shops. He had a likeable kind of personality that was surprisingly easy to talk to. It reminded her of chatting on the Internet, only live. "Well, for one thing, I can look at codes and see the patterns in them. Sometimes they jump out at me when I look at the figures, though not always. My boss says it's like playing the piano by ear instead of reading notes."

"Interesting. Did you know you wanted to do that kind of thing as a career?"

"No, actually I was going to school in Washington, studying criminal psychology when one of my friends told me about a contest on the Internet. She knew I liked cryptograms and thought I'd be interested. When I went to the web site it only had a brief explanation about the prize money and the contest rules, then a screen page that was filled with quarter-inch dots of color in tons of different shades. That was the code."

"Just dots of color?"

"Uh-huh."

"And you figured it out?"

"It actually had a pattern that seemed visible to me, though my friends couldn't see it. Anyway, the answer to the code was hidden inside the dots of color, which gave a web site address for Roy G. Biv."

"The color order of the rainbow?"

"Yes. At the time it seemed very clever and funny, and of course I wanted the $50."

"So you won the contest."

"Actually, there were eleven people who figured it out. Three of us ended up at NCS, the National Cryptologic School."

"They used the contest as a recruiting device?"

"Yes. I studied there for a couple of years on scholarship, but wasn't very happy. I didn't fit in good with all the math wizards, you know, being an idiot savant. I was ready to quit when my current boss contacted me and asked if I'd come work for him. That's how I ended up here in Portland."

"I'm impressed," Ross said, pulling the car over to the side of the road. "You're a fascinating woman, Meg. Now, how about if we take care of your cuts?"

"Okay."

He switched on the car's dome light and reached for the paper sack. "Why were you working undercover at Signet?"

Meg blinked at the harsh glare. "Isn't it my turn to ask a question?"

"Not yet, since I'm playing nurse." He pulled out one of the antiseptic towelettes and tore the foil package open. "Tip back your head and let me wipe that cut on your throat."

She did so, and he released his seatbelt, moving near. He carefully wiped at the dried blood, closely examining the cut. At first Meg felt overwhelmed by his nearness, but his movements were efficient and nonthreatening. A minute later he sealed the cut with a band-aid and she sat up.

"You can take that off in a few hours if you want, since the cut pretty much stays closed on its own. It'll just help protect it until the edges start to knit. Okay, time for the arm."

A car approached from behind and both of them paused. The sound of the engine increased, then ebbed to a whine as it drove by, making a forlorn echo. Meg slid her arm out of the sweatshirt and he carefully untied the bloodied handkerchief.

"You were going to tell me about your stint at Signet. Do you go undercover a lot?"

"No. It was my first time. Usually I stay at the office and work on codes, doing regular nerd stuff, you know."

He chuckled, thinking she was anything but a nerd. "Okay."

"For the last few months before coming to Signet, I'd been working on breaking through the DES—the Data Encryption Standard. Have you heard of that?"

Ross wiped at the blood around the cut with another towelette. This wound was far more tender and she flinched. "Sorry, I'll be more careful. No, haven't heard of it."

"That didn't hurt much. I'm just jumpy," she said. "In the seventies the government decided it needed a national encryption standard for protecting both government and private industry. IBM came up with an algorithm that NSA certified as free of any mathematical weaknesses. DES is a single-key cipher, which mean the sender and receiver use the same key to encrypt and decrypt a message. The DES keys are fifty-six bits long, which gives a zillion different possible codes. Is this boring?"

"Not at all." He finished wiping away the last of the dried blood and reached in the sack for a tube of antiseptic cream. "Isn't DES pretty old, if it's been around since the seventies? Especially considering how fast computer technology is growing?"

"It's ancient," she said, watching him unscrew the tube's lid. He squeeze a bead of antiseptic into the gash. "The government wants to replace it with what's called the Clipper Chip. That's a cryptographic device made to protect private communication using what are called keys. Once set up, the government would become escrow agents of the keys, enabling them access to encrypted communications in both the private and industrial sectors. There's a lot of hot debate about it going on right now."

"I'll bet," Ross said, opening the package of butterfly bandages. "Is this all common knowledge?"

"Yes. I'm not telling you anything you couldn't find out at the library or on the Internet. In fact there's lots of stuff written about it because people are campaigning to stop the Clipper Chip from being used."

"You said you were trying to break through the DES. You mean actually break it's encryption?"

"Yes. My boss wanted me to look for a back door. It's been suspected for a long time that the cryptologists who wrote the DES program might have left an intentional mathematical vulnerability, their own back door, although it's never been proven. The creators of it were very smart. I mean light years ahead of everybody else. When they made the code they chose an arbitrary method of mixing up the bits they selected, so cracking the DES's unusual algorithm has proven impossible, even for the new mathematical attack systems that have been developed using computers."

Ross applied one of the adhesive ends of the butterfly bandage, then pushed the wound together with his fingers. He applied the second part, pulling it tight to make a good seal. Half the gash was closed, and he opened another bandage. "I'm guessing that your boss was hoping you could find a back door into the DES to show it was vulnerable. Once that happened it would make switching to the Clipper Chip a lot more acceptable by its critics."

"Yes, that's very good," Meg said, surprised and pleased. "See? You're not an ape."

Ross chuckled. "I feel like one, just hearing you talk."

"It seems like I'm lecturing, and I don't mean to be, but if I didn't tell you about the DES and Clipper Chip, I couldn't explain why they sent me to Signet." Another car drove by and she tensed, but it passed with the same lonesome whine as the last. "Anyway, I was never able to find a back door, even after searching for a long time."

"There," he said. "All done, and it wasn't too excruciating."

"Actually, you did a very good job. To be honest, I was kind of nervous about having you do it. How did you get your first aid training?"

"Boy scout merit badge." Ross clicked off the dome light and turned on the engine, pulling out into the street. "You were explaining?" He let his voice dangle, prompting her to continue.

Meg slipped her arm back inside the sweatshirt sleeve, noting the bandages were more comfortable than the knotted handkerchief had been. "My boss also knew I could be pretty good at breaking passwords, and so sent me to Signet where I was to search for a set of codes. Now, back to the Clipper Chip, which is actually a cryptographic algorithm known as Skipjack. NSA has classified Skipjack on national security grounds, which is meant to stop independent evaluation of the system's strengths. It was important for us to learn if Signet had developed a series of codes to evaluate Skipjack."

"Which would be illegal."

"Right."

"Is that what you stole off Willis Dent's computer system?" He stopped at a red light.

"No," she sighed. "I made a mistake. I saw a folder full of code files on his system and thought it must be the Skipjack codes. I meant to copy them to the CD, but instead moved the files by mistake. I was nervous, you know, since it was my first undercover job."

"So what files did you accidentally take? Dent came totally unglued about your stealing them, you know. He called me about an hour after you took them."

The light turned green and he moved ahead, paying little heed to the car with two antennas which approached from behind.

What Ross had just said was new information for Meg, and she was surprised. Until Alan Scorzato had shown up in her apartment, she had been eager to forget about the codes. "I don't have a clue what they are. If we're playing twenty questions, you're way past your limit," she said, smiling.

A bullet hit the Buick's roof, sounding like the loud thud of a rock. Another hit the rear fender. Meg cried out and scrunched down as Ross slammed his foot on the accelerator. They bolted through the intersection, nearly ramming a car driving crosswise through the green light. It screeched to a halt, its horn blaring as a truck behind it also slammed on the brakes. Ross' Buick shot forward and continued accelerating. He made a sharp turn and Meg slammed into the side door as the tires squealed on the wet pavement. The car behind them followed, it's front tires jumping the corner curb with a jolt.

"They're shooting at us!" Ross said in amazement, his fingers gripping the steering wheel as the speedometer needle steadily rose. He was still coming to grips with Alan's attack on Meg, and was stunned by this new assault.

He made a sharp left turn as another shot was fired. The rear driver's side window shattered, spewing glass pebbles across the back seat. Cold, wet air imme-

diately entered the car and Meg gripped the armrest on the door next to her, trying to brace herself against the car's zig-zagging movements. The engine of the
other car roared as it leapt after them and attempted to pull even. Oncoming
headlights swerved off the road, a horn blaring, and Ross slammed his foot all
the way to the floor. The Buick gave a quick scream of protest, then shot forward
even faster. The car behind increased its pace, pulling forward, too.

The windshield wipers slapped at the rain, their once-rapid pace now seemingly lazy in comparison to the speed of the headlong race. In front of them was
a grassy area with a few shade trees and benches. Ross made a right-hand turn,
hopping the curb face-on and using the open lawn to give him a big enough space
to make a wide turn. His tires dug into the grass and spewed up sod, but he did-
n't roll the car. He turned off onto the narrow boulevard going east, then stepped
on it. He watched in the rearview mirror as the Signet car behind him tried to follow and took the turn too fast, sliding on the rain-slick street. The driver turned
the steering wheel sharply instead of taking the curb head-on, which caused the
driver-side wheel to slam into the curb. The car backed away, then headed after
them, but this time Ross smiled. They were still in the chase, but their car was
limping.

Meg looked up at him, her face fearful. He saw she was scared, but trying to
be tough. They caught sight of two rapid muzzle flashes; one of the bullets
lodged in the trunk with a loud thud. Ross kept his foot on the accelerator, desperately trying to put distance between themselves and the Signet car.

*　*　*

"Put that gun away, you idiot!" Wimer yelled. "You can't drive and shoot, so
stop it!" It was the same thing he had been saying since Leo had first started
sticking the gun out the window and firing at the Buick. "You're going to have
the cops all over us!" This last he added in an effort to make the bodybuilding
jock control his adrenalin and stop driving and shooting at the same time.

Leo Fromm let off a string of swear words and pulled his head back inside the
window. "Reload it," he said, dropping the hot muzzle in Wimer's lap, who
immediately shoved it onto the floor as the car lurched forward.

The sideways slam of the wheel against the curb had bent the axle, and the tire
now emitted a whine as it rubbed against the fender. Fromm continued to accelerate and the pitch of the whine increased. The car vibrated but he didn't slow,
determined to keep Ecklund's car in his sights. He didn't trust Wimer's tracking
equipment after their last fiasco.

While Ross had been calmly driving through the Portland streets, and had even
stopped to bandage Meg's arm, the trio in the Signet car had become increasing-

ly stressed and irritated with each other. After a wrong turn they had lost the signal from the transmitter and had to set up a grid search, crisscrossing the city streets. Just when they were at their peak of frustration, the receiver had started beeping again. Wimer was then able to navigate the car back onto the track of their prey and they'd actually made a visual, though his momentary excitement had come to a screeching halt when Leo had stuck his gun out the window and fired. From that moment on the car had been filled with screaming, cursing, and general ill-will as the chase took off. Leo Fromm's steering became erratic as he tried to shoot and drive, and several times the car had fish-tailed on the wet roads, making the other two men yell at him in alarm. The jarring movements had also made Alan Scorzato sick, and he started screaming at them to stop. Wimer had turned around in his seat and viciously told Scorzato to shut up his whining or get out of the car. The supervisor had then fired him, and Wimer had immediately threatened to go to Dent about Scorzato's having gotten, and then lost, the stolen CD. A grudging, unspoken truce settled in, though both of them had continued yelling at Fromm to stop shooting until they got in range.

Now that the gun was out of Leo Fromm's hands, his driving was less erratic, although the car was not doing well. The Buick ahead of them had disappeared around a corner. A few seconds later they reached that corner and the driver turned the wheel sharply, the tires protesting as two of them left the pavement. For a horrifying few seconds it seemed as if the car would roll, though half a second later the wheels slammed down onto the road. The vibrating increased.

"Slow down before you get us killed!" Scorzato shouted.

"You're going to blow that tire if you keep it up," Wimer pointed out.

They passed a pickup coming from the other direction. Its lights were on high, which shone harshly in their eyes. The men blinked and looked away.

"Where are they?" Fromm cried. "I don't see them!"

Wimer looked down at the dial. "They're ahead of us and over a street. We've got the tracking device, so take it easy and let them think they've lost us."

"I want to keep them visual," Fromm said, turning left despite Wimer's instructions. His adrenalin was high, along with his excitement. He secretly enjoyed the helplessness of his two passengers as he made the decisions because of having control of the steering wheel. "And get that gun reloaded."

"We're losing the signal, Leo! Will you stop turning until I tell you to? Head down this road, and see if we can spot them."

Fromm obliged, running a series of red lights without looking, while Scorzato cringed in the back seat, glad there was little traffic.

*   *   *

"I don't know Portland well, so you need to navigate," Ross explained as they headed out of the city center and crossed a bridge. "Where's the nearest golf course?"

Meg was staring out the back window, grateful the Signet car wasn't still on their tail. Rainy air swept in through the shattered side window, chilly but invigorating. She pulled up the collar of her sweatshirt, looking back at Ross. "Golf course?" she repeated, unable to comprehend why he wanted to know.

"Yeah. Is there one around here, or some other place nearby with a chain-link fence?"

"I think so. Go up two or three stop lights, and I'll tell you where to turn." She looked back over her shoulder. "I think you've lost them."

"No, they're tracking us. Somewhere on this car is a transmitting device, which is how they found us back there."

"How do you know?"

"Did you see the antennas on the car? They weren't there before when I saw it in the parking lot at your place. Those antennas are attached to a receiver inside their car, which means they're picking up radio transmissions from my car. That must be how they found you. They put the tracking device on my car, probably while I was at a meeting yesterday at Signet, then this morning tracked me to your apartment when I started following you."

Meg stared at him. "You were following me today?"

"Yes. Did I leave that part out?" She was gazing at him with parted lips, a dismayed expression on her face. Even though he was afraid it would make her mad, he couldn't help but chuckle. "Okay, well, you can have your twenty questions, too. I just didn't have time to tell you everything yet. Does it upset you?"

"Turn here," Meg said. He took the turn sharply and she held tight to the armrest, hoping he didn't wreck the car. "I guess not, considering you've already searched through my bedroom drawers. Why do you want a chain-link fence?"

"Because it causes havoc with tracking devices. The signal our car is sending out right now bounces off interfering structures, which is probably why they didn't get to us right away when we were downtown. For some reason, chain-link fences are the worst at bouncing the signal back, and so that's why we want to find one. Just long enough to get us away from them so we can stop and find the transmitter. Knowing it's there makes me really edgy, especially since they were shooting at us. I have to tell you, this whole night is something else! It almost doesn't seem real to me. Imagine if your supervisor ended up being someone who was out there trying to rape and murder. I never cared much for Alan, but I didn't expect to see this side of him."

"You never know what kind of monster hides inside people," Meg said, staring bleakly at the slush of water being bladed away by the wipers. "I learned that when I was still a kid."

Ross gazed at her, seeing the vulnerable expression she wore. Somewhere along the way she had been hurt badly. It was in her face and posture, and in the way she hugged herself against the damp cold. He turned up the heater to combat the brisk air streaming in through the shattered passenger side window.

"Turn left, and then go straight about a quarter of a mile. I'm pretty sure there's a golf course up there."

He stepped on it and soon they were driving along a wide expanse of chain-link fence. He drove to the edge of the golf course and around it's fenced perimeter, turning on a road that separated the wide lawns from condominiums. He pulled up in front of one of the houses and shut off the engine and lights, grabbing a flashlight from the glove box. "Come on, help me search. If we don't find it in a couple of minutes, we'll have to start driving again."

They both hurried out of the car. He opened the hood, shining the flashlight beam down inside, while Meg dropped to her knees, searching in the meager streams of light that sieved through the engine. The minutes ticked away as she looked, the wet ground soaking the knees of her jeans. Ross slammed the hood and also dropped down, shining the light under the car's frame. Rain fell in thin sheets, soaking them. They continued to search the underside of the car, tension mounting.

Meg wondered how well the chain-link fence would work at distorting the signal—if it worked at all. If it didn't, how soon until the Signet car pulled up and the men got out with guns? She ran her hands along the underside of the car, desperately searching, blinking her eyes against the rain that blurred her vision. She was terrified of seeing Alan Scorzato again, and of what he might try to do. There was also the image of the bodybuilder with the angry, brutish expression. Last time there had been a car window between his fist and her face. Next time she might not be so lucky. Her heart was hammering.

"Ross, we've got to go," she called out in a hoarse whisper. "They're going to find us!" He didn't answer, his flashlight beam scanning the belly of the car. "Please, Ross. I'm scared."

"I got it!" he said, standing up. "Hurry, get inside the car."

Meg needed no urging, leaping up and climbing back inside. He jumped in and shut the door, his wet hands fumbling with a narrow black box. He slid the side panel open and popped out two heavy-duty batteries which immediately stopped the box from transmitting. Ross dropped it onto the seat between them and started the engine, this time leaving the lights off as he pulled back onto the roadway. He took a different route out, winding his way through a residential area.

She picked up the box and looked at it, shivering because her clothes and hair were soaked. "This is it?"

"That's it. Looks harmless enough, doesn't it?"

He was driving much slower, hardly able to see now in the rain and darkness, depending on the outside lights on the houses to light his way. In the far distance they could see headlights coming towards them. "Is that them?" Meg managed to ask, her throat constricting with fear.

"Good chance," he replied, backing into a driveway beside a large boat and turning off the ignition.

"What are you doing?" she asked, alarmed. "We've got to go!"

"We'll be fine. Right now this boat is blocking us from their view. Besides, they'll probably turn off before they get here."

"What if they don't?"

"You're panicking, hon. You're wanting to run because your adrenalin's back up, but I think we're better off hiding for the moment. If that's them, then right now they're having a fit because the signal that's been guiding them has quit."

"Then we should take advantage of that and leave."

"They're looking for a moving target. If we move, I have to turn on the lights to go fast enough to get away from them. That would be like sending up a flare."

Even though what he said made sense, Meg still felt overwhelmed by fear. "The lights!" she whispered, pointing out the approaching beams from the oncoming car.

"Get down," he said, his hand going to her head. She immediately scrunched onto the floor, his hand still atop her head. He was bent low, too, his face next to hers as he reached under the seat with his free hand.

"I'm scared," she whispered, overcome with claustrophobic fear.

He slid out a dark shape from under the seat, and she saw it was a gun. He clicked the safety off. "Don't be scared. I'm not going to let them get you."

Meg was breathing heavily, staring at the gun that had been concealed beneath his seat. Was that legal? The lights of the car slid near as the vehicle gathered speed. Through the open rear window she could hear the sound of tires crunching on wet pavement, making the car seem dangerously close. The lights brightened the interior of the Buick and she knew they would be seen. When the men got out and came after them, would Ross start shooting, and would they? It was the kind of freakish occurrence that sometimes happened in peaceful neighborhoods, and then made the evening news. Meg didn't want to be part of a shootout and the evening news, but feared she would be. His hand still rested on her damp hair, the heat of his palm surprisingly comforting during this moment of apprehensive fear. A few seconds later the headlights passed by, disappeared around a corner as the car shot past. Everything was very quiet, the muffled sound of the rain the only noise.

They both held still a minute longer, Ross seeming to listen for sounds of the car possibly returning. Eventually he re-engaged the safety on the gun and slid it back under the seat, then removed his hand from her head and sat up. Meg sat up also, staring across the layout of the quiet residential neighborhood. Ross started the engine and pulled out of the driveway, heading in the direction from which they had come. He left the lights off, driving slowly until they came to a street exiting the neighborhood for the main road. After checking to make sure it was clear, he switched on the headlights, flooding the rainy roadway ahead of them with white light. He stepped on the accelerator and soon they were traveling on a main road where there was more traffic.

"You okay?" he asked, turning up the heat. The warm air didn't do much against the chill of their wet clothes and the rainy wind swooping through the back window.

"Yes," Meg answered, feeling ashamed. She glanced out the side window at the night-time scenery. "I'm sorry about panicking."

"Don't be. It makes us ape types feel at least somewhat useful when the geniuses in the place get nervous."

Meg looked over at him, not knowing what to think. She had never met anyone like Ross Ecklund. "Shouldn't you be going in the other direction, away from those guys?"

"I will in a minute," he said, falling in behind a couple of cars. There was a red light ahead and Ross slowed, grabbing the transmitter and reinserting the batteries. He pulled the car in close next to a black pickup in the turn lane, and hit the button that lowered his window.

"What are you doing?"

He stuck his arm out the window, attaching the magnet side of the transmitter to the rear fender of the pickup. He rolled the window up and brushed the rain from his sleeve. A couple of seconds later the green arrow in the turn lane lit up and the truck took off. Ross grinned at her.

"I don't want our boys to be disappointed because they lost the signal. This will keep them busy, if they're close enough to pick it up again." The light ahead of them turned green and he pulled through the intersection, changed lanes, and entered an empty parking lot. He turned the car around and re-entered the street, heading away from the golf course.

* * *

It was almost one in the morning when the large Samoan agent, Brian Moses, drove his boss to the apartment complex where Meg Parrish lived. When he and Richard Hammond arrived there, two police cars were in the parking lot, the flashing lights of one of them like a homing beacon marking the place where disaster had struck. They parked and got out of the car, and Brian showed his ID to the officer in the parking lot. Half a minute later they were inside her apartment, where they saw an officer taking blood samples from the carpet. Another took prints from the sliding glass door using fingerprinting dust mixed with iron filings and a special magnet that acted like a delicate brush for detecting prints on glass.

Daniel Trenery and his assistant, Jake Cornel, were already there, talking with a police detective. Richard nodded at them. "What's going on? Is she okay?"

"She's not here," Trenery explained. "This is Detective Rosanbalm."

"You're Richard Hammond? Her supervisor?"

"Yes. I was told a 911 call was placed from here more than an hour ago."

"That's right. There's signs of forced entry at the glass door, and the front door was left unlocked. It looks like either she fled or was possibly taken from here against her will. Her car is still in the parking lot. The neighbors didn't hear anything, and there's not many signs of a struggle except for the blood stains."

Hammond leaned heavily on his arm brace, noting the dark red blotches on the couch, floor, and quilt. "It's not a substantial amount," Trenery stated. He meant there wasn't a pool of blood that indicated a slit throat. It wasn't really much comfort, though.

"If you could answer a few questions, it would help us," the detective said. "We'll be done here in a few more minutes, and then Mr. Trenery has indicated you'd like to bring in your own team."

"Yes," Hammond responded. "What do you want to know?"

It took another forty minutes for Detective Rosanbalm and his officers to finish what they were doing, and for the NSA team to move in. They then began a meticulous search of every square inch of the apartment. For most of the time Hammond walked around, observing. He was looking for clues out in the open, where the others were searching for what was hidden. Over and over again the same question came to mind: what had happened to her?

He remembered how miffed she'd been at him, almost teary at one point because he wouldn't confirm her suspicions about the Briggs boy and his family being telepaths. She'd been upset, he knew. But how did that tie in to this current mess, or did it at all? He looked at the neat apartment decorated in pale colors and with watercolors and pieces of fancy glass. The crimson stains on the gray carpet and couch were garish in contrast. He couldn't stand looking at them anymore, so turned and walked through the rest of the place. Her bedroom was a surprise to him with its draped bed and flowered prints. It made her seem more sensitive and feminine as opposed to the reserved cryptographer who was driven to break codes.

The team finished their search, turning up nothing unusual. "Her computer system is down," Brian said. "It might have been reformatted or had something else done to it, because we can't even get it to boot. Trenery said to take it in and have our computer specialists look at it."

"Yes, go ahead." Hammond felt a momentary hope. Meg seemed the most likely candidate for making sure her computer was inaccessible to the average user, and she definitely had the know-how to keep others from getting into her files. That meant she might have left under her own volition.

"We're about finished," Trenery said, coming over to him. "I'm sorry to say we haven't found anything else to give us an idea of what happened. We'll have to wait for the blood samples to come back, and the fingerprints. I'll make sure the place is sealed with evidence tape." He had the file on Parker Briggs in his hand, and indicated it. "We'd better take this."

"Do a debugging search, will you?" Hammond said off the top of his head, reluctant to leave the apartment with no shred of information as to what happened to her. "Let's see if we pick up anything."

"It's a long shot, but you never know," Trenery responded, willing to give Hammond what he asked for, considering the circumstances. "Jake? Let's check for microphones."

"Sure thing," his man answered, heading out to the trunk of his car.

Jake returned with a piece of equipment that looked a lot like a small metal detector, activating it and carefully making a sweeping search of the apartment. He had been working at it for a few minutes when the indicator beeped in response to a radio transmission. The beeping increased in speed the closer he came to an end table beside the couch. Brian Moses stepped forward and removed the lamp and houseplant on top of the table, then upended it. He and Jake both spotted a small black transmitter the size of a nickel but twice as thick. Now that the bug had been found, the detection equipment emitted a signal which scanned through the frequencies until it zoned in on the specific one being used by the transmitter.

"The receiver has to be within thirty feet," Jake said. "Let's look outside."

The team of agents headed out both doors, looking on either side of the apartment for something that might house the receiver. They began searching in the obvious places, the sites where they would have chosen to hide it themselves. One of the men got equipment out of the trunk of his car and began to scale the nearest telephone pole, searching through the cluster of wiring boxes. He ignored the rain dripping from the brim of his hat and began prying the boxes open. Eventually he found a phoney one with a small dish inside. It was receiving transmissions from the bug.

"Got it!" he called, and the others quit their search, heading for the parking lot. The agent climbed down, bringing the receiving dish with him, and the men studied the pole. He indicated the direction the dish had been pointed, which immediately narrowed their search. It had to be re-transmitting to another hidden device set up in line-of-sight, and not very far away.

They started examining a row of trees that were in line with the pole, the men scouring through the branches. A couple of minutes later one of them discovered a birdhouse with a hinged lid. Inside was a voice-activated tape recorder.

*   *   *

Hammond and Trenery were back at the CSS office, sitting in the small conference room where they had interviewed Meg earlier that evening. Brian Moses brought them coffee.

"Head on home and get some rest," his boss said. "You can come back in at six. I'll call if I need you before then."

"I'd rather stay," Brian said. "I'll be at my desk if you need anything."

He left the room and Trenery's assistant, Jake Cornel, entered. He put the tape recorder in the middle of the table and sat down. "Okay. We've got something, though I haven't listened to it all. The tape is new, only recording since this evening. I'm guessing it was just changed, or that the whole system had barely been set up. It's hard to tell."

"What about the devices they used?" Hammond asked.

"The same stuff we use, which doesn't mean much. People can buy just about whatever they want now days. Anyway, you'll want to hear this tape. I'm skipping the first part. It activated when she checked her answering machine in the evening. One of the messages was from Brian, who told me he called today from downtown, and also your office called her. The next time it activated was when the t.v. came on, and so I've bypassed the news and part of a late-night show. This is where something happens."

He turned on the recorder and they heard a man's voice say, "This could hurt." They listened to the dialogue between Meg and an unknown man, and Hammond felt his heart sink in apprehension as the male voice explained about the knife. A short time later she cried out, and the man nastily explained about giving her a taste of how sharp the knife was. Hammond immediately recalled the blood stains in her apartment and felt sick. He glanced up at Trenery, who for once didn't seem impassive. His face was also alarmed.

A few minutes later and the assailant said something which blew them out of the water. He asked for the Kronek codes. The two men glanced at each other, stunned by this unexpected turn. The voice asked about the CD she had with the codes on it, which apparently she found for him and he tested on her computer. In the background the t.v. host was doing a monologue, the audience laughter tinny and out of place. The intruder wanted to know who she worked for. When he didn't like her answer about working for the government, she lied, and he accepted it. Next he wanted to know why she had taken the codes, and her explanation surprised them. Trenery stared at Hammond, his expression full of unspoken queries.

The CSS supervisor turned his attention back to the tape, gazing at the small black box as if it also held visual clues. The dialogue continued and his concern deepening because the man's voice took on a sexual tone. Hammond's mouth went dry and he gripped the table edge when he heard her ask the intruder not to hurt her, and when the man instead made crude sexual remarks. She sounded so frightened and hopeless. The three men at the table listened to the noises of the attack, to the sounds of a struggle and of the assailant's voice alternately swearing and making filthy comments.

Trenery stared at Hammond, whose face was white. He looked sick, and Trenery felt much the same. Both of them recalled Meg's past which had been full of tragedy, and the thought of still another cruel event seemed excruciatingly unfair.

Suddenly the man yelped and cried, "What are you doing here?" There was the sound of a quick scuffle, and then the man began screaming about his nose being broken.

Another man spoke. His voice was deeper than the attacker's had been, and he was talking to Meg about not passing out, and later asked if she were alright. A new, hopeful kind of expression surfaced on Hammond's heavy features. Trenery lifted his eyebrows and mouthed, "Who's that?"

The next minute there was nothing but the first man's moaning, then Meg's voice took on a wild, nearly insane edge. She screamed about the man killing her sister, and was apparently attacking him. There was more scuffling and then the assailant must have fled. They listened to the rest of the tape, to the voice of the man who called himself a "friend" and more time elapsed. Then Meg made curt comments about safeguarding her computer. They heard the sound of a door opening, then nothing but the television. A few seconds later there was the scrape of the glass door sliding open and a quick curse. After that there was nothing but the noise of commercials from the t.v.

The CSS supervisor looked at the two NSA agents, his face full of relief. Whoever the second man was, Hammond felt grateful to him for interceding.

"He must have also been from Signet," Trenery stated, reading his co-worker's thoughts. "The attacker knew him and asked what he was doing there. Those men were both from Signet, and they came after her because she had the codes. Why didn't she tell us?"

"You heard what she said. Meg thought she'd gotten the wrong codes, and didn't want to get in trouble. This comes down on your head, Dan, for not letting me tell her the truth about what she was looking for. I tried to explain to you that she was too smart and inquisitive, and that she would know the difference between a Skipjack and something like the Kronek codes."

"I didn't expect her to actually steal them from Dent, just to find them and tell us where they were hidden! We figured they would be encrypted, so all she needed to do was find the folder full of codes and tell us where to look. She wasn't authorized to actually break into the files holding the codes and read them, you know. But since she did end up taking them, why couldn't she have just given us the codes? If she had, none of this would have happened."

"Meg is a cryptographer, not an NSA agent. When she got those files and they were encrypted, it was like finding a candy store. Making and breaking codes is what she does for a career. She would never ignore the challenge to break the passwords, unless given a direct order, which you failed to do. If you would have leveled with her, and told her the name of the folder and what kind of codes were in those files, you'd have had them in your hands a week ago."

"We've got to find them. Let's do whatever it takes to track her down."

"Meg is my concern," Hammond said, his face grim. "Right now I don't give a damn about those codes. I want to make sure our girl gets back safe."

"Nothing's going to happen to her. She's with some kind of Lone Ranger type who stepped in and broke the other guy's nose. We'll find out who those men are, and then find her."

"I hope you're right," Hammond growled, reaching over and shutting off the tape.

Chapter 12

The all-night laundromat was brightly lit, which made Meg nervous because she felt exposed. She stood beside a dryer that tumbled her sweatshirt and Ross' jacket in a heated cycle, while Ross himself was outside. He had pulled the car directly in front of the door and under the overhanging eave, which deflected the rain. Now he was using his pocket knife to slice up a cardboard box, which he eventually taped inside the broken window with some duct tape retrieved from the trunk of his car. He really was a boy scout, she reflected. One who was now wearing a gun in a shoulder holster.

A moment later he signaled her to come, and Meg hurriedly opened the drier. She put on the hot sweatshirt, which felt wonderful, and grabbed Ross' jacket, tossing it to him as she came through the door. Soon they were driving down the road again, in much better shape. The cardboard blocked the rain, and the heater dispelled the rest of the damp air.

"Do you want to find a payphone and call someone from CSS?" Ross asked. "I'm guessing that would probably be the smartest thing to do, as far as getting help."

"I suppose so," Meg sighed.

"What's wrong?"

"I had a fight with my boss tonight, and think I quit. I was pretty upset. Even if it is best to call him, I still need a little time to think things through. Is there any way I could get to my car, do you think?"

"Not without the risk of getting shot at again, or chased down. Those guys will probably go back to your place once they figure out we switched the transmitter. That would be the logical thing to do, anyway. There's a slim chance they won't, but do you want to risk it? Look, I don't mind driving you where you want to go. It's not exactly like I can go back to my place, either. They'll be looking for me, too."

"I didn't think about that."

"So, where do you want to go?"

She wanted to go to Benicia, California, but didn't dare say so. "Can we get something to eat? I know it's two in the morning, but I'm hungry."

"Me too."

About ten minutes later they found an all-night restaurant at a truck stop off the freeway. It was surprisingly busy, with large semis coming and going, and gas pumps continually in use. The truck engines emitted deep purrs, and men talked in loud voices over the noise. Ross parked the car in the rear and they entered the restaurant, choosing an unobtrusive booth near the back. Plastic daisies in a vase sat atop the Formica tabletop, surrounded by salt and pepper shakers and a bottle of ketchup. A thin strain of country music issued from a radio in the kitchen, and there were appetizing smells coming from a hot griddle.

The waitress took their orders, then Meg went to the ladies room, grateful for a chance to take care of physical needs that had been a nagging priority for the last half-hour. When she washed her hands, she noted it took several squirts of the pink soap to get rid of the dirt and grease she had picked up from beneath the car when they had searched for the transmitter. She stared at herself in the mirror, seeing a wary expression and dark smudges beneath her eyes. Her hair was windblown and wild-looking, which she managed to tug a comb through. A few minutes later she was back at the booth, waiting for Ross. He sat down beside her as the food arrived. Soon he was eating a chicken-fried steak with potatoes and gravy, while she had vegetable soup with thick noodles and toasted slices of bread on the side.

They ate in silence for a while, both feeling the draining effects of the adrenalin finally ebbing from their systems. The images of attackers with knives, chasing cars, and shooting guns, began to seem oddly out of place in the well-lit restaurant.

"Is it my turn to ask a couple of questions?" Meg queried, looking up from her half-empty bowl of soup.

"Sure. Ask away."

"Did Willis Dent talk to you about the codes that I took? Do you know anything about them, or what they're used for?"

"No. He was secretive, and wouldn't say anything when I asked him. He was just dead-set on getting them back. Apparently they're worth a lot to him. More than I realized, if his men were willing to kill us to get them back."

"You must be right, though to be honest I've checked the codes out and don't know what they might be used for. In fact, my gut instinct says they're unbreakable." She took a bite of the bread, her mind setting that topic aside for the moment. "Okay, since that's a dead end, let's move on to question two. When I said you could have the CD with the codes on it, you said you didn't want it. You said you'd had a 'major change of priorities,' if I remember your exact words. You also said you didn't care if Signet got the CD back or not. Yet you'd spent the better part of a week looking for me. After finding out where I lived, you broke into my place, searched for the CD, and eventually ended up following me. All of that to find a set of codes you don't even want now because your priorities have changed."

Ross scooped potatoes and gravy onto a piece of steak and popped it into his mouth, thoughtfully chewing. "Yup."

"So explain."

The waitress came over to check on them, refilling their water glasses. Ross ordered two pieces of apple pie, heated and with ice cream. When she had left he put his fork down and looked at Meg, his brush-stroke eyebrows coming together in uncertainty.

"You're asking me to give you a one-paragraph review of *War and Peace*. I'm not sure I can do it."

Meg smiled and finished her soup. "I'm not going anywhere."

Ross glance out the rain-spattered window at the night sky. "I used to have a family," he said at last. "There was my dad, and mom, and little sister." A familiar feeling of dread touched Meg upon hearing the words 'used to'. He continued. "In the beginning it was just me and my dad. My real mother left when I was a baby, and I never knew her. That might bother most kids, but I had the world's greatest dad. When I was five he remarried, and I ended up having a mom, too. Marilyn wasn't a stepmother to me. She became my real mother, and we didn't have problems the way everyone always thinks step-moms do with step-kids. It wasn't threatening to me for them to get married, because my father had this boundless kind of love and I knew nothing could change that. The three of us had some great times together. Then six years later my little sister was born. I was crazy about Sissy, and we all spoiled her. The four of us had this great life, until I was seventeen and my dad came down with something called sarcoidosis."

The waitress came to the table with their pie, setting the plates in front of them along with clean forks. A few seconds later she left. "I've never heard of that," Meg said.

"No one has. It was so rare that even the doctors didn't know much about it. The disease caused lesions on his brain stem that were inoperable, and it attacked his central nervous system. They used chemotherapy and steroids to shrink the lesions, which bought us a couple of years." He stared at the vanilla ice cream melting atop the apple pie.

"I'm sorry," she said, the words sounding trite.

"Me too. We had some great years, though. Afterwards, Mom, Sis and I got along okay. Marilyn was a rock." He picked up his fork, taking a bite of the dessert. "Eat your pie before the ice cream becomes soup."

She took a bite. It was delicious, but she wasn't much in the mood for eating dessert at the moment. When she glanced up from the plate he was studying her. "I told you, *War and Peace*."

"I want to hear the rest."

"When I was a senior at UCLA, our mom was killed in a car accident. A few days later, after the funeral, my little sister disappeared."

Meg stared at him, not knowing what to think. "Was she kidnaped?"

"No. She ran away. Before she did, she told me that Mom's death hadn't been an accident, and if she didn't get away, the people who had killed our mother would kill me, too. Because of my parents' will, I became her legal guardian when Mom died. Sis was sure they would kill me, and then our grandparents, until no one was left in the family to be her guardian and she would become a ward of the state. So she ran away. That was ten years ago, and I haven't seen her since."

Meg stared at him. "Why did your little sister believe that?" she finally managed. "Was she in shock because of losing your mother? I know shock can make us think all kinds of strange things, and have unreasonable fears." The logical side of her mind immediately brought up her own phobia of five-year intervals.

"No. She knew what she was doing."

"You believed her?" This seemed even more implausible.

"I always believed her," Ross answered, pushing away the pie that he no longer had an appetite for either. "Shannon was different from most kids. It's hard to explain."

"Shannon?" Meg slowly repeated.

Ross nodded. "Sissy for short. From the time she was little, she just knew things. She was very smart, and had what Mom called a sixth sense. We would tease her about it sometimes because it was so funny and weird. Dad used to call her our little wizard."

Meg nodded and he stared past her, as if looking at a picture from a long time ago. "She had this way of helping us over the hard things we went through, like Dad's death."

"How old was she when you last saw her?" Meg asked, trying to keep her voice calm. It had to be a coincidence.

"Twelve."

"And that was ten years ago?"

"Yes. I got postcards sometimes, maybe once or twice a year. They came from all over the country, and once from Mexico. She was letting me know she was okay, but that was all. It wasn't enough for me, though. I was determined to find her. In the beginning I decided to hire a firm of private investigators to help me, and ended up using all the money from the sale of my parents' house. Eventually I dropped out of school with one semester left, and worked with the agency full time until the money was gone. By then I figured it had at least been a good education, and started using their resources myself. They even offered me a job, which I took for a while. I learned a lot from them about how to find people. Apparently, though, I never learned enough, since I wasn't able to find Shannon."

"And you've been searching for her these last ten years?"

"Off and on. I traveled some, trying to find her, but eventually slowed my pace. It was expensive. Finally I went back to school and got my degree, but decided to stay with being an investigator. It seemed to pay better than being a social worker would have, anyway, and it let me keep looking for her. A couple of years ago I started to let my search for her slide because there didn't seem much hope left that I'd ever find her. Then six months ago I came across something that started me looking again. I followed that lead to Portland, but it turned out to be a dead end, too. By then I had the job with Signet, and pretty much decided to stop looking for her. Until this afternoon."

The waitress brought the tab and asked if something were wrong with the pie. They both assured her it was fine, relieved when she moved away.

"So what happened this afternoon?"

"I was following you in the market, and you were with that Deaf boy. The surveillance profile in your night stand said his name is Parker Briggs."

"Yes."

"I was trailing you when you came to that stall with geraniums."

Meg glanced away, looking outside the window where tall pole lights illuminated the falling rain, making it appear as fingerprint whorls against the black sky. He paused and was staring at her, waiting for her to look back at him. Finally she met his gaze.

"You were upset," he said. "I don't need to paint it out for you. It's your experience. But when you sat down on the bench, Parker Briggs did something with his hand. He put it on the side of your head and you started to calm down. He was doing something to help you, wasn't he? Something you've probably never experienced before."

Slowly Meg nodded. Her discomfort at his observation of the incident with the flowers began to evaporate in the light of what he was saying. "Yes, Ross. He was doing the same thing that Shannon can do, too." She lowered her voice and leaned in, her excitement increasing. "And that's what you recognized in the market today, and why your priorities have changed. You know all about what they can do!"

Meg was on the brink of something big, and had been since this afternoon when Parker and Shannon had changed everything. Until now there had been no one who would substantiate her findings, or explain them, but very possibly Ross could. It was a wildly bizarre coincidence, but her logic had been so frequently suspended during the last few hours that she was willing to let it be suspended again. "Does your sister have red hair?"

His gaze intensified. "How do you know that?"

"Does she have green eyes and freckles, and a little half-moon scar in the hollow of her throat, right here?" Meg asked.

Ross reached out, grabbing her arm. He was staring at her, unable to find his voice.

* * *

Martin Wimer stood beside a black pickup in the parking lot of a bar. Light from the pink neon signs diffused the darkness and allowed him to spot the transmitter stuck to the truck's fender. He angrily snatched it off and walked back to the Signet car. Before he got in, he unhooked the antennas and put them back inside the car. Once inside, he turned off the receiver and shut the briefcase.

"How'd they know we were tracking them?" Leo Fromm asked.

"How do you think, dummy? You pulled right up behind them, which let Ross see the antennas. Let's get out of here."

"You two have screwed this whole thing up!" Alan Scorzato said from the back seat. "Now we'll never find her."

Wimer resisted the urge to tell him to shut up. "It ain't over yet. Not by a long shot. Let's get you to an emergency room so they can take care of your nose. We'll drop you off, and you can take a taxi home."

"What are you two going to do?" Scorzato asked, trying to keep his voice from sounding relieved at the prospect of finally getting the medical attention he needed.

"We'll divide up and see if we can spot them. Leo, go back to the girl's place."

"Okay."

"I'm going to head to Ross' apartment and see what I can learn. He might even take her there, and if he does I'll be able to get them both. If not, then maybe there'll be something in his place that can give me a clue about where they might go, or at the least something on how he's tied into Zytex. I'll bet Dent will want to know if he's always worked for Zytex, or if they just bought him out."

"One thing's for sure. Willis is going to want them both taken care of and this mess cleaned up, but only after you get the CD back," Scorzato reminded.

"I took care of Phil Black after he swiped those papers, didn't I?" Wimer testily asked. "You can trust me to take care of these two. It's what Signet pays me for, remember?"

Leo guided the car onto the freeway and stepped on the accelerator.

*   *   *

Meg took a sip of water as Ross stared past her and into the distance. She had just finished telling him the abbreviated version of her experiences that afternoon, and had tried to keep it as succinct as possible. She had explained about the different members of the family she had met, and about Parker and Shannon's efforts to help her with problems from her past. She didn't give details. Meg then ended the story with the police raid and all it had entailed. Ross hadn't interrupted, letting her tell the whole story.

"That's pretty much everything," she said, picking up her fork and stabbing at the soggy pie. "Another condensed version of *War and Peace*."

"It might not be the same Shannon."

"It might not," Meg agreed.

"There's probably no way of knowing until I see her, but to be honest, I think it really could be. Maybe I've been hoping to find her for so long now that I'm just snatching at another straw. What are the odds that it's really her? Especially since I was tracking you for completely different reasons than trying to find her. I wasn't even looking for Shannon, which makes the coincidence pretty strange. But all the things you describe happening are the kind of things that went on with her."

"What kinds of things?"

"Like I said, she was different from other kids. She had a way of sensing things. It got more that way the older she became, too, and sometimes I really worried about her. Nearly six months before Mom died, Shannon started having nightmares. They were always the same, she said, about being chased by men in dark clothes. They were hunting for her, and she was trying to hide from them. It affected her and she started being unnaturally careful, always locking doors or looking out the window when an unknown car drove by. It had us worried."

"Did you believe her?"

"Yes, because her forecasts were almost always right."

"You don't mean she could predict the future?"

"No, not predict. Mom called it being sensitive, having a kind of sixth sense about people and their thoughts. I used to tease Sis that it was because her skull was thinner than ours, and that she was picking up microwaves." He smiled at the memory. "Shannon lots of times told us things about ourselves she shouldn't have been able to know. For example, when I had a bad day at school, she'd come and talk to me. I didn't even have to give her details because she already seemed to know them. When something sad happened she had a way of comforting us, similar to what happened to you this afternoon. We weren't the only ones, either. I can't tell you how many times I had to go looking for her in the neighborhood because she was visiting with somebody we didn't even know very well. Sometimes she was with other kids, but lots of times she was visiting adults. There was this elderly man whose wife had died in a plane crash, and Shannon spent a lot of days with him. There was another family with all kinds of troubles. For one thing, they had two little kids with genetic problems, and the parents were really struggling with it. She was over there all the time. She'd look out the window and say, 'Mrs. Gordon isn't doing very good today. Maybe I'll go see her.' Then off she'd go, and be gone all afternoon. There was another woman down the street that had a multiple personality disorder. Shannon loved her, and kept going there even when Mom and Dad forbid her because they felt nervous about it."

"You think she was helping those people?"

"I know she was. A few of them talked to me about her."

Meg stared at him, her expression concerned and excited. "I think Shannon could do those things, and what she did with me, because she's telepathic."

Ross slowly nodded. "I came to that conclusion years ago. Lots of times she knew stuff that no one had told her, and that she couldn't have possibly guessed at. In fact, she was the reason Dad went to the doctor in the first place. Even though Shannon was only seven at the time, she kept worrying about him and said there was something wrong with him. Soon after that he started getting headaches and went right in for an exam. That wasn't like him, since he was the kind of man who usually just took a couple of painkillers and toughed it out. But Shannon was so concerned that it worried us all. After we found out about the sarcoidosis, she was even more distraught. She kept saying there must be someone who could help him, someone who was better than the doctors. Maybe she was right, but now that I look back on it, I'm grateful that we at least had the extra time with him that we did. In some ways it was a lot harder losing Mom because her death was so sudden. I didn't have time to say goodbye."

"I know." They were both quiet for a moment, and she put her fork down. "How did Shannon take your mother's passing?"

"It was awful. She blamed herself, and said the men wouldn't have done it if it weren't for her, whatever that meant."

A few theories began to come together and Meg's expression grew tense. "Maybe it means men like that phony Agent Warner, and his cohort who planted the drugs, wanted to get their hands on Shannon. Maybe they still do." Meg told him about her one-sided discussion of telepathy with Hammond and Trenery, and all it had entailed. She included her angry suggestion that she quit working for them if they wouldn't level with her.

"They wouldn't admit or deny anything about the telepathy?"

"No, but I was hitting a few hot spots when I asked my questions. It's obvious that national security would be a concern if there's some people walking around out there who can read minds, you know."

Ross felt himself grow tense. A couple of missing pieces had just been added to the jigsaw puzzle of his past, and it seemed as if they were being slammed into place with a sledge hammer. "What this all means is that she's on the run again, only this time she's pregnant and due to have a baby any time, if the woman you met really is my sister." The thought of Shannon in that condition made her seem no less vulnerable than she had as a girl. "I have this mental image of her as a twelve-year-old. It's hard for me to think of her as twenty-two and having a baby." He picked up the tab and reached for his wallet. "Let's get out of here."

They left the restaurant and got into the car, driving back towards Portland. "You're worried," she said, looking at his tense jaw.

"Worried, yes. And excited at the possible prospect of finding her, and also feeling scared to get my hopes up again. Look, if you're up to it, I want to do something. Would you mind taking me to the house where you met her so I can snoop around?"

"You think you might find something?"

"I'm guessing that the place has already been gone over with a fine-tooth comb, and that there's not going to be anything to tell me where she is. What I'm looking for is something that might help me know if it's really Shannon or not. If it's another dead end, then I'll just have to chalk this up to one more weird event during my search for her, and then get on with my life. If it is her, though, I'd sure like to know. Are you up to going? After listening to your story I'm guessing you must have been exhausted even before tonight's joy ride started."

Meg smiled at him in amusement. "Actually, I'm beyond that point. Everything, including our conversation, is starting to become surrealistic."

The rain began to ease until there was nothing more than a few drops periodically landing on the car's windshield. The streets were still wet, though, with heavy puddles in the gutters. They drove in silence for a while, both trying to assimilate what they'd pieced together. Meg gave him directions to get to the house, which took a little effort since she had been on a bus and signing with Parker, which had been distracting. At the time she had tried to pay attention to the bus route, but it hadn't been easy. Eventually, though, they found it and he pulled the car up in front and turned off the lights.

"This is pretty shabby," he commented, getting the flashlight out of the glove box.

"You should see it in daylight."

Quietly they got out of the car and went up the cracked walkway and onto the steps. Once inside the screened porch, Ross turned on the flashlight and muted it with his hand. He studied the torn evidence tape left by the police, and noted the door was slightly ajar. "We're not the first ones to try this," he said in a low voice.

They stepped inside the kitchen and he shone the beam across the messy counter tops and appliances. Meg noticed two loaves of bread still in their baking pans. Gram must have managed to get them out of the oven before the police came. The rest of the kitchen was the same, except that it was quiet. There were no voices or the sound of a running washing machine. The only noise came from their footsteps and the ticking kitchen clock. They moved into the living room. It was extremely dark, with almost no light coming through the draped windows. The flashlight beam was like a flitting firefly, touching on the furniture, bookcase, and walls. Ross spotted a floor lamp close by and switched it on. Dim light leapt from beneath the stained silk shade and cast odd shadows around the room. The corners of the livingroom were still dark, but the lamp gave them enough light to see by.

It looked the same as it had this afternoon, Meg thought, staring at the worn velveteen couch where she had sat with Parker and Shannon, and where something monumental had happened to her. "They said they were a family," she commented in a quiet voice. "Parker told me Shannon and Leah were his sisters. Doesn't that seem odd, if Shannon is really your sister?"

"Not if they're telepaths. If you found someone else who could read minds, like you could, wouldn't you tend to think of them as family? Especially if you went into hiding together?" He walked over to the wall mural. "Wow."

"I know. It's really weird, but beautiful, too. Leah painted it."

"The little kid? Didn't you say she was only eight?"

"I didn't believe it at first, either. I thought Parker did it. But look at this." She pointed to an island with a castle on it, and the penciled outline of a fairy. Meg struck the same pose, lifting her arms. "What do you think?"

"It looks like you. Except for the wings, of course," he teased.

"She drew it while I watched. That convinced me pretty fast."

"Considering it's three in the morning, and all the strange stuff we've already talked about, I pretty much will buy anything. Let's check upstairs."

*   *   *

Eunice Finch climbed out of her creaking bed and went for a glass of water. She was having trouble sleeping because her arthritis was bugging her again, and because she was afraid that dirty little Asian girl would come back and set her house on fire. On the way to the bathroom she paused, catching her breath at what she noticed. There was some kind of light moving around in the upstairs window of Mabel's house where the police had been today. She stood watching it, mesmerized by how it seemed to move through the rooms, pausing now and then. It must be a flashlight, Eunice decided. She shoved the curtain aside and pressed her face against the far edge of the glass pane, barely able to catch a glimpse of the porch. There was a car parked below, just in front of the walk.

She stepped back, staring at the flitting beam of light again, then hurried into the bathroom. Feeling her way through the semi-darkness, she grabbed her false teeth out of the orange cup which was crusted with hard water stains, and slipped them into her mouth. Then she marched back to the sagging mattress and sat down heavily, reaching for the phone on the night stand. Beside it was the card the FBI man had given her, and she fumbled with it before being able to pick it up. Once she had it in her fingers, Eunice had to squint to read the penciled number. She carefully dialed, listening to the satisfying whir of the rotary dial as it slid back into place after each number.

*   *   *

"Does it strike you as odd that there's not many personal items here?" Meg asked.

Ross looked around the bedroom filled with black walnut furniture. "The place is fully furnished. In fact, it seems overcrowded."

"That's not what I mean. There's furniture and housewares, but not many clothes or personal items, and almost no toys. Leah said something about them renting this place, and one of her brothers being concerned because she was painting on the wall and it wasn't their house. It just seems to me that this is the kind of place to rent if you're on the run. It's rundown and not really noticeable, and comes furnished with someone else's things. That way when you have to go at the drop of a hat, you don't worry about what you're leaving behind."

"Makes sense. You'd make a good investigator. Let's check the other rooms."

They found more of the same, and Ross made little progress in his examination of the drawers and closets. He was very thorough at what he was doing, and Meg wondered if this was how he had gone through her things when he'd been inside her apartment.

"It doesn't make you uncomfortable to go looking through people's drawers?"

"Not when I have a job to do. Especially not if I think there's something that will prove to me that the Shannon you met this afternoon is my sister. I'd pretty much do just about anything to find that out."

He closed the bottom drawer of a large dresser and stood, opening the closet door. After a few minutes more he came back out and shut the door. "Maybe this is a waste of time. There's nothing here that can give me a clue if it's her."

"Did you think there would be?"

"Yes and no. I have this tendency to be optimistic in spite of bad odds."

They went back downstairs and passed through the livingroom, where Ross stopped at the quilting frame as if seeing it for the first time. He stared down at the baby quilt, saying nothing. Meg came and stood beside him, looking down at the pattern which Shannon and Gram had been hand quilting with needles and thread. There were five calico cats appliqued onto a pink background.

"What's wrong?" Meg asked.

"I must be losing it. I didn't even look at this thing."

"Shannon and Gram were working on it when Parker and I came in. They talked about making it for the baby."

"I've seen this before," Ross stated.

"This quilt?"

"Actually, I've seen one like it, only bigger. Mom made a quilt for Shannon's bed, and it had cats cut out of material like this. Her whole room was decorated with cats," he added.

Meg looked up from the baby quilt. "You're sure it's the same?"

"Yes. Flowered cats on pink material, with thread whiskers and dots for eyes. Mom and Sissy bought the material and worked on it together. I remember her being all excited about it."

"This means your sister, and the Shannon I met today, really are the same person," she said with growing excitement. "Wow."

"Wow is an understatement," he commented.

"That's the proof you were looking for."

"It must be," Ross said. Suddenly he pried up one of the thumb tacks which held the quilt to the frame. "Help me get this off, will you?"

She started removing the tacks, careful not to tear the fabric. When they were finished she picked the quilt up and folded it in fourths. "If we find her, she'll be happy to get this back."

Ross walked over to the lamp, clicking it off. The room was plunged into darkness and he turned on the flashlight, pointing it at the floor. They walked into the kitchen and he clicked it off. A little outside light filtered in through the windows.

"I think we can find them," Meg said.

"How? If they're on the run, they aren't exactly going to leave clues that the men trailing them could pick up. I know, because I've been looking for ten years and haven't been able to find anything."

"They left me a clue," she said softly into the darkness.

Ross paused, turning to look at her through the dim light. He could barely make out her features even though she was only a couple of feet away from him. "Are you kidding?"

"Of course not."

"They left you a clue?"

"I think so."

"Why would they do that? It would be risky."

"I'm guessing it's because they weren't able to finish helping me. Shannon was very upset when the police came in and their telepathic link was broken." She paused, thinking it was much easier to talk about things like telepathy in a darkened house that was full of mysteries itself.

"What kind of clue?"

"Parker finger-spelled the name of a town to me as we were leaving, and I think it's maybe where they're going. Before everything happened tonight, and we ended up on the run from those creeps, I was planning on leaving for there tomorrow."

"Why didn't you tell me?"

"What was I supposed to say? Drive me to California, will you? Until an hour ago I didn't even know you and Shannon might be related, and until ten minutes ago we weren't sure it was the same Shannon. I didn't want to get your hopes up."

Their conversation was interrupted by the sound of tires crunching on gravel and the sight of headlights fanning the outside yard. A car pulled up in front of the house and Meg's heart began to hammer with fear. "Is it Alan Scorzato?" she whispered.

Ross stood to the side of the window and barely moved the curtain. "It's not the Signet car," he answered.

"Good," she managed, the single word hardly audible.

"It might be someone worse," Ross added, sliding his gun out of its shoulder holster he had donned at the laundromat and giving her the flashlight. The headlights were shut off, and he watched two men get out of the car. Ross reached over to the kitchen door and quietly slid the deadbolt in place. The men were examining his Buick and checking out the license plate.

Meg felt her fear deepen. "Do you think it's those fake FBI agents?"

"Probably."

"Then let's get out of here," she said, her whisper harsh. "There's a front door off the livingroom."

"We can get out, but they're by the car. I don't want to take off on foot."

Another vehicle turned onto the road, it's lights passing over the house as it pulled up beside the first car. The doors opened and two more men got out. Meg watched them through the curtain, seeing them reach into shoulder holsters. "They've got guns!"

Ross had a gun, too, she remembered, but there was only one of him. A new wave of fear washed over Meg, and she thought that she must be the most disaster-plagued person on the continent.

Ross crouched down, quickly moving his way across the kitchen to the refrigerator. He opened it a crack and found the button that activated the lightbulb. He pressed it in with the end of his gun, shutting off the light, then pushed the door open. His free hand was fumbling through the contents.

"One of the men is heading around the house," Meg harshly whispered. "Two others are coming up the walk."

"That leaves one man by the car?" He asked, grabbing an egg from a half-open carton and quickly shutting the refrigerator door.

"Yes."

Ross moved to the microwave and jerked it open, smashing the inside lightbulb with the butt of his gun. He stuck the egg inside and pressed the button that read 'High.' The oven started to purr and he turned to Meg, grabbing her hand. They ran through the dark livingroom, almost colliding with a chair, then worked their way to the back of the house and to a ground floor bedroom. Ross led her to a window on the side of the house, and flipped the latch on top of the frame, shoving it upwards. It squealed in protest, but the noise was masked by the sound of the kitchen door being kicked in and wood splintering as it banged open. A similar noise was coming from the front door.

Meg needed no urging to climb through the window, though the drop was surprisingly far because the window in this older home was fairly high up. She landed on an overgrown oleander bush, dropping the quilt. The twigs of the bush stabbed her legs and she scrambled forward, catching up the little blanket and running across the lawn. Ross was right behind her, and they hopped a low wooden fence, scurrying across a neighbor's back yard. A couple of seconds later they were moving through a gate and out onto the neighbor's front lawn.

It wasn't raining any more, but the air smelled heavy with moisture. A night wind stirred the leaves on the trees, which rustled like scraps of tattered silk. The whispering sound seemed to warn Meg of danger.

"This way," Ross said, pointing down the block lined with overgrown trees.

They had run past several houses when he suddenly grabbed her shoulder and pointed across the street. "Cross over, but stay in the shadows and away from the porch lights," he whispered. "Head back to the car. If we hug the trees, then we probably won't set off any motion detector lights. Go now."

"They'll find us!"

"We've got a ten-second distraction coming up, so get moving!"

His hand was firm on her arm, and Meg found herself doing what he said even though every nerve in her body told her to run as far away from those men as she could. Soon they were on the other side of the road directly opposite from where Ross' car was parked.

She crouched behind a tree and hugged the quilt to her chest, afraid to look at the man across the street. Ross did the watching, nervously glancing at his watch. About five seconds later there was the muffled sound of a grenade going off, and the reflex answer of a gun being fired inside the house. The man by the car bolted forward, running up the porch stairs and disappearing inside.

"Go!" Ross said in a harsh whisper, pushing her ahead of him. The damp wind whipped against Meg's face, the cloudy darkness surrounding her during the panic-filled flight.

Ross opened the driver's side door and she dove in ahead of him. He was right behind her, putting the key in the ignition. He turned it over so hard that the starter screamed, then one second later he jerked the shift bar down and stepped on the gas. Gravel spewed from beneath the spinning tires which soon grabbed hold and caused the car to leap forward onto the pavement. They were speedily moving away when two men ran out of the house and fired shots, bullets slamming into the trunk and shattering one of the tail lights as the car careened away.

Ross rounded the corner at full speed, the car sliding on the damp pavement but making the curve without too much of a problem. Hitting a straight stretch he floored it, then turned sharply on another side street. No doubt those other men were already in their car and following him, ready to shoot again. This time, though, he was more in control. The previous chase with the Signet car had been good practice, he thought. It was almost as if a high-speed chase were now the norm, and slamming the accelerator to the floor was what felt natural.

"Is there anybody in town who doesn't want to chase you down and shoot you?" he asked with a grin.

Meg stared at him, dumbfounded. How could he think this was funny? "I guess not," she managed, turning to look over her shoulder. "What was that loud bang?"

"My specialty. Egg in a microwave. I learned that on my mom's new oven when I was ten. She about had a heart attack."

It was probably funny, but even Meg's black humor wasn't able to kick in. She had been scared too many times tonight, and felt like screaming. She continued to check behind them. "Do you think they'll catch us?"

"Nope. They don't have a transmitter hidden under the car like Alan did." He sounded sure of himself, but Meg didn't feel even marginally comforted.

Too much had happened tonight, and her ability to analyze situations was shot. Her nerves were shot, too, and she was angry at all the creeps out there. Alan Scorzato and his men, and those FBI fakes, were just a sample of the rotten people out there, skulking in the dark and ready to pounce on innocent victims.

After they had been driving for more than fifteen minutes, with no sign of the other cars, Meg finally started to calm down. Perhaps Ross was right about losing them. Eventually he turned the car south on the interstate.

"Where are we going?" Meg asked.

"California, of course."

Chapter 13

Ross looked at Meg, who was dozing with her head tilted back against the headrest. It gave him a better view of the band-aid across her throat where Alan's knife had sliced her. He was too tired to feel the same kind of outrage he had experienced several hours before, but he still had enough energy to sincerely hope that Alan's nose was permanently screwed up.

She looked exhausted and had purplish shadows under her eyes. Ross, himself, felt completely beat. He took the exit to Salem and drove around for a while until he spotted an out-of-the-way motel with a vacancy sign. The Wagon Wheel Inn looked like it had been built in the fifties and never remodeled. He pulled up in front of the office and Meg roused, opening her eyes but not lifting her head.

"Where are we?" she managed.

"We've only made it to Salem, but I'm shot. I thought we should try and rest before heading to California."

"Okay," she murmured, closing her eyes and drifting off again. She had never felt so completely exhausted in her life, and it seemed as if her body was on some sort of shut-down.

Ross returned a few minutes later and drove the car around to the rear. "Come on, let's get you into bed," he said, opening the car door and guiding her into one of the motel rooms.

Meg blinked and stared around the small room which had two double beds covered with ugly bedspreads that matched the brown carpet. She dropped her oversized purse onto a chair as Ross locked the door behind them.

"I wanted to pay with cash instead of a credit card because the past few hours have made me kind of paranoid, but I only had enough money for one room. You okay with this?"

"You're a boy scout, aren't you?" she replied, gratefully heading for the tiny bathroom.

A few minutes later she came out and washed her hands at the sink area. They traded places and while Ross was using the bathroom she stripped off her sweat-shirt which garnered an immediate stab of pain from her arm. Next she tossed off her shoes, socks, and jeans, leaving them in a pile on the floor. Throwing back the covers on one of the beds, she climbed in wearing her oversized t-shirt and panties. The sheets were cold, the mattress hard, and the pillow too thick. Nothing had ever felt so good in her life, she decided, turning on her side and pulling the covers in close around her.

She was already half asleep when Ross came out and used the sink, then switched off the light. The room was plunged into darkness and soon she heard a creaking noise from the other mattress as he climbed into bed. Meg's last thoughts were about how strange her life had become. In the past she had rarely even dated, but tonight she was sharing a motel room with a man she had only met a few hours ago.

*   *   *

Ross had been solidly asleep for several hours when strange noises began to invade his dreams. He was so deeply asleep that it was hard for him to wake, and he felt much like a scuba diver in the depths of the ocean trying to swim the long distance to the surface. The strange noises increased, and even in his sleep he began to feel alarmed. Someone was making fearful, suffering sounds, and before his dreams had completely drifted away, he had images of Shannon being hurt. A few seconds later he opened his eyes, staring into the gray light. The room was dark except for a soft feathering of light at the edge of the latex-backed curtains. He felt disoriented before remembering where he was, then recalled the layout of the motel room and groped for the lamp, switching it on. It was only a forty-watt bulb, but the light seemed piercing and he blinked, looking over at the other bed.

Meg was scrunched up against the headboard, staring across the room with sightless eyes. Her face was ghostly white, and her expression made his skin crawl. It was similar to the look on her face yesterday at the geranium stall, only worse. Far worse. She wore a mask of such horror that it filled him with dread, especially because it was accompanied by terrible grief-filled sounds issuing from her parted lips.

Ross threw back his covers and went to her. He touched her arm but she recoiled, shuddering. "Meg, wake up. You're having a nightmare."

She took in a deep gasp, as if she had been unable to breathe until now. Her eyes slowly focused as she began to wake. "It's over," she choked. "It's over!"

"That's right, Meg. It's over."

Disoriented, she stared at him, gasping. The horror was still on her face, and it spoke of such utter devastation that it shook him. It was like happening on a train wreck, and not knowing what to do when faced with so much carnage.

"Don't...look...at me," she managed between shortened gasps. He stared at her, not sure if she were awake yet. She turned away from him. "Please...don't look," she managed, her voice thick with humiliation.

Her panting gasps increased, and Ross realized she was hyperventilating. He moved off the bed, looking around the room. The paper sack filled with first-aid supplies was sticking out of her purse. He grabbed the bag and dumped the contents on the floor, then hurried over to her. "Here," he said, sitting down beside her and putting the bag over her mouth and nose. "You're hyperventilating. Try to slow your breathing."

Meg held the sack, watched the brown paper being rapidly sucked in and blown out as she panted. With difficulty she forced herself to calm down, even though her body was screaming in pain. Her lungs felt like they were rupturing, and her calf was knotted in a muscle cramp. Every part of her hurt, and this time it seemed almost more than she could bear. Worst of all, though, was Ross sitting beside her on the bed in his t-shirt and boxer shorts, staring at her with uncertainty and concern. Deep humiliation dug at her and she looked away.

The bag smelled greasy from the antiseptic gel that had leaked onto the paper, and it also had a stringent odor from the discarded, bloody towelettes that had been stuffed inside. The first-aid smell overwhelmed her with memories of a disinfected room and a t.v. monitor displaying the dead face of her mother. She gagged. A few seconds later Meg discarded the bag, heading for the bathroom, her progress slowed by the cramped calf muscle. She slammed the door, going to the toilet and throwing up.

Eventually she was able to rest her head against the seat, feeling fairly sure there would be no more heaves. The vomiting had subsided, but her humiliation and shame clung to her like a fetid odor. She wanted to die. Eventually she stood, feeling shaky. She flushed the toilet and stared longingly at the shower. It was part of her ritual, after the nightmare, to stand beneath the sharp spray of hot water until the misery had faded. Glancing at the door she saw there was no lock. She felt uncomfortable at the thought of showering with Ross in the other room. Besides, she no doubt owed him an explanation, if he were still there. She wouldn't blame him if he thought this was all too weird to deal with and just took off.

Slowly Meg opened the door and saw Ross standing by the sink. He handed her a damp washcloth which she accepted, pressing it to her mouth.

"You okay?"

"I'm fine."

"Better come sit down."

She followed him into the main area, limping over to the bed. Why didn't he just take off, exiting her life the way everyone else had? It would save her a lot of humiliation, knowing she'd never have to see him again.

"What's wrong with your leg?"

"It's got a cramp."

He came and sat down beside her on the bed, the mattress squeaking under his weight. "Let me see," he said, reaching for her leg and bending it at the knee. His fingers felt the knotted muscle. "That's a bad one. Here, I think I can help."

He set her leg out straight, then grabbed her foot and pulled it forward, stretching the calf muscle. At first it hurt worse, but eventually the pain ebbed. Ross released her foot, then had her bend her knee up again. He massaged her calf with slow, circular motions, kneading the taut muscle.

"When my dad was in the hospital, he used to get cramps because his nervous system was so messed up by the sarcoidosis. It kind of made everything on him go haywire. I got to be pretty good at this." He looked at her face which was still white. "Want to tell me about it?"

Meg slowly shook her head, then looked away. "I don't want to tell you, but guess I owe you an explanation, since I woke you up." She waited, hoping he would make the polite statement about her owing him nothing. He didn't, though, and she bit her lip until it hurt.

"I'll help you along," he offered. "I already figured that Shannon and Parker had a reason for helping you, so there must be something ugly in your past. Remember, I saw your reaction at the geranium stall, though I don't know how that ties in. Anyway, that's why you want to find them, so they can finish what they were doing, which is also why you're willing to join forces with me, so to speak. I also know that both your parents are dead. You slipped up and told Shirley at Signet about that, even though your personnel file said your mother lives in Denver, which was probably your CSS pre-decided excuse for exiting Signet when the time came. And I figure something pretty bad happened to you when you were fifteen or sixteen, because your photo album, which I found while searching your closet, didn't have any pictures of you in it after that age, except for your senior picture. My guess is that your sister, Robyn, was murdered, because when you flipped out and attacked Alan you accused him of killing your sister. Am I right on any of this?"

Meg stared at him, both awed and annoyed by his deductive reasoning. It was hard not to be impressed, though at the same time her sense of privacy was shrinking at an alarming rate.

"Yes, you're right. I've lost some people close to me, and it's been difficult. When I was six my father was electrocuted. That left three of us. There was me, my mom, and my older sister Robyn, who was Deaf. I also had two best friends, Stacey and Claire, who lived next door. When I was eleven, they were killed when their house caught on fire. I saw them through their bedroom window, dying in the flames. Their dad died, too. Their mother went to prison for setting the fire to collect life insurance."

His expression showed he was appalled, but she didn't want to stop and encourage his comments. She swallowed hard and hurried on, anxious to finish the explanation. "When I was sixteen, Mama and I came home from shopping. We had been buying decorations for Robyn's graduation party. While we were gone, someone broke in and attacked her. Robyn was raped and murdered. I found her body."

Ross slowly shook his head, speechless, and Meg continued. "She had struggled with the attacker, and a potted geranium was knocked over on the floor. The geraniums at the market triggered a flashback, which is what you saw happen. After Robyn died it left just the two of us, Mama and me. When I was twenty-one, Mama decided she couldn't go on. I found out later that she wouldn't use the insulin her doctor prescribed. She was driving home one night and went into a diabetic coma. The car rolled and she died. I had to identify her body."

"I'm so sorry," he said, the words inadequate but his expression telling volumes.

"My past hasn't been any worse than yours," Meg stated.

"I don't agree. For one thing, I had Shannon to help me cope with losing my parents. You got a taste of what that was like yesterday when she and Parker started working with you. As for losing Shannon, that's been miserable, but it's also been survivable and I've learned a lot along the way. Besides, I knew she was alive and at least getting by because of the postcards."

Meg stared down at her hands lying idle on the sheet. "You know, when I was going to college in Ellensburg, I met this woman who had been molested by her father. She told me a lot about it. That seems way worse than what I've been through. And there are people who have survived wars and concentration camps, what about them?"

"It's not fair to compare. We all suffer at our own levels."

She sighed. "To be honest, I'm ashamed. And angry at myself for being such a baby."

"You've got to be kidding," Ross said. He was staring at her, his dark eyebrows moving downward with concern. "You systematically watched everyone you loved get cut away from you, just like a big carving knife slicing off pieces of your life. Not only that, but if I caught your ages right when you talked about it, I think those events happened every five years. That seems like a pretty hellish joke."

Meg stared off into the distance, as if there were more to the dimly lit room than four walls and a set of cheap furniture. "Yes, that's true. Last night, when Alan attacked me, I thought it was time for another terrible thing to happen. I thought he was going to rape and kill me, just like some sick creep had done to my sister ten years ago. For the first time in my life I thought it was a good thing my mother was dead. I've missed her so much because we were friends and did stuff together all the time, and I loved being with her. But last night I remember thinking it was good she was gone, so she wouldn't have to suffer through losing me, too." Her voice paused, and she drew her attention back to Ross. "Somehow the disaster got diverted, though. It was like having a two-ton train barreling down on me, and suddenly it was derailed. I owe that to you."

"Glad to be of service," he said with a quirky half-smile, continuing to massage her leg.

They were both quiet for a few seconds, then she slowly pulled away from his touch and flipped the sheet over her bare legs. "My calf doesn't hurt now. Thanks for doing that. I'm sorry I woke you up."

"Do you have these nightmares often?"

"No, not too much. Mostly when I'm under stress."

He slowly nodded. "I would say that the last few hours would count as high stress."

"I haven't been bothered by the dreams for maybe two or three months, except for having one a week ago last Friday."

Ross thought back through the week. "Your birthday," he slowly stated. "Yeah, I could see how that would do it. You turned twenty-six, which means it's been five years since the last awful thing happened to you."

"How do you keep doing that?" she asked, puzzled. "What are you, a fortune teller?"

"Your photo album, remember? I saw your baby picture, with your birth date written underneath. At the time I realized you'd just had a birthday, and that it had been on the day you were at Signet when I first saw you at that meeting. You were a beautiful baby, by the way."

Meg's puzzled expression cleared and she smiled. "Thank you."

"You're still beautiful."

Her smile faded and she ran her hands self-consciously along the sheet. "No I'm not."

"Yes you are," he quietly replied, lowering his head a little to maintain eye contact with her now that she had dropped her chin. "Don't you know that, Meg? In fact, I'd say you are drop-dead gorgeous. I won't push the issue, since you're uncomfortable with it. I'm guessing that after what happened to Robyn you didn't think being pretty was safe. And after what that slimy jerk, Alan, did to you last night, it might be impossible for you to feel safe again. All I'm saying is there's nothing wrong with you being a beautiful woman, and with me noticing it."

He decided to quit there, not wanting to mention what it had been like for him to massage her calf while trying to ignore her long, bare legs. "Are you going to be able to go back to sleep? We have a couple more hours before checkout."

"I think so," she said, feeling more relaxed than she would have thought possible, all things considered. He doused the light and climbed back into his own bed.

Meg lay down and pulled up the covers. "Ross?" she said into the darkness.

"What?"

"Do you think we'll find them?"

He was quiet for a while. "I don't know. I'm hoping so."

"Me too. For a couple of minutes yesterday I felt what it might be like to be normal. I'd like a shot at that."

"I don't blame you, Meg. We'll do everything we can to find them."

She closed her eyes, a sudden sting of tears brought on not by sadness, but by hope.

* * *

At nine o'clock on Monday Morning, Daniel Trenery showed up at Signet with an NSA team and a search warrant. Willis Dent stood helplessly by while two computer specialists began work on his system. He felt outraged and coldly furious. He also felt sick with dread.

"While they're busy with that, why don't you and I have a little talk," Trenery said, guiding Dent towards the conference room next to his office.

The president of Signet glanced across the corporate floor, seeing two uniformed officers standing at the elevators. He also noted the frightened gaze of Beverly, his secretary. His own stomach tightened into a knot of nerves as they entered the room which seemed suddenly confining. Dent unconsciously clenched and unclenched his jaw.

"I'm not saying anything until my lawyer arrives," he icily commented.

"No problem," the NSA agent calmly responded. "I'm not expecting you to say anything. I'll do the talking. Have a seat, Mr. Dent."

Willis complied and Trenery shut the door before sitting down. The NSA agent studied the executive's defensive posture, and how his eyes scanned the room like those of a nervous ferret. Dent felt trapped, which was a positive thing as far as Trenery was concerned. No doubt his mind was running in ninety-mile-an-hour circles. He might have been able to stay unflustered if this had been a visit from the police, or even the FBI, but Trenery knew there was just enough of the unknown about the NSA that Willis Dent had to be seriously worried. He opted to play on that factor.

"My agency is concerned with the security of our nation, Mr. Dent. It's our job to keep our country safe from certain things that might be a threat. We work under the Department of Defense by direct order of the president, and our directive is to make sure that our government stays safe. We are willing to go to extraordinary lengths to be certain of that. So of course you can understand how something like the Kronek codes would be a definite threat to the security of our country."

Dent's face grew even more pale, if that were possible, and his eyes bulged, though to his credit he was able to keep his lips tightly clamped together. Trenery displayed a small, mirthless smile. "You know, right now it's just you and me having a talk about those codes. I'm more than willing to keep this conversation down to the two of us, and to see if we can take care of it. Soon, though, this will be out of my hands, and into those of the Director of Central Intelligence. If it goes there, we're looking at intelligence priorities that make this fall under attempted treason against the United States."

"You're crazy!" Dent blurted, a sudden flush of color creeping up his neck and infusing his pale face.

Trenery watched the executive's complexion change from pasty white to crimson during the course of a minute. He kept his own expression calm, hiding the satisfaction he felt at the visual evidence of Dent's guilt.

"I'd like to help you while this is still in my hands," Trenery explained. "We only have a relatively short time before it moves upstairs, and then there's nothing I can do."

"You don't have proof of anything against me," Dent retorted.

"Of course we do. Why do you think we're here?" Trenery's voice was solid, and the truth of what he said was obvious in his clipped words. The audio tape from last night was proof enough to him that Signet had the codes. Unfortunately, that was all he knew.

"What do you want?" Dent finally managed, his voice sounding hoarse because his throat was now tightly constricted.

"We want all your copies of the Kronek codes, and we want to know who you've sold any other copies to. We need to know what other countries or agencies might have them, that sort of thing. We also want to know which of your employees were involved in searching for Margaret Wilson, and we want to interview them. That's all. Just a couple of easy things. You let us have the codes and information, and we can probably wipe the slate clean. If not, then I can assure you treason charges will be brought against you."

"I haven't done anything wrong! I came by those codes legally when I purchased Kronek's company!"

Trenery stared at him, his eyes taking on the same expression of superior intolerance he had learned from his years of serving as a commander in the military. He meant the gaze to be intimidating, even though inwardly he was triumphant at Willis Dent's admission of ownership of the codes. "Maybe you'd better wait for your lawyer to get here before we talk further." He stood and headed for the door.

"Wait!"

Trenery saw Dent's tongue flick across dry lips. The guy's mouth probably felt like the Sahara. He decided to take on the role of empathizer, and see if it got him any further. Going to the door, he signaled his assistant through the glass.

Jake opened the door a crack. "Yes boss?"

"Could you bring us some water?"

"Sure thing."

Jake closed the door and Trenery returned to the table. He sat down, staring at the man who had been arrogantly aloof and angry at the beginning of the conversation, but who now looked whipped. "We have about another half-hour or so until my team is finished with your files and computers. Once we coordinate with the team at your house and learn what they've found, then it's out of my hands."

Willis Dent's mind was spinning. They were at his house, too? "You have no right..." he croaked, his voice disappearing as his throat tightened further. They were the government, and the government had more rights than anybody. He knew they wouldn't find the codes on his computer, but were there other pieces of evidence he had carelessly left behind, such as those which had involved getting rid of Phil Black? And would they find further information in his files about his search for Margaret Wilson? How the hell did she figure into all of this, anyway? And what would happen if they found the safe in his den and broke into it? These weren't local cops, or even the FBI. These were the big guys in charge of national security, just like this agent Trenery had explained, and they might very well have the technology to easily find and get into his safe. If they did, then they'd have their hands on the CD full of codes, which meant definite proof they were in his possession. After that, there would be nothing to bargain with. He tried to think through it all, but his normally organized thoughts were in a jumble. It had never occurred to him that the government would want the codes. He didn't know that much about them himself, but clearly they were even more important than he had originally thought. Somehow the government had also gotten the information that he had taken possession of them, and now they wanted to take them from him. Dent managed to control his outrage because a stronger sense of survival had kicked in.

Where was his stinking lawyer? Two-hundred bucks an hour, and the guy couldn't even get off his duff and get over here in a crisis! "I want immunity," he finally managed, his mouth so dry that his lips stuck to his teeth.

The NSA agent thoughtfully stared at him as if weighing possibilities. After what seemed like an agonizing thirty seconds to Dent he said, "I'll see what I can do."

*   *   *

The jewelry store clerk stood at the counter, his limp hands on top of the glass display case. His eyes stared sightlessly ahead, as if there were nothing but a blank, endless horizon stretching before him. He was no longer aware of the young man dressed in jeans and an imported silk shirt who stood in front of him looking through the assortment of exclusive watches recently removed from the display case.

Benny picked up a thirty-five hundred dollar Buliva Acutron with a fourteen-carat gold case and band. The clerk had just been explaining that it was the store's top-of-the-line watch, with a twenty-five year guarantee. Now, however, the clerk wasn't explaining anything. Instead he was just staring off into space, as was the woman sitting behind the counter with her jeweler's tool still in hand. The young man slid the watch on and admired the way it looked.

"I think it's definitely me," he said out loud. "I'll take it. Don't bother to wrap it, since I think I'd like to wear it home. No thanks, I don't need a receipt."

He chuckled, then walked out of the store. He headed down the street, away from the exclusive jewelry shop with its fashion-dressed clerks and high prices, whistling tunelessly to himself. Prices never bothered Benny since he was not only rich, but could take whatever he wanted. Another block further and he felt the mental hold on the occupants in the store begin to falter. He held on a few minutes more, even though it gave him a headache. He didn't do it because he felt afraid they might catch him. That was never a fear. Instead he preferred to do it to test himself, to see how much further he could stretch the control before it finally gave way.

A couple of seconds later it snapped like a rubber band stretched to the limit. He was disconnected from those weaklings at the store. Smiling to himself, he brushed away the trickle of sweat that had formed at his temple despite the cool air. Afterwards he felt pleasantly revived, the way someone else might feel after a physical workout. He arrived at the prearranged restaurant and sat down at an outdoor table, then ordered a large meal, sensuously enjoying each bite. He took time, now and then, to admire his new watch.

Benny was gifted. That's how he thought of himself. Above others, and gifted. There was a bitter edge to his talents, however. He regretted being unable to do more with his mind. It was true he had a marvelous ability, though. He could go inside someone's head and cloud their thoughts, just block their thinking the way a lead panel blocks x-rays. He had always used his ability to get whatever he wanted, even when he was young. His parents had never been happy with his gift, though, especially his old man. Even after all these years, Benny still felt anger when he thought of the mean jerk who had been his father. Duane had never really liked him, and that had come to a head one day when Benny was thirteen.

He could still remember overhearing the fight. Duane was angry with Benny's mom, Teri. "I tell you, he's not my son," the man's voice seemed to echo from the past. "I don't know what that damned doctor did, but that kid isn't mine. He doesn't look like me, or act like me, and sometimes he gives me the creeps."

"How can you say that?" his mom had cried. "He's your son!"

"No," Duane had coldly stated. "He's not."

Benny had felt the hurt as if it were a knife, and the hole it cut in him oozed out anger. Duane had walked into the livingroom and paused, seeing his son. They had stared at each other for a few seconds, and in those seconds Duane had sealed his fate. If he had said he was sorry, or even given a look of embarrassment at being overheard, then Benny wouldn't have been forced to do what he had done. But Duane did neither of those things, only stared down at his scrawny teenage son with disgust before heading out the door.

The anger had become a flood, and Benny had gone to the window and watched his father drive away in his sporty new Fiat. The anger had been too much, and so Benny had sent a cloud into Duane's mind as he turned onto the freeway. He hadn't been as good with the gift back then. The threads were tenuous, but he had still been able to do it. Duane had entered the freeway and unknowingly driven his sports car under the wheels of a semi. Benny had allowed consciousness to return to his father a few seconds before impact, just so Duane would know he was going to die and that there was nothing he could do about it.

At the memory of that day, Benny felt both vindicated and sad. He didn't grieve for Duane. How could you feel sorry about a cold fish like that dying? The reason he felt sad was because of the changes that had followed Duane's death. His mother had never looked at him the same way after that, and some of the time she had looked scared. He didn't get rid of Teri the way he had his father because, after all, she was his mother. But neither could he stand being around such a pitiful mouse of a person. Eventually he left, using his gift in so many ways that he had even surprised himself. He found that stealing was a snap. Fighting was fun, too, especially if he started a row with some kind of gang member. It was hilarious to let them throw the first punch, then make them stand there frozen while he turned them into mince meat.

In those out-of-control teenage years, Benny had tried his hand at practically every illegal thing, including rape and various forms of murder. Unfortunately, his spree had come to a halt when Oscar and Felix had intervened. Those weren't their real names, of course, but were the names he knew them by. They had managed to get him locked in a cell which had scared him to death, though at the time he had only been a fifteen-year-old kid and was more easily intimidated than he was now. Eventually they had let him out, after setting down some guidelines and promising that next time he wouldn't get put in a cell, but would get a sniper's bullet through the brain. Other than those first unsettling days, it had turned into a fairly good working arrangement. He could pretty much do whatever he wanted, as long as he kept a low profile and went on jobs for them when they needed him. They paid him well for going on those "walks" as they called them, and his bank account was almost a million bucks now. Not only that, but he got to travel all over the world and go into high-security places no one else ever got a chance to.

Life was a kick for Benny, except for one thing. It really bugged him that he couldn't do more. He dreamed of reading people's minds instead of just clouding them, and of being able to make them into human puppets, doing whatever he willed them to. If he could have done those things, then Oscar and his brown nose, Felix, would never have been able to put him in a cell in the first place. But that wasn't the case.

Sometimes Benny's dreams of doing more filled him with longing. At different times he thought about the others out there, like himself, who could do more, and who might make him obsolete and no longer of use to Oscar. He dreaded the day that might happen, and wished he could find carloads of the others driving down *the freeway. Then he would cloud their minds and get rid of them the way he'd gotten rid of Duane. Benny wasn't quite sure if such a thing were possible, though. The minds of his detested siblings, as he thought of them, might be impenetrable. He worried about that.*

A man came to the table and sat down opposite Benny. He had attractive features marred by a scar running lengthwise through his eyebrow. "Hi, Ben," he said.

The younger man barely glanced up. "Felix," he verbally acknowledged. "Like my watch? It's fourteen carat gold."

"Nice. How much?"

"More than you can afford on your salary. Too bad you don't have the ability to go shopping for great bargains the way I do." Benny snickered at his own cleverness. "So what's up, Felix?"

"Remember the walk you took last week? We need to go back there again."

"To the CSS office?"

"Yeah."

"Didn't you get what you were looking for the first time?"

"Guess not."

"Okay. Well, you're paying the fare, so I don't care if we go there again or not, though it was a little boring. You government types are no challenge when it comes to brain power. Just let me finish this steak first, okay?"

Felix nodded and leaned back in his chair, studying the man with pale eyes who was only a few years younger than himself. Although Benny might have wished he could read minds, Felix was glad Benny's telepathic talents were limited to keeping people distracted. If Benny could have read his mind, he would have learned that Felix thought of him as a complete loser with an underdeveloped personality and no social skills. Felix thought Benny was also a classic sociopath with no true sense of loyalty to anybody. The guy didn't have a family, a girlfriend, or friends in general. He took whatever he wanted, and Felix despised him for it. He hoped the time might come when they could persuade some of the others to join their ranks, and at that point he would happily see that Benny was gotten rid of.

Chapter 14

Check-out time at the Wagon Wheel Inn was noon. Ross and Meg left the motel shortly after eleven and drove to a nearby grocery store where they picked up bananas, bear claws, and a carton of juice. Next they stopped at an ATM and each of them drew out a couple of hundred dollars.

"Do you think we're being paranoid?" Meg asked, stuffing the crisp twenties into her wallet and climbing back into the car.

"Yes. But those guys last night were spooky."

"The first or second set?" she asked, peeling a banana.

"Both," Ross answered. He poured two cups of juice. "The second set are the ones who might be tied into the government, though, and I'm not sure what their tracking abilities are. I'm guessing they wouldn't have any trouble picking up a credit card trail, so we might be smart to act a little bit paranoid."

"Not a problem for me," she said, taking a bite of banana and accepting the cup of orange juice he handed her. "I've been just left of paranoid for years."

Ross chuckled and opened the package of pastries, picking up a bear claw and taking a bite as he started the engine. He pulled out into the street and headed west. "You seem more optimistic this morning."

Meg looked up at the sky which had cleared. It was a pristine blue decorated with wispy clouds. The city looked clean from the heavy rains, and the air smelled sweet. "There's nowhere to go but up, is there?"

After the previous day and night, and all it had entailed, the world looked good to her this morning. The sunlight lent itself to a false sense of safety, as if dangerous events could only happen in the dark. Not only that, but she was well aware of having escaped another tragedy, and hope of continued survival went a long ways towards lifting her spirits. Physically she wasn't doing great, though. She hurt in a dozen places, and muscles that had been strained during her fight with Alan Scorzato were making their aches known. Her neck and back were stiff, the cut on her arm tender, and her calf still sore from the previous night's cramp. For a moment she had a quick memory of Ross sitting beside her on the bed, his large, warm hands gently kneading her calf. Meg turned her mind to other things.

"Where are we going?" she asked, noting he was heading the car into the heart of Salem.

"The business section downtown. I want to find a parking garage with a lot of cars. If we can find another blue Buick, it would be a good idea to switch the license plates. Those men at the house last night got a good look at this car and the license. If they're serious about finding us then that's the first thing they'll use. They'll already have my name from DMV by now, but we'll be harder to track with a different set of plates."

"You're good at this. Have you been on the run before?"

"First time. I'm usually on the other end of things. To be honest, I prefer to be the one doing the tracking instead of the one doing the running."

To Ross' frustration, it took them almost an hour of searching through parking lots and garages before they found a similar car with Oregon plates. It was on the fourth level of a hospital parking garage, and Meg kept watch while Ross switched the plates. She was nervous and wanted to just take them before someone came back, but he explained that if he did that, the car owner would report them stolen. They had a better chance of going unnoticed if they just switched the plates.

Once this was accomplished, they left the garage and headed for the interstate. Fifteen minutes later they were on their way to California.

*   *   *

Alan Scorzato was having a rotten day. The doctor who had examined and taped his nose during the early morning hours hadn't been optimistic. He had talked about long-term problems with the septum and a possible surgery. His nose was still swollen and throbbing, despite the painkillers, and he also had two black eyes already forming. These physical problems were the least of his worries at the moment, though.

Currently he was sitting in a chair in one of the conference rooms at Signet while two federal agents stood staring down at him as if he were a worm. The underarm areas of his shirt were soaked, displaying two large circles of sweat, and beads of perspiration ran down his neck.

"I don't know what you're talking about," he protested again. "I'm telling you, I never stepped foot in her place. This happened in a bar fight last night," he said, indicating his face.

Daniel Trenery stared down at Scorzato with distaste. It was obvious he was the kind of self-serving and morally weak man most people automatically disliked; added to that was the knowledge that he had attempted to rape Meg Parrish last night, with possible plans for murdering her, too. The guy had been protesting his innocence for ten minutes, stubbornly stupid in his refusal to admit anything. They had been playing him along, letting him set up elaborate lies he couldn't keep track of.

"Who broke your nose?"

"For the tenth time, some jerk at a bar."

"Which bar?"

"I don't remember."

"That's because you were never in a bar last night. You don't know which one, and you don't have any eyewitnesses, either, because there weren't any. At least not any you want us to contact. The game-playing is over, Alan. It's time for you to tell us the truth. We know you were in Meg Parrish's apartment last night, and that you tried to rape and kill her. We also know someone stopped you. Who was it?"

Before he could protest further, Jake Cornel brought over a tape recorder and set it on the table. He pressed the play button and Alan heard his own voice making sexual comments. A minute later he heard the ensuing scuffle with Ross Ecklund, and then his own voice high-pitched and screaming about his nose being broken. Alan's mouth plopped open like a fish caught on a line. They let it play for another half-minute before shutting it off. He stared at the recorder as if it were a spaceship from Mars, trying to fathom how it had come to contain his voice. He tried to say something, to find a few words of protest, but nothing came out. His face had grown bright red, his cheeks and the top of his head crimson against his carrot-hued hairline and goatee. The black and purple discoloration around his sockets stood out even more, in dark contrast to the rest of his coloring.

Daniel Trenery leaned forward, resting his hands on the table and staring down at Alan with distaste. "We know you were there, and what you were trying to do. It's all on this tape, every last bit of it. If you'd gone through with it, we'd no doubt be arresting you for rape and murder instead of only attempted rape."

"Where'd you get that?" Scorzato finally managed, unable to fathom why a tape had been running, recording the incident in the first place.

"Don't you think the important question really is how this will affect your future, Alan? Everything you did is right here on this cassette."

Trenery doubted the guy was together enough to remember that his name hadn't been spoken aloud on the tape. They had figured out who he was strictly because of the broken nose. It had made him easy to pick out.

Overall, Trenery felt good about how things were going. Willis Dent had crumpled. He had agreed to hand over both copies of the codes, and after an hour of grilling was able to convince them he hadn't sold copies of the codes to anyone. He had been pathetic in his reassurances that he'd wanted to study them first, and learn more about them. He had even been in the process of hiring a scientific team to look them over, and had the hiring profiles sent up from personnel. Trenery was pleased about the containment and the further imminent possession of the codes. The third copy was either with Scorzato or Meg Parrish. It hadn't been clear on the tape as to who had it, though he was guessing it was with Meg. Regardless, he knew it was only a matter of time until he got his hands on that one, too.

Dent had agreed to hand over any paper files involved with the codes, including the copies of those which CSS agent Phil Allred had managed to take. They hadn't been able to find more of a tie-in there, and of course Dent was adamant that he'd had nothing to do with the hit-and-run which had almost taken the agent's life, so that was a disappointment. Other than that, the situation had worked out well. By the end, Dent was submissive and fully cooperative. He gave them the personnel list of his security staff, most of whom were currently being interviewed. Of those, Alan Scorzato had been their biggest find so far.

Although they wouldn't hold him long after this initial interview, Trenery reflected that there had been two different blood types found at the crime scene. He was positive one of them belonged to Scorzato. When Meg showed up, they would encourage her to press charges. For now, though, he was more concerned with getting the CD with the codes on it.

"We know you're the one who was in her apartment," Trenery stated. "And we know you took the codes from her."

"I didn't take the CD," Scorzato protested, wiping at the sweat on his forehead with the back of his hand. "It got left there. I swear it! I just wanted to get out of there."

Trenery turned away from him, his feigned posture one of disbelieving. Even though he knew the guy was probably telling the truth for the first time this morning, it was important that Alan feel the need to convince them. "You take care of him," he said to Jake. "I've got some calls to make."

After another glare of disgust at Meg's assailant, Trenery left the room, allowing Jake to play the sympathizer. Thirty minutes later they had as much information as Alan Scorzato could give them, including the identity of the man who had rescued Meg and taken her on the run. His name was Ross Ecklund.

* * *

The man with hawk-like features sat at his desk, sorting through the information he had recently gathered. It wasn't much help, he reflected, closing the folder with irritation. His real name was Ed Gless, though he had gone by several fake names during the past week. Yesterday he had posed as Agent Warner of the FBI. This morning he'd been called Oscar by their telepathic contact, Benny, when they'd gone to the CSS office. He got tired of switching identities, but also realized Benny was one person he definitely didn't want to know his real name.

Ed's assistant, Paul Espinosa, known as Felix to Benny, had also gone with them to the CSS office. It had been a nearly fruitless expedition. The satellite director, Richard Hammond, hadn't been there, and in fact the office had been fairly empty, which had made it easy for Benny. Despite this, they had come away with little information. Hammond's pertinent data was probably now secreted away somewhere, which meant he was being cautious because of the last time Benny had helped them investigate the CSS office. The only thing they had found was a memo which substantiated that Meg Parrish was more involved with Parker Briggs than they had previously suspected. Her name had now moved up on Ed's list from that of a possible lead to a probable one. His agents had seen her at the Brigg's house last night, and this morning Paul had learned that someone had discovered and removed the wiretap he had arranged to have set up at her apartment. Since he and Paul hadn't found out much more than what they already knew, and they were now facing a series of dead-ends, Meg Parrish became their main focus in the ongoing investigation.

Paul came into Ed's office and sat down. He handed his boss a blowup of a DMV photo, retrieved via the license plate number of the car spotted in front of the Briggs' house last night. "The guy's name is Ross Ecklund. He works as a security specialist for the Signet Corporation, a software engineering firm."

"What's he doing with the woman?"

"I don't know. Maybe he's a boyfriend or something. Harrington was checking out their personal credit histories and other information on the computer, including detailed financial records. He was using our special tap into the ATM traffic lines, and learned that about a half-hour ago they both hit the same machine in Salem."

"They're going south, it looks like. We'd better get on it."

"One of our units is already on the way," Paul said, then paused. "It might be nothing, you know. They might just be going on a trip together or something."

"They were at Briggs' house last night, weren't they, and had a run-in with our men? I think they're running scared, and now they've left Portland and stopped to get cash. Maybe Meg Parrish is tied into the ones we're looking for after all. What if my first guess was right, and she's actually one of them?"

Paul was thoughtful. "She didn't get away from the car like the others did. She's an undercover agent for CSS, that's all. I don't think there's more to it than that."

Ed slowly shook his head. "Benny couldn't get away when we had him. Some of the others might not be able to, either. Maybe we're missing something here. If she's really an agent for CSS, and the material we got from their office today makes it look that way, then perhaps she's going to continue working undercover on this case, which means Hammond knows a whole lot more than we do. If she's not, then maybe there's some different kind of tie in. Until we get a better lead, I'd say she's the one we've got to follow."

"I agree with you. We'll track her down and see if she'll lead us to them. My guess is that she will."

"I hope so," Ed said. "If not, I'm going to be really pissed."

*   *   *

Meg studied the map of California that had been in the car's glove box. It looked like they would get to Benicia in a few hours. She folded the map and put it away, gazing at Ross's profile which was etched by a bead of sunlight. He was more attractive than she had originally thought when seeing him for the first time at the Signet meeting. Not that his features were more handsome than she had originally assessed, but rather that his personality went a long ways to enhance them. He had a strong, likeable personality and she found it hard to believe he was single. She was trying to get up the courage to ask him the question that had been at the back of her mind for a while now. When he looked her way and smiled, it gave her the momentum she needed.

"You're not married, are you Ross?"

He raised his eyebrows at the query and then shook his head. "Divorced."

"That's too bad."

"Actually, it was probably for the best since I was young and brainless at the time."

"High school sweethearts?"

"No, but almost." Ross was inwardly pleased that Meg was interested enough to ask. "I met Kristen when we were both sophomores at UCLA. She was passionately studying archeology, and I decided to passionately study her. We were crazy about each other at first, but the relationship was doomed."

"Why?"

"It was pretty much based on hormones and not much else. We didn't have a whole lot in common, and it was a stormy first year of marriage. Then Mom died and Shannon disappeared. Kristen was sympathetic at first, but she was also very involved in her studies. I was suffering and needed more comforting than she wanted to give, or at least it seemed that way. I've since read that a lot of marriages break up when there's a tragedy, because the one hurting the most isn't getting what they need from their partner. I'm explaining this because a lot of time has passed, and I don't have any grudges against Kristen."

"That's good."

"Yeah, well, time is supposed to be the great healer. I don't know if that's true, but it was hard for me to maintain resentment after a couple of years. Just never saw the value in it. At the time, though, it hurt. Our relationship was already strained before the accident. Then the more involved I got in looking for Shannon, the less Kristen understood it. She was appalled when I dropped out my senior year and didn't graduate with her, since that was everything to her. She couldn't understand why I couldn't get over losing Mom and Shannon, and why I just didn't get on with my life instead of looking for my kid sister. And I couldn't understand what the big deal was about her sitting in the dirt patiently removing dust with a brush, just to find some broken pieces of pottery belonging to a dead civilization. I said that once and she flew off the handle," he grinned.

"Anyway, I went searching for Shannon, and Kristen went on a graduate expedition to Guatemala to study pre-Columbian societies. While I was following leads on my sister's disappearance, she was enduring hot jungle nights and apparently couldn't resist the charm of her team leader, who had also been her professor. They've been married for several years now, and travel all over the world together digging up the past."

"Does it bother you?"

"Nope. Kristen and I didn't want the same things, anyway, so there wouldn't have been much hope for our marriage. I wanted a family—a house with kids and pets, stuff like that. She didn't. Guess I was pretty stupid not to bring up that kind of thing until after we were married and it was too late, but like I said, our relationship was very hormone-based and we were young."

"You never found anyone else?"

"Came close a couple of times, but no. I was really busy with work, and following leads, and somehow the time slipped by and here I am, thirty-two and still no house filled with kids and pets, and no kid sister, either. Kristen was probably right. I should have just learned to get over it and get on with my life. What about you? Ever married?"

"No, never even came close."

"Why not?"

"No one was interested, I guess."

"Sorry, Meg, try again. I'm not buying that."

She stared at him in surprise. "Don't be rude."

Ross chuckled. "I'm not. Let's be honest. Wherever you go, guys must follow you around with their tongues hanging out."

"That's not true," she said, feeling a flush of embarrassment. She preferred asking the questions far more than she did answering them.

"What about work? No guys at work interested in you?"

"Actually, when I first came to CSS, a lot of the other cryptographers didn't even like me, especially the mathematicians. Some of them started calling me 'teacher's pet' because my boss made a big deal out of some of the codes I broke, and a few more that I put together. I wasn't surprised when no one exactly asked me to go with them to the Christmas party, you know."

"Huh...I get it. You showed up with your gift for codes and knocked them out of the water. Their brainiac egos could have handled it if you'd been mousy, with coke-bottle glasses or a massive over-bite, but it wasn't that way. Adding insult to injury was the fact that you're also gorgeous, and the kind of woman that's always scaring those nerd types to death. I'd say it wasn't very fun for any of you. They were intimidated by you, and you were rebuffed by them, through no fault of your own, I might add. Okay, so if that eliminates work, what about your social life? There had to be other guys who didn't care if you were smarter than them, and who were anxious for a relationship with you."

"Maybe I'm the one who's not interested in a relationship."

"Really? Why not?"

Meg sighed, looking out the window at the trees and scrub grass rushing past. "I guess I just got tired of losing everybody I ever loved. I got tired of feeling bad because my family and friends kept dying. Eventually you get to the point where being alone seems like the safest way to live."

"Don't you get lonely?" he asked, his voice softer now, and empathetic.

She felt a quick sting of tears and blinked hard. What was wrong with her? Why was she feeling overwhelmed by emotions during a simple conversation? "Can we talk about something else for a while?"

"Sure. What do you want to talk about?"

"How about if you tell me more about Shannon. Last night you said that you got some information which brought you to Portland looking for her, but it ended up being a dead end. Can you tell me about that?"

"Sure, but let's pull into this rest stop first and stretch our legs."

Ross guided the car off the freeway and drove into the area marked for cars. They got out and used the restrooms, then walked around for a while. The cool breeze felt good on Meg's face and she stretched her arms out in front of her, still feeling stiff from yesterday's fight. She thought about how much her life had changed in the past twenty-four hours, in awe not only of all the experiences she had been through, but also by how quickly Ross had been able to establish a rapport with her. A few days ago she could never have envisioned having any sort of conversation with a man like him, and yet during this morning's drive she had been sharing confidences and actually felt fairly comfortable doing so.

Meg concluded that although Parker and Shannon's healing endeavors had been incomplete, they had still alleviated a portion of the pain which had kept her isolated for such a long time. This new step towards emotional freedom was both exhilarating and a little bit scary. She watched Ross buy two cans of pop from the overpriced coke machine before heading back to the car. She joined him and soon they were on their way again.

"Where were we?" Meg quizzed.

"You wanted to know about the lead that brought me to Oregon," he reminded, opening one of the cans and taking a sip. "It started about a year-and-a-half ago. I was still living in San Jose and working for an investigative firm that handled corporate background searches, that kind of thing. In my spare time I ran a little moonlighting business that helped people look for missing persons. I stuck with personal situations so it wouldn't be in conflict with the company I worked for." He paused and took another sip.

"Anyway, I was approached by this lady named Yvonne Dillard. Her only daughter, and her son-in-law, had been killed in a car wreck two months before. Their little boy, her grandson Evan, had disappeared from the scene. He was only eight at the time."

"She must have been frantic."

"Actually, she had a pretty good handle on it. Yvonne is a neat lady and I've come to know her well. At the time she felt certain that Evan was okay. Not only had Yvonne gotten a hand-written note from him in the mail, but he'd been sending her thought messages to let her know he was safe. She'd been afraid to tell the police this last part, because they would have thought she was nuts, but she and I ended up with a pretty good rapport right off the bat because of our similar case histories."

"He was telepathic, like Shannon?" Meg asked, intrigued.

"I'm sure of it. Yvonne and I spent a lot of time comparing notes, and I ended up knowing quite a bit about Evan and his parents. He was Yvonne's only grandchild. His parents had tried for quite a while to have a baby, and had been thrilled when he was finally born. From the age of two, though, he had started to behave differently. Not in a bad way, or anything. He was like Shannon, only with a lot stronger abilities, or at least I'm guessing so, because he was able to mentally contact his grandma from far away."

"What do you think happened to him?"

"My theory is way out on a limb, but I'm still standing by it because my gut instinct says it's right. Yvonne and I believe the same people who were after Shannon were also after Evan. We didn't come to this conclusion at first, but after we learned more it seemed to make sense. Remember that Evan had been contacting his grandma telepathically? He let her know that he was with others who were like himself. They had managed to get him away from the accident before the men looking for him moved in. According to Evan, the others he was with were good people and he was safe with them."

"How many of these telepaths do you think there are?" she asked, amazed.

"I don't know. Maybe a handful, maybe lots."

"And they're just walking around among us, using their telepathy while we're mostly unaware of it? Where do they come from? It's as weird as if they were aliens from another planet, but since I don't believe in aliens, that theory is out the window. I've always thought Big Foot and the Loch Ness Monster were nothing but hoaxes because I've got this pragmatic mind. When I was a kid it was clear to me that magic tricks were only illusions. I never believed in the Easter Bunny or clapped for Tinkerbell, so do you know how weird this all seems? The idea of telepathy is so hard to believe."

"I know."

"If I hadn't experienced what I did with Parker and Shannon yesterday, I'd think this whole conversation was crazy. Since yesterday I've been trying to be more open-minded than before, but it's still not easy."

"I lived with it for years because of Shannon, but it's not the kind of thing you want to tell the guys on your baseball team."

"No kidding. I didn't mean to go off on a tangent. What happened next?"

"Nothing. We ran into a dead end. Yvonne and I still kept in contact, but after a while there was nowhere left to go. Then something else turned up when I least expected it, and from my own family. My grandma had to go into an assisted living center. Granny Anne is pretty old and had been widowed and on her own for more than fifteen years. Eventually she had to have more care, so my Aunt Cecilia moved her into an apartment that offered assisted living. She had to sell

Granny's house, and while getting everything ready she was sorting through all of the papers and letters that Granny had kept over the years. Our family has always been a bunch of pack rats. Anyway, Cecilia found a couple of letters from my mom and sent them to me. That's when I got what seemed like a big break."

"What was in the letters?"

"The first one was dated a year before Shannon was born. In it Marilyn was telling Granny Anne, who was her mother, about how much she wanted to have a baby. She and my dad had been trying for a long time, it seems, and out of desperation they were going to a special fertility clinic in Concord. The place had an extremely high success rate, and so it was their last hope. Although it was costly, they had decided to try it. The second letter was three months later, thanking Granny Anne for helping with the medical costs, and also talking about how thrilled Mom was because she'd finally gotten pregnant. She was full of praise for the doctor and clinic, and grateful for what they'd been able to do for her."

"And you hadn't know about any of this?"

"It was all news to me. Of course at the time she went through it I was still a little kid, and Marilyn had always been sort of shy when it came to talking about anything of a sexual nature, even pregnancy and childbirth. It wasn't exactly the type of thing she would have sat down and chatted with me about once I got older, either. At first glance it didn't seem that important, until I remembered how Yvonne had talked about Evan's mother and father trying so hard to have a baby. I called her and we discussed it. She remembered the name of the clinic, and the doctor who had helped them. They were the same as in Marilyn's letter. From that point on, it seemed like too much of a coincidence to ignore."

"Did you go to the clinic?"

"The very next day. Unfortunately its doors were closed, and it was no longer in business. The doctor directing the clinic had died in an accident a year or so before, and the clinic had eventually been bought by a corporation six months before it had closed down. I was surprised by this, and it seemed unusual. Why would a company buy a medical facility if it had no plans for keeping it open? That's what made me want to look further."

"Who bought it?"

"Signet."

Meg raised her eyebrows in surprise. "You've got to be kidding. What would a software engineering firm want with a fertility clinic?"

"That was my question. So, I packed my bags and headed for Portland. It didn't take long to get hired onto Signet's security team, considering my background and the fact that security is such a high priority of the company. I spent every spare minute trying to find out why they had purchased the fertility clinic and then shut it down, but I never found out anything, and I can be a pretty thorough investigator. All I came up with was that the clinic was just another acquisition of the growing Signet corporation. Since I'd abandoned my job in San Jose, there wasn't much else for me to do but stay in Portland and continue working at Signet."

"The whole thing about them buying the clinic doesn't make sense."

"Yeah, well, that's where I've been stuck at for six months. It doesn't make sense to me, either, but after being around Willis Dent and watching him operate, a lot of what he does is strange. He seemed more driven by paranoia than common sense. Even so, I keep asking the question that has no answer: why would he acquire a fertility clinic in another state and then close it down?"

"Maybe as a tax write-off? Businesses do that all the time."

"Maybe," he said, shrugging at the same question that had bothered him for months.

"It's just such an odd coincidence that both Evan's parents, and yours, had ties to the same medical facility."

"No kidding. Before coming to Portland, I found out everything I could about the clinic. There wasn't anything weird going on that I could tell, and it had a good reputation. It was small, but doing well. The staff members and clients I'd been able to get a hold of had nothing but praise for the clinic, and especially for its head doctor, William Kronek."

"Kronek?" Meg repeated, her mind glazing over the familiar name. "Kronek!" she suddenly cried, reaching over and grabbing Ross' arm. "The codes, Ross! That's the name of the codes I stole from Dent's computer!"

Chapter 15

They stopped in Medford, a town just north of the California border. While Ross filled the car with gas, Meg searched through the yellow pages at a phone booth, looking for a listing of computer stores. After asking directions they headed to the mall area of the city. Fifteen minutes later they found a large computer store and went inside. They went straight to the software aisle and Meg grabbed an Excel package. She was peeling off the shrink wrap and opening the package when a store clerk came over, asking if he could help.

"I'm buying this," she explained. "But I want to look at it on one of your computers."

He obliged and let them test it on an IBM. Once it was installed, the clerk was distracted by a customer looking at printers, and he left them to their own devices. Meg immediately took the CD with the codes on it from her purse and popped it out of the jewel case, inserting it in the computer's ROM. A couple of minutes later she had the Kronek folder open and they were scanning the files. She opened the first one, showing Ross the strings of coding.

"See? This is what I was telling you about."

"Q, S, C, and Z. Just those four letters?"

"In repeat groupings of one or more. Some of the multiples go quite high on the scale. Look at these right here. See how there are five Z's and then fourteen Q's, then two Z's and six C's and so on? I'm thinking it makes for probably millions of different variations, if not infinite possibilities."

And there's no way to decipher it?"

"Not necessarily. I just said that I couldn't do it. Maybe someone out there who has a different edge than I do could break it. If they did, I don't know what they would get, though, because I'm pretty sure it doesn't break down into language, either human or computer."

"You're certain?"

"No, I'm not certain of anything. It's just my semi-educated guess."

"You're top of the line at what you do, so I'll trust your judgment."

She closed the file and typed in the password encoded date beneath the second file, opening it. "See? More of the same, only different. Same code, different pattern."

"It looks just like the first file to me."

"They're different. I've checked each file, and they all have different patterns of the same four letters. When I stare at the strings of coding as a whole, and not as individual parts, they each take on their own sort of appearance. Their pattern structure is kind of pretty, don't you think?"

Ross stood close to her, peering over her shoulder at the monitor. He couldn't see what she was talking about, but it was fun to watch her at work. "It's interesting, that's for sure."

"I kind of think of them as strands of jewelry. Some of the codes seem to have more delicate patterns, while half of them seem thicker, in a way. It's weird."

"You can really see that?"

Meg glanced up at him, for the first time noticing how close he stood. "Sure," she answered, trying not to feel flustered.

"Those files are each labeled with a date," he observed.

Meg exited the file and looked at the many icon files with their individual numbers. "Right. I've been assuming they were dates based on the origin of the codes, since they're set in chronological order starting from the seventies. But I'm not sure of that anymore, especially since I now know who Kronek was."

"Maybe they're birth dates. Check and see if Shannon's is there. August 30, 1976."

Meg scrolled through the first of the files until she reached 1976. Half-way through the year she found a matching date.

"What's the odds of there being a birth date in here that would match Shannon's?" she pondered. "Are you good at statistics?"

"Not good enough. I'd say it's not very likely, though, and that it's probably more than just a coincidence. I'm guessing this is Shannon's file."

They stared at the screen, and after a few seconds Meg typed in the password which opened the file. To Ross the code looked no different than the other two had, but Meg studied it with growing interest. "Hers is one of the more chunky codes. You know, kind of like Aztec jewelry, so to speak? That's how I think of it anyway."

Ross smiled, thinking about how much her Escher-like tendency to see patterns, and to associate them with physical articles, must bug the mathematicians she worked with. He pointed to the full-page spreadsheet of patterned lines. "What do these jumbled rows of letters have to do with Shannon?"

"I don't know," Meg sighed, closing the file. "What about that little boy, Evan? Do you remember his birthday?"

Ross was thoughtful. "No, I don't think so...wait a minute. Yvonne talked about him being born on Christmas, and how excited they all were. Check the year 1989."

Meg did so, and found a file labeled 25 DEC 89. They stared at it. "What do you think?"

"I think that one file matching a birth date might be a coincidence, but two wouldn't be."

"What kind of codes would tie into people, though?" she queried.

Ross studied the monitor, a sudden idea coming to him. "Hang on a second. Open that file and let me look at it." She obliged and he intently studied the code. "I've got it! I know what it is. Take the CD out and buy that program, will you? Let's get going and we can talk in the car."

A few minutes later they were back in the Buick and on the interstate heading south.

"How many files did you say there were?" Ross asked.

"A hundred and forty-three."

"Then I'm guessing that means there are a hundred and forty-three telepaths, all of them tied in to what Dr. Kronek did at the fertility clinic."

"What he did? Do you have it figured out?"

"I think so."

"You're saying you can break the codes?" Meg asked, trying to hide the uncertainty in her voice since code breaking was her profession and she hadn't been able to crack them. "You know what they say?"

"No, but it's possible I know what they are. In fact, it's so obvious I feel like an idiot for not figuring it out right away. Kronek was a medical doctor, which means those codes are medical. What kind of coding is associated with the human body?"

"I don't know."

"Come on, stop thinking lateral."

Meg's expression was puzzled, then her eyes widened. "Genetic?"

"Right."

"No way."

"I think so."

They drove in silence for a full minute, both of them thinking. "What do you know about DNA?" he finally asked.

"Nothing."

"Not even from high school biology?"

"I had very selective learning. Idiot savant, remember?"

"Well, I don't know a whole lot either, except for what I learned in one of my classes at the university. If I remember right, genes carry all the DNA information for making the proteins in our bodies. Those proteins decide how we look, how our bodies functions, and even some of our behaviors, stuff like that. The DNA has four chemicals, or bases, that scientists abbreviate by using four different letters."

"Like in the Kronek codes? C, Z, Q, and S?" Meg asked, her excitement growing.

"I think they're actually A, T...C, and one other. Oh yeah, G. Anyway, what if Kronek changed the letters for his own purposes, so only he would know which letter represented which base? Out of those four bases there are tons of pattern combinations, just like you saw in the strands of coding. The human genome has something like three billion pairs of bases that are the blueprint for who we are, so to speak."

"Three billion? The file codes were no way that big."

"What if the files only contain the specific strands of DNA that affect these people's mental make-up, or the physical structure of part of their brains? Maybe it's the specific coding for what makes them telepaths."

"I don't know, Ross. Those file folders go clear back into the early seventies. How could this Dr. Kronek have been doing that kind of thing so long ago?"

"Maybe he was ahead of his time." Ross glanced down at the Kenny Loggin's jewel case which held the CD that had suddenly become very important to them. "When I work a case, and am investigating, there are times it's important to take a leap of faith in making conclusions. Almost never do you have all of the puzzle pieces. A lot of the time you have to guess, and hope you've got it right."

"But why would Kronek do this kind of genetic engineering, and how could he pull it off so many different times? A hundred and forty-three is a lot."

"I don't know why he did it. Maybe he wanted to make this mess of human pottage we live in better by adding a new ingredient to the soup, or maybe he did it just because he was an egomaniac who had the ability to pull it off. Who knows? After finding the link between Shannon and Evan, I did some research. The clinic focused on in vitro fertilization, where the egg is fertilized outside the mother's body and then reinserted into the uterus. It used to be called having a test tube baby, and there was a big uproar about it when they started doing it in the 70s, though it's become far more commonplace today. Dr. Kronek's special-ty was working with fertilizing the ovum, or eggs, outside the mother's body. Maybe that was the opportunity he took for changing the genetic make-up of kids like Shannon and Evan."

"And these are the codes for each one of them," she slowly stated, indicating the CD.

"I thought you weren't buying this?"

"I'm starting to, even though there are a lot of things left unexplained," she ceded. "In some ways it tends to appeal to my sense of order to at least have an explanation, even if it's far-reaching. I like logical answers for things, and this theory has some scientific reasoning behind it, not just a bunch of new age hocus-pocus. But how does this tie into Willis Dent, and Signet's ownership of the codes?"

"You've go me there. Though doesn't it seem likely that Dent knew what these codes were, which is why he wanted them in the first place? I'm guessing it's the reason he bought the clinic. He was only looking for specific data. Once he got it, he shut down the clinic."

Meg nodded, seeing more of the pieces fall into place. "The codes might be valuable. Maybe there are people out there who would pay big for this kind of information. If so, no wonder he was determined to get this CD back from me."

"Do you think the codes were valuable enough for him to order Alan to kill you?"

A slight shudder ran through her. "Maybe."

"When I was with Dent in his office, and he was stressing how important it was for us to find you and get the codes back, he said something that bothered me. He was angry, but in a cold kind of way that was weird. He said he wanted you 'taken care of.' Those were his words. At first I thought it sounded threat-ening, but then assumed he meant we needed to make sure you were arrested. After everything that happened yesterday, though, I'm guessing my first impres-sion was right."

"I'm not surprised he would order Alan to get rid of me, though the thought is creepy. Our office suspected Signet of trying to kill one of our other agents."

"You had another agent there?"

"Yes. He was working undercover at Signet, too, though I didn't know him personally. I'd actually only seen him in the hallway at CSS. Apparently he was new, and had just come down from NSA to our division. He was working under-cover at Signet in a different area, until he was nearly killed in a hit-and-run acci-dent. That's why I was pulled out of Signet. My boss didn't have any proof Dent was responsible, but he felt it was too dangerous for me to stay there any longer."

At the mention of her boss, Meg felt a slight pang of guilt for taking off without calling Richard. She should have let him know she wouldn't be coming in to work today, but then decided that maybe he would think she had quit, or was just angry and needed time off. It might be a good thinking through time for them both, she decided.

"There were two of you working undercover," Ross stated with growing interest. "Who was the other agent?"

Meg thought for a minute. "I think his cover name was Phil Black. He was one of the men in that Friday meeting with you when I brought Willis Dent those papers. That's the first time I recognized him as having come from CSS."

Ross looked at her in surprise. "The friendly blond guy? Sure, I remember him. Late that afternoon Alan told me he was going to be fired for stealing company information. It was the first clue we had that there might be corporate espionage going on inside Signet. What it sounds like, though, is that they didn't fire him. Instead they tried to kill him because they wanted to make sure he didn't pass on the information he'd taken." His voice showed increasing excitement at the discovery of these new facts. "That's the tie-in, Meg! That's how the rest of this falls into place."

"What do you mean?"

"It's been bothering me about what a coincidence it was that I had been tracking you for the stolen codes, and yet you ended up leading me to information about Shannon. But this is the rest of it! When Alan and I talked about firing Phil Black, he was holding the file folder that Phil had supposedly taken a copy of. I got just a quick look at it, maybe a few seconds is all, before he noticed I was checking it out and shut the folder. The paper I saw had a list of names with birth dates and some other information on it. Of course I didn't see Shannon's name there, but maybe if I'd had more time I would have. That file must have held the paperwork on the people who are listed in the codes. If Phil was able to get a copy of it back to your boss, that's probably how they got Parker's name, and why they were having you go undercover with him. If they put those names from the file into a state-wide search, his might have come up as having applied for a vendor's license to operate his artist's booth at the market."

Meg's expression was one of dawning revelation. "That has to be it! It makes sense! Ross...what if my boss didn't tell me what I was really looking for at Signet? What if he was just telling me I would be looking for a Skipjack program for security reasons, because I don't have a very high security clearance? What if the codes he really wanted were the Kronek codes that I ended up taking off of

Dent's computer? Once CSS got the list of the hundred and forty-three people, and Phil was almost killed, they pulled me out of Signet, never knowing I'd accidentally taken the coding information off of Dent's computer."

"Makes sense."

"Oh my gosh! Richard is going to have a total cow. I'm in big trouble." She flipped open the jewel case, staring at the CD as if its smooth metal surface might reveal something more. "What do we do now?"

"That depends," Ross said, his voice thoughtful and serious with concern. "You know, I'm thinking those codes would not be good in the hands of the government. All they need is a reason to start engineering telepaths. I can't even think of how many ways that could go wrong. So far we've only run into people like Shannon and Parker who want to do good for humanity. I don't see that as the direction the government would want to go with this, though. They would probably try to use telepathic people as a secret weapon, maybe even form a special army that would make our country secure, at least within their bureaucratic way of thinking. I doubt it would turn out good, though, because look at the kind of people in charge. They'd probably be the same men that tried to get their hands on Shannon and Evan, like that fake FBI agent you met. What do you think he'd do with the codes? Not exactly raise up a bunch of loving kids. Imagine an army of sociopaths who had been made that way by being reared in military installations instead of homes. They'd have the ability to get inside people's heads, but with government officials as the puppet masters. Not only that, but how long would it last before the telepaths got powerful enough to take charge? I can't help but wonder how many generations it would take to screw up this planet if something like that happens."

Meg thought about how Parker and Shannon had so easily entered her mind, and how traumatic it was even when their intent had been good. What if people with Alan Scorzato's tendencies also had telepathic powers? She thought of Robyn's rapist, and of the Donna Greens of this world, who were evil and without feeling. It was horrific to imagine their kind walking around with telepathic powers, and no doubt the ability to kill at will. Meg slowly closed the CD case, staring at Kenny Loggin's friendly face on the cover.

"If the government does what you're suggesting, then God help us all," she said. "Because he'll be the only way we'll get out of this without destroying ourselves."

* * *

It was after five o'clock when Martin Wimer and Leo Fromm climbed into the back seat of their boss' car. Willis Dent started the engine and drove towards the far side of the park across from the Signet building. Fromm started to say something, but Dent signaled him to be quiet. Eventually he stopped the car and they got out, walking away from the parking area and into a tree-lined section of the park.

It had been an extremely stressful day for Willis Dent. The NSA agents had left Signet several hours ago, but he still felt shaken to the core. He managed to look serene, though. It was important to him that his aloof personae stay in tact.

"I've sent Alan home," he explained. "I'm leaving him out of this for the time being, since he's too high profile with those government agents right now. Tell me about Margaret Wilson."

"Her real name is Meg Parrish," Wimer explained. "We tracked her down by following Ross Ecklund to her apartment yesterday. When Alan questioned her, she admitted to working for Zytex. We're guessing he's on their payroll, too. Probably has been all along."

The thought of another betrayal filled Dent with renewed anger. It seemed he wasn't able to trust anyone. "Alan said she had the CD with the codes on it. Does she?"

"Yeah," Wimer answered. "Alan checked it out on her computer."

"Why didn't you get it from her last night?"

"That was Alan's doing," Leo Fromm interjected. "He wanted to go in and do the job himself. I think he had a taste for her, if you know what I mean. Ecklund showed up in the middle of it, broke Alan's nose, and nabbed her. We're guessing the two of them are still together and that they have your CD."

"How do you know she hasn't turned the codes over to her boss at Zytex?"

"Because it's been a week," Wimer said. "If she was gonna do that, she would have done it already instead of still having the CD. Maybe they decided to sell the stuff on their own, since they probably figure they could make a lot more money than by turning it over to Zytex."

"Where do you think they are now?"

"I checked Ecklund's place last night, but he didn't come home. Leo went over to her apartment, too, but cops were there. Somebody must have called them when Alan and Ross started fighting. My guess is that Ross and the girl are gonna keep a low profile for a while, at least until they make a profit from your stolen codes."

"Then that's it," Dent said, discouraged. "There's no way of finding her and getting the CD back, is there?"

"Not necessarily. Leo and I still have some things we could do. Remember, I spent a lot of time on the police force, and also was a private investigator after that. If you want us to keep looking, we can do it. No telling what we might turn up."

Dent's eyes narrowed, his harried mind sorting through the facts. He had been given no recourse but to turn over his two CDs with the Kronek codes on them to the NSA agents, along with everything else he had. The whole incident filled him with cold rage, and he felt more violated than when Margaret Wilson, whose real name was apparently Meg Parrish, had broken into his computer system. He also felt afraid, and that fear was weighing against his intense desire to regain what was rightfully his.

"You'll have to be careful. Those NSA agents are looking for her, too. They asked both Alan and myself about her, and they're going to want the CD she's got. If you can find her, and get the codes back for me, then I'm willing to give you each twenty-five thousand dollars. Of course that would include getting rid of her, and Ecklund, too. Do you want the job?"

"Sure," Wimer managed after a moment of surprise. He tried not to act shocked by how much money Dent was offering them, but it was hard to hide his excitement.

"Sounds good," Fromm chimed in, grinning.

"Starting today I'm taking you off payroll. According to Signet records you're both laid off. I'll make sure you get money for expenses, and a cashier's check in the mail on payday. Work with cash. Don't use the company credit cards anymore. There can't be any tie-ins to our company, understand? I can't risk another run-in with those feds."

"What if we don't find her?" Fromm asked, concerned. "I don't want to be out of a job."

"Either way, I'll make sure you get reinstated. It's only going to be a temporary layoff until you've found her and bring me back that CD. Do you want the job or not?"

"We'll do it," Wimer said.

"One other thing. The feds took my copies of the codes. I don't have anything left, which makes the CD she has very important to me. Before you kill her, I need to see it for myself to make sure it's the real set of codes. Once I have them, then you can eliminate her."

"What about Ross?" Fromm asked.

"Kill him on sight."

*   *   *

The small city of Benicia was situated on the northeast bay shoreline, thirty-five miles from San Francisco. Named after Captain Vallejo's wife, it had once had the prestigious honor of serving as California's capitol for thirteen months starting in 1853. A few generational residents were still resentful at having had that honor stolen from their town.

It was late afternoon when Meg and Ross parked the car on First Street, a shop-filled avenue which had no parking meters. The street started with St. Paul's Church and ran the length of the small town, ending with an enchanting view of the bay.

They got out of the car, feeling stiff from riding for so many hours. "We're here," Ross announced, looking up and down the street at the small, colorful shops. Most of them were two story with brickwork or stucco faces in tan, pale green, and terra cotta. Others had decorative tiles and bay windows, most had awnings.

"What a darling town," Meg said with enthusiasm. "This is going to be fun."

He glanced at her and smiled. "I hate stores like these. You're not going to drag me inside any of them, are you?"

Meg laughed and stretched, grateful to be out of the car. "Probably every one, until we find what we're looking for."

"Okay, where do we start?"

Her smile faded as she scanned the tree-lined street, shops, and tourists strolling by. "I'm not sure. All I know was that Parker told me to come here. Maybe that was kind of naive of me, to just think I could take off and head for this town, hoping to find them here somewhere."

"Maybe they'll find us."

"I hope so," Meg answered.

Ross joined her on the sidewalk. "Let's go for a stroll and see what's here," he suggested.

They passed by shops that sold antiques, collectibles, clothing, and jewelry. Meg was interested in most of the stores, stopping to look at the window displays. They both took special notice of the people, hoping to see a familiar face. All they encountered were strangers.

Diverted by the displays, Meg dragged him into several shops. Ross patiently stood beside her as she examined the items for sale. He usually detested shopping, but found himself focusing on Meg and therefore enjoying it considerably more. It seemed odd to him that he had spent yesterday following her in a similar routine at the Portland market, while today he was the one walking beside her. The only predictable thing about life, he decided, was that it was seldom predictable.

A cool breeze blew off the bay as they strolled down the sidewalk, and they paused at one of the street corners decorated with tile artwork. The mosaics in the sidewalk depicted events from local history, and this square focused on Jack London, who had once lived in the area. Meg stared at it but her mind was focused elsewhere.

"Ross, what if we can't find them?"

"Then we chalk it up to another interesting experience, and get on with our lives."

Meg looked up at him. "I don't want to go on with the kind of life I've had," she impulsively confessed. "I'm tired of my stagnant, boring life, and of living the way I do."

Ross reached out and took her hand, staring down at the delicate fingers against his own thicker ones. "We've only been here a half-hour. Let's give it more time. Come on, we'll try the other side of the street."

They walked along, holding hands and looking like most of the other couples who were window shopping. It felt good to Meg. She couldn't recall another time when a man had held her hand like this. His fingers were warm, and it gave her a fleeting sense of security.

"Even if things turn out for the worst and we don't find them," Ross commented. "I've still had a very nice time."

"Me too," Meg admitted, surprised by the suddenly obvious fact that she had been enjoying herself. "Except for getting shot at."

Ross chuckled. "Yeah. That part stank. Are you hungry? There's several cafés along here. Let's get something to eat."

They strolled past an antique store with window boxes overflowing with ivy. Another shop had blue dome-shaped awnings and trees set in terra cotta pots. They came to a café with a crimson door and dark green trim. Overhead was a matching awning. Through the windows Meg saw small, circular tables topped with glass, beneath which was lace layered over flowered fabric. In the window was a chalkboard menu which declared, Today's Special: 'crab melt.' The words were thickly printed in different shades of colored chalk. Beneath, in smaller print, it read: Today's Thought: 'For as a man thinketh, so is he.'—Proverbs, 23:7.

Meg stared at the sign. "Let's go in here."

"Good idea," Ross agreed, also noticing the sign.

They opened the door, causing a string of bells hanging from the inside knob to jangle. The narrow café had a long counter and crimson bar stools. Two couples sat at the tables, while an older lady was perched at the counter. For the most part, the café was empty. Ross and Meg chose to sit at one of the tables, and soon a man came over to them. He was short and round with a pleasant face. Probably in his mid forties, he wore a white apron over a green plaid shirt. "How are you folks?"

"Good," Ross answered.

The man set down two glasses of ice water. "Our menu's on the wall," he explained, indicating the large chalkboard with a list of entrees and other items.

"We're interested in today's special, the crab melt. What is that?"

"A toasted English muffin topped with grilled crab, cheese, and tomato, and it comes with your choice of soup or salad. Today's soup is clam chowder."

"Is the crab good?"

The man grinned, his gaze piercing. "You bet! Besides, you know what they say about seafood being brain food. Good for you that way."

"We'll go for it," Ross said.

The man left with their order and Meg leaned over to Ross. "What do you think?"

"I think it sounds tasty."

"That's not what I mean. Do you think we're onto something here?"

Ross stared into her earnest brown eyes enhanced by a serious expression. "You know what I think?" he whispered, leaning in closer.

Meg drew in, lowing her voice. "What?"

"I think we should have the cheesecake for dessert."

She drew back and frowned at him. "Very funny."

While they were waiting, Ross used the payphone in the back of the café. He dialed Yvonne Dillard's number in Concord, but to his disappointment got an answering machine. He decided to leave a message.

"Hi, Yvonne. This is Ross. I'm going to be in California a few days and want to know if I can impose on you, like last time. Hope it's not a problem, but I'd like to see you. I'll try back later, okay?" He hung up the receiver and returned to the table.

The crab melt and chowder were delicious. As Ross suggested, they finished with the cheesecake and ended up feeling stuffed. They went to the counter to pay the bill, waiting for the party ahead of them to leave. At the counter a woman in her sixties was enjoying quiche. Her pale yellow hair had a tarnished look, no doubt from years of coloring over gray. Her face was heavily lined, and she wore fancy amethyst earrings in contrast to her light blue jogging suit. The lady smiled at Meg, who returned the greeting.

"How was everything?" the man in the apron asked.

They both assured him it was good. Meg studied his face. "I like your thought for the day. 'As a man thinketh.' That one."

He smiled at her, counting back the change to Ross. "It's not really our thought for the day. We pretty much leave it up year-round."

"Do you know my friend, Parker Briggs?" she impetuously asked. "He told me to come to Benicia."

The man gazed at her a long time, and it seemed to become quiet in the small café. "We're closing soon," he finally said. "Everything in town shuts down early on the weekdays. Why don't you come back tomorrow? Our special is going to be angel hair pasta with clams."

Disappointment filled Meg and she turned to leave, but the woman's hand shot out and grabbed her arm. The lady stared into Meg's face, her faded blue eyes watery in their examination. "I'll bet your friend would want you to come back tomorrow and have the clams," she said, her strong voice startling Meg even more than her touch had. "Maybe tomorrow your friend will decide to try the clams, too."

Meg stared at her, then looked back at the rotund man behind the counter. Ross was looking at them, too. "What do you think?" she heard Ross ask the man.

"I think Lana knows what she's talking about."

"Okay," Ross slowly replied. "We'll come back."

They left the café and almost immediately a 'closed' sign was put in the window.

It was after six-thirty when Ross and Meg drove away from Benicia, heading for Concord. "We've got some time to kill between now and tomorrow," Ross said. "I'm hoping we can crash at Yvonne Dillard's place. She's invited me to stay with her whenever I come to California. I'd like you to meet her, too. She's a neat lady."

"That'd be great, Ross," Meg said, gazing out the window. "What do you think about those people at the café? Do you think there's really some connection there?"

"I don't know. Look, let's not make too much of it. One of the things I've learned in my search for Shannon is that you can't push things to work out. Let's take it easy and see what happens. We might go back to that café tomorrow and learn something new, or we might just end up with a plate of pasta and clams. In the mean time, is there anything you want to do before we go to Yvonne's house?"

"Yes. I'm starting to feel miserably in need of a shower and some clean clothes. I really want to go shopping for new jeans, underwear, stuff like that. Can we find a large department store somewhere?"

"No kidding. I'm ready for a change of clothes, too. Lets find a department store in Concord," he said, heading the car across the Martinez Bridge.

*   *   *

Yvonne Dillard hurried through the front door of her house, feeling a little bit harried. It had taken her longer to find a wedding gift than she had thought it would. She hustled upstairs and into her bedroom, quickly changing and gathering the last of her things. Her neighbor and friend, Myra, was waiting out in the car, ready to drive her to the airport.

Her luggage had been packed since the previous night, and she hauled the two pieces downstairs, passing the livingroom desk where the answering machine sat. It's light was flashing, and she punched the button, pulling on her jacket as she listened. She heard Ross Ecklund's voice and paused, trying to think what to do. She hoped to see him, too. He wasn't clear about when he would arrive or how long he might stay.

Grabbing her address book, Yvonne flipped it open and found his Portland number. She dialed it but got his answering machine, so left her own message. "Sorry I missed your call, Ross. It's Monday evening and I'm heading out the door for my niece's wedding in Arizona, but I'll be back Tuesday. I'm not sure when you're getting here, but make yourself at home if you get here before I arrive back tomorrow night. I'll leave the key with my friend, Myra, across the street, just like last time. It'll be good to see you again."

She hung up and grabbed a pencil, scribbling a brief note in case he didn't get the phone message but still showed up before tomorrow night. Then she hurried out the front door and locked it, stuffing the folded note in the screen where he'd be sure to find it. Myra came to help her with her suitcase, and a couple of minutes later they were on their way to the airport.

*   *   *

Meg bought two pairs of jeans, two plain colored t-shirts, a bulky blue sweatshirt, a pair of pajamas, several sets of underpants and socks, and her most missed item, a bra. She also purchased shampoo, conditioner, lotion, toothpaste, a toothbrush, floss, mascara, disposable razors, and a duffle bag to put everything in. Fortunately her purse had everything else in it that she required. It was amazing, she thought, how much a person needed just to comfortably get by in life.

Ross was waiting for her on the other side of the checkout aisle with his own purchases already bought and in a sack. The sun was setting when they headed out, and eventually they arrived at one of the residential sections of Concord. He pulled the car up in front of a two-story beige stucco house with deep-set eaves and coral trim. It had a small, neat yard and baskets of ivy hanging along the walkway leading up to the front door.

"It doesn't look like anybody's home," Meg said.

"I was afraid of this. Let's knock anyway."

They went to the front door and rang the bell. "Look," Meg said, pulling out a piece of paper that was wedged between the screen door and the jamb. It had Ross' name on it.

He unfolded the paper and read the note. "Yvonne is gone to a wedding until tomorrow night, but she got my message and says we can stay here until she gets back. Her neighbor's got the key. I'll be right back."

Ross went for the key and Meg got their packages from the car, depositing them at the front door and waiting until he showed up. A few minutes later they were inside the house, and Ross switched on the lights. "Myra, her friend, relayed Yvonne's message. She said to make ourselves at home."

Meg perused the large front room with its vaulted ceiling, comfortable couches, fireplace, and beautiful pieces of cherry wood furniture. The room was decorated in rich ivory with accents of pewter and cranberry. Ross led her upstairs, finding a guest room decorated in equally rich hues. He put her things on the bed and indicated the adjoining bathroom. Go ahead and shower, if you like. I'm going to use the room down the hall."

They looked at each other, the house seeming strangely quiet. "Thanks Ross," she said. "For everything, I mean."

He grinned at her, his face changing in that odd way it did, going from ordinary to appealing just because he smiled.

*   *   *

Martin Wimer decided to check out the apartment where Ross lived one more time. Maybe he had missed something the first time through, he thought. He let himself in the back door which he'd purposely left unlocked, then strolled through the apartment. Starting in the main bedroom, he felt less harried now than last night, though today he was still a bit high-strung. Maybe it was because of Willis Dent's new offer. There was so much to do with that extra twenty-five grand that the thought of it caused him to have ongoing feelings of anticipation.

Martin checked the closet and pulled out the tie rack, tossing it on the bed. He looked through the ties, choosing several he liked. He also surveyed other items in the closet, regretting that none of the suits, shirts, or shoes would fit him. In the kitchen he opened the fridge, finding a beer and some roast beef. He leisurely made himself a sandwich with all the trimmings, not bothering to put the mayo or other condiments back in the fridge. Next he checked the day's mail, opening a few pieces to see what was in them. The junk mail and bills were tossed on the floor. Once the sandwich was gone, Martin found a circular carton of ice cream in the fridge. He got a spoon from the sink and ate the pecan fudge swirl right out of the carton. When he was full, he left the rest of the ice cream sitting on the table, not bothering to put it back in the freezer.

He checked out the livingroom, going for the answering machine. There were several hang-up calls, probably from salespeople, and Red Cross calling to ask if Ross could come in and donate blood. "Yeah," Wimer snickered under his breath. "He's gonna donate blood, all right." His thoughts were interrupted by the last call on the machine. It was Yvonne Dillard's message.

Wimer moved to the Caller ID, checking through the names. He came to the last number on the display, a Y. Dillard who had a California area code. Grabbing his notebook, Wimer jotted the information down. A thrill of anticipation ran through him, and a momentary vision came to mind of Dent handing him twenty-five thousand dollars.

Chapter 16

Meg felt considerably better after showering and dressing in clean underwear, jeans, and the new sweatshirt. She had managed to get rid of the sticky adhesive left by the band-aid on her throat, and had also replaced the butterfly bandages on her arm with a couple of regular band-aids. Her hair was fluffy and clean, and she had put on some mascara and lip gloss. The sound of soft music drifted up from the livingroom, and she went downstairs. The stereo system was playing Enya, and Ross was in the kitchen.

"Yvonne doesn't drink, but there's some juice in here, or pop," Ross said from the open refrigerator. "Come see what you'd like." He had shaved and his hair was still a little damp from the shower. He was wearing new jeans and a blue cotton shirt with the sleeves rolled up. Blue was a good color on him, she reflected.

She picked out a bottle of cranberry juice, which he poured over ice. He had a Coke. They wandered back into the livingroom and Meg pointed to the pictures on the mantle. "Is this Yvonne's daughter?"

There was a family photo of a couple and a little boy. "Yes. That's Jenny and her husband, Ethan, about six months before they died. The little boy is Evan. Here's another picture of him."

Meg studied the child with an acorn cap of blond hair, a heart-shaped face, and giant blue eyes. "He's so darling. She must miss him terribly. Is that Yvonne?"

"Yes. I'd say the picture is a couple of years old, though."

The photo showed an attractive woman in her fifties, with light brown hair and glasses. "She's not married?"

"Divorced a long time ago. Raised Jenny by herself."

They walked over to the couch and sat down. Meg placed her half-filled glass on a tile coaster. Ross finished the last of his drink and did the same, then leaned back against the couch. "It's been a long day," he said, slipping his arm around her shoulder and encouraging her to rest against him. "Driving always takes it out of me. Are you tired?"

"Yes. There's just been so much to think about, the codes, and the clinic, all of that. I can't stop wondering about it and if we're going to find Parker and your sister."

"Don't worry about that tonight," he said, moving closer. "It'll wait till tomorrow."

Meg became very aware of how near he was, and noticed the smell of his cleanly shampooed hair. It should have made her feel panicked to have a man this close, she reflected, much as she had always felt when someone got too near. It didn't, though, and she half-wondered if Parker and Shannon had achieved more success with her than she had realized.

"I want to kiss you, Meg," Ross said.

"It's only our first date," she playfully murmured, studying the deep hazel color of his eyes. Why hadn't she noticed what great eyes he had right from that first meeting at Signet?

Ross studied Meg as she rested her head against his arm. He was hesitant to push her too quickly, yet he was also increasingly enticed by her. Being around her was exciting, but not simply because she was a desirable, attractive woman. He was coming to realize that her vulnerability was intensely appealing to him, far more than if she had been sophisticated or aggressive.

"First date? Hmm...how many hours do you figure a date lasts?" Ross asked. "I'm guessing about three, don't you think?"

"That's probably right," Meg agreed, realizing this was one area where she had little information to draw from.

"Well, do you realize we've been together for almost twenty-four hours? That's like having eight dates. It seems like we've established a fairly substantial relationship."

She slowly smiled at him. "I guess you're right."

He moved closer, his mouth finding hers as if it were a beacon drawing him in. His arms slid around her, pulling her against him.

Meg had been kissed before, though it had never been like this. Until now she hadn't understood what the big deal was. That perception was quickly changing. At the moment Ross' mouth was gently plying hers with such sensuous warmth, and his arms were encircling her in such a masculine hold, that she felt overwhelmed. She began to realize there was a whole lot more to kissing than she'd thought. Eventually he started to pull away, but she followed him back onto the couch, not willing to let him go. The kissing continued for several more minutes until Ross tenderly disengaged her.

She blinked hard, staring at him. Her face was flushed and she was breathing in short, quickened gasps. Ross grinned at her. "I think we'd better quit here, sweetheart, or this is going to turn into a whole lot more than just a first date."

Meg looked flustered and embarrassed. She sat back, staring across the room at the fireplace. He reached out with his hand, running his fingers down her jaw line. "You are one completely delightful woman, Meg Parrish. Just when I think I've got you figured out, you throw me another curve."

She turned her head to look at him. "The problem with dating is that you can't exactly plan it out on a spread sheet, can you?"

Ross chuckled, fighting an intense desire to take her in his arms again. "To be honest, this is the best date I've been on in years."

*   *   *

The next morning Meg awoke feeling far better than she had the day before. A good night's rest had worked wonders. She dressed and went downstairs, finding Ross already there. He was in the kitchen, looking through the pots and pans.

"Hi," she said, feeling a little shy recalling the previous night's session on the couch.

He stood up and put a large pan on the stove, coming over to her. "Good morning," he said, kissing her lightly on the lips. "Feel like breakfast?"

"Sure. What's on the menu?"

"How about omelets?"

"I've never made them before. Do you know how?"

"Of course. I happen to like cooking."

She raised her eyebrows. "I'm impressed! A man who is cool-headed in a crisis, great at high-speed chases, and can also cook." She didn't add the part about kissing, though it came to mind.

"You bet. Every woman's dream. Fill that pan half-full of water and put it on to boil, will you?" he asked.

"I take it back, at least about the cooking," Meg teased. "I know enough to realize that boiling an omelet makes for very soggy eggs."

"You genius types think you know everything, don't you? Try to follow directions, and maybe you can learn something."

"From the guy who makes eggs blow up in microwaves?"

He stared at her with a threatening expression. "All right!" she said, grabbing the pan and heading to the sink.

Meg put the water on to boil and cut up pieces of ham, while Ross cracked four eggs in a bowl and whipped them with a fork, then added a little water. He got out grated cheese, a measuring cup, and zip-top freezer bags. "Put a half-cup of the cheese and ham mixture in each of those freezer bags," he said.

She did so, then he dumped half a cup of the egg mixture into each bag, squeezing out the air and zipping them closed. He tossed the bags into the pan of boiling water, then toasted bagels while Meg set the table and put out orange juice. After the eggs had boiled in the water for ten minutes, Ross retrieved them and unzipped the pouches, dumping the fat, fluffy omelets onto a couple of plates. They sat down to eat.

"This is delicious," Meg said after the first taste of omelet. "Where did you learn how to make these?"

"It's an old boy scout trick," he answered.

Meg had never thought that dating a boy scout would be even remotely interesting, but since meeting Ross she was starting to have a whole new appreciation for what that might really entail. They enjoyed the rest of the meal, making plans for the day.

*   *   *

Tuesday afternoon Beautiful Bob walked through the Mall in Concord, keeping a fair distance between himself and the couple who were just leaving the Internet rental store. He'd been waiting around for them quite a while now, and was relieved they were finally on their way. A security guard had already approached him about loitering, and he was glad to be moving out of the area. It was a hard task for Bob to stay inconspicuous in such a preppie place because of his appearance.

His real name was Robert Ferris McKinley, but a group of cops had given him the nickname of Beautiful Bob years ago, and it had stuck. It wasn't meant as a compliment. He knew he was ugly. He'd known it from the time he'd been an acne-scarred kid, and the corrupt life he had lived during the past two decades had only made his looks get progressively worse. His stints in and out of jail hadn't helped, either. At the age of thirty he looked years older. He had straggly black hair that hung in ratty-looking threads, and an equally unkempt beard. There were tatoos up and down his arms and some on his back. It was this part of his anatomy that was the most hideous. One of the cops had taken a picture of his back to show school children during anti-drug assemblies, just so they could see what a drug dealer was like and the kind of people they would deal with if they tried drugs. Bob figured that the sight of it, and the other photo of his frightening face, should be enough to keep a whole slew of kids from ever even trying drugs.

Seven years ago his back had been tattooed with the words 'Hell's Angels' in an arc above and below the group's insignia of a skull and cross-bones. Four years ago he had been in a drugged stupor and really crossed their leader. They had decided to kick him out of the group, which ended up being a very unpleasant experience. Hell's Angels didn't exactly tear up a person's membership card when they expelled someone. Instead, a few of their toughest guys dragged him outside and beat him up. Then they held him down and tattooed black squares over the eleven letters spelling out the words 'Hell's Angels.' They'd also put a large X on his back, officially dissolving his membership in the group. The skull and cross-bones hadn't been so easy. They'd used a hot iron to remove it, and now he had a shiny patch of scar tissue on his back in the shape of an iron.

After that episode he had become even more isolated, doing drugs, dealing drugs, and not caring much about anything else. Three months ago he had hit rock-bottom, finding himself in jail again. The cops had stripped him naked and shaved his beard and his head which made him look like he was wearing a white bald cap in stark contrast to his leathery forehead. They'd had a good laugh because of it, and labeled him a freak. Bob had agreed. He was a freak. He must have been a freak his whole stinking life, or why else would his own father have tried to kill him numerous times, and why hadn't Bob been able to stop that sack of filth from molesting and killing his sisters while he was forced to watch? His father went to prison, but it didn't get much better after that. His mother's string of boyfriends had taken him on terrifying emotional joyrides with multiple episodes of physical abuse that turned him into an even bigger freak. His mother had apparently seen what a freak he was, too, and had forced him into prostitution to finance her drug addiction. She'd rewarded him with marijuana joints, until he'd decided he could do better on his own and left home. Bob had been eleven at the time.

When he'd gotten out of jail the last time, he'd decided to put the freak show to an end by taking quantum doses of heroin. That was his plan, and he had set about getting the stuff together. It had never come to fruition, though, and now he found himself in the strangest situation he'd been in for a long time. He was currently shadowing a man and woman in the mall, determined not to lose them. The guy he was tailing was a good looking man, the girl very pretty, and they seemed like a happy, normal couple walking along and shopping together. He felt a stab of jealousy, but pushed it aside. He had a job to do, and he wasn't going to let anything deter him from it.

* * *

While their car's rear window and tail light were being replaced, Meg and Ross spent several hours in the Concord Mall. They rented Internet time on a computer, learning what they could about genetics and in vitro fertilization. They learned a lot, but not much more of anything that could help them. Ross had been close to the mark in his explanation of genes and the four DNA base chemicals, and although they read through a number of articles on the subject, a lot of which Meg felt was over her head, there wasn't much to substantiate their theories. If anything, it seemed highly unlikely that Dr. Kronek would have been able to do what Ross and Meg theorized. For one thing, the study of genetics, and the classification of the different DNA combinations, was only recently becoming more clearly identified because of the use of computers. How could Kronek have been that advanced in genetics so long ago?

Even more confusing was the other piece of information they learned. The first documented case of in vitro fertilization had occurred in England in 1978, with the birth of Louise Brown. Some of the file names on the Kronek CD, however, were dated as early as 1975, a full three years before the first IVF birth became a world-wide sensation.

"We must be wrong," Meg sighed. "Kronek wouldn't have been doing in vitro procedures three years before the first documented case made history."

"'Documented' is the key word," Ross argued. "Who's to say the concept of in vitro, and the testing of it, wasn't done privately before knowledge of the process was ever presented to the public? According to this article, in vitro experimentation has always been privately funded because it falls under the category of embryo research, which the government doesn't underwrite. That means the procedures wouldn't have the same oversight that government research would, and the documentation would be private. What if Kronek was experimenting on his own?"

"Maybe," Meg said, still unsure.

"Did you notice the increasing frequency of the file folder birth dates with each year? There were only a couple in 1975, then the dates in each following year began to increase, almost like a pyramid. They more than doubled with each new year. Look at this," he said, pointing to a paragraph on the monitor. "'In vitro may have been controversial twenty years ago, but in the last decade it's been routinely accepted. There's been 300,000 IVF babies born worldwide in the last ten years, and nearly 60,000 of them were in the U.S.' I'm still standing by my theory that Dr. Kronek was playing around in the petri dishes, and that somehow he was able to manipulate the genetic material before returning the embryo to the mother's uterus. Why else would he have file folders full of DNA codes on Shannon, Evan, and the other kids?"

"That's the million-dollar question, isn't it?" Meg said.

By one-thirty they decided to quit and get something to eat from the food court. Once the car was fixed, they spent the rest of the afternoon sight-seeing a couple of places Ross was familiar with in the Bay Area before heading to Benicia. It was a little after five when they went into the café on First Street. The round-faced man was there, working behind the counter. A few other people sat at the tables, but none were Parker or Shannon. Meg felt disappointed.

"You're back for the clams," the man said in his friendly, open way as he set down the glasses of water. "Two plates?"

"Sure," Ross said.

He left and they both fell silent. Meg didn't want to voice her disappointment at not seeing Parker, and Ross felt there wasn't much to say. A few minutes later the man set down steaming plates of angel hair pasta with clams. "This is one of our best entrees," he said. "I'm sure you'll enjoy it."

They ate in silence for a while. "I don't even like clams," Meg eventually stated, staring down at the plate.

The bells on the door handle jangled and she looked up, seeing the older woman from the night before enter the café. The proprietor had called her Lana. She was wearing lavender polyester slacks and a flowery top, along with the amethyst earrings from yesterday. "Well hello," Lana said, coming to their table. "You're having Fred's pasta with clams, it looks like. It's the house specialty."

"Would you like to join us?" Ross encouraged.

"Thank you," Lana said, sitting down. Almost immediately Fred brought her a plate of pasta, too, then left. "You're tourists here, I take it?" she asked, digging into the noodles.

"I am," Meg said. "Ross used to live in California, though."

"Then you're lucky because you've got a tour guide. Have you taken her into San Francisco yet?"

"Not yet."

"Oh, you must do that! Take her to the Palace of Fine Arts. That's my favorite place to visit. My friends and I go there for a picnic lunch sometimes and feed the birds. The pigeons will just flock to you if you toss them some bread or popcorn, you know. Tomorrow would be a very good day for it, since the weather is forecast to be clear."

"We'll do that," Ross promised, noting Meg's increasingly pleased expression.

Almost immediately Lana changed the subject, telling them about Benicia and it's marine history. Then she talked about her years in real estate and her husband, Louis, who loved gardening. She also told them of her twin sons, Gary and Greg. Eventually the topic moved to a new baby granddaughter born last year, which was her first experience with being a grandmother. Lana explained all about the infant and showed them pictures, lamenting that she didn't get to be near the baby because the parents lived far away. It was nice, friendly chatting that became increasingly boring.

"I always thought how lucky I was," Lana continued, ignoring her plate of pasta. "It seemed like God was very good to Louis and me, letting us have two boys at once, especially after trying for years to have a baby. I was older, you know. Nearly forty-three when they were finally born. Maybe it was just because I was a first-time mother and wanted to have children for so many years, but they seemed like quite exceptional boys, even from the first. Both Louis and I realized we were very lucky to have these remarkable sons. They were just special, know what I mean?"

Both Ross and Meg were gazing steadily at her, no longer bored.

"My dad and step-mom had a hard time being able to have a baby, too," Ross carefully commented. "Mom ended up going to the Childbirth and Fertility Clinic in Concord, and that's how we got my little sister, Shannon. We always felt she was special, too."

Lana beamed, her eyes sparkling. "Well she would be, wouldn't she, if that's how you got her? Some of us joke about it being the Concord water that makes for marvelous kids."

"Where are your sons now?" Ross asked.

Her smile faded. "Don't get to see them too often, you know. They're busy traveling, and studying medicine. They both decided long ago to enter the healing arts. Louis and I think it's going to be great having sons who are doctors."

Fred brought them their tab before they were finished eating. It was like a silent request for them to leave, and they couldn't help but notice his concerned glances at the other patrons and at the door.

"Well," Lana said, standing. "I've got to go. Don't forget about tomorrow. Be sure to take some popcorn with you, right? You'll want to feed those birds, as it's quite fun to watch them eat their lunch right along with you."

"We will," Meg promised.

A few minutes later the tab was paid, and they left the restaurant. Ross and Meg strolled back to their car which was parked one block over. The streets of Benicia were much busier because of an open-air market set up along the sidewalks. There were tables offering breads, fruits, vegetables, hand-dipped chocolates, and many of the merchants' wares from inside their stores. Ross and Meg stopped and bought some mangos and a loaf of sunflower seed bread, then headed to the car.

They climbed in and Ross calmly reached under his seat, sliding out the gun.

He put it on the seat between them. "Lock your door, Meg."

She immediately complied, then looked at him with a worried expression. "What's wrong?"

"We're being followed," he said, starting the engine and pulling into the street.

Meg glanced over her shoulder, seeing a throng of people dressed in nice clothes and carrying shopping bags. Among them stood a large man with scraggly black hair and a beard. He looked incredibly out of place.

A moment later they were headed down the street, the crowds shrinking in size and the man eventually disappearing from view. "Did you see him?" Ross asked.

"The guy with the beard?"

"Yes, that was him. He was also back in Concord, in the mall."

"The same man?"

"Absolutely. Maybe I'm jumpy, but what are the odds that he'd show up in Benicia, when I spotted him earlier in Concord?"

Meg sank down into the seat. "What's going on, Ross?"

"You've got me. All I know is we're playing a whole new game, and I want to be cautious," he replied, looking down at the gun which lay between them on the seat.

* * *

The sun had begun to set by the time Ross and Meg pulled into Yvonne Dillard's driveway. They had stopped to buy ammunition for his gun, which he now kept in his shoulder holster. They went inside the house. Meg was carrying the bag of bread and mangos, and talking to Ross about possibly calling her boss, Richard Hammond. When they entered the livingroom, she saw a woman sitting in one of the chairs. From the pictures on the mantle, Meg assumed it must be Yvonne. She wasn't smiling, though, like in the photos. In fact, her expression was nervously alarmed.

"Hi, Yvonne," Ross said, his voice fading. He sensed something was wrong, all his instincts coming suddenly on guard. He started to reach for his gun.

"If you draw that, I'm going to have to put a hole through your head," Martin Wimer said, stepping out of the kitchen. He was holding a 45 automatic and with a sinking feeling Ross knew he would never be able to withdraw his own gun in time.

"I think you'd better put your hands where I can see them," Martin added.

Ross did as he was told, turning to face Wimer and the other two men who stood beside him. Leo Fromm was there, and so was Willis Dent, whose pale eyes were glinting like those of a reptile. It surprised Ross to see him here; it seemed odd that the president of Signet had somehow managed to show up in

Yvonne's livingroom with two of his thugs. How had they found him?

Leo Fromm hurried forward, sliding the gun out of Ross' shoulder holster and putting it against his temple. He grinned, his face changing from that of a handsome bodybuilder to an evil gargoyle. "Bye-bye, Ross!"

Meg and Yvonne both cried out, but Wimer was the one who interceded. "Are you nuts? This is a residential area. You shoot that gun now and some nosy neighbor will dial 911 for sure. Hang on and we'll finish them all off at once, then get out of here before any cops have a chance to show up."

Fromm shrugged, choosing to club Ross with the gun instead of shooting him. The blow knocked Ross down and he fell to the floor, his head reeling. It wasn't a hard enough hit to knock him out, but he still felt disoriented and his head was throbbing. A trickle of blood ran down his temple from where the gun's muzzle had torn his flesh. He slowly sat up but didn't try to stand. At the moment there wasn't much he could do, though he was concerned because Dent was moving towards Meg.

She was staring at Ross, feeling horrified and afraid. Her eyes were focused on the thread of blood trickling down his temple, and her own temples pounded with fear. Willis Dent came and stood in front of her, his lean features sharp with simmering anger. He slapped her hard and she staggered back, her ears ringing from the blow and her face stinging.

Ross started to rise but Fromm put the gun to his head again. "Don't matter to me what Martin says, you give us any trouble and I'll blow your brains out right now. Bam! All across this lady's carpet." Ross complied with the demand.

"Sit down," Dent said to Meg, indicating a chair. She did as he suggested, trying not to show how frightened she was. She willed herself not to raise her hand to her cheek which was stinging with pain. A small smile perched on Dent's mouth and he looked smug.

"I'm going to ask you some questions, and you're going to answer them. If I think you're lying I'm going to hurt you. Do you understand?"

Meg nodded and his smile widened. "Good. You work for Zytex, right?"

Hesitantly she studied him. Would Dent react to the truth the same way Alan Scorzato had? "I told Alan I work for Zytex because, when I tried to tell him the truth, he thought I was lying and threatened me with a knife. I told him Zytex because it was the first company that came to mind, but I've never worked for them. I'm an agent for the Central Security Service under NSA. I was sent undercover to look for the file codes and accidentally moved them off your computer instead of copying them." Dent was studying her, his face clouded with what was either apprehension or anger. "That's the truth, I swear it," Meg hastily added.

"Where's the CD?" he stonily asked, upset that she was involved with the federal agents who had stormed his office yesterday.

"In my purse." She pointed to where it lay on the floor. Fromm went over and dumped the contents out onto the floor, picking up the CD jewel case. He gave it to Dent.

"I brought a computer with me to check it out. If you're trying to stall, I'm going to have Leo break some of your fingers," Dent said.

Meg didn't answer. She sat still, trembling inside. In spite of what had happened with Shannon and Parker, and the hope of healing that had been held out to her, she wasn't able to throw off the superstitious fear that had ridden her for years like a demon jockey. Maybe the close call with Alan Scorzato had only been a red herring, just one of fate's tricks to let her think she was going to get through this year unscathed. In some ways it was worse, like giving a prisoner the key and telling him he could go, but then at the last minute saying, 'Oh, by the way, you have to go through the gauntlet, first. If you survive, then you're free.'

It was worse because she now had more to lose. She had come close to being truly happy for the first time in years, and to feeling as if she might hope for a normal life after all. Under the pressure of the moment, Meg was able to be starkly honest with herself. Even though she'd only known Ross a couple of days, she was falling in love with him. Until now she had never been able to envision herself even having the courage to fall in love. It was like winning the sweepstakes, only now that she was ready to turn in the winning ticket it was stamped as void.

She looked over at Ross who was sitting on the floor, bleeding. He had become a kind of hero to her, and she had felt safe with him in spite of the car chases and shootings. Now he was in as much danger as she, and it didn't seem like there was going to be a way for either of them to get out of this alive, or poor Yvonne Dillard who was an innocent bystander.

Martin Wimer went to get the computer, and Dent walked over to Ross, staring down at him. "You a fed, too?"

"No," Ross said, looking up at Dent with a gaze that obviously said what he thought of him. "I was tracking Dr. Kronek and ended up at Signet."

Dent's expression showed he was startled. "Why? Who's Kronek to you?"

"My kid sister is on his list."

"She's one of them?" Dent asked with sudden excitement. "Tell me what you know about them."

Ross stared at the man he had come to despise. Even though he knew it was risky to defy him, he figured they were all going to die anyway, and he'd rather go out of this life with a few pieces of dignity left. "No thanks."

"Do you want me to have Leo blow your head off?" Dent crossly asked.

"I'm not going to hand out information you can use to hurt my sister."

Dent walked over to Meg and grabbed her hair, jerking her head back. A small, involuntary cry escaped her, and she bit down on her lip to make sure she made no other sounds.

"Maybe you would like us to work her over for a while and make this pretty face into mush. We can start by breaking her nose, just like you broke Alan's."

"Leave her alone," Ross said, his voice heavy with anger.

Dent released Meg's hair but he didn't move away. "They can heal people, can't they? Kronek could do it, and those hundred and forty-three people listed in the codes can do it, too, I'm willing to bet. I saw it with my own eyes, and the thing I want to know is, how do they do it? How can they take somebody who is dying and make them okay again in just a short time? It's the strangest thing I've ever seen, and I want to have access to that. I want to know how they do it and how I can use it."

Ross didn't answer, realizing Dent was confused and didn't have the full picture. He hadn't said anything about telepathy, or about the mental healing that people like Shannon and Parker did. At this point there was no way Ross was going to give the guy any information.

Dent shrugged. "I guess it doesn't matter if you talk or not. I wouldn't believe much of what you said, anyway, since you've been sneaking around inside my company like a thief. Now that I'm getting the codes back, I'm going to set up a scientific team to study them. I'll figure it out and this time the feds aren't going to get their hands on my codes. They're looking for you, too, but after you guys die in a house fire, I guess they'll stop looking."

Martin Wimer produced Dent's laptop for him and they set it up. A couple of minutes later he inserted the CD into the computer, while Leo Fromm announced he wanted to check the fridge for a beer. It only took Dent a couple of minutes to verify it was the real thing. He took the CD out of the laptop and smiled, putting it back into the jewel case. "Get Leo," he said.

"Leo!" Martin barked over his shoulder as he turned off the laptop and folded it closed. "Forget the beer, we gotta go."

"Leo's not coming," a deep voice said, and everyone turned in the direction of the kitchen. A man was standing in the doorway, pointing an M-16 automatic rifle at Dent and Wimer. It was the dark stranger Ross had seen at the mall in Concord and later in Benicia. He looked even more frightening with the weapon in his hands. "Put down your gun, fatso, and don't do nothin' funny or you're dead meat."

Wimer's eyes were bugging out of his head, and he slowly set the gun down on the coffee table. All five people in the livingroom stared at the man, trying to figure out what was going on. He glanced at Ross. "You, on the floor, check 'em for guns." He motioned to Dent and Wimer. "You two hold still and don't try no tricks, 'cause I'd just love to blow your guts across the room."

Ross stood up, surprisingly steady on his feet in spite of the blow. He patted down Wimer first, finding a 38 Special in his coat pocket and a knife in an ankle holster. He tossed both items on the coffee table, then shoved Wimer away from them. Next Ross searched Dent, roughly checking him for any weapons, but the guy was clean. Apparently he liked leaving the dirty work to his thugs.

"Where's Leo," Wimer asked, not because he was concerned but because Leo's condition might be a forerunner to what they could expect from the ugly man with the M-16.

"He's got neck problems." There wasn't any sound of joking in his voice, just a matter-of-fact tone that made them realize there were worse ways of dying than being shot. "You," he said to Ross again. "Move those guns away so they don't try no tricks." Ross obliged and the man then looked at Yvonne. "You okay, Ma'am?"

She nodded, trying to find her voice. "They didn't hurt me."

"Good thing," he said, glancing towards the kitchen. "Okay, kid, come on in," he called.

A couple of seconds later a little blond boy came running into the livingroom and straight for Yvonne. "Grandma!" he cried, his voice full of happiness.

Yvonne slumped from the chair and onto her knees, embracing the child. "Evan," she said, her voice breaking. "Oh, Evan!"

Chapter 17

Yvonne Dillard was hugging her grandson, and they were happily chatting with each other. "You've grown so much! I can't believe how big you've gotten," she exclaimed, tears running down her cheeks. "Where have you been, Evan?"

"I been staying with some friends, some people who are like me. They take good care of me, Grandma, and I been learning lots of things. I don't want you to worry. You know what? I been worried about you, though, and your friends. That's why I got Bob to help me."

The large man came forward, putting his hand tenderly on the little boy's head. "Evan, we can't stay long."

"I know," Evan sighed. "There are worse guys out there than these, and we need to be really careful."

Reluctantly he left his grandmother's embrace, walking over to Willis Dent who was on the floor where Bob had told him to sit. Evan smiled, but the man didn't return the greeting. He moved in closer, but Dent shrugged him away, having always detested children. "Get away from me."

"Shut up," Bob angrily said. "You sit still and shut up while the kid checks you out."

Dent glanced up at the threatening stance of the man holding the gun. He did as he was told. Evan knelt beside Dent, studying him. He touched him on the side of his head, and Dent's scowling eyebrows lifted in startled surprise. Evan reached out with his other hand, putting it on the man's jaw and turning his face so they could stare into each other's eyes.

Ross and Meg watched in growing amazement as the president of Signet sat in frozen panic, his gaze suddenly unfocused and unseeing, his expression frightened and bewildered. A few seconds later he started to weep. Meg felt a chill run through her. Dent wept pathetically, sobbing in jagged breaths. Eventually he was able to move, and he pushed Evan away from him. The weeping didn't stop, though, and he fell over, his fingers digging into the plush carpet.

Meg couldn't help but feel alarmed by his bizarre behavior. Willis Dent was a cold-hearted and miserable man who had slapped her, threatened to have her fingers broken, and had definitely planned to kill her. In spite of these factors, it was hard to ignore what a mess he had dissolved into. His level of distress was alarming to watch and incredibly intense. His hysteria was worse than any she had even experienced in her nightmares. What was happening to him, and what had the little boy done? Dent's misery was so evident that she actually found herself feeling sorry for him.

Evan stood and Bob came over, putting his hand on the child's shoulder. He looked up at his large friend with concern. "He doesn't want me to help him. I've already started it, though, and the doors are opening. What should I do, Bob?"

"Let him alone for a while. Maybe you can finish it later. Check out this other guy."

Evan walked over to Martin Wimer who was staring at his boss. What was wrong with Dent, that he was bawling like that? It was the oddest thing he'd ever seen, and it got freakier by the minute as Dent curled into a fetal position, quietly sobbing. Wimer glanced at the boy who knelt beside him and he drew away in sudden fear. What kind of kid was this, and what was he going to do now?

The boy knelt down, staring at Wimer for a while, then he shook his head and stood up. Bob came over to him. "You can't do nothin'?"

Evan's brows drew together in concern. "I can't find anything in him to fix."

Bob nodded, then looked at Evan's grandma. "Ma'am, will you take Evan upstairs for a little while? We'll call you to come down in a few minutes."

Yvonne took no urging, grabbing Evan's hand and going upstairs. Once they had gone, Bob walked over to Ross and handed him the gun. He then headed for Martin Wimer, his face growing harder with each step. "The kid can't fix you. Know what that means? It mean you're a walkin' sack of human garbage, just like my old man was."

Wimer was fixated on the ugly's man's face, and alarm bells started going off in his head. He scrambled backwards but Bob was on him, grabbing him by his jacket and plowing his fist into Wimer's face. With more efficiency than would have seemed possible for his size, Bob also grabbed his leg and quickly set to work. Using a strategically place foot and his oversized hands, Bob snapped Martin Wimer's femur bone.

The flabby security man from Signet began screaming in pain. Ross stared at the scene as if he had just stepped into the weirdest episode of his life. The large, scary-looking guy had broken Wimer's leg. Dent was curled into a ball, sobbing in a way that made an eerie, discordant harmony with Wimer's howls of pain. What the heck was going on? Less than five minutes ago Ross had been desperately hoping the police might show up, or that he might be given a chance to somehow get his gun back from Leo. A dozen schemes had surfaced and been discarded during Dent's questioning of Meg and himself as he had tried to think of a way out of their predicament. Yet in his wildest imaginings, Ross hadn't been able to foresee this kind of rescue.

The howling screams were increasing in volume. "Shut up," Bob said, grabbing Wimer's head and banging it into unconsciousness. The sudden silence was a relief. Bob looked over at Ross. "We need to get this fat guy, and the muscle guy in the kitchen, out of here. Evan's grandma don't need the hassle of trying to explain this to the cops. You gonna help me?"

"Sure," Ross managed.

"Good." Bob came over, took the automatic weapon back, then set the safety. He handed it to Meg. "Here's the safety, see? Switch it off and it's ready to go. I don't think those feds are gonna come here, but just in case they show up you better be ready. You don't let nothin' happen to Evan, you hear?" He voice was darkly threatening.

"Can you shoot it, Meg?" Ross asked. "It'll have a real kick."

"I think I can," she said, finally able to find her voice.

"Don't let them get their hands on that boy. They ain't never gonna have a chance to pick his brain apart, if I can help it. He better be safe when we get back."

"Okay," Meg answered.

"Good," Bob said, seemingly pleased she was going to do what he told her. "We ain't gonna be gone long, and you can call Evan to come downstairs after we leave." He turned to Ross. "Come on, help me lift this guy. I got a pickup on the side of the house, so let's go through the kitchen and garage."

It was a struggle to carry Martin Wimer's limp body out to the truck, especially since his broken femur bone made his leg flop around like a dead fish. Bob said a few choice swear words along the way. Ross carried Wimer under the arms, and they struggled to get him through the side door of the garage. They came to a new red pickup truck and Bob dropped Wimer's legs, then lowered the tailgate. They tossed him into the back and Ross nervously scanned the neighbors' houses. It didn't seem as if anybody were watching, but the sky was dark and he wasn't sure who might be hidden behind lightless windows.

"Let's hurry," he said.

"Now for the other one," Bob stated, heading back to the house with Ross in his wake. They found Leo Fromm lying like a large rag doll on the kitchen tile.

"Is he dead?" Ross asked.

"I wish!" Bob snorted. "Only karate-chopped his neck instead of breaking it. Evan don't let me do no killing now, if you know what I mean. Come on, let's get him out of here."

Fromm seemed nearly as heavy as Wimer, and by the time they finally put him in the back of the pickup, Ross was out of breath and a little dizzy. The blow to his temple was throbbing, and he felt a bruise growing there. He watched as Bob covered the unconscious men with a tarp and then closed the tailgate.

"It's gonna be easier to dump 'em off than it was to put 'em in," Bob efficiently observed, climbing behind the wheel. Ross got in the pickup, too. Bob started the engine and backed into the street, driving off through the peaceful neighborhood.

Ross found himself in the surrealistic situation of being inside a new, leather-scented truck with a weird stranger and a cargo of unconscious bodies. At this point there seemed little else to do but go with the flow. "I'm Ross," he said, extending his hand.

"Bob," the other man said, letting go of the steering wheel and shaking hands.

Ross wasn't sure what the handshake would do, but somehow it put a slightly civilized touch on an Outer Limits moment. "Can you explain why Willis Dent is back there bawling like a baby, and why you broke Martin's leg?"

"Sure. The first guy is a piece of crap, but he's that way for a reason. All scarred up inside, know what I mean? That's why Evan could work on him. The other two are way worse, though, 'cause they got no reason for being evil, and Evan can't do nothin' to fix 'em. They're just pieces of dirt that need to be thrown away. I figured if that fat guy's leg was broke, and the muscle guy needs a neck brace, then they won't be causin' no more trouble, specially if we drop 'em off somewhere. I would of liked to break both their necks, but Evan don't want me to kill now. After the changing started, I just don't do it no more. That was part of the deal. Evan would help me do the changing, but I couldn't do no more killing or drugs, or nothin' else against the law. He's such a little pris, sometimes," Bob said with a sudden grin.

"Evan is a healer, right?"

"Yeah. Weirdest thing, ain't it?"

"It's weird, all right. My sister is like Evan, and I always thought it was wild."

"You're sister? Wow, that's cool," Bob said, his expression showing that Ross had just gone up a notch in his opinion.

"You mind my asking how Evan ended up meeting you?" Ross queried.

"Well, I was kinda at rock bottom, and sitting on a park bench in Oakland this one day. I figured the best way out of my troubles was to sell the farm. I had the dope all ready, when Evan came over to me and climbed up on the bench. I tried to tell him to get away but he wouldn't go, know what I mean? Just insisted on talking to me and the next thing you know, I'm five years old again, watching my old man beat my kid sister's head in, and the pain is cuttin' my gut somethin' terrible. I thought I would die right there, my heart squeezed in half at seein' little Lucy's brains all spilled out in this pool of red and white jelly. But instead of it gettin' worse, Evan made it disappear. Next thing you know, I see Lucy smiling at me, and she's dressed in this real pretty pink outfit with little flowers on it. She never had a dress like that, but there she was, all prettied up and smilin' at me. After that Evan peeled out the scar and healed it. The inside scar, I mean. You get what I'm tellin' you?"

"I get it," Ross slowly answered. "Was all of your healing that hard, like the first time when you saw your sister killed, I mean?" He thought about Meg and wondered how much she still had to go through.

"Nope. After that I saw Lucy, and my other sister, Mary June, both happy and not hurtin' no more. Since then, Evan just peels the inside scabs off and puts a kind of mental band-aid on them and they go away. Course, the bad stuff I done is harder. I'm tryin' to make up for that, but it ain't easy. Like with that trash in the back. I could of killed 'em, no big deal. Six months ago I would of, if they'd crossed me. But now that I'm gettin' better it would be a whole lot worse if I killed again 'cause I'm changed and ain't the same. Course, if they come back and bother Evan's grandma, I got no choice."

He pulled the car alongside a sloped ravine filled with trees, up the hill from some new construction. The wood framework shone like a pale skeleton in the moonlight, and Ross thought it seemed a good place to dump Leo and Martin. When they got to the back of the truck, the bodybuilder was moaning, roused from his unconscious state. They took him out first and he started to swear. Bob was none too gentle as he dragged Leo out, and the muscle-bound man struggled and swore even more vile epithets than before. They tossed him down the ravine and he cried out, crashing into the bushes and rolling down the slope. His swearing stopped. Martin went next, but he was still unconscious. They heard him rolling down the hill, too, and hitting into the shrubbery. A couple of minutes later it was silent, except for the soft night breeze blowing through the trees.

Both men climbed back into the truck and Bob started the engine, pulling onto the deserted roadway. He turned the car around. "They might die down there," Ross unemotionally observed.

"Now that'd be a shame, wouldn't it?" Bob grinned.

Ross recalled how Martin and Leo had chased and shot at him. He remembered his close call with Leo a half-hour ago. The guy had been eager to shoot him, eventually settling for striking his temple with the gun. Martin had also made it clear that they planned to kill Meg, Yvonne, and himself. The thought of those two men rolling down the ravine, where they might or might not be rescued, actually filled Ross with a pleased sense of vengeance.

* * *

Evan was sitting on the couch between Meg and his grandmother. He held both of their hands, but his focused attention was now on Meg. He was seeing inside her, examining what Parker and Shannon had done.

"Do you know Parker and Shannon?" she quietly asked as he examined her. "Or their little sister, Leah?"

"I never met them, though I heard they're with our grandma," Evan said. "They do good work, though, it looks like." With a sigh he mentally pulled away. "That's a good idea, how they're taking care of it. They let you see it as a black sliver they can take out of you. Wish I could learn how to do that one."

"Can you finish what they started?" Meg asked.

He shook his head. "They were doing it fast. That's why it took two of them. I work slow. I never use just one picture. Maybe, when I get older, I can do that." He brightened with pleasure at the thought, and for an instant Meg was strongly reminded of Leah, even though they looked nothing alike.

"What do you use, Evan?" Yvonne asked.

"It depends. Sometimes I use band-aids."

"Band-aids?" Meg asked, thinking things were getting weirder by the moment.

"It's like with Bob. He's got all these bad scabs inside, and I pull them off and put a band-aid on so they can heal. I started using Winnie-the-Pooh and Tigger ones, cause he never had any kid band-aids when he was little. This week I been using Tweety-bird and Sylvester the Cat ones, though. Bob likes them the best."

"I don't understand any of this, Evan," Meg said with sudden exasperation. "What are you talking about?"

"It's hard to explain in words. I thought you would understand, with what those other two did by trying to heal you. It's pictures. At least that's what I use. It's not really band-aids. It's just a way to let Bob see inside, and help heal his own scars. We get the pain out and put a band-aid on it, and then it starts to get better. I don't know why it works. It just does."

He looked at Willis Dent who was no longer crying. Instead he was huddled in a curled-up ball, staring at the pattern in the carpet as if it were a treasure map. "I used doors with him. He's inside a house with these closet doors he's kept shut, and now they're opening. He doesn't like what's in them. I wish he'd let me help him." Evan hopped off the couch and went over to Dent, kneeling beside him. He reached out and touched the man who was in a fetal position. Meg and Yvonne watched in fascination. After a minute of fierce concentration, Dent shuddered and Evan looked up with a pleased smile. "Good! He's going to let me help after all. Come on, Willis, let's clean out the closets and get the doors shut for good. You must get real tired of them popping open all the time."

*   *   *

Bob pulled the pickup into the driveway; he and Ross hurried inside the house, both men anxious at having been gone longer than planned. They found Willis Dent sitting up, looking at Evan. His eyes were puffy and his face red, but the tears were gone. He held a soggy handkerchief in his hands. Bob walked over to them.

"Evan, we really gotta go. I told the others I'd get you back safe, remember? It probably ain't safe to stay here much longer."

"Okay."

The boy started to stand, but Dent stopped him. "Don't go. I still need help."

Evan worriedly shook his head. "I can't do more, Willis. You have to clean out the rest of the bad places yourself."

"I can't," the man faltered.

"You gotta try," Evan said. He may have been a child, but his stance and voice were eerily adult. "Do you see how bad you've been? You were going to kill my grandma, and Meg and Ross. You can pay for some of that by working the rest of it through yourself. It's not going to go away unless you do."

Ross came and stood over Dent, holding his gun which he had retrieved from the kitchen where Leo had dropped it. "How did you learn about Dr. Kronek and his codes?"

"What..." Dent managed, trying to focus on Ross. "Oh, that. Two years ago I was driving through Sonoma County on a country road. There was a one-car accident blocking the lanes. The car had rolled several times just a few minutes before I pulled up. I got out to see, and found there were four injured people. Two of them were dying. One was cut up, and another had his legs practically severed. It was bad, and I went to my car and got my cell phone and called for help.

"When I got back, the man with the mangled legs had dragged himself over to a teenaged girl who was nearly dead. He had his hands on her chest, and I swear she started to get healed. I saw some wounds close up and her eyes open. I'd never seen anything like it in my life. The other girl that wasn't hurt so bad was crying. She was begging the man with the severed legs to let her help him, but he wouldn't. He told her to take care of the boy, and so she did. She worked on this teenaged kid and he came back around, too. I swear he was dying, then suddenly he was able to talk and sit up. By the time the paramedics came, the two dying kids were alive but the man with the crushed legs was dead."

"Physical healers?" Meg asked, amazed. She and Ross looked at each other, then at the boy. "Evan, are some of the healers able to make people physically well?"

"Sure," Evan said. "There are two kinds of us. Sometimes it takes one kind to help somebody, and sometimes it take the other kind. With a few, like autistic kids, it takes both."

"Who were the people in the accident?" Ross asked Dent.

"I didn't learn the names of the three that lived because they vanished from the hospital. But the man who died was William Kronek."

Ross and Meg stared at each other at this unforseen turn. Kronek, himself, had apparently been a telepath.

"I found out who he was, then tracked his name to the clinic in Concord," Dent explained. "When I got the chance, I bought the place. I wanted to know how they had done that healing. I had to know, because I've always had this fear of death. Because of her," he said, his voice growing bitter and his expression turning inward.

"I've been scared everyday of my life about dying, which is why when I found those DNA codes, they became so important to me. I figured they were the key to what I'd seen. At the least they must have been valuable. Imagine what people would pay to become like those healers, or to be saved from dying?" He didn't sound excited about the discovery, though. If anything his voice was defeated.

"Change of plans, huh?" Bob empathized. He helped Dent stand. "I'll take you out to your car. You're a lot luckier than them other guys. We're lettin' you off easy, since Evan could do some work on you. I'm gonna let you drive away from here, but I gotta warn you, if you come back again I'll have to kill you." His voice wasn't threatening or hostile. It was matter-of-fact, which in some ways made it even more frightening. "You understand?"

"Yes," Dent managed.

"Evan, say good-bye to your grandma. We really gotta go."

Bob retrieved his gun and grabbed Dent's arm. The president of Signet shakily managed to walk out of the house. Evan ran to Yvonne, who was already fighting back tears. Ross put his gun back in the shoulder holster while Meg grabbed the dumped-out contents of her purse and put them back inside, including the CD with the Kronek codes. Ross came over to her as she stood.

"Are you okay?" she worriedly asked, touching the dried blood on his temple.

"I'll be fine, except it's been a lot of information to grasp. The more we learn, the weirder it gets, don't you think?"

"Like looking in a kaleidoscope and trying to make sense of it," Meg sighed.

Bob came back into the house and retrieved Evan. A couple of minutes later they were gone, driving down the road in his red pickup. Ross went over to Yvonne and gave her a hug. "Why don't you see if you can spend the night with your friend, Myra? That or go to a motel."

"Are you leaving?"

"I think we better," Ross said. "I'm sorry how this all turned out."

"I'm not," Yvonne said. "Not even for a minute. I got a chance to see Evan, and to know he is going to be just fine. It's more than I've hoped for in a long time." She hugged both Ross and Meg goodbye.

A few minutes later they climbed in Ross' Buick, driving off into the night.

*   *   *

It was late Wednesday morning when Paul Espinosa sat glumly listening to the rasping voice on the other end of the receiver. His boss, Ed Gless, was on the line, and neither of them were happy. Although unable to see his superior's hawkish features, Paul could well imagine how Ed's eyebrows must be pulled into a scowl at the moment. What did he expect, anyway? Paul wondered, nervously rubbing the scar in his eyebrow. His team were good at what they did but they weren't miracle workers.

"I know," Paul defensively qualified. "Well, we're doing everything we can at this point, aren't we?" He wasn't able to keep a note of frustration from creeping into his voice.

The line went dead, which was usually the way his boss exited a phone call, and Paul hung up the receiver. Benny was sitting across the room, his chair tilted back, his feet propped up on a desk. He was smiling. "Trouble at HQ?"

Paul Espinosa said nothing, preferring to look away from the man he thought of as an oily sociopath. It was no picnic having Benny along, either. Even though they might need him, it didn't please Paul to have to be around him this much.

Yesterday afternoon they had traced the use of Ross Ecklund's Visa card to an auto body repair shop in Concord where he had paid for a new tail light and rear side window. His photo had been verified by a store employee, which had been enough information for them to decide to set up a control post in Concord. They had temporarily confiscated a couple of government offices, and also had satellite teams established in both Oakland and San Francisco, linked via computer and phone lines. Since then, however, they had done nothing but wait.

"If they're on the road, and were maybe just passing through Concord, then we've probably lost them," Benny observed. He was cleaning his nails with a file, scraping beneath each nail tip with meticulous precision. It was a constant habit and it annoyed Paul, who thought it might be nice to actually shove some dirt under Benny's nails so he would have something to dig out. "This is probably a waste of time, though of course you're paying my tab," Benny added.

Paul ignored the younger man, walking over to one of the computers where a specialist searched sources of information. He decided they would give it until the end of the day, but then he would have no choice but to assume their quarry had fled the area.

"Hang on," one of the computer specialists said. "I've got something."

Paul hurried over to where the young woman with wire-rimmed glasses and a boyish haircut sat. "What is it, Dinah?"

"Ecklund just accessed an ATM in San Francisco."

The room erupted into sudden activity, and Paul Espinosa leapt for the direct line to the San Francisco satellite team. A triumphant thrill ran through him as he shouted into the phone.

*   *   *

Ross slid the twenties into his wallet, retrieved his card from the ATM, then climbed back into the car. He smiled at Meg, who was gazing with interest at the unique city life of downtown San Francisco. Even on a Wednesday the streets were full of bustling activity.

"It's so different here," she said. "I like it."

"The Bay Area is fascinating," he agreed.

They drove away from the bank while Meg looked at a city map and located the Palace of Fine Arts, telling him which street to turn on. They had spent the previous night at a Motel 6 in Alameda, where they had talked late into the night about their discoveries. Meg had even charted the events out with notes, but there were still some unexplained gaps in their information.

They now knew there were two kinds of telepathic healers and that William Kronek had himself been a telepath with physical healing abilities. Meg had theorized that the differences in the appearance of the genetic codes she had noticed must be indicators of the two different kinds of telepaths that both Evan and Leah had referred to. Some of them were able to heal people with physical problems, while others could heal psychological disorders.

They recalled Lana's discussion of her twin sons, Greg and Gary, who were training to become medical doctors. Meg gave Ross a detailed account of the scene with Shannon and Leah. She told him about his sister's onset of labor, explaining how the child had seemed to physically take care of Shannon during the contractions. Much of what she had seen three days ago was starting to make sense. "Turn here," she said, pointing to a street, and Ross obliged.

"Maybe that was why Shannon was so upset when our dad was sick," he mused, unconsciously touching the bruise on his temple. "She kept saying there must be someone out there who could do more than the doctors. She was probably right."

"They might end up giving the medical industry a run for their money. Not to mention making psychologists obsolete. Parker and Shannon did more for me in one afternoon than a therapist did in a year of sessions," Meg confessed. They were both thoughtful for a while.

"You know what I'd like to figure out?" he commented. "I'd like to know which part of the government is after them. Somebody in the system must have found out about these kids, and they're trying to get their hands on them. But who? The NSA or Department of Defense, do you think?"

"I don't know, but Bob made mention of federal agents last night, and Evan said someone other than Dent was after them."

"How do you figure the agents found out about the telepaths in the first place? It wasn't through Kronek's records, because Dent ended up with those."

"Maybe they actually happened onto some of the telepaths themselves. If you found someone who could do the stuff these kids can, wouldn't you want to know where they came from? Or find out if there's more of them?"

"You're probably right," Ross thoughtfully stated. "If you end up finding the goose that lays the golden egg, and it can make you rich, how much richer can you get if you end up with a whole farm full of special geese?"

"Somehow those government agents must have discovered Shannon was telepathic."

"It wouldn't have been hard. She was flitting around the entire neighborhood working with people. They were talking to each other about her, and talking to us. One of them even wanted to tell her story to a magazine, but my mother really ly put her foot down about that. So what if someone out there was watching for that kind of thing and found out about her? We might never know how they tracked her down. Maybe it doesn't even matter, but it's clear to me that they came after her. Shannon was sure of it herself. She felt they were evil enough to eliminate anyone in our family who would become her legal guardian, so that she would eventually become a ward of the state. That's why she ran away."

A small shudder passed through Meg. "It's so creepy. Last night Bob said there were worse men out there than Dent and his two thugs. He was nervous about it."

"Yeah, well, it's worth being nervous about."

Meg dug into her purse and pulled out the CD. "What about this, then?"

They sighted the Palace of Fine Arts and Ross headed for it, eventually pulling the car along a curb near the grassy area. He turned off the ignition and stared at the jewel case in Meg's lap. "I don't know. How important do you think it is?"

She shook her head, uncertain. "If it were the only one, I'd say it was very important. But last night Dent told us federal agents took his two copies. That means it's fallen into the hands of the government, just like we were afraid it might. And you know they'll want to use it. Worst case scenario is probably going to happen after all," she soberly stated.

"I guess you're right, depending on which faction of the government has it. If it's in the hands of the kind of men who killed my mother to get at Shannon, then I'd say we need to go buy some land in Alaska and homestead there."

Meg wasn't sure if he were serious or not. She slid the CD into the inside breast pocket of her denim jacket. "If they've got their hands on the codes, then this CD is worthless unless the group of telepaths want it. It seems like it should rightfully belong to them, don't you think?"

They climbed out of the car and Ross opened the trunk. He took out a blanket, their picnic lunch, and a plastic bag full of popcorn as Meg threw her purse in the trunk. He closed it and they walked to a shady spot, gazing at the beautiful architecture of the decorated columns and arched dome surrounded by trees and water.

Ross spread out the blanket as Meg unpacked the sandwiches and drinks. It was a cool, pleasant day with a clear sky and slight breeze. They ate in silence, watching a group of Japanese tourists feeding a flock of pigeons. Droves of the birds surrounded the young people who were attired in nice suits and dresses. They took pictures of each other, chasing the birds who would then fly up, surrounding the person feeding them. Great effort was put into the picture-taking, and no doubt the background of flying birds would make for picturesque photos. There was much chattering excitement from both the tourists and the birds, and it was fun to watch. Eventually the photographers left and things quieted down.

A few of the birds then focused on Meg and Ross, sensing they had food. He opened the bag of popcorn and threw out a handful. That was all it took for the flock of pigeons to invade the grassy area. A few seagulls and small blackbirds joined the hunt, cawing excitedly at the find. The birds began the wary dance of darting in for the pieces of popcorn before flapping out of harm's way. In time, though, the birds moved in close enough to be fed by hand.

The pleasant interlude continued until the birds became startled, flapping away at the movement of someone walking near. Meg looked over her shoulder, seeing a dark-haired woman approaching them. Without saying a word she sat down on their blanket, took a handful of popcorn, and threw it to the flock. The birds eagerly came back for the food.

Ross and Meg studied the woman who had short black hair and sharp, attractive features. She was dressed in black pants, a cropped suede jacket, and a crimson turtleneck. Ross guessed she was probably in her mid thirties. Her intelligent eyes seriously studied them, and then she smiled. "I'm Daria."

"This is Meg, and I'm Ross." He held out his hand and she shook it.

"Shannon's brother," she said with a widening smile.

"You know my sister?"

"Yes, of course."

"Meg and I both have a lot of unanswered questions about what's going on," he said.

"We don't have much time," she stated.

Meg nervously glanced around. "Are we in danger?"

Daria sighed. "What I mean is, I don't like to stay in the open for long periods of time. Ten years of being on the run has helped me become cautious."

"I was hoping to see Shannon and Parker again," Meg explained. "I mean, Parker told me to come to Benicia, then we were told to come to San Francisco. I thought they'd be here."

"I know. We've run into a bit of a problem, though. Shannon went into labor."

"Is she okay?" Ross asked, concerned.

"She's fine. It's just delayed things, which is why you've been getting the runaround, so to speak. I know it must seem like some odd sort of scavenger hunt you're being sent on, but it wasn't meant to be that way. If you can be patient a while longer, you can see them again. Parker explained to us about what happened at the house in Portland, and they were both upset they weren't able to finish what they started with you. Most of us have a strong tendency for closure," she said, suddenly smiling. "It doesn't sit well with us to start a work that doesn't get taken care of. Shannon was especially concerned that it might be worse for you to be interrupted once it had started...worse than if they'd never done anything in the first place."

Meg stared at the noisy flock of birds whose cawing masked their conversation from the people passing by. "It was worth it to see there's a light at the end of the tunnel."

"Good. I'm glad, then." Daria reached into her purse, taking out a piece of paper and handing it to Meg. "Put this in your pocket. When you're on your way, you can look at it. It's got instructions on where to find Parker and Shannon. It'll probably take a couple of days, but they've promised to be there and to finish what they started."

"Thanks," Meg said, her hopes soaring. She slid the paper into her pocket.

"You're one of them," Ross said, surprised because she was at least ten years older than Shannon, and therefore couldn't be one of the people whose birth dates were listed on the file codes. "You're telepathic."

Daria studied his face for a couple of seconds. "Yes."

"Physical or psychological?"

"Physical. You know a lot." She stared at him, slowly nodding as if she were reading text, and he wondered if it were his thoughts she examined. "You know more than most. And yes, you're right, I am older than the others. That's because I'm not one of the infertility kids. William Kronek was my father."

"Your father," Meg said, studying her with renewed interest.

"He was telepathic himself," Ross commented.

"Yes." She paused, staring off into the distance. "I wouldn't talk about this with just anyone," she explained. "But I can tell what kind of people you are. Besides, you're Shannon's brother, and you've been through a lot. Maybe you deserve an explanation. My father used his mental telepathy to alter my DNA at conception. By the time I was five I was exhibiting advanced abilities as a physical healer, far more than even his own. When I was only four we were walking along the beach one day and found this dying bird with a broken wing. I healed it in a matter of minutes and sent it flying away. At that point he realized what I could do. Dad decided the world would be a better place if there were more of us in it. After that it took him five years of research, but he was able to do it."

"He altered DNA during in vitro procedures, didn't he?"

"Yes. In the beginning he was working within the uterus, as he'd done at my conception. But the growing acceptance of in vitro procedures made it much easier for him. He was able to do many more embryonic changes before his death two years ago."

"And he made two kinds of healers."

"He didn't know everything," she said. "Some of that was a mistake. For half of the IVF procedures he used his own sperm instead of the donor's. Those became physical healers like himself. The psychological healers were the biological children of the fathers who raised them."

Ross stared at her, increasingly bothered by what he was learning. "He was playing god."

Daria looked away. "My mother had died in a plane crash three years before, and I was his only child. Her death was horrific for him, and he never got over losing her. Dad couldn't stand the thought of marrying again, but at the same time believed the world would be a lot better with more children in it who could carry on his work. He could see no other way."

"He didn't have the right to do such a thing."

"My father recognized that history would either see him as a villain or a hero," Daria defended. "Those of us who have come together, the Shannons and Parkers of our family, think of him as a hero."

"If all of these telepathic kids have ended up wanting to help other people, then maybe it's all fine and well. But what are the odds of that, I'm wondering?" Ross theorized. "I don't think it could turn out as rosy as you're painting it."

"Most of us are dedicated healers," Daria explained.

"Most," Ross echoed. "Not all?"

"No, not all." Her expression became grim.

"It's a lot of power to give a kid," Ross finally commented.

"The percentages of problems are low. We've corrected many of those who've gone awry." She seemed uncomfortable with this aspect of the discussion.

"It's tampering with nature," Ross said, feeling a growing anger. "It's not right. Why couldn't Kronek have just left Shannon alone? She would have been normal, and we'd still be a family. At least she wouldn't be on the run and having to hide for the rest of her life."

"I think your sister is remarkable," Meg softly commented, placing a hand on his arm. "Would you want her to be different than she is? There's no going back, Ross." She looked at Daria. "Why was your father telepathic? I mean, was it just a quirk that he was born that way?"

"That's another story," Daria sighed. "I think you've been given more information than you want. Besides...." Her voice trailed off and her face grew suddenly tense.

Ross saw her expression and became alarmed. "What's wrong?"

The woman's eyes widened and she stood, her body stiff with fear. "They're here," she managed, turning away from them. The birds flew up in a cloud of flapping wings as she headed through them, disappearing into a group of tourists who were passing along the walkway.

'Get away if you can,' she warned them, the message echoing inside their minds.

Chapter 18

Ross and Meg ran for the car, abandoning the blanket and picnic lunch. They climbed in and Meg locked her door, staring back through the rear window as Ross fumbled with putting the key in the ignition. Three men were running towards them. They were casually dressed in jeans and sun glasses, but she caught a glimpse of walkie-talkies in their hands.

The car leapt away from the curb and a horn blared as Ross cut into the stream of cars. He quickly turned a couple of corners, but was impeded in his flight by the afternoon's growing traffic. It wasn't going to be as easy to get away this time, he reflected. Not like it had been in Portland during the middle of the night. He headed the car up a steep hill with a sudden drop off.

Meg gasped as her stomach dropped with the descent of the vehicle, and she grabbed for her seat belt. Frustration mingled with her fear. They both still had so many questions, and they had been on the verge of getting those needed answers from Daria. Not only that, but the CD with the codes on it was still inside her jacket pocket. It had been her plan to give it to one of the telepaths, and Daria had actually seemed like the right one to have it, since she was William Kronek's daughter. Now, though, it sat like a hot potato burning a hole in her side. She most definitely did not want the men who were after Parker and his family to have it.

Most worrisome of all, though, was the folded piece of paper in her hip pocket that Daria had given her. Meg hadn't looked at it yet, but it supposedly gave directions for meeting with Parker and Shannon. If those men back there caught up with her and Ross, they would definitely take that information and use it. Perhaps the right thing to do would be to destroy the paper, sight unseen, so that even under duress she couldn't tell them what they wanted to know. Even as the thought surfaced, Meg shrugged it away. She must wait until the very last minute before surrendering her hope of seeing the healers again.

Ross took a corner too fast and almost hit a couple of jaywalking pedestrians. Their mouth's stretched in ugly shapes of cursing protest, then half a second more and they were a disappearing blur. Meg looked over at Ross. His jaw was clenched and his entire body looked tense. She wondered if this aspect of their time together were becoming as gratingly exasperating to him as it was to her.

*   *   *

The helicopter passed over the Palace of Fine Arts, moving east. The men inside were listening with focused attention on the information they were receiving. According to the agent on the other end of the radio transmitter, the San Francisco team had the suspects in their sights and were trailing them at a distance.

Paul Espinosa pressed the button on the mike. "Good. Keep them in your sights but don't spook them. We should be on top of you in a couple of minutes."

Benny sat in the back seat of the helicopter, feeling both excited and annoyed. He had gone on a lot of missions with Felix before, whose real name he had learned this week was Paul, but he had almost never gone with a team, and it was exciting. The annoying part was that he was crammed in the back seat and ignored, which was really stupid, in his opinion. He was the one who would be able to stop the fleeing suspects when the time came, so why weren't they showing him more respect or asking for his input?

"There's the team car," the pilot pointed out.

"We have you in our sights, Team B," Espinosa confirmed.

"Suspect is ahead, due east," the voice crackled over the radio.

A couple of blocks ahead of the team car, racing up a steep hill, was the Buick they had been hoping to find ever since their encounter with it Sunday evening at the house in Portland. "We've spotted her, too," Espinosa told team B, then turned to the pilot. "Let's close in!"

Benny craned his neck to try and see the car, not able to view it well from where he was sitting. It made him irritated, and so he decided it was time to show the team why he was along. He ignored the conversation in the helicopter and the loud whir of the overhead rotary blades, focusing instead on the suspects the team was following. It wasn't easy, because usually he came in direct contact with the target persons, then kept them frozen while the work was done and departures were made. This was a little different, but still doable. Excitedly he made tenuous contact with the driver. A few seconds later he was grinning.

"What the hell...." the pilot said.

"What're they doing?" one of the team members asked. They watched the car in their sights accelerate, going over one of the hilltops with too much speed. It cleared the ground then landed hard on the roadway that had dropped away in a steep decline. A couple of seconds later it began swerving out of control.

*   *   *

"Ross!" Meg screamed, grabbing the wheel. The car was increasing in acceleration, his foot seemingly frozen to the floorboard. His hands gripped the steering wheel and made it immovable, and she caught an eerie image of a blank expression, as if he were a sleepwalker who heard none of her pleas. Meg's attempts at guiding the car were useless, and half a second later the Buick impacted with a pole on the driver's side door, jarring them. There was a shriek of metal and Ross' door buckled in towards him, glass shattering in a spray of pellets across them both. The car continued forward, moving sideways up the pole before it stopped, and before the banshee screech of metal-on-metal was finally silenced. The engine died.

Meg sat gasping, a sudden flash of memory haunting her. It was of another car she had seen at the impound office five years ago. The driver-side door had been the instrument that had killed her mother. It hadn't been a gun or a knife, but a lethal car door that had buckled inward on her mother and crushed her when the vehicle had rolled. Shakily she turned towards Ross, unable to take a breath. She felt as if she were inside a vacuum where there was no air to breathe, and for a terrifying moment she feared he would be dead. But when she turned her head Ross was there, looking at her with a pained and confused expression. His face was white, but at least the sleepwalker stare was gone.

"Ross?" she managed, more an exhaled breath than an actually word.

He blinked hard and grimaced, finding his voice. "What happened?"

"I don't know. You went into some kind of trance or something. Not driving, just staring." Her voice cracked with emotion.

"Hey!" a man shouted, opening Meg's door part way and looking at them. "You two okay?"

"Yeah," Ross managed. "Help us get out of here, will you?"

"Sure thing! Wow, did your brakes give out? It looked like you couldn't stop. I saw the whole thing."

Since the car was tilted up against the pole on the driver's side, the passenger door wouldn't open all the way. Meg squirmed out through the opening, then turned to watch Ross who seemed to be moving painfully. He undid his seatbelt and slid across the seat, slowly managing to get out of the car. The streets were crowded, and a large group of people had gathered at the scene. Behind them horns blared, and overhead was the whirring sound of rotary blades. They looked up as a helicopter made a pass above them.

Ross grabbed Meg's hand, pulling her into the crowd. They darted into one of the many stores that lined the streets, moving quickly. He snatched up two baseball caps as they went through, hurrying past a startled woman at the counter who shouted at them. They headed out the back door. Soon they were on the street again, weaving through clusters of people and heading past touristy shops.

Meg pulled on the cap Ross handed her, taking time to glance at him. His face was ashen and he was moving awkwardly. It was clear he was in pain from the accident, but neither of them could talk right now because there was only time to run. Even so, a sick feeling of dread filled Meg. What new and vicious trick was fate playing on her? She was getting tired of finding bad guys around every corner who were trying to hunt them down. Not only that, but first she had narrowly escaped Robyn's fate of being raped, and now had barely escaped her mother's fate of being killed in a car wreck. It was a cosmic joke that wasn't funny, and she felt helpless at the rug being jerked from beneath her feet on such a regular basis. Like rats in a maze with trap doors, she angrily thought.

Ahead of them was a city bus just ready to head out. The driver waited as they hurried up the steps and paid the fare; they sat in an empty seat near the front. Ross and Meg stared at each other, both gasping for breath even though they hadn't run that far. A few seconds later the bus was underway.

"You're hurt," she whispered, barely able to push the words out because she felt afraid to give verbal support to her observations.

Ross was still holding her hand and he squeezed her fingers. His face was drained and he was trying hard not to grimace. "I'll be okay," he said, panting for breath. "Just rest, don't talk."

Meg nodded, watching the street life of San Francisco whip by. It seemed charming and full of life, which felt somehow inappropriate for their circumstances. Less than five minutes later the bus slowed and stopped, its brakes groaning and the door swishing open. "Let's go," Ross said, standing.

Her body wanted to scream in protest that they had just sat down, but instinct told her they were trapped on the bus and would be easy to catch. They headed out the door and merged with the crowd again. Ross dropped her hand, faltering as if in pain. His stride became more awkward and Meg slid her arm around his waist, glancing at the clusters of people passing by. She didn't see any suspicious men or hear the whipping blades of a helicopter, but the intensified fear inside her still spoke of danger.

The crowds deepened, and all around them were unique little shops with signs written in Chinese. Odd, steamy smells assaulted them as they passed by tables with cooked foods. The stalls next to those had vegetables, fruits, and herbs. The sound of the voices in the crowds changed in cadence and pitch as Chinese became more prevalently spoken; a couple of blocks further and they were in the heart of Chinatown.

Ross was gasping. His steps slowed and Meg led him through a doorway and into a small store. It was narrow but deep, with glass counters on either side which were filled with oriental wares. There were also many racks of items for sale in the center aisle of the store. The shop was full of not only a great deal of saleable clutter, but also many customers. Meg and Ross headed to the back of the store, moving slowly now. He was walking slightly hunched over, but his breathing was less ragged. It was hard to pretend to be a customer, Meg thought, when each of her senses was primed for a flight from danger. She stood staring down at dust-covered trinkets that looked like ivory carvings but were probably plastic.

The door opened again and they caught a glimpse of two men entering the store. She wasn't sure if they were the same ones she had seen in the park, but their sharp glances and demeanor showed they meant business. Ross tugged her hand, unobtrusively leading her through a curtained doorway in the back wall of the store. Her heart was hammering with fear. Did those men have guns? Ross hadn't been wearing his gun at the picnic site, and hadn't retrieved it from the car after the accident. She couldn't help but think of the fake FBI agents chasing after them at Parker's house, their gunfire hitting the car's trunk and shattering the tail light. She stared at Ross who was peeking through the curtain, watching the men. Were they coming this way?

Meg glanced around the back room which had a work table and was stacked with dozens of small cardboard boxes. To her surprise she saw an old woman sitting on a stool, a tiny cup of tea delicately balanced in her hand as if she were uncertain whether or not to sip it. Her skin was as thin and shiny as oiled paper, and age lines scored her lips. She was staring at Meg with two onyx-black orbs. They gazed at each other until Meg finally pulled her eyes away, scanning the back room for an exit. Her glance fell on a door leading outside, but then her attention was drawn back to the woman who shook her head with a slight movement. The black eyes moved slowly to the right, staring at a side door which had crates on either side.

Ross' posture grew tense and he closed the tiny gap in the curtain. Meg didn't need him to tell her the agents were coming towards them. She grabbed his hand, leading him to the side door the old Chinese woman had indicated with her eyes. To Meg's dismay it opened into a small, dark bathroom with no other exit. The woman stood and hurried to them, pointing inside. Ross and Meg followed her suggestion and stepped in because at this point hiding was the only real alternative.

By now the old woman was moving with speed surprising for her age, shoving them behind the door and pushing it back so that they were standing in the dark room with their backs to the wall and the door at their faces. Through the hinged crack Meg saw the woman hurriedly return to her stool. She couldn't see all of the woman, but caught a glimpse of her leg and the teacup in her hand. A couple of seconds later there was the sound of movement, of the curtains being pushed aside and of someone entering the room. Efficient, hostile-sounding footsteps moved quickly, and Meg felt her heart thudding like that of a snared rabbit. Her throat constricted and she couldn't breathe, which was perhaps the best thing since a gasping breath would surely give them away.

Too late she thought of the paper in her pocket. Why had she been so selfish and refused to destroyed it once the chase began? Would this information now be taken from her and used to capture the others? Her fingers ached to reach into her jean pocket and retrieve the slip of paper Daria had given her, to shove it in her mouth and chew it up, and choke on it if that's what needed to be done to protect them. But to do so would be to sound an alarm, and so she stood still, her body pasty with sweat, her lungs and heart and stomach all protesting at the resurgent injections of adrenalin.

There was the sound of the back door being opened, a pause as if the agent scanned the alley behind the street, and then the sound of the door closing. There were more footsteps and the rustling of the curtain fabric being parted then swishing back in place. After this there was silence, except for the slight noise of the old woman sipping her tea. Even though there were no more footsteps, Meg and Ross stayed behind the door. She felt a movement at her side and realized he was reaching for her fingers. She slid her hand into his, immediately feeling how slick his fingers were. He was drenched with sweat. A minute more and he slowly guided her out from behind the door which he partially closed, making the room even darker. He sat down on the toilet, leaning against the wall.

"You're hurt," Meg whispered, kneeling beside him.

"Yeah."

Neither of them said anything for a couple of seconds. Finally Ross looked at her through the dim light. "I'm going to tell you what to do, hon," he whispered. "And I want you to listen carefully to me and not argue. First of all, get that paper out of your pocket and look at it. Read what Daria wrote down, and then destroy it."

Meg nodded, getting the note out of her pocket and looking at it, tilting the paper to catch the light from the doorway. Her eyebrows came together with uncertainty and she started to say something but Ross stopped her. "Don't tell me what's on there. Hurry and memorize it, okay?"

She read it again, committed it to memory, and then tore the paper into tiny pieces.

"Good girl. When I'm able to stand up we'll flush it," Ross said, indicating the toilet he was sitting on. "Now you have the address of where to go, and you're going to need to get there without me."

"No," she said, her shocked whisper harsh.

"Listen, Meg! I'm hurt and can't go with you." His voice was low but firm. "I'm not hurt bad, though. There's no way I'm going to die from this, do you understand?"

"I'm staying with you! Let me see where you're hurt, Ross." She crouched down beside him, looking up into his face.

He opened the left side of his jacket and showed a lump beneath his shirt where a broken rib was pushing hard against the skin. Flecks of blood darkened his shirt and she stared at it, unable to believe he had come this far in what must have been severe pain.

"If you have internal injuries..." she managed, her voice trailing off.

"If I have them, and there's a good chance I do, then they're still not bad enough to do me in." He let the jacket fall closed. "I'm going to have to go to the hospital, though. If you go with me, there's a chance they'll get you, which is why you can't stay with me."

"I'll risk it."

"Will you risk them using sodium pentathol on you, or whatever high-tech truth serum they've got now days? Will you risk letting them get there hands on Shannon? And Parker, and Evan?"

"Why did you have me look at the paper, then?" she accused, the sound of angry tears filling her voice.

Ross reached out, brushing her cheek and jaw with his fingers. "Because you have to go to them," he said. "You've got to let them help you get over being hurt, so you and I can go on and have a life together."

A tear slid from the corner of her eye, welling at the place where his thumb rested on her cheek. She couldn't say anything for a few seconds. "How will I find you again?"

"Go back to Portland. I know where you live, and I'll come straight to your place as soon as I can. It's only going to be a couple of days at most. That's a promise."

"They'll find you...."

"We're not sure of that. I'll dump my I.D. and go in under a fake name. Remember, they probably don't know I'm injured. Why would they look for me at a hospital?"

"But what if they do find you?" she persisted.

"If they do, they'll make me tell them what I know. But how much is that, anyway, and how much do they already know? Probably a bunch of it. One thing I don't know is where to find Shannon and the others, which makes me not so important."

"They're dangerous," she whispered, distraught. She couldn't bear the thought of them hurting him. There are worse men out there, Evan had said.

"There's nothing else I can do at this point," Ross stated. "Not if I'm bleeding inside from splintered ribs. I have to go get it taken care of. The game plan has changed and I'm done hunting for Shannon. I don't need to find her, Meg, but you do."

"Not without you," she managed.

He let out a slow, exhausted breath and closed his eyes. "You're so stubborn. I hate falling in love with stubborn women." Slowly he reopened his eyes. "Where do we go from here, then? Are you going to be able to put away the past and start a new life? Are you over your fears yet?" Even though his words were laying down sharp directives, his voice was gentle.

"Those fears have kept you crippled for a long time, Meg. You know as well as I do that it's necessary for Shannon and Parker to finish the healing. You wouldn't have come on this trip in the first place if it weren't true."

"I know," she managed.

"Then go find them," he pleaded.

Meg slowly nodded but her words were hesitant. "There isn't any other way?"

"No, sweetheart, there isn't. Not that I can see." He stood, grimacing from pain, and she saw that it required effort for him to even stand at this point. The short rest had caused his muscles to tighten in pain, and he seemed to be growing weaker. In the dim light his face was very pale, and she felt afraid it was from the internal bleeding. He lifted the toilet seat and she dropped the paper scraps with the info on them into the bowl, pushing the handle and watching them swirl in the water before disappearing. Ross slid his right arm around her, pulling her close. He caught a whiff of her hair and thought she smelled sweeter than any flower or perfume ever could. Meg lifted her face and he kissed her softly. Reluctantly he pulled back and let her loose from his hold. "Hurry up now, before they come back."

Meg stared at him with tear-wet eyes. She desperately did not want to leave him. It seemed as if every muscle in her body were screaming that the two of them had to stay with each other, that this was just another mean trick, another trap door in the maze that must be avoided. Despite the emotional turmoil, the logical side of her mind countered that she must go, that if they were ever going to really be together then she had to find Parker and Shannon and let them finish what they had started.

She slid from his grasp, not looking at him. If she looked at him, she wouldn't be able to leave. Stepping out of the darkened bathroom and into the workroom, she saw the old Chinese woman still sitting and drinking her tea. After only a slight hesitation Meg headed for the door leading outside.

"Thank you," she whispered to the woman, going through the back door and into a sunlit alley which looked blurry through her tears.

*   *   *

"What do you mean you're the one who did it?" Paul Espinosa said with growing anger, standing not far from where the helicopter had set down. "Did I tell you to do anything to that car? Did I say, 'hey, Benny ol' boy, why don't you just use your stupid little mind tricks to screw up this assignment?' Did I authorize you to make that decision on your own, you geek!"

"You better be careful!" Benny shouted, his face red with humiliation. "You better be careful, Felix, or you're gonna just not pay attention one day and find yourself walking right in front of a bus!"

A couple of the team members were staring at them where they stood together beside the helicopter. Paul grabbed Benny's shoulder, guiding him away from the others. "Let's have a talk, Benny boy," he angrily stated. His grip tightened on Ben's shoulder, who squirmed away from him. "Let me explain the facts of life to you. Of your life, if you want to go on enjoying it. You had better make sure that I stay healthy. In fact, you better hope and pray that I never so much as stub my toe. You know why? Because if anything happens to me, it's all set up that you follow in my footsteps. Got it?"

Benny's sullen expression disappeared, and he stared at Paul Espinosa with uncertainty. "What are you talking about?"

"I'm talking about your plans for me, Benny," he explained, his voice now satiny, which made the words even more threatening. "You can be real creative in trying to get rid of me. You can plan your accidents, but none of that will matter. If I go, you go, no matter what the circumstances. Just like being joined at the hip. I'm your zookeeper, and if the zookeeper dies mysteriously, then the baboon has gotta go, too. Do you get it, punk?" He was looming over Benny. His face was red, the scar in his eyebrow a contrasting white streak.

"I'm not like you, Benny. I don't spend my time being creative. Instead, I'm much more straightforward. It's already set up, nice and simple. It'll be a bullet." He put his finger in the center of Ben's forehead. The younger man immediately reeled away but it didn't stop him from continuing. "One way in, one way out. With a lot of smashed brain matter in between."

"Stop threatening me," Benny said, his voice cold with hatred.

A small smile touched Paul's lips, giving him a nasty expression of superiority. "You made the first threat, Ben. You. Not me. And you're the one who screwed up the team's plan."

"I stopped them. That's what you wanted, isn't it?"

"Sure. Except we wanted to stop them when the situation was exactly right, so we could take them into custody. The way it happened, though, they got away in the crowd because of the traffic mess-up from the accident. Now we're not even sure we can find them. Can you find them for us?" This last query was laced with sarcasm.

Benny wished with all his heart he could pluck that one out of the air, like David Copperfield on a stage snatching up magic objects, but he didn't have the ability to do so. Instead he had to shake his head. It was a quick, annoyed movement that Felix seemed to take as an admission of weakness.

"Okay, then. From this moment on, you don't so much as scratch your head without my telling you to. You take orders like the rest of the team. Got it, Benny?"

The younger man didn't answer. He couldn't bring himself to even acknowledge this kind of treatment, but neither did he have the courage to say anything else in his own defense. It appeared that Paul was taking his silence as agreement. Of course Paul didn't realize that Benny was beginning to feel the same kind of hatred for him that he had once felt for his father.

*   *   *

Ross leaned against the worktable in the backroom of the Chinese shop, scissors in hand. The contents of his wallet lay before him, and he was cutting up his credit cards as quickly as he could. In a couple of minutes they were plastic confetti, which he slid off the table and into a wastebasket full of paper. A normally easy task, he felt drained just from lifting the scissors. He was lightheaded and weak, but not so weak he was going to pass out. At least not yet. He tried to work quickly, aware of the young Chinese man carrying on a hushed conversation with the old woman. The guy was warily eyeing Ross and didn't sound happy.

Harvey Po turned back to his grandmother and continued speaking in the

Mandarin tongue he had known since infancy. "Those men were looking for him. They might have been from the government."

"Maybe just bad men with guns," his grandmother said with quiet aplomb, rinsing out the tea pot. He had seen her discuss the price of vegetables with more steam than this.

"Or the government," he repeated.

"Then all the more reason, if it was men from the government."

Harvey was well aware of his grandmother's total distrust of any governing power. The rules she lived by were the cultural ones which governed Chinatown. "Is that why you helped hide this man?" he asked.

"He was with a girl. Very pretty for a Caucasian. Too big boned, though."

"Not a good enough reason, Grandmother," Harvey said. His patience was wearing thin, but he kept any sound of annoyance from his voice since he'd always had a great deal of respect for her. He might think many of her old-world opinions were strange, but he never said so.

"When I was a girl," she began, her voice taking on the storyteller lilt he was so familiar with, "The emperor fell because the communists came, and my father's family had to hide. Someone hid me. I thought, ah! This is just like when I was a girl, cowering in the back of the butcher's shop. So, now it is my turn to hide someone else."

Harvey nodded but said nothing else. His grandmother usually ended up having the last say in things.

The table held brown wrapping paper, string, and mailing supplies, which Ross thought fortunate. He picked up a pen and shakily managed to write on an envelope, addressing it to his place in Portland. Then he put his driver's license and a couple of other important papers inside. He sealed the flap, which took some effort since his tongue was dry, then also affixed a stamp to the envelope. He buried it in a pile of outgoing mail. Afterwards he closed his wallet and slid it back into his pocket. There was cash inside, but that was all. He finished with a quick search of his other pockets, throwing away a dry cleaning receipt he found which had his name on it. At this point he was free of anything that might identify him. His hope was that as long as his name wasn't typed into a hospital computer, he had a better chance of not being discovered by the men who were after him.

He turned to the young man. "How do I get a taxi?"

The woman smiled at him before her grandson could answer. "You not need a taxi. Harvey, my grandson, will drive you."

They both looked at her with uncertainty. "Grandmother," Harvey said, focusing on her instead of making eye contact with Ross. "That is not possible."

His grandmother looked back at him with her unwavering stare. "He goes soon," she managed in English. The words didn't come easy, but her voice was flint-hard. "He is hurt. Need go to hospital soon."

Ross realized she had been listening to his conversation with Meg. The woman must have ears like a rabbit. She also seemed to be building up enthusiasm for his cause, because now she was scowling at her grandson.

"You want him pass out and then we need call ambulance? You think your father would like to see ambulance in front of his fine store? Very bad for business, I think. Everyone say, 'What wrong at Po Ling's store? What bad business go on? Maybe gang lords there.' That what you want happen?"

Harvey couldn't think of what to say, and his grandmother didn't give him a chance. "You put him in back of delivery truck and make a delivery to hospital. He can get out there, no one even see you. No men come here to ask questions. No men ask why Grandmother hide him in back, and maybe take her to prison where she dies like your uncle, my brother, back in China communist prison."

When she took a breath, Ross stepped in. "I can pay you," he managed.

"How much?" the grandmother asked. He could see her expression showed that it might be a very good thing to do a good deed and also make a profit.

"Fifty dollars."

"Yes," she said. "Fifty dollars fair price." She turned to Harvey. "See? Okay deal, then. My family also make good deal with boatman when we leave China. That fair."

Harvey studied Ross uncertainly, then shrugged. "Okay, but the money first."

Ross retrieved his wallet, shakily removing the cash and handing it to Harvey. The young man took it and stuffed it in the front pocket of his jeans. "Come on, then, let's go."

He turned and headed out the door and Ross followed, moving as quickly as he could. It wasn't easy, though, and for a few seconds he thought he might pass out in the alley, bringing to fruition the old woman's fears of an ambulance being called. Yet in spite of the dark haze drifting across his eyes, he was able to make it into the back of the delivery truck. There wasn't much room but he climbed in, grateful for a chance to lay down.

The young man peered in at him. "I'm letting you know now, if you die I'm tossing you out on a road somewhere."

"If I die, guess it won't matter to me," Ross managed.

The Chinese fellow grinned and slammed the door.

Chapter 19

After an hour of wandering through Chinatown and other districts of the city, Meg hopped on a bus. She didn't know where it was going, only hoping that she had managed to avoid any of the agents still looking for her. Eventually she got off the bus, finding herself in the heart of San Francisco. She walked past high-brow art shops, eateries, and theaters, feeling in a daze. Her mind was constantly turned to Ross and her separation from him.

Her feet ached and she was exhausted. Not only that, but her left knee was sore from where it had hit into the dashboard during the accident. Her shoulder was achy, too, because it had rammed into the door when the car hit down on the road after flying through the air. If this was how her body was feeling after the experiences in the car wreck, what was it like for Ross? Had he made it to a hospital by now? Meg wondered why she had ever agreed to leave him, and thought of going to some of the local hospitals to try and find him. Would that put Ross in even more danger, though? She felt afraid, both for Ross and for herself. Meg also recalled his blank sleepwalker gaze right before the accident. Something had happened to him, and she knew it had to be tied into the telepaths, but how?

A passing trolley car, loaded with people, dinged its bell, startling her. Meg soon found herself at the underground entrance to the BART, but her attention was diverted by a large man in ragged clothes who approached her with an aggressive stride.

"Help the homeless!" he demanded. "Buy this magazine they print and help the homeless." Meg stared at him and he scowled. "What's the matter? Didn't you hear me?"

Meg used a few signs as if she were Deaf, showing she wasn't interested. His mouth gaped and he seemed stumped at how to use his forceful selling tactics if she couldn't hear him. With a shrug he turned away and she went down the long flight of stairs, disappearing into the cavernous hold of the Bay Area Rapid

Transit system. She bought a ticket from one of the vending outlets and then entered the turnstile gate. A minute later a train pulled up and she stepped inside, finding a seat. The windows were streaked with grime, looking dingy in contrast to the bright theatrical posters which advertised several plays. She watched the tile walls start to slide past as the train moved out of the underground depot, picking up speed and eventually emerging into the open. Before long the train had left San Francisco behind.

She stared at the industrial scenery whipping by and tried to sort things out in her mind but found it hard to focus. Her thoughts kept turning to Ross and to the things he had said. He had talked of being in love with her. Well, she was in love with him, too. Never could she have believed something like this could have happened so fast, especially because she had kept her life so orderly and safe during the past ten years. She hadn't allowed anyone inside her protective circle for a reason. Now it was too late, though. Meg reflected that she had never felt more alone than she did right now. Maybe a person had to actually have love and a hope of happiness first before genuine despair and loneliness could actually set in.

The BART headed into the tunnel which lay beneath the bay. According to the electronic information posted by the door, she was on her way to Oakland. With a sigh she thought about the instructions on the paper Daria had given her. Meg had told Ross she would find his sister and Parker, and that she would get their help. How was she going to do that, though? Her purse had been left in the trunk of his car, and they'd had no chance to retrieve it once the helicopter showed up. After buying the ticket for the BART, Meg only had a ten dollar bill and some change in her pocket. She had no credit cards or photo ID, and no checkbook, either. So how was she supposed to get from here to Albuquerque, New Mexico on ten dollars?

The train stopped in Oakland and she got off with a crowd of people, finding a helpful young couple who told her where the nearest postal outlet was. She hopped on a bus and headed the short jaunt there. Once inside, she bought a small, padded envelope and addressed it to Parker Briggs in care of general delivery in Albuquerque, New Mexico. The postal worker helped her come up with the right zip code. She then took the CD out of her inside jacket pocket and slipped it into the envelope, sealing it and paying for the metered postage. A few seconds later the CD was on its way to New Mexico and she felt better. Meg had decided somewhere between San Francisco and Oakland that she didn't want to carry it with her any longer, and that it was better to risk losing it than to chance it being taken if she were captured. Unfortunately, by the time she had paid for the envelope and postage, her ten dollar bill was down to eight ones.

Learning directions for reaching the library, she hopped on another bus, arriving there after a twenty minute jaunt. She headed into the building, welcoming its quiet atmosphere and surroundings. This would be a good place to do some research, and to see if she could come up with a few more answers. It was also a quiet, comfortable place where she could safely think about what to do. If she were going to make it to New Mexico, then she would need help.

*   *   *

Ross lay unconscious on an examining table in a curtained-off area of the emergency room. X-rays and vital signs had been taken, and he was scheduled for surgery. Two physicians examined Ross further, assessing his injuries from what they had seen so far.

"The spleen has the worst damage, although there's also some trauma to the liver and internal bleeding in several places."

"Yes, but it's that splintered rib I'm more concerned about, and the way it's pressing on that vein."

"Excuse me," a man's voice said from the other side of the curtain.

The first physician moved to the side, peering around the edge of the hanging curtain. He saw a man dressed in jeans and a polo shirt, with a small walkie-talkie attached to his belt. "Can I help you?"

"I was told you have a patient in there who might have been injured in a car accident. The receptionist said he was brought in about an hour ago and has no ID."

"Are you a relative?"

The man in jeans paused for just a second. "Sure. He might be my brother. I'd like to see him if you don't mind. To make sure it's him."

"Okay," the doctor said, parting the curtain. "This him?"

The man in the polo shirt stared down at Ross' pale, unconscious face. "Yes!" The physician looked at him with an odd expression and the man hurried to explain. "I mean, I'm relieved I've found him. Can we talk to him?"

"We?"

"My...other brother and me."

"He has some major internal injuries and is scheduled for immediate surgery."

"We're taking him there now," the second physician explained, pulling back the curtain the rest of the way and releasing the break on the Gurney. "You can take care of the paperwork out at admissions, though." They began wheeling him from the room and the man moved out of the way.

"There was a woman with him," he said, following them from the room and down the hallway. "Did you see her?"

"Check in the waiting area," the first doctor said over his shoulder.

Frustrated, the agent watched the Gurney disappear behind an elevator door. He snatched the walkie-talkie from his belt and headed to the waiting area.

The elevator didn't stop at the surgery floor, but headed up two more flights. When the doors slid open, the two doctors pushed the Gurney down a hallway leading to patient recovery rooms. "In there, Jack," the first young physician said, indicating an empty private room with no patient's name on the schedule sheet. They guided Ross inside and closed the door. "Did that scare you, being so close to one of them?" Keith asked.

"No kidding," Jack replied, setting the brake on the Gurney while Keith set out the Do Not Disturb sign. He then called surgery and canceled the planned emergency operation, explaining that the patient had expired.

"Let's hope that's the word which gets back to Mr. Walkie-Talkie downstairs," Keith commented.

"Let's also hope nobody comes in here and asks what we're doing," Jack added. He looked down at Ross. "Okay, buddy, we're gonna do some things to help you feel a whole lot better, so you can go see Shannon. By the way, I'm your brother-in-law."

"Good, Jack," Keith said with a grin. "Now that the formal intros are finished with the unconscious, let's get on with this before somebody comes in."

"Okay. Do you ever feel like we're sneaking inside a witch doctor's hut with a hypo of penicillin?"

"All the time. I keep wondering when they're going to figure out it's incredibly dumb to slice open the human body in an effort to repair it. Not all that far removed from leeches and bleeding, if you ask me. So, which part do you want to do?"

"The rib, I guess," Jack answered. "Bone takes so much longer to re-bond, and that'll be what keeps us here the longest. Why don't you work on the rest?"

Keith stared down at Ross' body cavity, letting his sight move inward beyond skin, muscle tissue, and eventually the stomach. He focused on the spleen. Most of the internal bleeding was coming from several tears in the small organ. He moved his sight deeper into it, focusing as if his gaze were the lens of a microscope. Now the fun part started. He began working on a cellular level, repairing the damaged cells of the spleen. He meshed and bonded them together, stopping the flow of blood in the process. It was a work which never ceased to fascinate him, though most of it he had to do quickly and in passing, since his intern experiences hadn't yet allowed him into an operating room. He was looking forward to that day. Keith was a unique healer who loved and hated his learning experiences in hospitals. There were times it seemed as if he were in a house of horrors where ghastly decision were made with everyday aplomb, but even so he was learning a great deal. Jack, on the other hand, loathed them and refused to intern. He was planning on becoming a naturopath.

Forty minutes later, Ross regained consciousness. He looked up into the smiling faces of two young men. "What's going on?" he managed.

"You feeling okay?"

Ross slowly lifted his hand, reaching for his side. There was no longer a protruding lump of bone threatening to shove its way through the skin. Not only that, he felt surprisingly good in comparison to how he'd been back in the Chinese shop. He was weak, even lethargic, but definitely not in pain.

"I couldn't run a race or anything." His voice was a little thick from having been asleep.

"How about a wheelchair race to get out of this hospital," one of them grinned. "You up for that?"

With their help he slowly sat up. At first he was lightheaded, but that soon passed. "The pain is gone, and from the looks of it, my rib isn't broken any more. You must be healers."

"I'm Keith, and this is Jack."

"Thanks for helping me."

"It's the least I can do, considering we're related," Jack said, smiling.

"Related?"

"I'm married to your sister."

Ross gaped at him, feeling a little slow on the uptake. "Shannon?"

"She made it clear that nothing better happen to you. She's the sweetest girl I've ever met, but man, she can be hard as iron when she's worried about someone."

Ross offered his hand, which Jack shook. "It's very good to meet you. Where is she?"

"Well, we're going to be heading there soon if you're up for it."

Keith was bringing around a wheelchair. They helped him move into it from the Gurney. "Do you know where Meg is?" Ross asked.

Both young men looked hesitant. "There's kind of a problem. She's on her own for a while," Jack explained. "Right now, you're our priority."

"We have to find her," he said, the sound of his voice anxious, even to his own ears.

"Actually, Ross, we're hoping she'll find us."

Meg slowly opened her eyes. She was sitting at a table in the library and had been resting her head on her folded arms. Having felt drained and worn out, she had planned on only letting her eyes rest for a few minutes. It wasn't clear how long ago that had been, but it was now dark outside the windows of the library. She raised her head and stretched, looking down at the books on the table. Despite researching the human gene, Meg had learned nothing new. She thought this had probably been a waste of her time.

She stood and went to the circulation desk, checking in with the librarian to see if her name had finally come up for available time on one of the computers. It had, and so she anxiously sought out the computer and sat down. She accessed the Internet, using several different search engines to try and find out which faction of the government was involved in genetic research. After more than an hour, and having had no luck, she decided to turn to her most pressing need, finding help in getting to New Mexico.

Although it had been only a few days since she had entered the CY-FY chat room where she usually talked to her Internet friends, it seemed like a month. She had chatted with them almost daily for a couple of years, but that hadn't happened for several days in a row now. Cyber Guy was there but XenX wasn't, and it was the latter of these two that she really wanted to talk to. Cyber Guy noticed she had entered the room.

Cyber Guy: Wow, did you drop off the face of the Earth or what?
CodeBreaker: Actually, I've been on a trip. I need to ask XenX something. Is he around?
Cyber Guy: I think he was heartbroken you didn't show up. He's been hanging out at Darth Vader.
CodeBreaker: Thanks. Gotta run.

Meg left CY-FI before Cyber Guy could ask any more questions, and headed to the Darth Vader chat room, immediately spotting XenX. She logged on just as the front desk made an announcement that the library would be closing in five minutes. She glanced at her watch, surprised to see it was almost nine. She didn't have much time and so started typing.

CodeBreaker: Hate to interrupt, but I need to talk to you.
XenX: Sure, now you want me.... Where you been?
CodeBreaker: Actually, I'm in your area, if you really do live in Berkeley.

XenX: You're here? In CA?

CodeBreaker: Been doing some traveling. Can I talk to you in person?

XenX: Sure. Follow me to a private room.

CodeBreaker: Thanx. We alone now?

XenX: You bet. So, since you're here, do I get to meet you at last?

CodeBreaker: Why don't you code me your number and we'll talk in person.

XenX: Great! Call me at ZOGA QUOTE.

Meg logged off, grabbing one of the pencils and scraps of paper that the library provided by the computers. She wrote down ZOGA QUOTE, noting there were nine letters if she combine the two words. A regular phone number had seven digits, unless the area code was included, then that would be ten. ZOGA QUOTE had one letter/number too few, or two too many. A few of the lights in the library dimmed and she pushed away from the computer, standing. No one was at the circulation desk, so she hurried there and picked up the phone, looking at the numbered buttons. There were no letters on the number one, but the two had ABC, number three had DEF, and so on. She searched for the Z, finding none, since the number nine ended the alphabet with WXY. There was no Q, either. The number seven had PRS printed next to it's number. Until now she'd never realized that the phone dial omitted Q and Z. That meant that those two letters in the words ZOGA QUOTE were blanks. That left seven remaining letters. The O in ZOGA must then be the first digit of his phone number. It converted to a six, and the G was a four. She went through the remaining letters, transferring them to numbers on the paper.

"May I help you?" a man asked, coming up behind her.

She jumped, startled by the deep voice. Glancing up she saw a large African American man holding several books in his arms and quizzically looking at her. Hurriedly she put the receiver down and shook her head, feeling a little shaky at being startled. Maybe that was a natural tendency because of her recent experiences of being pursued. She headed to the front door, moving out with the last of the stragglers, most of whom were holding books. One of the library workers was standing by the front door with a key, ready to lock it.

"I need a phone," Meg said.

"There are two payphones outside the main door," the woman answered.

Meg passed through the exit and headed for one of the phones. She put in some coins and pressed the converted numbers, hoping she had gotten XenX's phone number right. The library worker was locking the door and there would be no access to the computer, so she wouldn't be able to double check with him in case she had his number wrong. The phone rang three times before being picked up.

"What took you so long?" a voice on the other end of the line asked. "Thought I'd stumped you."

"Hi," Meg managed, feeling suddenly shy. She may have spent a lot of time chatting with XenX on the Internet, but she didn't even know his real name, or if he had been truthful about being a professor's assistant at Berkeley. He was someone she'd never met, and now she was going to ask him for help. "I had to find a pay phone," she explained.

"Where are you?" he asked.

"In Oakland."

"No kidding?"

There was a pause, and she took in a slow breath. "Thanks for giving me your number."

"What's brought you to California?" His voice didn't sound nearly as playful as his usual Internet demeanor. Maybe talking person-to-person made that happen.

Meg decided to be candid with him. It was only fair if she were going to ask him to help her. "Do you remember the last time we talked? A few days ago? I told you there was some trouble at my work."

"Sure, I remember. You were kind of down, you said. I figured that's why you haven't shown up at CY-FY."

"I don't exactly know how to explain this, but I figure I should be straight with you. If this sounds too weird, and you hang up on me, I'll understand."

"I won't hang up. We've been typing to each other too long for that." Despite his words, his voice was now hesitant.

"When I told you I work for the government, I wasn't joking. For the past three years I've been a cryptographer for CSS. That's why I chose the name CodeBreaker."

"A cryptographer?"

"Not anyone important, you know, just someone writing a few codes for the government. Things like that. My level of classification is pretty low, and I haven't dealt with anything that was highly classified. Until a couple of weeks ago, what I spent my time doing would have been boring to most people."

"What happened a couple of weeks ago?"

Meg felt encouraged by the question. At least he hadn't hung up on her. "I got my hands on something I wasn't supposed to. It was a mistake."

"Are you in trouble?"

She said nothing, feeling her throat constrict at hearing her situation put into such a simple phrase. "Yes," she managed.

"Can I do anything to help? Without getting myself in trouble, that is?"

"Thanks for asking," she said, feeling a flood of relief. "And for not making any James Bond jokes."

He chuckled at her attempt at humor, but she could sense it was more from politeness than anything. She hurried on. "You won't get in trouble. First of all, I need some information. I was working on the Internet at the library when they closed, so I couldn't finish looking. Do you think you'd have time to scan for me?"

"No problem. What do you want to know?"

"I'm not sure you can find it out, but I'd like to know which faction of the government is involved with genetics."

"Genetics?"

"Yes, specifically genetic research. Can you check on that for me?"

"Okay. Anything else?"

"Can I meet with you?" She figured if there were a chance of getting him to pay her way to New Mexico, then she should ask for that in person.

He paused, and she didn't know if he were surprised or hesitant. "Sure."

"Unless it would be a problem," she added.

"No, it's not a problem," he said, and his voice sounded jovial. "It's just that every time any of us asked to talk to you in person, or see a photo or something like that, you acted like we had leprosy."

"I did not," she defensively answered.

"Yes you did. And here you are, calling me from my own backyard, asking to see me. Can I tell Cyber Guy about this?"

"Not till after we've meet and I've left."

"Okay. You know what? We had a side bet going that there was a chance you were a guy. That happens sometimes."

"Well, I'm not."

"I can hear. So, how about meeting me for breakfast?"

"That'd be fine."

"You been to Berkeley before?"

"No, but I can ask directions once I get there. Tell me where to meet you."

"Okay. There's a little place not far from the college called the Dutch Oven. They have great pancakes. Meet me there at 9:30?"

"Sure," she said. "See you tomorrow, then."

"Uh, CodeBreaker? You are going to come, aren't you? This isn't a joke or anything?"

"No joke. I'll be there."

A few seconds later she hung up the phone, walking away from the library. She buttoned her jacket against the cool night air, the breeze whipping the few strands of hair which stuck out from beneath the baseball cap she was still wearing. Despite the fact that XenX had agreed to meet her, and would possibly help her get to New Mexico when she asked him, she still felt flooded with melancholy. She also felt drained and exhausted. Her short nap at the library had only managed to make her long for more sleep.

After walking down the road, heading away from the library, she eventually came to a small café. The lighting was dim and candles flickered atop the tables in sconces of dark glass. A singer performed with a guitar while people talked in low voices or listened to the music. She was seated at a table in the back and given a menu. Looking at the list of items to eat, Meg realized she was very hungry. She ordered soup and pie, the same thing she had eaten with Ross on their first night together.

Meg stayed in the café for a couple of hours, which was as long as she felt prudent. Then she paid for the food and headed out again. She only had a couple of dollars left to pay for bus tokens, so of course there would be no motel tonight, not even an inexpensive one. After leaving the café she walked the streets of Oakland, passing rundown convenience stores that were bright with activity. She began to realize she had chosen a somewhat dangerous town to hide out in. For a cautious person, she was living on the edge in a way she never would have dreamed possible before.

There were a number of hills in the city and she looked up, seeing residential areas in the distance. It seemed smarter to head there than into the inner-city districts where gangs might be. She walked for more than an hour, ending up in a rundown residential area. At this point it was well after midnight, and she felt so tired she thought she couldn't take another step. She passed by a number of houses, many of which had cars parked in front. She began to check the car doors but all were locked. Eventually she came to a large station wagon. It was in poor condition and had a flat tire, but the back door was unlocked. Being careful to make no noise, she opened it and climbed inside. It smelled dusty and was clutter with so much junk that she couldn't see the floor. None of this mattered to her, though. She locked the doors, fearful that the owner might jerk one of them open in anger if he saw her inside. Next she rolled down a window just a crack to let in some fresh air. In the front seat she found an old sweatshirt that was stained with paint. She turned it inside out and made it into a pillow, gratefully laying down on the seat and putting it under her head. It was necessary to lie on her side and bend her knees, but even so it felt good to assume a resting position. She closed her eyes which felt gritty and strained. Her head was pounding, her arms and legs felt weak, and her face and ears were cold from her long walk in the cool night air. It took a while to fall asleep, but eventually she was able to drift off.

*   *   *

It was almost nine-thirty when Meg got off the bus near the sprawling Berkeley campus. She had to ask a couple of people before finding someone who knew where the Dutch Oven was. She walked quickly, afraid to be late for fear that XenX would leave. Pausing only a minute upon seeing her reflection in a store window, she ran her fingers through her hair, wishing she had a comb. The baseball cap had accidentally been forgotten in the station wagon where she'd spent the night, so she could do nothing but try to smooth her hair with her fingers. She also wished she had a toothbrush, settling for one of the breath mints that was in her jacket pocket.

It had still been dark when Meg had awoken with a start. She had been dreaming of Ross, seeing him staring into the distance with a zombie-like gaze. In her dream he had been a sleepwalker who wouldn't wake up, and he'd ignored her pleas to recognize her. After that she had been unable to doze off again, so had headed out in search of a bus route schedule. All along the way she had thought of Ross. Even though she had been frightened several times during their travels together, she had still felt safe because he had been so capable. A variety of mental images kept surfacing.

She remembered their first encounter and his angry glare when he'd slugged Alan Scorzato, and how he had told her he was a friend. She remembered how he had been waiting for her with a damp washcloth when she came out of the motel bathroom after throwing up, and later massaged her aching calf while he sat beside her on the bed. She thought of how he'd acted during their last minutes together in the back of the Chinese shop. He had been in a lot of pain, but his concern was for her well-being. Now, more than ever before, Meg realized she must make it to New Mexico to meet with Parker and Shannon. It was what Ross wanted, and what she wanted, too. She hoped with all her heart that XenX would agree to help her.

Meg found the small café which had a brick face and faded brown awnings. The name of the place was painted in an arch across the large front window, and when she stepped inside she saw that the café was busy. There were people at nearly every table and booth, and the aromas drifting from the kitchen were mouth-watering. She stood by the front door, scanning the tables, but wasn't sure where XenX might be. Most of the people were college age, and sitting in clusters, but she also saw several men sitting alone. She focused on one man who was looking at her. He was short, stocky, and wearing a Hard Rock Café t-shirt. He stared at her as she approached and she smiled.

"Hi," she said, coming to his table.

"Hi," he answered, smiling back at her.

"Why did the rhinoceros cross the road?" she asked, thinking that since it was the joke XenX had typed to her a week ago, he would know the answer.

"I don't know?" the man said, grinning at her. "Why did it?"

"Sorry to bother you," Meg said, turning away. She caught his disappointed expression as she did so, and wondered if this were going to be harder than she had at first thought.

"The rhino crossed the road because there was a chicken on its back," a voice said from behind her.

Meg turned and saw a man sitting in a booth not far from where she stood. He looked to be in his mid twenties, one of the college crowd, and was sitting with a physics book in his hands. He closed it and smiled. "CodeBreaker?" he asked with raised eyebrows.

Meg nodded, sliding into the seat across from him. They studied each other. He had ordinary features beneath a partially receding hairline and wore small, oval glasses through which she glimpsed blue-gray eyes. He wasn't handsome but had an intellectual look that combined well with his lanky physique. She found it amusing that he had turned out to be pretty much as he had purported himself to be. In part she had assumed that most of her Internet buddies made themselves out to be more than what they really were. She realized how lucky she was that her last hope for assistance hadn't turned out to be a fourteen-year-old kid who's mother had to give him a ride to the café.

"So, you're XenX," she said. He nodded but didn't say anything, so she held out her hand. "Meg Parrish."

He shook her hand and then found his voice. "Barry Lowe."

"Thanks for meeting me."

"Sure."

They sat in silence for a couple of seconds, and it seemed to her as if the previous night's partially stilted phone conversation had been a rapid dialogue compared to this. He was staring at her with a quizzical expression and she became nervous. "Is something wrong?" she finally asked, glancing around the café.

"No. Sorry. This isn't a joke is it? Something Lenny and Doug set up to get even with me for that video prank I pulled on them?"

"A joke?"

"Uh...I mean, you're not really CodeBreaker, are you?"

"Yes, of course. We talked on the phone last night."

"Okay." His voice didn't sound even a little convinced. He reached over to a newspaper that had been left on the table next to them and made a quick search, pulling out one of the pages. He folded it and got out a pencil, handing it to her along with the newspaper. He pointed to the jumble puzzle. "Can you do that?"

"The puzzle?" she asked, wondering where he was going with this.

"Give it a shot."

She looked at the jumbled words, rearranging the letters for each of the six words and quickly writing down the correct answers, including the final answer to the pun. Afterwards she handed it back to him and he scanned it.

"Eighteen seconds," he said, looking up from his watch.

The café door opened and she glanced over at it, seeing a college-age girl enter wearing a short jumper and hiking boots. Meg returned her attention to Barry and asked, "What's this all about, anyway?"

"I figured if you were a cryptographer, and the real CodeBreaker from CY-FY, it would be easy for you. I guess you are who you say you are."

A waitress came over to their table and he ordered a couple of breakfast specials and coffee. When the woman left, Meg looked back to him. "You didn't believe me?"

"No, of course not."

"Why?"

He seemed hesitant to answer, then shrugged. "The way you look. I didn't expect you to be so...pretty, I guess. The way you were so determined not to let us see you, I always assumed it was because you were a really smart person with two heads or something. Not looking like this, though."

"Sorry to disappoint you," Meg awkwardly replied. "How about we change the subject, so both of us can stop feeling uncomfortable. Were you able to find any of the information I asked for?"

"I found something, but I don't know if it's what you're looking for." He slid a manila envelope out from under the physics book and handed it to her.

Meg opened the envelope and pulled out papers stapled together in several individual packets of information. She began to read about the Human Genome Project, a fifteen-year effort to identify the 80,000 genes in human DNA, and determine the sequences of the three billion chemical base combinations.

"A project like this would take some major funding, don't you think?" she asked, shuffling through more of the papers.

"No doubt."

The waitress arrived with a syrup dispenser and two plates stacked with pancakes. After pouring the coffee the woman left.

"Here's something interesting," Meg said. "Listen to this description of what they've been doing inside this project. 'The genetic map is complete, the chromosome physical maps are within eighteen months of completion, and pilot programs to begin sequencing the entire human genome are under consideration.' What do you think of that?" she asked, glancing up at him.

"What should I think of it?" he asked with a shrug. "I'm not sure where you're going with this."

"No, of course not," she murmured, flipping through more pages. It made sense to her, though. The Kronek codes would be useless unless the human genome was sequenced. Once the mapping was done, would they then be able to implement Kronek's same procedures of genetic manipulation? she wondered.

"They must be using massive computer systems to analyze the DNA bases," Meg commented. "It can't be an independent study, so what I want to know is, who's holding the purse strings?"

Barry reached out, sorting through the papers. He pulled out one sheaf, pointing to the third paragraph. "Right there."

"Coordinated with the National Institutes of Health and the DOE? Department of Energy?" her voice trailed off and she stared into the distance, not even seeing him.

"It's odd, I know," he said, taking a bite of pancake. "Why would the Department of Energy be involved with a genome project? I'm not sure what the reasoning is behind that."

"Me either, but I've found the tie-in I've been looking for, and it suddenly makes sense to me. DOE is part of the Intelligence Community. Most people just don't realize it. The position of Director of Central Intelligence, or DCI, was set up by the National Security Act clear back in 1947. The DCI is actually the head of the CIA and the rest of the Intelligence Community. Under the DCI there are thirteen different agencies, including the Department of Defense, which heads NSA and hence CSS, who I work for. I don't remember all of the thirteen agencies under DCI, but I know it includes the Department of Justice, Department of the Treasury, and also Department of Energy. DOE is actually a faction of the Intelligence Community. And now you're telling me that they're involved with this huge fifteen-year genome project?"

Meg skimmed through more of the papers, then stuffed them back into the manila envelope and picked up her fork. She took a bite of pancake, not saying anything else. So now she knew who the guys searching for the telepaths were.

Not that this piece of knowledge really gave her an edge. Had Hammond and Trenery known, and was that why they'd been so reluctant to say anything the last time she'd talked to them? After all, the NSA and DOE were sister organizations, all part of a big family protected under the DCI. Perhaps they'd felt they couldn't come out and tell her that the Department of Energy had this big genetic research project going with a possible secret secondary project underway to identify the genetic anomalies of telepathic DNA. She wasn't classified to know that kind of thing, was she?

Meg realized her mind was a hundred miles away, whirring like a gyroscope. She looked up at Barry who was studying her. "I'm being rude," she said. "I tend to get caught up in a puzzle and then I can't let go of it until the last piece is in place. You've been great to help me."

"So what kind of trouble are you in, that you're running from the DOE?"

She put her fork down, staring at the half-eaten pancake. "The less you know, the better off you'll be. Ignorance can be bliss." The door opened and she glanced over at it, watching a couple of men enter together. They were young and had trendy clothes and haircuts. She looked back at Barry.

"You're scared."

"Does it show?" she asked, managing a tentative smile.

"You've checked that door almost every time it's opened."

"Have I? I didn't notice. To be honest, I've been looking over my shoulder a lot."

"Isn't there somebody who could help you? I mean, if the government is the problem, then what about the press? Sometimes news media can help."

Meg smiled and shook her head. "Not with this. There is someone out there who can help me, though. I'm supposed to meet with them soon. That's where I'm in a bind, though, and why I've come to you, XenX. I hate to ask you for this, but when I ended up on foot, I also ended up without my purse. It's back in San Francisco somewhere, and so I've been getting by since yesterday on the change in my pocket. In the mean time, I've got to get a bus ticket to New Mexico. It's out of line for me to ask you, I know that, but is there anyway you could help me? The minute I get back to Portland I'll send you a check."

"Sure," he said after only a slight hesitation. "But we'll have to hurry, I need to be back for a class by eleven."

"Thanks," Meg said with great relief. "I owe you big for this."

He paid for breakfast and they headed out the door. Once inside his aging Honda they headed for the bus depot. She pushed aside the concerns she had about the genome project and the Department of Energy. The knowledge really didn't do anything except prove her theory that the government was involved, plus answer Ross' question about which agency it was. Instead she turned her attention to Barry, asking him about his work and the classes he was taking. He was friendly and nice, but she felt they had a more challenging rapport over the Internet than in person.

At the bus station he bought a ticket for Albuquerque, plus gave her a twenty dollar bill so she had some cash. "Thanks," she said, offering her hand. "You've been great, XenX."

"Can I see you again sometime?" he asked, shaking her hand and hanging on to it for a few seconds. "I mean, you're not dating someone, are you?"

"Actually, I am," she said, glancing away.

"Is it serious?"

"It's become that way very quickly."

"Oh. Well, hey, guess I'd better get back to the university so I'm not late for my class."

"Sure. When I get back to Portland I'll give you a call and get your address, so I can reimburse you for this."

"No problem," he said, lifting his hand in farewell and heading out of the depot.

He hadn't been gone long when the bus she was supposed to be on was ready to head out. She would have to make a transfer along the way, but had been lucky in getting to the depot when she did, since the next departure wouldn't have left until five in the afternoon.

Meg settled into a seat, opening the manila envelope and taking out the information that XenX had downloaded from the Internet. She read everything, not only to help pass the time but because she wanted to be sure that her theories were right.

*   *   *

Daniel Trenery and his assistant, Jake Cornel, were standing in the university hallway with Richard Hammond and Brian Moses. The four of them were in the science building on the Berkeley campus, near the room where a class on advanced physics would soon be taught. Students streamed through the hall, heading to a variety of classrooms. The four of them stood out in definite contrast with their dark suits and button-down collars. Jake and Brian glanced at the photocopied picture from Barry Lowe's transcript, studying the male students who passed by. They caught sight of him at the same time. He was talking to a friend, nodding his head and chatting until he saw them. His steps faltered. They didn't wait for him to finish his stroll to the classroom.

"Barry Lowe?" Jake Cornel said, walking up to him and showing his ID. "Federal agent, NSA. We'd like to talk to you."

Even though Cornel's voice was low, the act of flashing his ID had caught the attention of several students and they began to pool around him, at a safe distance, of course.

"What's going on, Barry?" his friend, Doug, asked.

Barry's face looked pale but he nodded, ignoring Doug. "Sure," he managed, looking at the other two agents who were also approaching. One of them was heavy-set, wore an arm-brace cane, and walked with a limp. The other was late forties with a military haircut and demeanor. Neither of them looked happy.

The fourth of the group, a large Samoan agent, pointed across the hall. "Your professor said we could use his office. This okay with you?"

"Sure," he repeated, walking in that direction and trying to ignore the curious stares of his friend and the other students. He also tried not to look scared, but was certain he was failing miserably at this last task.

A couple of minutes later he found himself inside his professor's office with the four agents. It seemed very crowded, and he leaned against the desk as the Samoan agent shut the door. He decided to take the bull by the horns. "You working with the Department of Energy?"

Trenery and Hammond glanced at each other, trying not to show their surprise. "Why would you say that?" Trenery asked.

"No reason," Barry said with a shrug. "What's this all about, anyway?"

"We're here about Meg Parrish. You've had contact with her."

"How do you know that?"

"Let me explain," the one with the arm brace said. "My name is Richard Hammond, and I run a satellite program for CSS out of Portland. Meg works for me. A few nights ago something happened to her, and she ended up running away because she was scared. Right now we don't know where she is, but we figure she's in trouble. We've been trying to find her, and during our search we took information off her computer. We learned that you and she have been talking on the Internet for a while now, and so a couple of our agents started watching for her to show up at some of the chat rooms both of you frequent. Seems you had a very short conversation with her last night, isn't that right?"

Barry's mind was in turmoil, and he stared at Hammond who sighed. "She's worked for me for three years, Mr. Lowe. I'm very fond of Meg, and very worried about her. My main goal in finding her is to make sure she's protected. Can you help us?"

"She said I wouldn't get in trouble for helping her."

"You're not in trouble," Trenery put in. "Not as long as you tell us what you know."

"Is she in trouble?"

"Not yet. We'd like to keep it that way, if you're willing to help us."

Barry swallowed hard, the morning's breakfast of pancakes and syrup beginning a gurgling war inside his stomach. "Okay," he finally said. "What do you want to know?"

Chapter 20

Ross was holding the tiniest baby he'd ever seen. He didn't realize how small babies started out, since the few he'd ever chanced to come across were usually either crawling or screaming. This one made little mewling noises, though, if it cried at all. Most of the time it just slept. He touched the head which was covered with fuzzy red down.

"Isn't she beautiful?" the child Leah asked. "Our little Nicole. Gram says we should of named her Penny because her hair is red, instead of Nickel." Leah smiled at the joke.

Ross smiled, too, then looked at Shannon. He'd been looking at her a lot, ever since arriving at the sprawling stucco house in Albuquerque the night before. He was finally getting over the shock of her being so grown up, since for the last ten years she had been frozen in his mind at the age of twelve. There were similarities to the old Shannon, especially when she smiled, but there were differences, too. Her hair wasn't as bright red now and had more auburn in it. Her freckles had faded, too. Overall, she was very grown up. The ten years had slipped away and she'd become an adult. She also looked remarkably energetic for having just given birth; the work of physical healers, no doubt. He felt very glad she was safe and well.

It had been a consoling few hours. They had talked long into the night, and for the first time since her disappearance he was able to lay some issues to rest. Meg had been right about not being able to change the past, and he was finally coming to terms with accepting it.

The house was a hive of activity. In the last couple of days it had become a gathering place for nearly twenty of the Kronek kids, many of whom weren't kids at all. It was an odd group of people who seemed to complete each other's sentences and have a silent, ongoing rapport. Parker was there, too, and the first thing he asked Ross was when Meg would come. Unfortunately, Ross didn't know the answer. All he could do was sit and wait for her.

The baby began to fuss and Shannon took her. He stayed in the kitchen with the older woman everyone called Gram, offering to help her make lunch. He was curious about her, and wondered at the role she played with the young people. "Are you telepathic, too?" he finally asked while coating pieces of bread with mayonnaise.

"Good grief, no," Gram said, opening a couple of giant cans of tuna. "I feel like it, sometimes, though. I've gotten very in tune to them stepping inside my head for a conversation. Guess they feel Grandma is free territory." She smiled when she said this, so he knew it didn't bother her.

"You're really their grandmother?"

"I am. William was my son. Open that jar of pickle relish, will you?"

"William Kronek was your son?" he asked, surprised.

"Quite the honor, isn't it?" she laughed with a deprecating glance. "These kids all but have him memorialized, though I can tell you that my fondest memories of him are when he was an ordinary boy. He had such a messy room, you know. I could never get him to clean it."

"When did you learn he was a telepath?"

"When he was still a child. By the time he was a teenager it became even more obvious, though. His father and I were both amazed in the beginning, but even so I never foresaw how far-reaching it would be. Or that he would die so unexpectedly. Once Will was gone, I felt it was necessary to carry on his work, the work he'd started. I've tried to be a gathering point for the kids."

"I met Daria yesterday. She told me some of his history."

"Oh, I miss that girl! She was my first grand-baby, you know. Course, now she's thirty-seven and hardly a little grandchild."

"Do you know why your son was telepathic? I mean, was it just a fluke of nature, or was there more to it than that?"

"Well, there's no way of knowing for sure," she said, mixing a large dollop of mayo into the tuna. "It could have just been a misstep of nature, but I've always assumed it was from the research my husband and I were doing. Frederick was a pioneer in the field of genetics, and I was his assistant. He was definitely ahead of his time, and the work he was doing preceded the explosive work in molecular genetics that eventually happened in the fifties. You see, in the first half of the century it was thought that genes consisted of proteins. That was before Watson and Crick deduced the structure of deoxyribonucleic acid, or DNA.

"Frederick's focus was on those proteins, and so we were working in the laboratory extracting genetic material from bacteria and marking the proteins in that bacteria with radioactive tracers. I was working with a lot of protein chemicals and radioactive materials in that lab, not realizing until it was too late that I was expecting. I've always thought it was my exposure to the contents of the lab during my early pregnancy that made William different, but maybe I'm way off. Maybe it's just a mother's need to find an explanation for something that ended up being so life-altering. Who knows; it could have just been an act of God. It's always been my belief that God has a marvelous sense of humor."

She thoughtfully stirred pickle relish into the tuna, then placed dollops of the mixture on the bread for Ross to spread with a butter knife. "I guess it doesn't matter," she said. "William was William, just like each one of the grand-kids are themselves, and I wouldn't have it any other way, you know."

Out of politeness Ross didn't say what he was thinking, that he still believed William Kronek's decision to alter the genetic make-up of embryos had been a major assault against nature. The doctor had created a breed of children destined to struggle because their ability to intrude into the human mind was a tremendous threat, even if they usually meant to help. It seemed to Ross that the human mind was the one last place which was meant to be safe from intrusion. It was the way life on Earth had always been, but because of what William Kronek had done, that was now changing. If history were on the threshold of a great change, Ross didn't want to be here to see that first major step. He wanted to go on with the illusion of life being what it was meant to be, a mundane, ordinary world where the only mind readers out there were fakes working in carnivals or hawking their phony promises on t.v.

*   *   *

Meg found the sprawling university town of Albuquerque to be surprisingly picturesque. It was nothing like Portland, or San Francisco, either. Instead it was a desert clime with a definite southwestern look. Most of the houses she passed were stucco haciendas with rock gardens and cacti. It was late afternoon, and the bright sunlight gave everything a golden look. Meg was only partially able to enjoy it. She felt drained and very tired.

The cab she'd hired at the bus depot pulled up in front of a ranch house made of peach-colored stucco and surrounded by a low stone wall. She did a mental double-check of the address, then decided she must be at the right place. She paid the taxi driver and got out, walking up to the front door as the cab drove away. Almost immediately the door was opened by Leah, and Meg knew she was in the right place.

The little girl grabbed her around the waist and hugged her. "You're here! We been waiting for you! You're going to be so surprised. I'm not supposed to tell, though," she said, releasing Meg and then taking her hand, pulling her inside the house and shutting the door. She led her into the livingroom where more than a dozen young people sat conversing or studying. Meg couldn't help but stare at them, knowing they must be more of Kronek's children. Parker was sitting with them, but stood when she entered the room. He came over to her.

"We are very glad you made it," he said, his voice unflawed.

"You can talk?" she asked. "I mean, without a Deaf accent?"

"Yes, of course."

"Then you're not Deaf?" she queried, puzzled.

"Profoundly Deaf," he replied, this time without speaking. She heard his words inside her head. "Being telepathic allowed me to learn English because I heard the words of others inside my head. That didn't stop me from being Deaf, though."

"Why the sign language, then?"

"Because I am Deaf," he smiled with amusement. "Why would I want to abandon my heritage? It seemed only right for me to accept Deaf culture, you know. Besides, there's been a lot of work I've been able to do there. I've met so many others who have spent their lives in isolation because they can't hear, and because their families were unwilling to learn their language. It was a natural venue to follow, for a healer."

Meg thought about Robyn, then lifted her hands to sign. "Good see you again."

"Same," he signed.

"Shannon here?"

"Yes. Upstairs. She anxious see you again."

"Hello, Meg," a familiar voice said from behind her.

With a gasp she turned around, staring at Ross. For a moment she stood frozen, unable to move, while Leah jumped up and down, clapping her hands and saying she had said there would be a surprise. Meg flew into his arms and he held her close.

"How?" she managed. "Ross, you were hurt...."

"Yes," he said, holding her close to him. "I'm fine now, though."

"How?" she repeated.

"Well, it helps if you've got a sister married to a healer," he grinned. "Shannon's husband, Jack, and another healer named Keith, came to the hospital. Let me tell you, the stuff they can do is pretty slick. No wonder Dent was impressed when he happened on that accident and saw those physical healers at work."

"You've traveled a long ways," Parker interrupted. "How about we get things taken care of, before there are any more interruptions?"

*   *   *

The den was a small, cozy room with shelves of books and overstuffed furniture in shades of corral and rust. Meg sat on a couch between Shannon and Parker, the same way she had the previous Sunday afternoon in the Portland house. Leah, who had promised to be quiet, sat beside Ross on a wicker bench.

"Can you see it?" Parker asked.

"Yes," Meg murmured, her eyes closed. "It's the black splinter, just like you showed me last time."

She studied the mental image as they lifted it away. This time it was more easily removed. "Good," she heard Shannon say. "You've been working on it."

Meg seemed to be standing at the edge of a large valley, watching the dark splinter from a distance as it was lifted out. The displaced happiness of early childhood flowed into the hole once made by the haunting memories, a kind of balm that helped her feel safe and content. She saw the black sphere start to spin faster, gaining more speed. In time it spun so rapidly that it began to melt. A few minutes later it had dissolved and was totally gone.

"It's disappeared," Meg stated, surprised it was so easily gotten rid of. Slowly she opened her eyes.

"That's it," Shannon said. "That's everything we can do."

"I think it's enough," Meg said, suddenly laughing. She felt eleven years old again.

Ross came to her and put his hands on her shoulders. "It's over now?" he asked.

"Yes," she sighed, feeling tired and yet relaxed, as if the world were now a calm, comfortable place. "Thank you," she whispered.

Leah slid off her chair, hurriedly walking over to Meg. Her demeanor was suddenly tense and she looked worried. "Uh-oh," she said.

"What's wrong?" Shannon and Meg asked at the same time.

She was staring at Meg, her eyebrows pulled into a scowl. "Your boss is here."

*   *   *

The puffy bags under Richard Hammond's eyes gave him a sad look, and Meg was shocked by how fatigued he appeared. He was leaning heavily on his arm brace, and his expression was stern. "Why didn't you call in?"

"Maybe because I wasn't sure who the good guys were anymore," she sighed, glancing over at Trenery. "I always thought we were on the side of right, you know. But recently it hasn't seemed like that."

"Where's the CD?" Trenery asked.

"I don't have it anymore. I got rid of it." She glanced over at Parker, sending him a mental image of shipping it to him via general delivery.

Don't worry, I'll pick it up, she heard him reply inside her head.

"Besides, according to Dent you took both his copies," she added. "Which means you already have the DNA codes."

"How do you know that?" Trenery asked.

"Dent told us," Ross interjected. "It's a long story," he added, noting their surprised expressions.

"It won't matter anyway," Jack commented. "You may have the genetic codes, but they're really worthless to you. There's no way to know which of the four genetic chemical bases those letters represent, or which strands of DNA they replace. William Kronek took that information with him when he died. Considering humans have three billion combinations of the DNA bases that aren't even identified yet, how could anyone know which strands they replaced to make us who we are?"

"A telepath might know," Trenery stated.

"We're no threat to you," Jack countered. "If we were dangerous, what you're fearing would already have happened."

"It's not just that," Hammond said. "You're in a position to help your government, you know. What you people can do would be invaluable to us, and to our nation's security."

"Doing what?" Keith asked. "Being spies? No thanks! You've got your little global shuffles going on, but we've got a bigger picture."

"It would be for peace," Hammond explained.

"Well, we have our own way of bringing that about."

The conversation was disrupted when several of the young people looked at each other, their expressions concerned. "What's going on?" Ross asked Amber, a young Asian American woman sitting beside him on the couch.

"Plan B," she murmured with a distracted expression.

* * *

"Okay," Paul Espinosa said with tense anticipation. He and the others had been tracking Daniel Trenery's vehicle, which was now parked in front of a ranch-style house. "Benny, if you could ever do your stuff, now's the time!"

"I can do it," Benny smugly stated, throwing out his mental blanket like a net spreading across a pond of hapless fish. There were lots of them inside, and it wasn't easy, but he was getting stronger all the time and would be able to do what was necessary.

"Is it done?" Ed Gless asked.

Benny slowly nodded, hardly able to talk. Already he was feeling the stress of it, and the beading of sweat that would eventually leave him drenched.

"Let's go!" Espinosa said to his two teams that were exiting the cars. "Start by getting the cuffs on them."

The teams moved quickly. There was no search warrant this time, and no legal pretense. At this point there was just too much at risk to bother with that. He led the way inside, stepping across the threshold and into a room where people sat in unmoving clusters. It was a truly exhilarating sight, the one brief moment for which Paul Espinosa was genuinely thankful for Benny's abilities.

He and his team members found most of the people sitting in the livingroom. They looked like mannequins having a meeting, with Daniel Trenery, Richard Hammond, and their two assistants at the center of it. He couldn't help but smirk. Those NSA dupes didn't have a clue what they were really up against.

"Get them cuffed," he heard Ed Gless demand from the doorway. Espinosa obliged, taking a pair of cuffs from his coat pocket. He headed for the young man he knew of only as Jack, reaching out and grabbing his wrist. The hand he took hold of suddenly grabbed him back and he let out a startled gasp, looking down into eyes that were angrily comprehensive.

'It's time we had a chat,' he heard a strict voice say inside his head. Two seconds later searing pain shot up the tendons of his neck and Espinosa heard himself give an involuntary cry.

Everywhere agents were dropping to the ground as if crippled by invisible bullets. It was a unique skirmish. The physical healers had previously discussed what to do; after much debate and a vote they had decided to put their oath of "do no harm" on hold. Their abilities had always been focused on healing, but used in reverse they were definitely able to cause pain. Dislocating a joint or hitting a nerve center worked effectively, and in a relatively short time the two teams of agents, including Ed Gless and Paul Espinosa, were writhing on the floor.

Benny stared at the scene in shocked amazement. He still couldn't comprehend that his first impression of a total blanketed control was wrong. In fact, at first it even seemed humorous to watch those macho agents mewling and squirming in pain. It wasn't until he felt someone grab his arm and spin him around that he began to feel fear. He found himself surrounded by several of the siblings he had always sensed were out there, but whom he despised.

"We need to take care of something for you," one of them said.

*   *   *

Daniel Trenery and Richard Hammond, along with their assistants Jake Cornel and Brian Moses, became aware of the turmoil happening around them at about the same time that Ross and Meg did. It was an eerie moment for the six people, because at first they had been quietly talking with the telepaths, when next they were caught in a strange, sleepwalking state. When they finally came out of the trance they found there were more people in the room than before, and a lot of shouting going on. Agents in suits were writhing on the floor, moaning in agony. A young man, surrounded by several of the telepaths, was screaming in rage and fury, cursing vilely and making threats. In time he quieted down, staring into the distance, his face bright red. A minute later the others stepped away from him.

"You didn't have a right to do that," Benny said with cold hatred. "You didn't have a right to take it away from me!"

"We had every right," Keith said. "We're not killers like you, though, so we'll give you a chance to get out of here. When those men you've been working for get back on their feet, and when they learn you aren't useful to them anymore, it's probably going to seem to them that you know way more than you should."

"I'll get you for this!" Benny screamed, staggering towards the door as if he were drunk. "I'll get even if it's the last thing I do!"

He grappled with the doorknob, his palm slick with sweat, finally managing to open it. He slammed the door back against the wall and ran out of the house with hobbled steps, screaming in fear and rage as he went.

*   *   *

The agents were sitting on the floor, clustered together like hostages. They weren't moaning anymore, because thankfully the pain had ended; however, they were worse for the wear and their weapons had been removed. They themselves now wore the cuffs.

Brian Moses retrieved a black box from the trunk of Trenery's car, bringing it into the house. He felt a little shaken by everything he'd seen this afternoon, and since Brian usually prided himself on the calm nature inherited from his Samoan race, it was doubly disturbing. He paused beside Meg.

"You okay, Brian?" she asked, sensing he was ruffled.

"Yeah," he said under his breath. "This is some weird stuff, though, isn't it?"

Meg smiled, watching him set the black box down on the coffee table. Jake Cornel came in behind him, carrying a Clipper-equipped telephone, which he set down beside the box Brian had just opened. He connected the phone to a wall jack and then to the box.

"Go ahead," Trenery said with a nod.

His assistant dialed the number of the other Clipper phone they wanted to reach, then pushed the red button to initiate the security feature inside the black box. They had to wait a few seconds for the two chips to synchronize and then read off a character string displayed on the telephone. This confirmed the security of the conversation with their other party. The conversation would be scrambled by a classified Skipjack algorithm which had been in development at NSA for more than ten years.

Once the connection was made, Trenery listened to the voice on the other end of the line. He then gave a succinct rundown of what had taken place. He listened for a few minutes more, then nodded, looking at the young people. "He wants to talk to one of you. Any volunteers?"

Several of them looked at Jack, who stepped forward. He took the receiver but didn't put it to his ear. "It's not necessary," he explained. What followed also ended up on Brian Moses' list of weird stuff, because it seemed clear that Jack was having a telepathic conversation with the person on the other end of the line. Though nothing was spoken, Jack's expression displayed a dialogue that was definitely occurring. "Thank you," he finally said aloud. "That's great." Jack then looked over at Ed Gless. "He wants to talk to you."

Ed stirred slightly, his hip aching miserably from where it had been pulled out of the socket and later returned. He hoped there was no permanent nerve damage. "Who is it?"

"DCI," Trenery explained.

Ed blanched, his countenance growing markedly pale when he realized that the Director of Central Intelligence, who was responsible for all activities in the Intelligence Community, was actually on the other end of the Skipjack phone. Despite his hands being cuffed he was able to put the receiver to his ear. "Yes sir," he said.

His dialogue became a series of yes and no responses, his face growing more grim with each passing minute. Finally he handed the phone back to Jake Cornel who disconnected it from the black box. Gless looked at Jack and Keith. "If you'll take these cuffs off, we'll leave now."

"Okay," Jack said, signaling the others.

"Is that wise?" Ross questioned, having only been an observer until now.

"We know their intent," Keith explained.

Paul Espinosa looked at his superior. "We just walk?"

"The project funding is in jeopardy," Gless commented without emotion. "We're through with trying to take them in."

Fifteen minutes later the DOE agents were gone. "Aren't you leaving, too?" Jack asked Trenery and Hammond. He was smiling sadly, as if he already knew the answer.

"We want you to agree to help us," Trenery said. "You can name your price. Otherwise, you're a threat to our national security. With people like you around, there is no security."

"You're just going to have to trust us," Keith said, coming up beside Jack.

*   *   *

Meg was having a dream. It was a strange, pleasant dream in which she knew she was sleeping, but seemed partially awake. In the dream she was saying good-bye to Shannon, Parker, and Leah. Ross was saying goodbye, too, and he was sad although accepting of the situation.

'When will I see you again?' she heard him ask his sister.

'You never can tell,' Shannon replied through tears. 'That's the marvelous thing about life. It's so unpredictable.'

Meg awoke to the sight of Ross sitting beside her on the floor. He was stroking her cheek with the back of his fingers. "Hello, Sleeping Beauty," he said. He tried to smile playfully at her, but she could see he had been crying. It embarrassed him, so she pretended not to notice.

She sat up, looking around the empty livingroom. "They're gone, aren't they?" "Yes."

They stood and walked through the vacant house together. "You okay?" she asked.

"Of course," Ross replied, pulling her into a hug. "Both of us are. You ready to start a life together, where bad guys aren't shooting at us, and there are no more car chases?"

Meg smiled up at him. "Can we get a cat?"

"Sure. I'd like some babies, too."

She became thoughtful, enjoying the feel of his arms around her. "I never thought about children before. I mean, it was always out of the question. If I could get hurt by losing friends and family, it seemed like loving a baby was no option."

"That's changed, though?"

"Yes," she answered, looking up into his hazel eyes. He bent his head, kissing her for a long time. Eventually they walked outside, surprised to see Trenery's car still there.

Hammond was sitting on the passenger side of the car, his door ajar. He saw them come out of the house and pushed himself erect, walking towards them. It took Meg a few seconds to realize what was different. He wasn't walking with his usual jerking limp, and his arm brace cane was nowhere in sight. In the three years she had known him, she had never seen him move with such natural ease.

A lifetime's damage from childhood polio was gone.

"Oh, Richard," Meg said with emotion.

"It's no use looking for them," he stated, his voice equally emotional. "They've left."

"That's okay," she said, slipping her arms around Ross. "They've left us better off."

Printed in the United Kingdom
by Lightning Source UK Ltd.
121874UK00002B/12/A